Jean François Paul de Gondi de Retz

Memoirs of the Cardinal de Retz

Vol. III

Jean François Paul de Gondi de Retz

Memoirs of the Cardinal de Retz
Vol. III

ISBN/EAN: 9783337018931

Printed in Europe, USA, Canada, Australia, Japan

Cover: Foto ©Raphael Reischuk / pixelio.de

More available books at **www.hansebooks.com**

MEMOIRS

OF THE

CARDINAL DE RETZ;

TRANSLATED FROM THE

FRENCH.

Vol. III.

MEMOIRS

OF THE

CARDINAL DE RETZ;

TRANSLATED FROM THE

FRENCH,

WITH

NOTES.

VOL. III.

LONDON:

Printed for T. BECKET, T. CADELL, and
T. EVANS, in the Strand.

MDCCLXXIV.

MEMOIRS

OF THE

CARDINAL DE RETZ;

WRITTEN BY HIMSELF,

To MADAM DE * * * *.

BOOK III.

MADAM,

I MUST beg of you not to be surprized, if in the sequel of this narration you do not find the same exactness which I have hitherto observed in what relates to the assemblies of the parliament. The court having removed from Paris to go into Berry and into Poitou, immediately after the king's being declared of age, which was upon the 7th of September 1651, and the Duke of Orleans keeping an even hand between the Queen and the Prince, there appeared not upon the stage of the parliament near so many actors as before; so that from the 7th of September to the opening of the parliament on the next St. Martin's day, which was on the 20th of November, it may be said that no considerable scenes appeared there, except those of the 7th and of the 14th of October. The Duke in the assemblies held on these days told the company that the King had sent him a full power to treat with the Prince, and that he had named to go along with him, and to assist him in this negotiation, Messieurs d'Aligre and de la Marguerie counsellors of state, and Messieurs de Mesmes, Menardeau, and Cumont, of the parliament. This negotiation came to nothing, becaufe the Prince refufed to accept the offer which the Duke had made him to go and confer * with him at Richelieu, as being a captious propofal of the court, made with a defign to leffen the ardour of thofe that were willing to engage with him. Upon the 26th of this month they had the news at Paris that the Prince was arrived at Bourdeaux on the 12th; and the fame day that the news came, the King went to Fontainbleau, where he was informed in the evening, that if the court would advance to Bourges, the partifans of the Prince would certainly leave that town. Meffieurs de Chateauneuf and de Villeroi preffed the Queen extremely not to give time to Perfan to throw himfelf into it with the gentry of the province; and the court going thither accordingly, and the chiefeft inhabitants having declared for the King, the reft furrendered without ftriking a blow. Palluau was left with a fmall body of troops to block up Montrond, which was defended by Perfan. The Prince of Conti and Madam de Longueville retired to Bourdeaux with all manner of hafte. Mr. de Nemours went along with them, during which journey he attached himfelf to Madam de Longueville, more than Madam de Châtillon and Mr. de la Rochefoucaut were willing he fhould. The Prince thought that he had engaged Mr. de Longueville to be of his party, in the conference he had with him at Trie; but it proved without effect, Mr. de Longueville ftaying at Roüen. The movement which the troops commanded by the Count de Tavannes about Stenay, made by order of the Prince after he had quitted the court, had not a much greater effect, becaufe the Count de Grand-pré, who

---

* Mr. de la Rochefoucaut fays in his Memoirs, that the end of that conference was not to make peace, but only to hinder the Prince from making war; at a time when the bodies politick all over the kingdom were about to declare themfelves.—The Prince befides was unwilling to truft his interefts in the Duke of Orleans's hands, becaufe of his union with the coadjutor his enemy, and of the union of that prelate with the court.

had

had left the Prince's fervice out of difcontent, made likewife a movement near Ville Franche, and another near Givet, which kept the Prince's troops in awe.

In compenfation for that, the defertion of Marfin in Catalonia was of great weight. He commanded in that province when the Princes were arrefted, and as he was known to be very particularly attached to the Prince of Condé, the court thought not convenient to confide in him. Orders were fent to the intendant to feize his perfon. He was fet at liberty at the fame time that the princes were, and he was even reftored to his poft. When the Prince left the court after his imprifonment, and took his way into Guienne, the Queen thought upon winning Marfin, and fent him a patent of viceroy of Catalonia which he had paffionately wifhed for, adding to it all manner of promifes for the future. But having been timely informed of the Prince's leaving the court, and of what he had refolved upon, he ftood in fear of being treated as he was the time before. He therefore quitted Catalonia before the Queen's difpatch had reached him, and got into Languedoc, with Baltons, Luffan, Monpouillan, le Marcouffe, and as many of his troops as he could get away. That defertion gave a wonderful advantage to the Spaniards in Catalonia, and it may be faid that it coft France that province.

The Prince in the mean while neglected nothing on the fide of Guienne. He brought over to his party the whole nobility and gentry of that province. Even the old Marefchal de la Force declared for him ; and the Count du Doignon, Governor of Brouage, who owed his fortune entirely to the Duke de Brezé, thought himfelf obliged to fhew his gratitude to the Princefs of Condé, who was fifter to his benefactor.

The Prince of Condé did not forget to feek for fupport abroad. Lainé was fent into Spain, where he concluded that Prince's treaty with his Catholic Majefty ; and the Arch-duke, who commanded in the Netherlands, and who had taken Bergue-St.-Vinox, made preparations on his fide, which afterwards coft

France

France Dunkirk and Gravelines, and which from the
time of thofe preparations obliged the court to keep
upon that frontier part of the troops, which had
otherwife been very neceffary in Guienne. Thefe
clouds however did not all the harm, at leaft within
the kingdom, that might have been feared from their
thicknefs and blacknefs. The Prince, in the levies
he made, was not ferved as his quality and his perfon
deferved. The Marefchal de la Force acted not in his
private capacity, in a manner anfwerable to the reft
of his actions. The forts at Rochelle, which were
in the Count du Doignon's hands, held out but a very
little while againft the Count d'Harcourt, who commanded the King's army. The Spaniards, who had
Bourg, a place in the neighbourhood of Bourdeaux,
put into their hands, fuccoured it but in a weak
manner. All that the Prince could do was only the
taking the town of Agen and that of Saintes. He
was obliged to raife the fiege from before Coignac ;
and the greateft general in the world, without exception, learnt himfelf, or rather taught to others on
all thefe occafions, that the moft heroick valour and
the moft extraordinary capacity, are able to fupport
but with a great deal of difficulty, new-raifed forces,
againft old difciplined troops.

Having refolved from the beginning of thefe Memoirs to infift only upon matters of which I have had
a particular knowledge, I touch upon what paffed in
Guienne, in the firft movements of the Prince, but in
a very flight manner, and but juft as much as the
knowledge of them is neceffary to you, for the con-
nection they have with what I am to relate of the
things that paffed under my eyes at Paris, and of
what I could difcover of the defigns of the court.

From Bourges, where I have faid that the court
went, it advanced to Poitiers that it might be nearer
at hand to oppofe the Prince's fteps. As they came
to perceive there that the Prince did not fall into the
trap which they had laid for him, by means of a
negotiation, in which, as they pretended, though
wrong-

wrongfully in my opinion, they had brought Gourville to be of their side, they ceased to keep any manner of measures with him, and the Queen sent a declaration * to the parliament against him, whereby she declared him guilty of high treason. This to my thinking was the critical moment that gave rise to the revolution that ensued. There are but very few people that have known the true mystery of it, though there was not one but thought that he had found it out. Some have fancied that that mystery consisted in the cabals which, as they would persuade themselves, had been made at court, for and against the King's journey. But nothing is falser. That journey was undertaken by the general advice of every one. The Queen longed with impatience to get free, and be at a place where she might recall the Cardinal when she pleased. The sub-ministers, by all their letters, encouraged the thought she had. The Duke wished more than any one the removal of the court, because his natural, and predominant temper made him always find a great pleasure in every thing that might diminish the respects which the King's presence obliged him constantly to pay. Mr. de Chateauneuf added to his desire of rendring the Prince, by some new step that would make a noise, still more irreconcileable to the court, the view of introducing himself into the Queen's favour, during a journey in which the absence of the Cardinal and the removal of the sub-ministers, gave him room to hope that he might still render himself both more agreeable and more necessary. The first president concurred in it to the best of his power, both because he thought that journey extremely useful to the King's service, and because the haughtiness with which Mr. de Chateauneuf treated him, was become insupportable to him. Mr. de la Vieuville

---

* Joli says, that the Duke of Orleans hindered for a fortnight together that declaration from being verified, but that the party of the court, to which the Coadjutor's friends joined themselves, carried it at last, so that it was read and regiſtered at the parliament on the 4th of December 1651.

was

was not sorry, as it appeared to me, not to be too narrowly watched during the first days of his exercising
his office of Superintendant of the Finances; and
Bordeaux, who was his chief confident, spoke to me
in a manner that expressed even some impatience that
the King was not already gone. The Frondeurs were
not less impatient for the King's going, both because
they saw the real necessity there was, not to give the
Prince time to settle himself beyond the Loire, and
because they thought that they might reckon upon
the Duke in a much surer manner when he was at
some distance from the court, than when he was near
it. This was what appeared to me of the disposition
in which every body, without exception, was in respect to the King's journey; and I cannot comprehend
what ground those could have, that have reported,
and even, if I mistake not, published in writing, the
diversity of opinions that were delivered at the council-
board, upon that subject.

You may therefore see that there was no manner of
mystery in the King's going; but in recompence,
there was a great deal in what followed that going,
because every body found in it the reverse of what he
had imagined. The Queen met in it, by the obstacles
which Mr. de Chateauneuf formed against the recalling of the Cardinal, more trouble beyond comparison,
than that which she had had at Paris. The sub-ministers
were mortally afraid that use and necessity should at
last settle in the Queen's mind, not only Mr. de Chateauneuf, but likewise Mr. de Villeroi, who seemed
weary of their advice. On the other hand, Mr. de
Chateauneuf did not find his hopes so well grounded
as he expected, the Queen continuing all the while in
an intimate concert with the Cardinal, and with all
those that were truly devoted to his interest. The
Duke soon became less sensible to the pleasure of being
free, which the absence of the court afforded him,
than to the jealousy which quickly arose in him from
the reports that were spread abroad of some secret
negotiations, which he thought the more dangerous
by

by reason of his being so far distant from the court. Mr. de la Vieuville, who was more afraid of Mazarin, than any body, told me a fortnight after the King had left Paris, that we had all been great fools in not opposing it. I owned it both in my name and in the name of all the Frondeurs. I still continue to own it now very sincerely, and I think this fault one of the greatest that any one could have committed on this occasion: I mean any one of those that did not wish for the return of the Cardinal Mazarin; for as to those that were in his interest, it is certain that they acted as they ought to do. What made us commit that fault, was the natural inclination which all men have to seek rather for present ease, than for what may bring them ease afterwards. I fell into it as all the rest did, and the example of others makes me not the less ashamed of it. Our oversight was so much the greater, and more unpardonable, because we had foreseen the inconveniencies of it, which indeed were not only visible but palpable; and because we chose to run the risk of the greater to avoid the smaller. There was beyond comparison less danger for us in letting the Prince take breath and fortify himself in Guienne, than in setting the Queen at full liberty to recall her favourite. This errour is one of those which has, I think, obliged me to tell you sometimes, that the most ordinary cause of people's mistakes are their being too much frightened at the present danger, and not enough so at that which is remote. It was not long before we felt, as well as learnt, that capital faults that are committed in a party which is opposed to the royal authority, confound the whole party so entirely, that it is hardly possible for those that have had a hand in committing those faults, not to be reduced to the necessity of committing new ones, let them behave themselves never so wisely. I explain myself. The Duke having properly put into the Queen's hands the recalling of the Cardinal, had now but three ways to follow; of which one was, to consent to his return; another, to oppose it in concert with the Prince of Condé; and the last, to form a

third

third party in the ftate. The firft of thefe ways was fhameful, after the publick engagements into which he had entered; the fecond had but little fafety in it, by reafon of the continual negotiations, which the fub-divifions of the Prince's party were daily and inevitably the occafion of; the third was dangerous for the ftate, and befides impracticable on the Duke's fide, becaufe it was above his genius.

Mr. de Chateauneuf being with the court at a diftance from Paris, had no other way but the flattering the Queen with the hopes of her minifter's return, or the oppofing that return by the obftacles which he might form by his court intrigues. The firft of thefe ways was ruinous, becaufe the prefent ftate of affairs fhewed the hopes of that return to be too near to pretend to find means to baffle them; the fecond was chimerical, confidering the Queen's humour and obftinacy.

As to myfelf, in what manner could I behave that might be accounted wife and judicious? I was neceffarily obliged, either to ferve the Queen according to her defire, for the return of the Cardinal; or to oppofe it jointly with the Duke; or to keep a middle way between thefe two. I was befides neceffitated, either to come to an accommodation with the Prince, or to remain upon the fame terms I was. But what fafety could I meet with in all thefe feveral ways? My declaring for the Cardinal's return had irretrievably ruined me, with the Duke, the parliament, and the people; and for my furety I muft have depended on Mazarin's word. My joining with the Duke againft Mazarin's return, would according to all manner of rules have occafioned a quarter of an hour after a revocation of my nomination to the cardinalfhip. As to the Prince, could I remain with him upon the terms I was, fuppofing the Duke joined with him, and I with the Duke? Could I come, on the other hand, to an accommodation with the Prince, at the time that the Queen declared that fhe refolved upon my nomination, merely upon my promifing her that I would

not

not come to an accommodation with him? The King's
stay at Paris must have kept the Queen within such
bounds as would have prevented many of these inconveniencies, and would have lessened the others. We
contributed to the King's journey, when it was in our
power to have obstructed it by many imperceptible
means. What happened of it is what always happens
to those that lose certain instants which are critical and
decisive in affairs. For finding now that we had not
any good way left, every one of us chose that wherein
he perceived the least evil; which never fails to produce two ill effects: the one is, that such a medley of
views is always confused; and the other, that the dis-
tinguishing of these views can never happen but by a
mere work of chance. I shall explain this, and apply
it to the matter now in question, after I have given
you an account of some pretty curious and remarkable
facts that happened at that time.

The Queen, who had always had in her thoughts the
restoring of Cardinal Mazarin, began, as soon as she
found herself free, not to constrain herself so much in relation to his return; and Messieurs de Chateauneuf and
de Villeroi found, as soon as the court was arrived at
Poitiers, that the hopes which they had conceived
were not, at least by the event, well grounded. The
success which the Count d'Harcourt had had in
Guienne; the conduct of the parliament of Paris, who
was against the Cardinal, but who forbad under pain
of death the levies which the Prince made to oppose
his return; the divisions which appeared publickly in
the Duke's family, between those that were attached
to the Prince, and those that were my friends; encouraged those that supported the Cardinal's interest
with the Queen. The Queen herself had but too
much courage in things which she was inclined to.
D'Hocquincourt, who went secretly to Breull, shewed
the Cardinal a list of 8000 men ready to receive him
upon the frontiers, and to carry him in a triumphant
manner as far as Poitiers. I have learnt of one who
was present at their conversation, that nothing touched
him more sensibly than the thoughts of seeing an army

bearing

bearing his colours (for D'Hocquincourt had taken green colours to honour the Cardinal) and that this weakness in him was observed by every body. The Queen, however, continued in the way of negotiating, at the same time that she projected to make use of that of arms. Gourville took several journeys in favour of the Prince. Bertet came to Paris to bring over to the Cardinal's interest Mr. de Bouillon, Mr. de Turenne and me. This scene is curious enough to dwell a little longer upon it. I have already told you that Messieurs de Bouillon and de Turenne had left the Prince's party. They lived very retired in Paris, and except their particular friends, they were seen but by few persons. I was of that number; and knowing, as well as any other at least, of what merit and weight these gentlemen were, I omitted nothing, both to apprize the Duke of it, and to engage the two brothers in his interest. His natural aversion to the eldest, which he could give no reason for, hindered him from doing what he owed to himself on this occasion; and the contempt which the youngest had for him, for a reason best known to himself, did not help to make my negotiation succeed. That of Bertet, who arrived at Paris just at this time, became but one between the two brothers and myself, by the means of the Princess Palatine, who was equally a friend to us three, and to whom Bertet had orders to address himself directly.

She assembled us at her house betwixt twelve and one at night, where she presented Bertet to us, who after a torrent of expressions worthy a Gascon, told us that the Queen, who was resolved to recal the Cardinal, was unwilling to execute her resolution without hearing what we had to say to it. Mr. de Bouillon, who swore to me an hour after in the presence of the Princess Palatine, that he had not to that day received any proposals from the court, at least in form, seemed to me imbarrassed; but he got off in his usual manner, that is, as a man that knew better than any body that I have ever seen, how to speak the most, when he said

the

the leaft. Mr. de Turenne, who was more laconick, and in truth much more frank, turned towards me and faid : ' I believe that Mr. Bertet pulls by the fleeve ' all thofe he meets with in the ftreets with black cloaths ' on, to afk their opinion about the return of the Cardi- ' nal, for I do not fee any more reafon to afk it of my ' brother and me, than of all thofe that have this day ' paffed over the Pontneuf.' ' There is much lefs ' reafon to afk it of me,' anfwered I, ' for there are ' perfons who have this day paffed upon the Pontneuf, ' who might give their advice on the matter; but the ' Queen knows that this is a fubject which I dare not ' enter upon.' Bertet replied to me bluntly, and without the leaft hefitation : ' And what will then ' become of your Hat ?' ' What it fhall pleafe Provi- ' dence,' anfwered I. ' But what return will you ' make the Queen for it ?' added he. ' What I have ' told her a hundred times over,' anfwered I. ' I will ' come to no accommodation with the Prince, if my ' nomination is not revoked. But I will be friends ' with him to-morrow, and be one of his party, if ' they continue fo much as to threaten me with it.' The converfation grew warm, but however it ended tolerably well; and Mr. de Bouillon obferved as well as I, that Bertet's order was to reft contented with what I had fo often told the Queen upon that account, in cafe he could get no more from me.

As to Meffieurs de Bouillon and de Turenne, the confabulation which Bertet had with them was much ftronger. I call it confabulation out of jeft, becaufe nothing was more ridiculous than to fee a little infig- nificant fellow, fprung from the borders of Gafcony, take it upon him to perfuade two of the greateft men in the world to commit the greateft piece of folly imagin- able, which was to declare for the court before they had taken any meafures there. They would not therefore hearken to what Bertet faid to them at that time ; but they entered foon after into fure meafures with the court. Mr. de Turenne had the promife of commanding the armies, and Mr. de Bouillon had

affurances

affurances given him of the immenfe recompence which he has fince had in lieu of Sedan. They were fo kind as to intruft me with the fecret of their accommodation, though I was of a contrary party, and their confidence in me proved quickly after the caufe that they were not taken up.

The Duke, who was informed that they went to ferve the King, and that they were to leave Paris upon fuch a day, and at fuch an hour, told me juft as I came to take my leave of them, that it was neceffary to arreft them, and that he was going to order the Vifcount d'Autel, captain of his guards, to do it. I leave you to judge what trouble this put me to, when I came on one fide to confider the juft occafion I fhould give to think that I had betrayed my friends fecret, and on the other what means I could make ufe of to prevent the Duke from executing what he had refolved. I began by expreffing the doubt I was in about the truth of the information that had been given him. I reprefented to him the inconveniency of offending upon a mere fufpicion, perfons of that quality and of that merit; and when I perceived that he relied upon his information, which in effect was very certain, and that he perfifted in his refolution, I changed my note, and thought only upon delaying the thing till they had time to get away fafe. Fortune favoured my defign: The Vifcount d'Autel that was fent for, could not be found. The Duke amufed himfelf about a medal which Bruneau brought him very a-propos; and I had time to fend Mr. de Turenne word by Varennes, whom I met with by great luck, to efcape without lofing one moment of time; and in this manner the Vifcount d'Autel miffed the two brothers by two or three hours. The Duke's vexation at it lafted not much longer; and five or fix days after, having found him in good humour, I told him the thing. He did not take it amifs, and he was even fo kind as to tell me, that if I had opened myfelf to him at the time that he mentioned the thing to me, he had given the preference to my intereft in the thing, which
    was

was much more confiderable than his was, by reafon
of the fecret with which I had been entrufted. This
adventure was not an obftacle, as you may think, to
the ftrengthening the old friendfhip that was between
Mr. Turenne and me.

You have already feen, in more than one place of
thefe Memoirs, that Mr. de la Rochefoucaut's friendfhip for me was not upon the fame foot. A mark I
received of it, which deferves not to be omitted, is
this. Mr. Talon, who is now fecretary of the King's
clofet, and was even at that time attached to the intereft of the Cardinal, came one morning into my
chamber as I was in bed; and after making me a
compliment, and naming himfelf, (for I did not fo
much as know him by fight) he told me that though
he was not in my intereft, he thought himfelf obliged
to give me notice of the danger which I ran. That
his deteftation for evil acts, and his refpect for my
perfon, obliged him to tell me, that Gourville, and
la Roche Corbon, who belonged to Mr. de la Rochefoucaut, and was major of the garrifon of Damvilliers,
had like to have affaffinated me the day before upon the
key which is over-againft the Pont-Bourbon. I returned thanks, as you may well judge, to Mr. Talon,
for whom I fhall certainly preferve fo long as I live a
heart full of gratitude. But being ufed to receive
advices of this nature, I did not make due reflection
upon the name and the merit of the perfon that gave
me this notice, and I was not prevented by it from
going the next evening to Madam de Pomereux's alone
in my coach, with no other followers but two pages,
and three or four footmen. Mr. Talon came again to
me the next morning; and after having expreffed fome
furprize, at the little attention I had to his firft advice,
he told me that the gentlemen he had fpoke to me of,
had again miffed me about a quarter of an hour, near
the Blancs-manteaux, the night before about nine,
which was juft the time I came away from Madam de
Pomereux. This fecond advice, which feemed to me
more particular than the other, awakened me from my
lethargy.

lethargy. I kept upon my guard, and walked abroad in
a condition not to be furprized. I enquired, by means
of Mr. Talon himfelf, of the whole detail. I got la
Roche Corbon arrefted and examined before the Lieutenant-criminel. He faid he was ordered by Mr. de la
Rochefoucaut to take me away by force and carry me
to Damvilliers: that for that purpofe he had taken
with him fixty chofen men out of the garrifon of that
place, which he had got into Paris one by one; that
Gourville and he having obferved that I came away
every night from the Hôtel de Chevreufe, between
twelve and one, with ten or twelve gentlemen only,
in two coaches, they had pofted their men under the
arch which is over-againft the Pont-Bourbon; that
perceiving upon fuch a night that I had taken a contrary way to that of the key, they lay in wait for me
the next night near the Blancs-manteaux, where they
had again miffed me, becaufe the man who was to
have watched my coming from Madam de Pomereux's
had fpent his time in drinking at a tavern that was
near. This is la Roche Corbon's depofition, of
which the Lieutenant-criminel fhewed the Duke of
Orleans the original in my prefence. You will eafily
believe that after fuch a confeffion it had not been a
difficult matter for me to get him broke upon the
wheel, and that if he had been put to the rack, he
had perhaps confeffed fomething more than a defign
of carrying me away forcibly. The Count de Pas,
brother to Mr. de Feuquieres, and to the prefent
Count de Pas, to whom I had a very great obligation,
came to intreat me to give him his life, which I
granted him. I obliged the Duke to order the Lieutenant-criminel to ceafe his proceedings, and as the
Duke was telling me, that it ought at leaft to be
carried as far as the rack, to draw from him the whole
truth, I anfwered him in the hearing of all thofe that
were prefent: ' 'Tis fomething fo brave, Sir, fo gal-
' lant, and fo extraordinary, to men that undertake
' things of this nature, to expofe themfelves to utter
' ruin, if they fail to execute an action as difficult as
                                                    ' that

' that of taking away forcibly a man who never goes
' by night unaccompanied, and of carrying him sixty
' leagues beyond the frontiers of France; I say, 'tis
' something so gallant to run that risk, rather than
' resolve upon assassinating the person; that 'tis best
' in my opinion not to penetrate too far, for fear of
' discovering something that disfigures a generosity
' which does honour to our age.' Every one laughed
at what I said, and perhaps you will do the like.
The truth is, that I was willing to shew my gratitude to the Count de Pas, who had obliged me very
sensibly two or three months before, by sending me
back, gratis, all the cattle of Commercy which was
his by the rules of war, having re-taken it after the
twenty four hours allowed. I was afraid that if the
matter was carried farther, and that the design of an
assassination, which was already but too visible, was
once fully proved, it would be no longer in my
power to get that unhappy gentleman out of the hands
of the parliament. I caused the proceedings to cease
by the instances I made to the Lieutenant-criminel.
I intreated the Duke to cause the prisoner to be by
his authority removed to the Bastille, the Duke refu-
sing to set him at liberty, though I pressed him to do
it. The prisoner however found means to escape
five or six months after, being but very slightly
guarded. A gentleman who belongs to me, whose
name is Malclerc, having got with him la Forêt,
Lieutenant to the Provost de Lille, arrested Gourville
at Montlhery, as he was passing through that place
to go to the court, where Mr. de la Rochefoucaut
had always some secret negotiations; for Gourville
had not been above three or four hours under arrest,
when an order came from the first president to set
him free.

It must be own'd that I could not have escaped that
enterprize but by a kind of miracle. The day that
they missed me upon the key, I went to Mr. de Caumartin, to whom I said that I was so weary of riding
always in the streets with five or six coaches full of
gentle-

gentlemen, and of fire arms, that I defired him to take me into his, and to carry me without any liveries to the Hôtel de Chevreufe, where I intended to be betimes, though my defign was to fup there. Mr. de Caumartin made many difficulties about it, becaufe of the danger to which I was continually expofed; and he confented to it only upon my promifing that he fhould be rid of his charge at my return, and that my people fhould wait on me in the evening at the Hôtel de Chevreufe, as it was their cuftom to do. Upon my promifing this, I fat myfelf down at the back part of his coach, the curtains being half way down; and I remember that meeting upon the key with fome men with buff-coats, he faid to me : " Thefe men lie perhaps here in wait for you.' I made then no manner of reflection upon it; I fpent the whole evening at the Hôtel de Chevreufe, and at my coming away it happened that I had but nine gentlemen to accompany me, which was a very unfit number to prevent my being affaffinated. Madam de Rhodes, who had that evening a mourning coach quite new, finding that it rained, defired me to take her into my coach, fearing her own would daub her. I excufed it at firft, bantering her upon her nicety. Mademoifelle de Chevreufe came running after me to the ftair-cafe, and obliged me to do it; and this was what faved my life, becaufe I paffed through the ftreet of St. Honoré to go to the Hôtel de Briffac, where madam de Rhodes lodged, by which means they miffed me upon the key. If you add to this circumftance, that of the Blanc-manteaux, and if you reflect on the uncommon generofity of Mr. Talon, who being of a party fo directly oppofite to mine, was yet fo honeft as to give me notice of this enterprize, you will confefs that no man has it in his power to difpofe of the life of another man. I now come to what I have promifed you in refpect to the confequences which the King's journey produced.

I think that I was telling you that being convinced in lefs than a fortnight's time, that after the fault we
had

had committed there was no way left for us to take but what was accompanied with terrible inconveniencies, we at laſt choſe one that was, as it always proves in like caſes, the moſt dangerous of all, becauſe we came to no general determination, but every one of us was left to follow the way he thought leaſt hurtful. The Duke did not take up arms with the Prince, and thought thereby that he did much for the court. He declared himſelf in Paris and in the parliament againſt Mazarin's return, fancying that that was ſufficient to ſatisfy the public. Mr. de Chateauneuf continued for ſome time, whilſt the court was at Poitiers, to think that he might amuſe the Queen by putting her in hopes of reſtoring her favourite at ſuch conjunctures as he thought remote. But when he came to perceive that the impatience of the Queen and the eagerneſs of the Cardinal had brought theſe conjunctures much nearer than he expected, he reſolved upon ſpeaking plainly, and upon oppoſing directly Mazarin's return; which he did with that ſort of freedom which always proves as uſeleſs as it is odious; when it is only made uſe of in default of ſucceſs in one's artifice. The parliament, who was too far engaged againſt Mazarin to ſuffer his being reſtored, appeared exaſperated at the leaſt ſigns that were ſeen of it. But on the other ſide, being unwilling to do any thing contrary to form and to the King's authority, thoſe of that body were themſelves breaking all the meaſures that might be taken in order to prevent Mazarin's being reſtored. As to myſelf, I was againſt it as much as any body; but being as much againſt the Prince's being reſtored, for the reaſons which I have mentioned before, I was forced againſt my will to contribute to the firſt, by a conduct, which, though judicious for the preſent, becauſe it was neceſſary, was inexcuſable in its firſt principle, which was the committing one of thoſe capital errors after which it is impoſſible to do any thing wiſely. This was at laſt the thing that undid us all, as you will ſee by the ſequel.

The

The Duke, who was the man in the world who loved best to invent reasons that might prevent his coming to any determination, had all along been persuading himself that the Queen would never bring to effect the intention, which he owned she had and would always have, of recalling the Cardinal to court. When is was no longer in his power to deceive himself, he thought that the only remedy would be to imbarrass the Queen without exasperating her; and I observed on this occasion what I have done on many others, That men are naturally led to fancy that they will amuse others by the same means that they would themselves be amused by. The Duke never came to act but when he was pressed to it, and Fremont used to call him the inventor of interlocutory decrees. Of all the means that could be used to press him to act, the most effectual and infallible was that of fear; so that when he was free from that passion he would naturally remain unactive: The same temper that causes this disposition, causes likewise a disposition to resolve upon nothing till you are necessitated to do it. The Duke judged of the Queen's disposition by his own; and I remember that one day as I was representing to him that it was not only prudent, but even necessary to change one's conduct according to the different minds of those one has to do with; he answered me in these very words: ' That's a mistake; every body thinks ' alike; but there are persons that can better hide ' their thoughts than others.' The first reflection I made on these words was, that the greatest imperfection that men have, is the pleasure they take in persuading themselves that others are not free from the imperfections which they perceive themselves subject to. The Duke was deceived in this occasion, more still than in any other; for the Queen's boldness was sufficient, without any further exasperation (which was the thing the Duke would avoid) to bring her to execute her resolution; and that same boldness made her likewise overcome all the obstacles whereby the

Duke

Duke thought to traverse her. He was still willing to fancy that by not joining with the Prince, and by sending sometimes Mr. Damville, sometimes Laumont to negociate for him at court, he should amuse the Queen, whom he thought he might restrain by the apprehension of his declaring against the court. He was likewise willing to fancy that by inciting the parliament against the return of the minister, which he did in a public manner, he should only give the court that sort of apprehension which is fitter to restrain than to hurry on. As the Duke spoke very well, he one day expressed his whole thoughts very finely upon that subject, to the president de Bellievre and to me, which however did not at all persuade us. We opposed a multitude of reasons to what he had said; but as he was destroying all our reasons, by repeating only what I have already mentioned, that is, by saying to us: ' We have committed the fault ' of letting the Queen go out of Paris; all our steps ' now cannot be but faulty, and we can resolve upon ' nothing that is good; we must only go on as each ' day's occasions shall require, and that being granted, ' there is nothing to be done but what I have said:' It was on this occasion that I proposed to the Duke to form a third party, for which I have since received so many reproaches, and which I had thought on but two days before. You have here the whole plan of it.

I can say truly, and without vanity, that as soon as I saw the Queen out of Paris with an army, I took it almost for granted that the Cardinal's return was infallible; judging that the weakness of the Duke, the disappointment of the parliament, the negotiations to which the several cabals that divided the Prince's party were altogether inclined, could not hold long against the Queen's obstinacy and the weight of the royal authority. I have no design to value myself for having betimes discovered this, because I am forced to own that having made this discovery only from the time that the court was got to Poitiers, I made it, too late. I have already mentioned, and I cannot do it too

too much, that a greater fault than ours was never
committed, in not oppofing the King's journey, which
was ftill aggravated becaufe nothing could be more
obvious than the confequences. This grofs miftake
into which every one of us fell in emulation of one
another, is one of the caufes that has fometimes
obliged me to tell you, that there are faults that can
hardly proceed from humanity, being fo very grofs that
creatures endowed with common fenfe could never,
one would think, be guilty of them.

After I had enough confider'd and weighed the confequences of this, I thought of fome means for repairing it as to my particular; and having made all the
reflections on the ftate of things which you have feen
difperfed in the preceeding pages, I found but two
ways to come off, one of which I have mentioned
before, the Duke, whofe genius it fuited with, having
from the firft and of himfelf entered into it. It might
have fuited with my intereft, becaufe the Duke, by it,
not declaring himfelf for the Prince, and continuing
his negotiations at Court, gave me time thereby to
follicit for my hat. But this way appeared good to
me no farther than neceffity abfolutely required it;
becaufe it could not procure the advantage which it
might perhaps give by the event to the poft of Cardinal, without being very fufpicious to all thofe who
were in the intereft of what was called the public.
I was altogether unwilling to lofe that public, and
this confideration, added to the others, which I have
mentioned before, made me be diffatisfied with a conduct, the appearances of which were not good, and
the fuccefs befides very uncertain. I therefore thought
of another way, which was greater and nobler, and
which I pitched upon for that reafon without any
hefitation : it was, to endeavour to bring the Duke
to form publicly a third party, apart from the Prince,
and compofed of Paris, and of moft of the great cities
of the kingdom, which were very much difpofed to
ftir, and in fome of which I had good intelligence.

The

The count de * Fuenſaldagne, who thought that the diſtruſt I had of the Prince's ill-will to me, was the only thing that obliged me to keep ſome meaſures with the court, had ſent Don Antonia de la Cruſa to me, with ſome propoſals that gave me the firſt hint of the project which I am now ſpeaking of. That gentleman had offered to make a ſecret treaty with me, whereby he engaged to aſſiſt me with money, without obliging me to any thing that might diſcover my intelligence with Spain. The notion which I formed to myſelf from many other circumſtances that happened at that time, was to propoſe to the Duke to declare publicly in the parliament, that finding the Queen reſolved to reſtore Cardinal Mazarin to his former poſt, he was reſolved on his ſide to oppoſe it by all the ways which his birth and his public engagements would permit him to uſe; that it would agree neither with his prudence nor his honour to content himſelf with the remonſtrances of the parliament, which the Queen would at firſt elude, and contemn at laſt; whilſt the Cardinal was levying forces to enter into France, and to render himſelf maſter of the King's perſon, as he was already maſter of the Queen's inclinations; that being the King's uncle, he thought himſelf bound to tell the company that they were obliged in juſtice to join with him in a conjuncture, when properly ſpeaking the thing in queſtion was only the preſervation of their own arreſts, and of the declarations which were owing to their inſtances; that their prudence did no leſs require it, the company being well appriſed that the whole city conſpired with him in a deſign ſo neceſſary to the good of the kingdom; that he was unwilling to diſcover his mind ſo openly to them, before he had put himſelf in a condition that might permit him to aſſure them of the ſucceſs, conſidering the good order into which he

* So much mention having been made in theſe memoirs, of the Count de Fuenſaldagne and of the court of Bruſſels, ſome account will be given of them in the fourth volume, from the lord Clarendon's hiſtory.

had

had put affairs; that he had fo much in ready money; that he was already fure of fuch and fuch places; and upon the whole, that what ought to move the company more than any other thing, and even oblige them to embrace with joy the happy neceffity in which they found themfelves to work jointly with him for the good of the kingdom, was the public engagement into which he entered from that moment with them, never to entertain any intelligence with the enemies of the ftate, and never to hearken either directly or indirectly, to any negotiation that was not propofed in full parliament, the chambers being affembled; finally, that he difowned all that the prince had tranfacted and was tranfacting with the Spaniards; and that for that reafon, and becaufe of the frequent and fufpicious negotiations of all thofe of the Prince's party, he would have no other communication with him than what common civility required in refpect to a Prince of his merit. This is what I propofed to the Duke, and what I fupported with all the reafons that might fhew the poffibility of putting it in practice, of which I am ftill altogether perfuaded. I enlarged upon the inconveniencies of the oppofite conduct, and I foretold him all that he afterwards faw of the conduct of the parliament, where at the fame time that they were giving out arrefts againft the Cardinal, they declared thofe that fhould oppofe his return guilty of high treafon.

The Duke remained fixed in his refolution; either becaufe he was afraid, as he faid he was, of the union of the great cities, which indeed might become dangerous to the ftate; or becaufe he was afraid that the Prince fhould come to an accommodation with the Queen, and unite with her againft him; to which evil I had however fhewn him more than one remedy. What appeared to me was, that the burthen was too weighty for him to bear. The truth is that it was beyond his ftrength, and that for that reafon I was in the wrong to prefs him about it. It is true, befides, that the union of the great cities, confidering

the

the difpofition they were in, might have fatal confequences. That made me fcruple the thing, becaufe
it is certain that I have always feared what might in
effect prove prejudicial to the ftate, and Caumartin
could never approve that project for that reafon.
What hurried me into it, if I may fay fo, againft my
common way of. acting, and againft my inclination,
was the confufion into which we were going to fall
by following the contrary way ; and the ridicule of a
conduct, whereby it appeared to me that we were all
going to fight after the manner of the ancient Andabatæ *.

The fecond converfation which I had upon this
fubject with the Duke in the great walk of the Tuill-
leries, was pretty curious, and by the event almoft
prophetical. I faid to his Royal Highnefs ; ' What
' will become of you, Sir, when the Prince is re-
' conciled with the court, or gone over into Spain ?
' When the parliament fhall give out arrefts againft
' the Cardinal, and declare thofe criminal that fhall
' oppofe his return ? When you can no longer, with
' honour or fafety, remain a Frondeur, or become a
' Mazarinian.' The Duke anfwered ; ' I fhall re-
' main a fon of France ; you will become a Cardinal,
' and keep your coadjutorfhip.' To which I replied
inftantly, as if I had been moved by fome enthufi-
afm : ' You will be a fon of France confined at
' Blois, and I a Cardinal at the caftle of Vincennes.'
The Duke was not moved, whatever I could fay ;
and fo we were forced from day to day to brufh on
blind-fold, for fo Patru called our way of acting. I
will enter into the particulars of our conduct, after
I have given you an account of a very vexatious thing
that happened to me at that time.

Bertet, who was come to Paris, as you have already
feen, to negotiate with Mr. de Bouillon, Mr. de
Turenne, and me, had likewife the Queen's order to

* The Andabatæ were a fort of Gladiators who, according to
Cicero, fought blind-fold, whence the Latin proverb, Andabata-
rum more pugnare.

fee

fee Madam de Chevreufe, and to try to perfuade her
to attach herfelf ftill more intimately to her than fhe
had hitherto done. He found her extremely well difpofed to his negotiation. Laigues was a man full of
himfelf, and of a temper, befides, the moft change-
able in the world. Mademoifelle de Chevreufe had
fome time before given me notice that he was every
day telling her mother, that it was time to end this
bufinefs, that all was run into confufion, and that we
were all of us at a nonplus. Bertet, who was a
fharp, piercing, and infolent man, having perceived
Laigue's foible, made a very cunning ufe of it; he
threatened, he promifed, and at laft he engaged
Madam de Chevreufe to promife him that fhe would
no way oppofe the return of the Cardinal *, and that
in cafe fhe could not perfuade me upon that article,
fhe would do her utmoft to hinder Mr. de Noirmoutier, who was governor of Charleville and of
Mont Olympe, from fticking clofe to my intereft,
though he had the government of thefe places only by
my means. Noirmoutier fuffered himfelf to be cor-
rupted by her, under colour of the hopes fhe gave
him from the court; fo that when I would oblige him
to offer his fervices to the Duke, at the time that the
Cardinal was entering into France with his troops,
he declared to me that he belonged to the king; that
in any thing that related perfonally to me, he would
always pafs over all manner of confiderations; but
that in the prefent conjuncture, when the matter in
queftion was only a falling out between the Duke and
the court, he thought it unfit for him to be wanting
to his duty. You may judge how much I refented
this action. I complained of him in moft bitter terms,
and I carried my paffion fo far, that though I went
every day to fee Mademoifelle de Chevreufe, who
declared herfelf openly againft her mother on this

---

* I find in Madam de Motteville's Memoirs, a treaty pretended
to be concluded between Cardinal Mazarin, Madam de Cheve-
reufe, Mr. de Chateauneuf, and the Coadjutor, for reftoring the
Cardinal, which fhall be inferted at length in the fourth volume.

occafion,

occafion, I faluted neither him nor Laigues, and I hardly opened my mouth to Madam de Chevreufe. I return to my narration.

Upon the opening of the parliament at the St. Martin's of the year 1651, the company deputed Meffieurs Doujat and Baron to the Duke of Orleans, who was at Limours, to defire him to come and take his feat upon account of a declaration which the King had fent to their bar upon the 8th of October, whereby he declared the Prince guilty of high treafon.

The Duke came to the parliament on the 20th of November, and the firft prefident having enlarged, even emphatically, upon all that paffed in Guienne, concluded for regiftering the declaration as a thing neceffary, in order to obey the King's command, which was extremely juft (that was his term). The Duke, who, as you have feen before, had refolved otherwife, anfwered the firft prefident, that this matter was not to be hurried on; that there muft be time allowed to bring it to an accommodation; that it was the thing to which he applied himfelf to the beft of his power; that Mr. Damville was on the road, bringing him news from the court; that it was furprizing that they fhould prefs a declaration againft a Prince of the blood, and that not the leaft notice fhould be taken of Cardinal Mazarin's preparations, for entering in arms into the kingdom.

I fhould tire you to no manner of purpofe if I enter'd into the detail of what paffed in the affemblies of the chambers, which began, as I juft now faid, upon the 20th of November; fince thofe of the 23d, of the 24th, and of the 28th of that month, and of the firft and fecond of December, were, properly fpeaking, employed only in repeating continually the neceffity of regiftering the declaration, which the firft prefident preffed in the King's name; and in hearing the feveral reafons which the Duke alledged to oblige the company to delay it. At one time he expected the return of a gentleman whom he had fent to court to negotiate; at another he affured the company

that

that Mr. Damville was to come very soon from the court, with alterations that softened it; at other times he raised difficulties about the form that ought to be observed, when the matter in question was the condemning a Prince of the blood; at others he maintained that the thing necessarily previous to all, was to think of taking proper precautions against the return of the Cardinal; at others he presented letters from the Prince, some directed to the King, and some to the parliament, whereby he demanded to clear himself. When he found that the parliament would not suffer these letters to be read, because they came from a Prince who was in arms against his King, and that most of the company were inclining to have the declaration registered, he gave the thing over, and he sent Mr. de Croissi to the parliament upon the 4th, to desire the company not to expect him when the registering of the declaration was to be put to the vote, having resolved not to be present on that occasion. The matter was debated without him, and was carried by a majority of 120 votes, there having been in the debate three or four different opinions, but more in respect to form than to substance; and it was decreed to have the declaration read and registered, that it might be executed according to its form and tenor.

What put the Duke into a consternation, was that Croissi having desired the company, after the debate was over, to name a day to deliberate about the return of Cardinal Mazarin, which was no longer questioned; he was hardly heard. The Duke spoke to me of it that evening, and told me that he was resolved to stir up the people in order to awaken the parliament; to which I answered in these very words; ' The parliament, Sir, will awake, only to make ' speeches against the Cardinal, and then will fall ' again into a lethargick sleep. Besides, I desire your ' Royal Highness to consider that the clock had struck ' twelve when Mr. de Croissi spoke, and that every ' body wanted their dinner.' He took this last for a jest, though I spoke it very seriously; he ordered
Ornano,

Ornano, mafter of his wardrobe, to raife a kind of commotion by the means of Maillard, of whom I have had occafion to fpeak in the fecond volume of thefe Memoirs. That wretch, to cover his game the better, went with twenty or thirty of his gang to make a noife at the Duke's Palace, from whence they went to the firft prefident, who ordered his gates to be opened to them, and fpeaking with his ufual intrepidity, he threatened to fend them to the gallows.

Upon the 7th the parliament in a full affembly of the chambers put out an arreft to prevent, for the future, thefe infolences. However the company thought fit to confider that it was neceffary for them to take off the pretences which occafioned them, and they affembled upon the 9th to deliberate upon the current report of the fudden return of the Cardinal. The Duke having faid in that affembly, that that return was but too certain, the firft prefident tried to fhift it off by propofing to call for the King's council, and to get the informations read, which, according to former arrefts, ought to have been made againft the Cardinal. Mr. Talon reprefented that the matter in queftion had nothing to do with thefe informations; that the Cardinal having been condemned by the King's declaration, there was no need of other proofs, and that if any informations were to be made, it could only be about the contraventions againft that declaration. His conclufions were, to depute to his Majefty to inform him of the current report of the Cardinal's return, and to intreat him to confirm what he had promifed to all his people upon this fubject, by his royal word. He added, that all governors of provinces and of towns fhould be forbidden to give paffage to the Cardinal, and that all other parliaments fhould be informed of this arreft, and exhorted to put out fuch a one. After thefe conclufions of the advocate-general, they went on to deliver their opinions; but having not time to go through it that day, and the Duke finding himfelf ill on the Sunday night, the affembly was put off to

Wednef-

Wednefday the 15th of December. The company upon that day agreed almoft unanimoufly to put out an arreft conformable to the advocate-general's con-, clufions, which, befides what I have mentioned, imported, that the King fhould be intreated to acquaint the Pope and other foreign Princes with the reafons that had obliged him to remove the Cardinal from his perfon, and from his councils.

There was an interlude that day which will convince you that it was not without reafon that I had forefeen how difficult it would be for me to act my part conformably to the conduct which we followed. Machaut and Fleury, two counfellors devoted altogether to the Prince, having faid in their fpeeches, that the diforders of the ftate were occafioned only by perfons who would by any means whatfoever carry the Cardinal's hat, I interrupted the firft to tell him, that I was fo ufed to fee Cardinal's hats in my family, that it was not likely that I fhould be fo much dazzled at its colour, as to be prompted by it to do all the hurt with which I was charged. As one ought not to interrupt any body whilft he is fpeaking, a great clamour arofe againft me in favour of Machaut. I begged of the company to excufe my warmth, which however, added I, does not proceed from want of refpect.

One of the company having faid in delivering his opinion, that they ought to proceed in refpect of Cardinal Mazarin, as was formerly done in refpect of the Cardinal de Châtillon, brother to the Admiral de Coligny, which was to fet a price upon his head, I rofe up, as did likewife all the other members that were clergymen, they being forbidden by the canons of the church to affift at any deliberations where the fhedding of blood is mentioned.

Upon the 18th thofe of the inquefts went by deputies to the grand chamber, to afk for an affembly of the chambers, on occafion of a letter which Cardinal Mazarin had written to Mr. d'Elbeuf, to afk his advice about his return into France. The firft prefident
owned

owned that he had that letter, which Mr. d'Elbeuf
had fent to him: that he had at the fame time difpatched an exprefs to the King to give him an account of it, and to let him know the confequence;
that he was expecting the return of his exprefs,
intending afterwards to affemble the chambers, if the
King's anfwer was not to his fatisfaction. Thofe of
the inquefts were not fatisfied with this. They fent
again the next day, which was the 19th, their deputies
to the grand chamber, and the firft prefident was
obliged to affemble the chambers upon the 20th,
having firft invited the Duke to be prefent. The firft
prefident having then acquainted the company that
the occafion of this affembly was the above-mentioned
letter, and the coming of Mr. de Noailles to Mr.
d'Elbeuf, the King's council were fent for, who, by
the mouth of Mr. Talon, gave their conclufions,
which were, that conformably to the arreft given upon
fuch a day the parliament fhould, as foon as poffible,
fend deputies to the King to inform his Majefty of
what paffed upon the frontiers; that his Majefty
fhould be intreated to write to the elector of Cologne
that he fhould order the Cardinal to withdraw from
his dominions; that the Duke of Orleans fhould be
defired to fend to the King in his own name, to the
fame effect, and to fend likewife to the Marefchal
d'Hocquincourt, and to the other generals, to give
them notice of Cardinal Mazarin's defign to return
into France; that fome of the company fhould be
named to go upon the frontiers, and make a verbal
procefs of what was doing there in relation to that
return; that the mayors and the magiftrates of places
fhould be forbidden to give the Cardinal paffage, or a
place of affembly to any troops that intended to favour
him, or any retreat to any of his relations or fervants;
that Mr. de Noailles * fhould be fummoned to appear
in perfon at the bar of this parliament, to give an

* I find Noailles in the French copy, but I believe it fhould be
Navailles.

account

account of the correspondence which he entertained
with him, and that monitory letters * should be published, the better to discover what that correspondence
was. This is an abstract of the conclusions conformably to which the arrest was given.

You think, without doubt, the Cardinal crushed by
this last arrest of the parliament, considering that the
King's council themselves had furnished all the mate-
rials towards his ruin? But you mistake, for at the
same instant that that arrest was agreed on, and that
people's passions were at the highest, a counsellor having said, that the troops which were assembled upon
the frontiers for the service of Mazarin would make
a jest of their arrest, if it was not signified to them
by men armed with good muskets and pikes; that
counsellor, I say, whose name I do not remember,
but who spoke, as you see, pretty much to the purpose, was repulsed with a general outcry, as if he had
said the most foolish thing in the world, the whole
company crying out aloud that the King alone had a
right to withdraw or to disband his own forces.

But I desire you to reconcile, if you can, that tender
regard for the King's authority, with an arrest that
forbid at the same time all towns to give passage to
one whom that authority would restore. What is most
wonderful is, that a thing that appears a prodigy to
future ages, is not felt at the moment, and that those
whom I have heard reason since upon this subject in
the same manner I do, would have sworn at that
time that there was nothing contradictory, between the
arrest and the restriction. What I have seen during
our troubles has explained to me in more than one
occasion, what I could not before comprehend in
history. You find there some facts so opposite to one
another that they become incredible; but experience
teaches us that all that appears incredible is not false.

---

* Letters from the spiritual judge to be read in all parish
churches, admonishing those who are informed of the truth of
any fact in question, to declare it on oath, under pain of excom-
munication.

You

You will still find this truth better supported by what passed after this in the parliament, which I intend to come to, after I have mentioned some circumstances that relate to the court.

There was some contest there in the cabinet council about the manner in which the Queen was to act in respect to the parliament; some said that she ought to manage that company carefully, and others that it would be best to abandon them to themselves; these were the words which Brachet used, speaking to the Queen. They had been inspired and dictated to him by Menardeau Champré, a counsellor of the grand chamber, and a man of good sense. He had charged Brachet to tell the Queen from him, that the best way that she could take was to let every thing at Paris run into confusion, it being always a means to restore the royal authority, when once that confusion is arrived to a certain pitch: that to that effect she ought to order the first president to come to court, and execute there his office of lord-keeper; to do the like to Mr. de la Vieuville, and to all those that were under him, in his post of the finances; and to cause likewise the grand council, &c. to come to the court. This advice, which was grounded upon the disappointments which an action of this nature would produce, in a city where it cannot be disowned, but that all the several establishments are linked in a very strict manner together, was opposed with a great deal of force by all those who were afraid that the Cardinal's enemies would make use against him of the weakness of the president le Bailleul, who by the first president's absence would be left at the head of the parliament, and of the animosity of the people which such an action would serve only to increase. The Cardinal was a long while in suspence about the reasons that supported these two opinions; though the Queen, who by her inclination was always led to think the most violent the best, had already declared for the first. What determined him, as I have learnt since of the Mareschal de la Ferté, was what Mr. de

Senneterre wrote to him in very strong terms, in
favour of the first opinion, and his frightening him
with the first president's manner of speaking in the
parliament, which was often very bold, and did sometimes, added Senneterre, more harm than his good
intentions could do good: but that was saying too
much by far. The first president at last left Paris by
the King's order, even without taking his leave of the
parliament, which he did by the advice of Mr. de
Champlatreux, pretty much against his inclination.
Mr. de Champlatreux was in the right, because he
might certainly have run some risk in the commotion
which such a step might have occasioned. I went to
take my leave of him the day before he left Paris, and
he said these very words to me: ' I am going to
' court, and shall there speak the truth; after which
' the King must be obeyed.' I am persuaded that he
really was as good as his word. I return to the parliament.

Upon the 29th of December the King's council
came to the grand chamber, and presented to the company a Lettre-de-cachet from the King, which in-
joined them to delay the sending the deputies who
had been named in the arrest of the 13th to go to
his Majesty, because he had more than sufficiently
explained his intentions to them formerly. Mr.
Talon added, that he was obliged by the duty of his
place to represent to them the commotion which such
a deputation might cause in a time so full of troubles.
' You see, continued he, the whole kingdom in mo-
' tion, and we have here a letter from the parliament'
' of Roûen, which informs us that they have put out
' an arrest against Cardinal Mazarin, in conformity
' to yours of the 13th.'

The Duke of Orleans spoke next. He said that
Cardinal Mazarin was arrived at Sedan on the 25th,
that the Marefchals d'Hocquincourt and de la Ferté
were going to join him with an army, in order to
bring him to court; and that it was time to oppose
his defigns, of which there was no longer any room

to

to doubt. I cannot exprefs to what degree people's minds were moved. They would hardly ftay till the King's council had taken their conclufions, which were to fend inceffantly their deputies to the King, and to declare from this moment Cardinal Mazarin and his adherents guilty of high-treafon; to enjoin the commons to fall upon them; to forbid the mayors and magiftrates of towns to give them paffage; to fell his library and all his houfhold goods. The arreft added to thefe conclufions, that the fum of 150,000 livres fhould be taken preferably, out of the fale, to be given to the man who fhould bring the Cardinal, dead or alive. At the mentioning of this all the ecclefiafticks rofe up, for the reafon I have already mentioned.

No doubt but you think affairs very much exafperated, and you will ftill be the more perfuaded of it, when I have told you that upon the fecond of January of the year 1652, a fecond arreft came out upon the conclufions of the King's council, and upon advice that the Cardinal had already paffed Epernay, by which it was farther ordered, that all the other parliaments fhould be defired to give a like arreft to that of Paris of the 29th of December; that two more deputies fhould be fent with the four already named, to the paffages, with an order to arm the commons; that the Duke of Orleans' forces fhould be commanded to oppofe the march of the Cardinal, and that orders fhould be fent for their fubfiftance. Is it not true that after thefe conclufions and this arreft, it was likely that the parliament was for a war? Nothing like it. A counfellor having faid that the firft ftep for the fubfifting the troops, was the having of money, which he propofed to take out of that part of the efcheats that related to the annual duty, he was repulfed with indignation and outcries; and the fame company that had juft before ordered the march of the Duke of Orleans' troops, in order to oppofe thofe of the King's, treated the propofals of touching the King's money with the fame fcruple of confcience,

as they would have done in a time of the greateft
tranquillity. I faid to the Duke, at our coming away,
that he might fee that I had not deceived him when
I had affured him fo often, that a civil war could be
but ill managed with the conclufions of the King's
council. He had another opportunity of being convinced of it the next day; for the parliament being
affembled, and the marquis de Sablonnieres, colonel
of the regiment of Vallois, coming in to him and
telling him that du Coudray-Giviers, one of thofe
named to arm the commons, had been killed, and
that Befaud, who was the other, had been taken prifoner by the enemies, the commotion was fuch in the
company, that it could not have been greater or more
general, if the fact had been fome horrible and detef-
table murder, committed with premeditated malice,
in a time of perfect tranquillity. I remember that
Bachaumont, who fat that day behind me, whifpered me thefe words in the ear by way of raillery
againft his brother counfellors: ' I am going to gain
' a mighty reputation, for my opinion fhall be to have
' Mr. d'Hocquincourt hanged and quartered for hav-
' ing been fo infolent as to fall upon perfons that are
' arming the commons againft him.' The paffion
which the company fhewed at this prevarication of
Mr. d'Hocquincourt's, againft which they made a
decree in form, was in my opinion the caufe of their
not refufing audience to a gentleman fent by the
Prince of Condé, with a letter and a petition to them;
for I can find no other reafon for it, after having
regiftered the King's declaration againft the Prince;
when this fame parliament had refufed to receive a
letter and a remonftrance, fent to them from that
Prince upon the fecond of December, which was a
time when there were as yet no formal proceedings
begun in the parliament againft him. Upon the
11th in the evening, being with Mr. Talon, I made
him obferve this circumftance; and he, who had
himfelf in his conclufions been for the receiving the
letter, made me this anfwer: ' We no longer know
                                        ' what

‘ what we are a doing; we are out of the beaten,
‘ road.’ That gentleman however infifted in his conclufions, that they ought not to touch the King's
money, which he affirmed to be facred, whatever
fhould happen. Judge, I befeech you, how that
could agree with the conclufions taken by him two or
three days before, whereby he was for arming the
commons and for ordering the Duke's troops to march
and oppofe thofe of the King. I have wondered a
thoufand times at the want of fenfe of thofe wretched
gazetteers that have written the hiftory of thofe times.
I have not met with any one that has fo much as made
the leaft reflection upon thofe contradictions, which
are however the things that beft deferve to be mentioned and obferved. I was at a lofs even at that
time in what I obferved in Mr. Talon's conduct, that
gentleman being certainly one of a refolute mind and
of a folid judgment, which made me fometimes believe
that what he did was affected. But I remember that
I loft that opinion, after I had well confidered of it ;
and that I had fufficient reafons (the particulars of
which are now out of my memory) to be perfuaded
that he was, like the reft, carried away by the ftream,
which in thefe fort of times ebbs and flows with a
violence that agitates men in fuch an oppofite manner.

This is exactly what happened to Mr. Talon, in
the deliberation of which I am now fpeaking; for
after his having concluded to give entrance to the
Prince's gentleman, and to have the Prince's letter
and petition read, he added, that both ought to be
fent to the King, and that the company ought not to
deliberate upon it till they had an anfwer from his
majefty. The Prince's letter to the parliament was
only an offer he made to the company of his perfon
and of his forces, againft the common enemy ; and
his petition tended towards having the execution of
the declaration againft him, which had been regiftred,
put off till the declarations and arrefts given againft
the Cardinal had had their full and entire effect.

They could not put an end to the deliberation that
day, though they had been upon it till three in the
afternoon.   It was made an end of the next day, and
an arreft was given, whereby it was ordered that Mr.
d'Hocquincourt fhould be required ·to fet Meffieurs
Betaud and Giviers at liberty, this laft not ·being
killed as it had been reported, but having only been
made a prifoner with the other; and that in cafe of a
refufal Mr. d'Hocquincourt and all his pofterity fhould
be made anfwerable for what might happen to them ;
that the declaration and arrefts given againft the Cardinal fhould be executed; that all his Majefty's fubjects fhould be forbidden to acknowledge the Marefchal
d'Hocquincourt and others that affifted the Cardinal
as commanders of the King's forces ; and that a ftop
fhould be put to the execution of the declaration and
arrefts given againft the Prince of Condé, till the
declaration and arrefts againft the Cardinal fhould be
entirely executed.

What paffed at the parliament on the 16th and 19th
of January is of no moment.   Mr. de Nemours arrived at Paris on the 19th in the evening, coming
from Bourdeaux, and defigning to go into Flanders,
to bring from thence fome forces which the Spaniards
had promifed the Prince.   It is neceffary to take up a
little higher the particulars relating to this journey of
Mr. de Nemours, which occafioned much jealoufy to
the Duke of Orleans.

I believe that I have already told you, that the
Duke was five or fix times in a day cruelly embarraffed,
being perfuaded that every thing went at random, and
that it was even impoffible to remedy it.   There were
inftants in which he was infpired with that fort of
courage that proceeds from defpair, and it was in thefe
inftants that he ufed to fay, that the worft that could
happen to him would .be to live in quiet at Blois.
But the Dutchefs, who did not like that kind of quiet
for him, often troubled the agreeable ideas which he
was forming to himfelf of it, and confequently often
gave him apprehenfions of the inconveniencies, which
                                                    he

he naturally feared already but too much. The ftate in which affairs were, did not help to hearten him, for befides his fancying himfelf always upon the borders of precipices, the fteps which he really was obliged to take and follow, were of a nature that might caufe the moft ftout and refolute to ftumble. The tranfactions that paffed upon Maundy-Thurfday, could not get out of his mind; and as he feared befides extremely to be under the dependance of the Prince, which he looked upon as infallible if he fhould unite entirely with him, he lived in fuch a conftraint that he was forced ten times a day to change his moft natural fteps, and at the time that he was in hopes that the Cardinal's return might be ftill traverfed by fome other means than a civil war, he had ufed himfelf fo much to preferve the regards proper to fuch a difpofition, that when he was obliged to change his meafures, his conduct became irregular, and altogether like that of the parliament.

You have already feen more than once that the company, in the fame fitting, ordered the marching of forces, and would not allow thofe forces the means to fubfift; that they armed the people againft forces, who had their commiffions and orders in due form from the King, and oppofed at the fame time with a mighty noife, thofe that propofed the difbanding of thefe forces; that they enjoined the commons to fall upon the Generals of the King's army that affifted Mazarin, and forbad at the fame inftant, upon pain of death, to make any levies without an exprefs commiffion from his Majefty. The Duke, who imagined that by remaining united to the parliament he fhould oppofe Mazarin independently of the Prince, gave way, by this union, ftill more eafily to his natural inclination, in which he was already but too much helped by his irrefolution. That inclination led him, as I have already faid, to keep the balance even on both fides, whenever he found any room to do it. This medium, to which he was before inclined, became neceffary by his union with a company whofe fteps
were

were always grounded upon the maxim of reconciling
the royal ordinances with a civil war. This ridicule
is in fome manner hid in refpect to the parliament, by
reafon of the majefty of that great body, which is
looked upon by moft people as infallible. But it
always difcovers itfelf very foon in private perfons, of
what rank foever, let them even be Princes of the
Blood, or Sons of France. It is what I was faying
every day to the Duke, who agreed to it, but had
always the fame anfwer in readinefs, which was : ' What
' better fteps can be taken ?' I believe that he repeated
that faying above fifty times in a converfation which I
had with him the day that Mr. de Nemours arrived at
Paris. The Duke expreffing a great deal of trouble
about the forces which he was going to fetch out of
Flanders, for fear they fhould make the Prince of
Condé too ftrong, and adding, that that Prince afterwards would make ufe of them to ferve his own turn,
I told him, that I was exceffively forry to fee him in a
ftate, wherein nothing could bring him comfort, and
every thing was able to, and muft, afflict him. ' If
' the Prince is beaten,' added I, ' what will you do
' with the parliament, confidering that that company
' would not move one ftep without the conclufions of
' the King's council, even in cafe that the Cardinal
' was with an army at the door of the grand chamber ?
' What will you do if the Prince is victorious, when
' you ftand already in fear of 4000 men that are
' fetching to join him ?'
    Though I fhould have been very forry, both by
reafon of the engagement I was in with the Queen
upon that fubject, and likewife upon account of my
private intereft, that the Duke fhould have united
intimately with the Prince, which he could not do,
befides, without fubmitting fhamefully to him, confidering the inequality of their two genius's, I fhould
have been glad however that his weaknefs fhould not
have filled him with that envy and fear which he fhewed
on his account, becaufe it feemed to me that medium's
might have been found to make the Prince ferviceable

to his ends, without giving him all the advantages which he was afraid of. I own that those mediums had in them a great deal of difficulty, and consequently that it was impossible for the Duke to make use of them, considering that he never made any difference between things difficult, and things impossible. It is incredible. to think what pains I took to persuade him that prudence required of him to do his best to prevent the parliament from declaring against these auxiliary troops that were to come to the Prince. I represented to him with vigour, all the reasons that obliged him not to deprive the Prince of that assistance, in the present posture of affairs, and not to accustom the company to condemn the steps that were taking against Mazarin. I agreed with him that it was necessary to blame in publick the union with the Spaniards, that there might appear no alteration in his conduct; but I maintained that he ought at the same time to elude the deliberations which the company would make upon that subject; and I proposed to him the means to do it, which by the diversions that would naturally offer of themselves, and by the weakness of the President le Bailleul, could hardly have been perceived. The Duke remained for a long time resolved to let the thing take its course, because, added he, the Prince is already but too strong: and after I had convinced him with my reasons, he did all that weak men never fail to do in like occasions. They turn so short when they change their opinion, that they cease to measure their steps, and run instead of walking. The Duke accordingly, whatever I could say to the contrary, resolved suddenly upon justifying the march of these foreign troops, and upon justifying it in the parliament by illusory arguments that deceive nobody, but serve only to shew the intention one has to deceive. This sort of fallacy has been in use at all times, but it must be owned that in the time of Cardinal Mazarin it has been studied and practised, more frequently and more insolently than in any other. It has not only been daily made use of in common affairs, but it has

3   triumphed

triumphed in publick edicts, arrests, and declarations;
and I am perfuaded that this publick outrage done to
probity has been, as I believe I have already faid in
the firft part of thefe Memoirs, the chiefeft caufe of
our revolutions. The Duke told me at the parliament,
that thefe forces ought not to be reckoned as Spanifh,
becaufe they were made up of Germans. You muft
obferve that they had been for three or four years in
the fervice of Spain in Flanders, under the command
of a Prince of the houfe of Wirtemberg, who was
paid by his Catholick Majefty, and that many perfons
of quality of the Low Countries were even officers
under him. I reprefented in vain to the Duke, that
what we were daily blaming the moft in the Cardinal's
conduct, was this manner of fpeaking and of acting
fo oppofite to the moft known truths. He laughed at
my fcruple, and anfwered me, that I might have obferved that the world defires to be deceived. This
faying is true, and was verified on this occafion.

I beg leave of you to ftop here for a moment, to
make this obfervation; that one ought not to wonder
if hiftorians, who treat of matters with which they
have had nothing to do, miftake fo often, when it is
impoffible for men who have been neareft to the facts,
not to miftake likewife, in an infinity of occafions,
mere appearances, fometimes falfe in every circumftance, for the real truth. There was not a man, not
only in the parliament, but even in the Duke's palace,
who did not believe at that time that my only bufinefs
with the Duke was to break the meafures which the
Prince kept with him. I fhould certainly have done
my beft to break thefe meafures, if I had fo much as
perceived the leaft difpofition in the Duke to enter into
any with the Prince, that had been folid and effential.
But I can affure you, that he was fo backward, even
to thofe, which the prefent ftate of affairs, and common prudence obliged him to hearken to, that I was
forced to labour hard in order to perfuade him to
preferve thefe laft meafures with fome fort of decency,
at the fame time that all the world imagined that I was
-　　doing

doing quite the contrary. I was not forry however for the report fpread about it by the Prince's partifans, though thefe reports coft me now and then fome rebukes which I received in delivering my opinion in the affembly of the chambers. I undertook at firft to turn thefe rebukes to my advantage, in keeping the Queen in good humour with me. But fhe was not long amufed by it; and having been informed, that though I kept ftrictly to the word I had given her, not to come to any accommodation with the Prince, I advifed the Duke however not to break with him, fhe caufed Brachet, who came to Paris at that time, to reproach me with it: I got him to write a memorial which I dictated to him, that made it clearly appear that I had not been wanting in any one thing of what I promifed her; which was true, becaufe I promifed her nothing that was contrary to what I had advifed the Duke. Brachet told me at his coming back, that the Queen was convinced of it, after having examined my reafons at his perfuafion; but that Mr. de Chateauneuf had exclaimed at them, and fpoke thefe very words to the Queen: ' I am not, Madam, no more ' than the coadjutor, for recalling the Cardinal; but ' it is fo criminal in a fubject to indite a memorial like ' this, which I have feen, that were I his judge, I ' would upon this fingle point immediately condemn ' him.' The Queen was fo kind as to command Brachet to relate thefe particulars to me, and to tell me that the Cardinal would be more true to me than that wretch, though I gave him no occafion: thefe were her words. I return to the parliament.

What paffed there from the 12th to the 24th of January 1652, is not worthy of your attention, nothing elfe almoft having been fpoken of but the affair of Meffieurs Betaud and Giviers, which was treated all the while as if it had been an affaffination committed in cold blood next to the parliament-hall.

Upon the 24th the Prefident de Bellievre, and the other deputies who had been at Poitiers, reported the remonftrances which they had made to the King, with
all

all the force and vehemence imaginable, in the name
of the company, against the return of the Cardinal.
They said that his Majesty, after advising with the
Queen and his Council, had caused the Lord Keeper
to answer to them in his presence, that when the Parliament had given their last arrests, they were not
apprized, without doubt, that Cardinal Mazarin had
not made any levies of forces but by the express command of his Majesty; that he had the King's orders
to enter into France, and to bring these forces along
with him; that the King therefore took not ill what
the company had hitherto done; but that he made
likewise no doubt that when they had learnt these particulars, and were further informed that Cardinal
Mazarin required only the means of clearing himself,
they would give an example to all his subjects of the
obedience which they owed him. I leave you to judge
of the commotion which an answer so little conformable to the solemn promises which the Queen had
repeated above ten times, must cause in the parliament.
The Duke of Orleans did not appease it, by saying
that the King had sent Ruvigny to speak to him in the
like manner, and to order him to send to their garrisons the regiments that went under his name. The
heat was still increased by the arrests of the parliaments of Toulouze and of Rouen, which were affect-
edly read at that instant, as well as a letter of the
parliament of Brittany, whereby that company desired
an union with that of Paris, against the violences of
the Marefchal de la Meilleraie. Mr. Talon spoke
against the Cardinal with a vehemence that had something of rage in it. He thundered against the Marefchal de la Meilleraie, in behalf of the parliament
of Rennes; but his conclusions went no further than
to remonstrances against the return of the first, and to
informations against the disorders committed by the
Marefchal d'Hocquincourt's forces. The heat evapo-
rated in words, the clock struck twelve, and the
deliberation was put off to the next day. It produced
an arrest conformable to Mr. Talon's conclusions, with
                                                    this

this addition only, made chiefly in view of the Marefchal de la Meilleraie, that they fhould not proceed in the parliament to the reception of any Dukes and Peers, nor of Marefchals of France, till the Cardinal was out of the kingdom.

An accident happened by mere chance in this fitting; which was looked upon as a mighty myftery. The Marefchal d'Eftampes in delivering his opinion, having faid without any defign, that the parliament ought to unite with the Duke for the expelling the common enemy, fome councellors fupported this opinion, without meaning any hurt, and others were againft it, moved to it merely by that fpirit which, as I have fomewhere told you, is oppofed to all that is, or appears concerted in thefe fort of companies. The Prefident de Novion, who was entirely reconciled with the court, took hold very artfully of this conjuncture to ferve the Queen; and judging very rightly that the perfon of the Marefchal d'Eftampes, who was of the Duke's family, gave him room to infinuate that there was a defign, in what had been certainly fpoken without any premeditation, he exclaimed with the Prefident de Mefmes, againft the word Union, as againft the thing in the world the moft criminal. He enlarged in an eloquent manner upon the injury done to the parliament, in thinking that company capable of an union which would infallibly caufe a civil war. The minds and hearts of moft perfons became of a fudden paffionate for the royal authority. Clamorous fpeeches were made againft the propofal of the poor Marefchal d'Eftampes, which was rejected with horror, as if the like had not been propofed perhaps above fifty times by thirty counfellors within fix weeks; as if the parliament had not returned thanks to the Duke in all their fittings, for the obftacles he put to the Cardinal's return; and, in fhort, as if the King's council themfelves in their conclufions had not been in two or three different manners, for praying the Duke to caufe his troops to march for that effect. This is a confirmation

of

of what I have already told you, that nothing is more
like the people than thefe companies.

The Duke of Orleans, who was prefent at that
fcene, was ftruck down with it, and it was that that
determined him to join his forces to thofe of the
Prince. He had for a long time kept him in hopes
that he would do it, both becaufe he had not the
courage to refufe them to the Prince, and becaufe
Mr. de Beaufort, who was perfonally interefted in the
thing, being to command thefe forces, preffed him to
the laft degree about it. But the Duke confeffed to
me that evening, that it was with a great deal of
difficulty that he refolved upon it, but that finding
nothing good to be hoped for from the parliament,
which was like to undo itfelf and to undo all thofe
that were joined to it; it was not fit to fuffer the Prince
of Condé to be ruined; and he was very near propofing to me that I fhould come to an accommodation
with him. He was however prevented from coming
fo far, either by reflecting on my engagements, that
were not unknown to him; or becaufe his fear of
falling into the Prince's dependency (and this was
what appeared to me) worked ftronger ftill upon him,
than that which this difappointment of the parliament
had put him into. You will fee the fequel of this,
after I have given you an account of what was paffing
at Court at that time.

I have, I believe, already told you that Mr. de
Chateauneuf had at laft taken the refolution to fpeak
plainly his mind to the Queen, and to declare againft
Cardinal Mazarin's return. This he did, in my
opinion, without any hopes of fuccefs, and with the
only view of gaining by it a merit with the publick
for his retreat, which he looked upon as unavoidable,
being very willing to make at leaft the people believe
that it was the confequence and the effect of the liberty
with which he had oppofed Mazarin's return. He
afked leave to retire, which was granted him.

Cardinal Mazarin arrived at Court, and I leave you
to judge in what manner he was received there. He
found

found there Mr. le Tellier, who had been already recalled by Meſſieurs de Chateauneuf and de Villeroi, for a certain reaſon which was made a myſtery of at that time, and the particulars of which I cannot remember. The Cardinal determined the King to go towards Saumur, though a great many adviſed him to march into Guienne, to make an end of puſhing the Prince. He thought it beſt to begin with Mr. de Rohan *, who being Governor of Angers, had, with the town and caſtle, declared for the Prince. ' Angers being beſieged by the Mareſchals de la Meilleraie and d'Hocquincourt, held out but a very little time, and coſt but few men. The Pont Sé, wherein Beauveau commanded for the Prince, ſurrendered immediately, and almoſt without any reſiſtance, to Meſſieurs de Noailles and de Broglio. The King left Saumur, and went to Tours, where the Archbiſhop of Rouen † laid the firſt foundation of the favour he was afterwards in, by complaining to the King, in the name of the Biſhops that were at court, of the arreſts given in the parliament againſt Cardinal Mazarin. Their Majeſties came afterwards to Blois, where Mr. Servien joined them. The Mareſchal d'Hocquincourt came near that town with his army, which committed incredible diſorders for want of pay. We ſhall ſee what progreſs this army made, after I have given you an account of what was paſſing at Paris.

I am perſuaded that I ſhould tire you if I ſhould enter into the detail of what was tranſacted in the Aſſemblies of the Chambers, from the 25th of January to the 15th of February. There was but one ſitting, or two at moſt, that were employed wholly in giving out arreſts for the reſtoring the funds that were appointed for the payment of the town-houſe rents, which the Court, according to its laudable cuſtom, withdrew one

* Henry Chabot de St. Aulaie, Duke de Rohan, Peer of France, and Governor of Anjou, who was much blamed by both parties for his behaviour at Angers.

† Francis Harlai de Chanvallon, Archbiſhop of Rouen, and afterwards of Paris.

day

day to put things into confusion in Paris, and restored
the next, for fear that that confusion should become
too great. The most considerable thing that passed
in the parliament at that time, was an arrest given by
the Grand Chamber, upon the 8th of February, at
the request of the Attorney-General, whereby any
person without exception was forbidden to levy any
forces without the King's commission. I leave you to
judge how well this could agree with seven or eight of
their arrests which I have mentioned before.

Upon the 15th of February the parliament and the
city received two Lettres de Cachet, wherein the King
acquainted them with Mr. de Rohan's rebellion, and
with the march of the Spanish forces led by Mr. de
Nemours, of which the letters shewed the inconveniencies, exhorting them to be loyal to the King.
After the letters were read, the Duke spoke and represented that Mr. de Rohan had made himself master of
the town and castle of Angers, only to execute the
arrests of the company that ordered all governors of
places to oppose the enterprizes of the Cardinal; that
Boisleur, Lieutenant-Governor of Angers, and a
zealous partisan of Mazarin's, had formed a design
upon that place, which Mr. de Rohan had been obliged
to prevent, and even to secure that gentleman; that
he could not conceive how the things that were trans-
acting daily in the parliament could be reconciled;
that they had given in a full assembly of the Chambers
seven or eight arrests one upon another, which enjoined governors of provinces and of towns to declare
against the Cardinal; and that but two days ago the
Chamber of Tournelle, at the request of the Bishop
of Angers, brother to Boisleur, had put out an arrest
against the Duke of Rohan, whose only guilt was the
executing those given in a full assembly of the Chambers; that the Grand Chamber had but few days ago
put out one to forbid the levying forces without the
King's commission, than which nothing could be more
contrary to the request made to him several times by
the whole body of the parliament, praying him to
employ

employ all his forces for the expelling of the Cardinal ; that he thought himself likewise obliged to inform the company that all the arrests which they had put out, had not yet been sent, neither to the several precincts, nor to the other parliaments, as it had been ordered. The Duke added, that Mr. d'Amville was come to him from the King, and had brought him Carte-blanche to oblige him to give his consent to the re-establishment of the Cardinal ; but that nothing in the world could ever bring him to it, or to disunite in opinion from the parliament, &c.

The Presidents de Bailleul and de Novion maintained stoutly, that the arrests of the Grand Chamber, and of the Chamber of Tournelle, of which the Duke complained, were legal, the number of judges that are required for putting out arrests in these Chambers being compleat. This reason, as impertinent as it will appear to you, considering the subject, satisfied most of the old councellors, drowned in, or rather swallowed up by their forms of law. The young councellors, inflamed by the Duke, rose up and forced the President le Bailleul to put the thing to the vote. Mr. Talon, the Advocate-general, avoided very artfully to give his conclusions upon the two arrests of the Grand Chamber and of the Tournelle, by turning his discourse, to the great satisfaction of the company, against the Bishop of Avranches, a man odious both for his infamous life, and for his slavish attachment to the Cardinal. This gave him an opportunity of making himself merry at the non-residence of Bishops, against which he really obtained a cutting arrest ; and his conclusions were, that all Mayors and Magistrates, as well as Governors of towns, should be forbid to give passage to the Spanish forces, led by Mr. de Nemours.

It was at that instant that the Duke executed what he had projected before, as I have already told you, and that he went even beyond what he had at first resolved. He maintained that he had taken these forces into his pay, and that they were not Spaniards. His speech, which he extended to a pretty great length, took up some

time ;

time ; the clock ſtruck twelve, and the aſſembly was
put off to the next day, which was the 16th. But
there was no aſſembly on that day, the Duke having
ſent in the morning to excuſe himſelf upon pretence of
a fit of the cholick. The true reaſon for this delay
was this.

The laſt diſappointment of the parliament had em-
barraſſed the Duke beyond what I am able to expreſs ;
and I believe that in leſs than two days time, I had
heard him repeat a hundred times the following
words: ' It is a cruel thing to find one's ſelf in a
' condition where it is impoſſible for one to act right.
' I had never conſidered of it before; but I experi-
' ence it and feel it.' His agitation, which, like a
fever, had fits, ſome leſs, ſome more violent, was
never greater than on the day that he commanded Mr.
de Beaufort, or rather gave him leave, to put his
troops upon action. And as I was repreſenting to
him that after the many declarations which he had
made both in the parliament and every where elſe
againſt Mazarin, it appeared to me that the ſtep of
cauſing his troops to move, againſt him was not ſo
great an addition to the diſlike which he had already
given to the Court, that he needed to apprehend it ſo
much : he anſwered me theſe memorable words, on
which I have reflected a thouſand and a thouſand
times : ' If you was born a ſon of France, an infant
' of Spain, a King of Hungary, or a Prince of Wales,
' you would not ſpeak as you do. Know that we
' Princes reckon words for nothing, but that we never
' forget actions. The Queen would not remember
' to-morrow at noon my declaiming againſt the Cardi-
' nal, if I would bear with him to-morrow morning.
' If my forces fire a ſingle muſket, ſhe will not for-
' give it me theſe 2000 years, let me act never ſo well
' to pleaſe her.' The general concluſion which I
drew from this diſcourſe, was that the Duke was
perſuaded that all Princes had the like ſentiments upon
certain matters ; and the particular one was, that the
Duke was not ſo much exaſperated at the Cardinal, as

to reject all thoughts of being reconciled to him, in
cafe of need. And yet a quarter of an hour after the
pronouncing thefe fententious words, he appeared to
me further than ever from it. For Mr. Damville
coming into his library-room, where I was alone
with him, and having preffed him very much in the
Queen's name, and by her order, to give him his
word not to join his forces with thofe of Mr. de
Nemours that were advancing, the Duke remained
inflexible in his refolution, and fpoke even upon that
fubject with a great deal of good fenfe, and with all
the fentiments that a fon of France, who finds himfelf
forced by the circumftances of affairs, to an action
of that nature may, and ought to preferve, at that
unfortunate time. You have here an abftract of what
he faid. ' That he was not ignorant that the part
' which he acted on this occafion was the moft uneafy
' in the world, confidering that he could gain no-
' thing by it, and that it took away from him before-
' hand all manner of quiet and fatisfaction : that he
' was well enough known to give no room to fuf-'
' pect that what he did was the effect of ambition :'
' Neither could it be attributed to hatred, to which
' paffion he was known never to have been inclined
' againft any one : that he was forced into it by the
' mere neceffity in which he had found himfelf, not
' to fuffer the ftate to perifh in the hands of a mini-
' fter unable to govern, and abhorred by all the world :
' that he had indeed fupported him during the fiege of
' Paris, but that he did it againft his confcience, and
' in regard only to the Queen ; that he had likewife
' fided with him, though with the fame fcruple of
' confcience, and out of the fame regard, during the
' whole courfe of the civil war in Guienne : That his
' lamentable conduct there for a while, and the ufe
' which he would afterwards have made of the advan-
' tages, obtained by his (the duke's) means, againft
' the Duke himfelf, had forced him to think of his
' own fafety, and that he confeffed, though to his
' fhame, that God had made ufe of that motive to

' oblige

'oblige him to follow the way which his duty had
'been for so long pointing out to him: that he had'
'not followed that way'in a factious manner, by can-
'toning himself upon the frontiers, and calling there'
'upon foreign aid: that he had joined only with the'
'parliaments, which are beyond comparison more'
'interested than any one in the preservation of the'
'state: that God had blessed his good intentions,'
'chiefly in permitting the expulsion of that bad
'minister without the shedding of blood, or any other
'harm done: that the king had granted to the tears
'of his people that piece of justice, more necessary
'still for his service than for the satisfaction of his
'subjects; that all the corporate bodies of the king-'
'dom, without excepting one, had expressed their
'joy by arrests, by thankfgivings, by bonfires, and
'other public rejoicings: that when we were upon
'the point of seeing union restored in the royal
'family, which would have repaired in a trice the'
'advantages obtained over us, occasioned by our'
'divisions, the evil genius of France had again
'brought this wicked minister upon the stage, to
'renew the confusion every where: that this was
'the most dangerous sort of confusion which we had
'as yet fallen into, because those who had the best
'intentions in the world, and the most remote from
'any private interest, were those that could the least
'remedy it: that in most other disorders which had
'hitherto befallen the state, people might have ex-
'pected an end of them by satisfying at last the defire
'of those whose ambition had occasioned them, so
'that what had been for the most part the cause of
'the evil, had however proved most commonly a
'remedy to it: that our present symptom was of
'another nature; that we were fallen into it by a
'general commotion of the whole political body,
'which made it impracticable for any of the mem-
'bers to help their own private cafe, there being no
'other remedy left than the expelling the venom
'which had infected the whole body: that the par-

'liaments

' liaments were so far engaged in it, that supposing
' that he, jointly with the Prince, should be willing
' to desist, they could not perfuade the like to these
' companies : but that they were so far from desisting,
' and so much obliged for their own safety to pur-
' sue the expulfion, that they would both declare
' against the parliaments, if these bodies should hap-
' pen to change.' ' Would you advife me, Brion,'
said the Duke of Orleans (for so he used to call the
Duke d'Amville, who bore that name when he was
the Duke of Orleans's first gentleman of the horfe)
' would you advife me, after what has paffed, to
' truft to Mazarin's word? Would you advife the
' Prince to do it? But supposing we could truft him,
' do you believe that the Queen ought to hesitate to
' give us the fatisfaction which all France, or rather
' all Europe, are asking her jointly with us? No
' body has a greater feeling than I of the deplorable
' condition which I fee the kingdom in, and I can-
' not without trembling fee the Spanish colours dif-
' played, when I confider that they are upon the
' point of joining those of Condé, and those of
' Vallois. But is not the present case, in respect to
' me, one of those that has given rise, with a great
' deal of reason, to the saying, That neceffity has no
' law? And can I difpense with following a way by
' which only I can defend myself and all my friends
' against the Queen's wrath, and against the ven-
' geance of her minifter? He has the royal authority
' wholly in his hands, he is mafter of all the towns,
' he hath all the veteran troops at his difpofal, he
' fhoves the prince to the furtheft part of the king-
' dom, he threatens the parliament of the capital
' city of the realm, he fues himself for the protection
' of Spain, and we know every particular of what he
' has promifed as he came through the country of
' Liege, to Don Antonio Pimentel. What can I do
' in this conjuncture, or rather what is it I ought not
' to do, except I bring difhonour upon myfelf, and
' am willing to pafs for the laft, I do not fay of

' Princes,

' Princes, but of men ? When I have suffered the
' Prince to be crushed, when I have left the Cardinal
' at liberty to subdue Guienne, when I see him at the
' gates of Paris with a victorious army ; will people
' say the Duke of Orleans is to be commended for
' having sacrificed his person, the parliament, and the
' city, to the revenge of Mazarin, rather than use the
' assistance of the enemies of the crown ? Will they
' not rather say the Duke of Orleans is a coward and
' a fool to entertain scruples, which even a Capuchin
' would reject if he was as far engaged as the Duke
' of Orleans is ?'

This is what his Royal Highness said to Mr. Damville, with that torrent of eloquence which was natural to him whenever he spoke without any preparation.
I have forgot to tell you that this Don Antonio Pimentel was sent to the Cardinal by Fuensaldagne, under
pretence of convoying him, and that the cardinal
gave him mighty hopes of an advantageous peace for
his catholic Majesty.   Don Antonio has since told me
that the Cardinal had spoke these very words to him :
' *Grabugio fo per voi :* I am making this bustle for
' your sake.   I require for payment that you would
' do for the Prince but half of what you are able to
' do ; or that you would tell me at this instant what
' your demands for a peace are.   France treats me in
' a manner which gives me leave to serve you without
' any scruple.'

The Duke, in all likelihood, had gone further in
his discourse, if he had not been told, that the president de Bellievre was in the bedchamber waiting for
him.   He left me in his library-room with Mr. Damville, who took me to task in respect to my own concerns, with a force of argument worthy of the good
sense of the house of Ventadour, to persuade me that
I was obliged both by reason of the hatred which the
Prince bore to me, and by the engagements into
which I was entered with the Queen, to hinder the
Duke from joining his forces with those of Mr. de
Nemours.   This is exactly what I answered him, or
                                                    rather

rather what I dictated to him whilst he was writing it down in his table-book, that he might, at my request, shew it both the Queen and the Cardinal.

' I have promised to come to no accommodation
' with the Prince ; I have declared that I could not
' abandon his Royal Highness, nor consequently for-
' bear serving him in all that he should undertake for
' opposing the return of the Cardinal. This is what
' I have told the Queen in the presence of the Duke ;
' this is what I have told the Duke in the Queen's
' presence ; and this is what I have faithfully done
' all along. The Count de Fiesque is every day
' assuring Mr. de Brissac, that the Prince will give
' me Carte-blanche whenever I please ; this I receive
' with all the respect which I owe the Prince, but
' without making any answer to his offer. The
' Duke commands me to give him my opinion of
' what he can do best, and to ground it upon his
' resolution of never consenting to the Cardinal's
' return ; I believe that I am obliged in honour and
' in conscience to tell his Royal Highness that he will
' give the Cardinal all the advantage, except he forms
' a body of troops considerable enough to oppose
' his, and to make a diversion of those with which he
' oppresses the Prince of Condé. In short, I intreat
' you to tell the Queen, that I do nothing but what
' I have always told her that I would do, and that she
' cannot have forgot what I have so often said to her;
' That there is not one man in the kingdom more
' sorry than I, to see things in a condition which not
' only gives leave to a subject, but even obliges him,
' to speak to his mistress in the manner I do.'

This gave me an occasion to acquaint Mr. Damville with what had formerly passed upon that subject, in the conversations which I have had with the Queen. He was touched with it, because he was well affected and devoted to the King's person ; and he was so much moved, chiefly at the effort, which I told him I had made to let the Queen know that it was wholly in her power, to become absolute mistress of all our concerns, and of mine more than any other; that that gentleman, out of affection to me, opened himself more than he had done, and said: ' This wretch (meaning the Cardinal) is going to ruin ' all; look to yourself, for he is bent upon hindering ' you from being a Cardinal; this is all I can say to ' you.' You will see by and by that I knew more upon that head than this gentleman.

As we were difcourfing, Mr. Damville and I, in this manner, the Duke came back to us, and leaning upon the Prefident de Bellievre, he acquainted Mr. Damville that the Dutchefs defired to fpeak with him; and fitting down after he was gone, he faid to me: ' I have informed Mr. de Bellievre of what I have ' told Mr. Damville in your prefence; but I muft ' difcover to you both a thing which it had been very ' improper for me to fpeak of to him. I am cruelly ' imbarraffed; for I perceive that the thing which I ' have maintained to him to be neceffary, and which ' is fo in effect, is however very bad, which I believe ' has never happened before in any other affair, ' except in this. I have been all night long reflect- ' ing on it; I have recalled to my memory the whole ' intrigue of the league, the faction of the Hugue- ' nots, the movements of the Prince of Orange; and ' I have found nothing in all of them fo difficult as ' what I meet with at every hour, or rather at every ' inftant.' At this he gathered up and enlarged upon all that you have feen hitherto fcattered up and down thefe fheets upon this fubject; and I likewife anfwered him all that you may have obferved there of my fentiments. It being impoffible to fix a converfation that runs wholly on uncertainties, the Duke inftead of anfwering me, anfwered himfelf; and what always happens in this cafe is, that he that does fo, never perceives it, which makes the converfation go on without an end. I intreated the Duke for that rea- fon to give me leave to fet down in writing my fen- timents on the ftate of things. I told him that I required but one hour to do it. To tell you the truth, I was

I was not forry to find at all events an opportunity of having what I had fpoken to him occafionally, con-- firmed to him by the Prefident de Bellievre. The Duke took me at my word; he went into the gal- lery, where an infinite number of perfons were wait- ing for him, and I wrote upon the table in the library, what you are going to read, of which I have ftill the original.

'I believe that the matter which is at prefent to' ' be difcuffed, is not what his Royal Highnefs might ' or ought hitherto to have done; and I am even ' perfuaded that it is inconvenient in great affairs, ' to repeat paft matters, except only with an intent ' to refrefh one's memory, in refpect to the relation ' they have to things to come. The Duke has but ' four ways to follow, which are; either to come to ' an accommodation with the Queen, that is, with' ' Cardinal Mazarin; or to unite intimately with the ' Prince; or to form a third party in the kingdom; ' or to remain in the ftate in which he is at pre- ' fent, that is, to hold a little with all fides; with the ' Queen, by remaining united with the parliament, ' who, at the fame time that they are railing at the ' Cardinal, preferve a regard for the King's authority, ' which breaks twice a day the Prince's meafures; ' with the Prince, by joining his forces with thofe of ' Mr. de Nemours; with the parliament, by fpeaking ' againft Mazarin, and not ufing at the fame time the ' authority which his birth and the love that the ' people of Paris have for him, give him, for pufh- ' ing on that company further than they have a mind ' to go. Of thefe four ways, the firft, which is to ' come to an accommodation with the Cardinal, has ' always been excluded from all his Royal High- ' nefs's deliberations, becaufe the Duke has always ' gone upon this fuppofition, that it was againft both ' his dignity and his fafety. The fecond, which is to ' unite wholly and intirely with the Prince, has not ' been admitted neither by the Duke, becaufe he has ' been unwilling even to imagine that he could be

D 4 ' capable

‘ capable of propofing to him (thefe were the words
‘ which the Duke ufed) to divide from the parliament,
‘ and abandon himfelf by that means, both to the
‘ difcretion of the Prince, and to the wavering ways
‘ of .Mr. de la Rochefoucaut. The third, which is
‘ to form a third party in the kingdom, · has been
‘ rejected by his Royal Highnefs, both becaufe it
‘ may be followed with confequences too dangerous
‘ for the ftate, and becaufe it could fucceed but by
‘ forcing the parliament to follow a conduct oppofite
‘ to the manner and forms of that company, which
‘ cannot be done but by means ftill more oppofite to
‘ the inclination and maxims of the Duke.   The
‘ fourth, which is that which his Royal Highnefs
‘ follows at prefent, is the very thing which caufes
‘ his prefent trouble and unquietnefs, becaufe by
‘ holding a little with the other ways, it has almoft
‘ all the inconveniencies of each, and has, properly
‘ fpeaking, not one advantage of any of them. In
‘ obedience to his Royal Highnefs, I fhall give my
‘ opinion upon thefe feveral ways.   Though as to
‘ my private concerns I might find my advantage in
‘ the Duke’s reconcilement with the Cardinal ; and
‘ though on the other hand, I have declared my-
‘ felf fo much againft that minifter, that my opinion
‘ upon any thing that relates to him, may, and
‘ even ought to be fufpected ; I do not hefitate to
‘ tell his Royal Highnefs, that he cannot without
‘ difhonouring himfelf, keep any medium upon
‘ that article, confidering the difpofition of all
‘ the parliaments, of all the· towns, and of all the
‘ people ; and that he can the lefs do it with any
‘ fafety to himfelf, confidering the prefent pofture of
‘ affairs, the difpofition of the Prince of Condé, &c.
‘ The reafons which fupport that opinion are fo ob-
‘ vious, that I need not explain them. I intreat his
‘ Royal Highnefs not to command me to tell him my
‘ thoughts on the fecond way, which is that of uniting
‘ entirely with the Prince ; and that for two reafons, of
‘ which the firft is, that the private engagements which
‘ I am

'·I am entered into, even with his own confent, with
' the Queen upon that fubject, are a fufficient reafon
' for him to believe that I might be moved by my
' private intereft in delivering my opinion. My fecond
' reafon for not meddling in this matter is, that I am
' convinced that if his Royal Highnefs was refolved to
' feparate from the parliament, the thing to be con-
' fidered would not be in that cafe, whether he ought
' to unite with the Prince, but what he ought to do to
' keep the Prince fubmiffive to him ; and this fubmiffion
' from the Prince to his Royal Highnefs is one of the
' chief reafons that has obliged me to propofe to him
' a third party, upon which I muft enlarge more than
' I have yet done, becaufe it is neceffary to fpeak of
' that third way, jointly with the fourth way, which is
' the holding a little on all fides. The Prince has taken
' fteps towards Spain, which can never agree, except
' by miracle, with the practice of the parliament ;
' and he, or thofe of his party, are every day taking
' fome towards the court, which agree ftill lefs with
' the prefent conftitution of that body. His Royal
' Highnefs ftands unmoved in his refolution of not
' dividing from it, which he would be obliged to do,
' fhould he unite intimately with a Prince, who, on
' the one fide, by his negotiations, or at leaft by thofe
' of his dependants, with Mazarin, keeps that com-
' pany in a continual jealoufy, and who, on the other
' fide, by his publick union with Spain, obliges them
' once or twice a-day, to declare openly againft him.
' It happens that at the fame time that the Duke, for
' the reafons which I have mentioned, cannot unite
' with the Prince, he finds himfelf obliged how-
' ever to prevent the Prince's ruin, which would give
' the Cardinal too much ftrength. Taking this for
' granted, there is no other choice left, but that of
' a third party, or that which his Royal Highnefs is
' following at this day. I think it therefore neceffary,
' before I enter into the detail and explication of a
' third party, to examine the inconveniencies and the
' advantages of the way which his Royal Highnefs is

' now

' now in. The first advantage which I find in it, is
' its carrying with it an appearance of prudence,
' which is always advantageous, because prudence is a
' virtue on which the generality of mankind is less
' able to distinguish exactly, than in any other, what
' is real from what is only specious. The second is,
' that this way not being decisive, it leaves, or seems
' to leave, his Royal Highness-always at liberty to
' make a new choice, whenever he meets with any
' thing that suits his conveniency. The third advan-
' tage is, that so long as his Royal Highness follows
' this way, he will not renounce his right of being a
' mediator, which he naturally has by his birth, and
' which alone may offer him an opportunity of re-
' trieving with advantage if he takes hold of it, all
' the disagreeable steps which he has already taken,
' or may for the future be obliged to take, in relation
' to the court. These, in my opinion, are the three
' sorts' of advantages, which are to be found in the
' way which his Royal Highness is now following.
' Let us now examine the inconveniencies, which are
' so many that I can hardly distinguish them all. I
' will therefore stick only to that which is capital,
' because it embraces all the rest. His Royal High-
' ness, by preserving a regard for the court, which,
' properly speaking, is the strengthening of Mazarin,
' with whom alone he refuses to be reconciled, offends
' the other parties enough in all appearance to cause
' the ruin, not only of his own, but of these other
' parties; and certainly he offends that of the Prince
' to a degree that will oblige those of that party to
' come to an accommodation with the court, con-
' sidering how specious a pretence his Royal Highness
' is giving the Prince for that accommodation, by
' assisting every day at the deliberations of a company,
' that condemns his taking up arms, and registers
' without any hesitation the declarations given against
' him. His Royal Highness sees the importance of
' this inconvenience, and feels the weight of it, more
' than any body else; but he believes, at least at cer-

1   ' tain

' tain inftants, that the guaranty of the parliament,
' and of the city of Paris, is able at all events to
' guard and to fecure him, which is the thing that I
' have all along taken the liberty to conteft with him,
' with all the refpect due to his high birth, becaufe it is
' impoffible but that the parliament by continuing to
' ftick clofe to their forms, muft fall to nothing at
' the end of a civil war, and that the city, which his
' Royal Highnefs leaves, according to its ufual courfe,
' attached to the parliament, muft run the fame fortune
' with that company, becaufe it muft follow the fame
' fteps. Thefe fteps are properly what will, in fpite
' of all France and even of all Europe, reftore the
' Cardinal, as they have already brought him back
' into the kingdom. He hath lately paffed through a
' great part of it with four or five thoufand adventurers,
' notwithftanding the troops of his Royal Highnefs,
' which are confiderable, and at leaft as good and as
' well trained up to war, as thofe which have brought
' this minifter to Poitiers; notwithftanding that moft
' of the parliaments have declared againft him; not-
' withftanding that there is fcarce any great town in
' the kingdom, on which the court can reckon; not-
' withftanding that all the people are enraged at him.
' This appears prodigious, and yet is not fo at the
' bottom; for there is nothing more natural, confider-
' ing that the parliament of Paris is contented with the
' arrefts iffued out from that company, which by for-
' bidding all manner of levies, and the feizing on the
' King's money, favour much more the Cardinal, than
' the declaring him criminal-can hurt him; confider-
' ing that the great towns, whofe natural motion is to
' follow that of the parliament, are acting exactly in
' the fame manner that company does; confidering, in
' fhort, that his Royal Highnefs's forces can only move
' by means, which, in refpect to his Royal Highnefs's
' regard for the parliament, have a very great affinity
' with the meafures of that company, which daily
' declares againft their moving. It appears to fo-
' reigners that his Royal Highnefs leads the parliament,

D 6   ' becaufe.

' becaufe that company declaims as he does, againft the
' Cardinal. The truth is, that it is the parliament
' that leads his Royal Highnefs, becaufe thofe of that
' company are apprized that his Royal Highnefs makes
' but a very flender ufe of the means he has in hand to
' hurt the Cardinal. The fear of difpleafing that
' company is one of the caufes that has hindered him
' from putting his troops in action, and from applying
' himfelf, as much as he had it in his power to do, to
' the levying new ones. The fame politicks will
' require of him to compenfate the joining of thefe
' forces with Mr. de Nemours' army, with the com-
' pliance and even the approbation which his prefence
' will give, to all the deliberations that will be taken,
' even with the greateft heat imaginable, againft their
' march. In that manner he will offend the Queen,
' he will exafperate the Cardinal, and that, without
' fatisfying the Prince, or contenting the Frondeurs.
' All thefe views will trouble him ftill more than any
' thing he has hitherto done, becaufe the objects which
' will occafion them, will magnify at each inftant,
' and the cataftrophe of the play will be the return of
' a man whofe ruin is thought fo eafy, that his re-
' eftablifhment cannot but appear extremely fhameful.
' I have taken the liberty to propofe to his Royal
' Highnefs a remedy to thefe inconveniencies, which I
' fhall again mention in this place, that I may not fail
' in any thing which he has commanded me to deduce.
' He has done me the honour to tell me feveral times, that
' the greateft obftacle to his coming to a final refolution,
' which he owns to be neceffary if it be poffible, is that
' he cannot do it of himfelf without falling out with
' the parliament, becaufe that company can never
' come to any fuch refolution, by reafon of their being
' fo much attached to their forms, and that they can
' much lefs do it in what relates to the Prince than in
' any other thing, both for that reafon, and for their
' juft diffidence of the feveral cabals which not only
' compofe, but which divide that party. Thefe two
' views are certainly very judicious and very prudent,
                                        ' and

' and it was from the like confideration that I had
' propofed to his Royal Highnefs a way which appeared
' to me to be almoft a fure remedy to thefe two incon-
' veniencies which are certainly very great and dange-
' rous. That way was, that his Royal Highnefs fhould
' form a third party, compofed of the parliaments and
' of the great cities of the kingdom; independent of,
' and even divided by publick declarations, from
' foreigners and from the Prince of Condé himfelf, by
' reafon of his conjunction with them. The proper
' expedient in my opinion to bring this about, was
' that his Royal Highnefs fhould in a full affembly
' of the Chambers explain his intentions clearly and
' fully, by faying to the company, that the regard which
' he had all along preferved for them, had obliged him
' to act contrary to his views, his fafety, and his repu-
' tation; that he commended their good intentions;
' but that he defired them to confider that the ambi-
' guity which it caufed in their conduct, would deftroy
' the good intentions with which the whole kingdom
' confpired againft Cardinal Mazarin. That that
' minifter, who was an object of horror to all the
' people, laughed at their wrath with 4 or 5000 men
' only, who had carried him triumphantly to Court,
' becaufe the parliament was every day giving out
' arrefts in his favour, at the time that the company
' railed againft him the moft bitterly; that his Royal
' Highnefs, in compliance to their body, had pre-
' ferved fome meafures which had conduced to the like
' effects; that finding the evil to increafe, he could
' delay no longer to feek out for remedies; that he met
' with enough, but that he was very glad to concert
' them with the company, whofe members ought on
' their fide to come to a good refolution, and to fix
' themfelves once for all upon fome effectual means of
' expelling Mazarin, having judged fo many times
' his expulfion neceffary for the fervice of his Majefty;
' that the only means to come to that end, was to
' manage well the war, for which effect they muft
' diveft themfelves of their fcruples; that for his part,

' the

' the only one which he intended to preſerve for the
' future was in reſpect to the enemies of the ſtate, with
' whom he declared that he would have neither union
' nor correſpondence ; that he looked upon theſe ſen-
' timents to be the leſs commendable in him, becauſe
' he knew his own ſtrength, and that he had no need
' of their aid ; that from this conſideration, but more
' ſtill from that of the evil which a conjunction with a
' foreign enemy is always able to cauſe to the crown,
' he neither approved of, nor concurred in any thing
' that the Prince had done in reſpect to that ; but that,.
' excepting that article, he was reſolved to do like
' him, and to obſerve no longer the meaſures which he
' had hitherto kept ; he would raiſe both money and
' forces, he would put himſelf at the head of affairs,
' he would ſeize upon the King's money, and would
' treat as enemies thoſe that ſhould oppoſe it in any
' form or manner whatſoever. I was of opinion that
' his Royal Highneſs might add, that the company
' was not ignorant that the people of Paris being ſo
' well affected to him as they were, it was eaſier for
' him to execute what he propoſed than to ſpeak it,
' but that the regard he had for them made him willing
' to acquaint them with his reſolution, before he carried
' it to the town-houſe, where he deſigned to declare
' his intentions that very afternoon, and to deliver
' commiſſions there at the ſame time. I entreat his
' Royal Highneſs to remember that when I propoſed
' this way, I took the liberty to aſſure him upon my
' life, that this ſpeech, joined to the circumſtances
' which I propoſed at the ſame time, which were to
' march to the parliament accompanied with a good
' number of nobility, gentry, clergymen and people,
' would receive no manner of contradiction. I re-
' member that I went ſtill further, and told his Royal
' Highneſs that the parliament, which would the firſt
' day come into this project only by ſurprize, would
' approve of it heartily the next. All companies are
' ſo made, and I have not ſeen one which in three or
' four days time would not naturally accuſtom them-
                                        ' ſelves

' felves even to what they received at firft only by
' conftraint. I reprefented to his Royal Highnefs,
' that after having put his affairs upon that foot, he
' ought no longer to fear that the parliament fhould
' forfake him ; neither could he any longer fear to be
' facrificed to the Court, by the negociations of the feveral
' cabals of the Prince, becaufe thofe of the parliament,
' who were of the court party, would be too nearly and
' perfonally interefted with his Royal Highnefs, to
' fuffer themfelves to be penetrated into, and be made
' tools of ; and becaufe the Prince himfelf would be
' fo much in the dependance of his Royal Highnefs,
' that his chiefeft care would be to have a fpecial
' regard for him. For in my opinion there would
' have been no manner of room to fear that the Prince
' fhould have come to an accommodation with the
' Court, had his Royal Highnefs followed that way,
' confidering the ftate of things, the ftrength of his
' Royal Highnefs's party, the declaration of the
' publick, and the fecret meafures which his Royal
' Highnefs might have preferved with the Prince. His
' Royal Highnefs knows better than any one whether
' he is not abfolute mafter of the people of Paris, and
' whether, when he is pleafed to fpeak peremptorily
' like a fon of France, and like one who is, and who
' knows himfelf to be the head of a great party, there
' is one man in the parliament and in the town-houfe,
' that durft, I will not fay refift, but contradict him.
' His Royal Highnefs will not without doubt have
' forgot that I had propofed to him at the fame
' time fome previous things to be done abroad, that
' were neither remote nor difficult : The rallying the
' broken remnants of my Lord Montrofs's troops, the
' taking into pay the difbanded forces of Newburgh,
' the declaration of eight or ten of the largeft cities in
' the kingdom. . His Royal Highnefs hath not thought
' fit to hearken to this propofal, becaufe he thinks that
' the confequences of it would be dangerous to the
' State. God grant that the way he is in proves not
' more dangerous, and that the confufion into which
' it

' it will in all likelihood throw him, be not more to
', be feared than the party I have propofed, which at
' leaft would have a fon of France at its head. I had
' in Paris 300 officers at my difpofal, and the Vifcount'
' de Lamet would have gathered up 2000 horfe out of
' the difbanded forces of Newburgh. I was likewife'
' affured of the towns of Limoges, Marville, Senlis,
' and Thoulouze.'

This is what I wrote upon the table in the library,
in lefs than two hours time. I read it to the Duke, in'
the prefence of the Prefident de Bellievre, who approved
of it, and backed it with a much greater force than I'
had done myfelf. The conteft grew warm, the Duke
maintaining, that without a clutter of this nature,
(for fo he called it) he would hinder the parliament
from declaring againft the march of Mr. de Nemours's
troops, which was the thing he feared moft, being
upon the point of joining his own to them. You will
find that he was not miftaken as to that, as I had
myfelf been, and as I was no lefs in another point ;
for I maintained all along to the Duke, jointly with .
the Prefident de Bellievre, who was of my opinion, that
it would not be in his power to hinder the parliament
from proceeding to the execution of the declaration
againft the Prince, though that company had put out'
an arreft whereby they engaged not to do it, till the Cardinal was expelled the kingdom ; for the Court found
fo little room for that execution, on the fide of the
parliament, that the minifters durft not fo much as
propofe it.

. Thefe fuccesses contributed much to the undoing
of the Duke, for they lulled him afleep, and prevented
his taking care of his own fafety. I will go on upon
thefe particulars, after I have given you an account
of what paffed in this converfation, in refpect to my
promotion to the cardinalfhip, which happened juft
at this time.

· The Duke, who was the man in the world the
fartheft from believing that it was poffible to fpeak
without fome interefted view, told me, in the heat of
our

our conteſt, that he could not conceive what intereſt I could find in a propoſal, which by breaking all manner of meaſures with the Court, would certainly cauſe my nomination to be revoked. I anſwered him, that I was by this time a Cardinal, or that I was not like to be one for a great while : but that I begged of him to be perſuaded, that ſuppoſing that my promotion depended upon that inſtant, I would in nowiſe change my ſentiments ; becauſe what I had propoſed was for his ſervice, without any relation to my intereſt : ' And I beg only, Sir, added I, in order to ' convince you fully of this truth, that you would be ' pleaſed to remember, that the very day on which ' the Queen granted my nomination, I declared to ' her Majeſty, that I would never quit your ſervice, ' but would adviſe you in the manner which I thought ' the moſt tending to your honour. I think that I am ' at this time acquitting myſelf faithfully of that ' engagement ; and to convince you of it, I moſt ' humbly intreat your Royal Highneſs to ſend to the ' Queen the memorial which I juſt now wrote.'

The Duke was aſhamed of what he had ſaid to me. He treated me with all the civility poſſible. He threw my memorial into the fire, and he left the library as obſtinate (ſaid the preſident de Bellievre to me, ſoftly) as he was when he came in.

I was telling you, that I had told the Duke that I was by this time a Cardinal, or was not like to be one for a long while. I was but very little miſtaken, for I was made one five or ſix days after. I received the news of it upon the laſt of February, by an expreſs which the Great Duke of Tuſcany ſent to me. I will tell you how that matter paſt at Rome, after I have made you ſome excuſes for having tired you ſo much, as without doubt I have done, both with the length of this laſt memorial, and with that of the Duke's diſcourſe to Mr. Damville, which are both full of a thouſand circumſtances that you have already ſeen diſperſed in ſeveral places of theſe memoirs. But moſt of theſe circumſtances having given birth to that body;

monſtrous

monſtrous in its form, and almoſt unconceivable,
even in that ſort of hiſtorical writing that may be
called marvellous; a body of which the members
ſeem to have had no manner of motion that was natural
to them, having acted in a manner even oppoſite to
one another; I have thought it even a piece of good
luck to have met in the courſe of this narration with
a ſubject that has obliged me to gather them all together, that you may with greater eaſe perceive at once
theſe circumſtances, which being only diſperſed in
ſeveral places, darken the truth of hiſtory by appa-
rent contradictions, which nothing can reconcile but
the ſetting in one view together the ſeveral arguments
and matters of fact. I return to my promotion.

You have ſeen, in the ſecond volume of theſe memoirs, that I had ſent to Rome the abbot Charrier,
who found the face of that court altogether changed,
by the retreat, rather than the diſgrace of the Signora
Olimpia *, ſiſter-in-law to Pope Innocent †, who had
been forced to take ſome notice of a kind of reprimand which the Emperor, at the inſtigation of the
Jeſuits, had cauſed the nuntio at Vienna to make in
his name to his holineſs upon that account. He had
ceaſed to ſee the Signora, and he allayed the cruel
vexation, which it was always thought that that had
cauſed him, with pretty frequent converſations with the
Princeſs de Roſſane ‡, his nephew's wife, who, tho'
very

---

* Donna Olimpia Maldachini, wife to Signor Pamphilio,
brother to Pope Innocent the Tenth, whom ſhe governed at pleaſure during his papacy. The complaints and the railleries which
were made againſt the Pope on that occaſion, obliged him to remove that lady. Amongſt other ſatirical pieces, a medal was
ſtruck, wherein Signora Olimpia was repreſented in all the pon-
tifical habits, and the Pope ſpinning at a diſtaff. Signor Olimpia
died of the plague at Orvietto in 1656.

† John Baptiſt Pamfilio, elected Pope in 1643, in the room
of Urban the Eighth, to the great diſſatisfaction of Cardinal Mazarin, and deceaſed in 1655.

‡ Wife to the Prince Camillo, nephew to the Pope. This
lady, the Signora Olimpia, and the Princeſſes Ludoviſi and Giuſti-
niani,

very witty, came not nigh the genius of the Signora, but who, in recompence, was much younger and handsomer. She acquired in effect an influence over the Pope's mind, and so great, that the Signora Olimpia conceived a cruel jealousy at it, which having set an edge to her wit, already very sharp and active, made her at last find out the means of ruining her daughter-in-law with the Pope, and of regaining her former credit with him. My nomination fell out just at the time that the Princess of Rossane was in her greatest favour, and it appeared on this occasion that fortune would repair the loss I had made in the person of Panzirolo. It was on this only occasion that I ever found it favourable. I have told you, in another place, the reasons I had to believe, that the Princess of Rossane would favour my pretensions, and that much more than the Signora Olimpia, who did nothing but by the help of money, and you will easily judge that it had been pretty difficult to persuade me to part with money for the buying of a hat. The Abbot Charrier found at Rome all that I had expected from the Princess of Rossane, and the first advice she gave him, was to distrust to the last degree our ambassador, who, to the secret orders which the court had given him against me, joined the immoderate passion which he himself had for the hat. The Abbot Charrier made an excellent use of this advice, for he amused the ambassador all along by appearing to put an intire confidence in him, and at the same time by shewing my promotion as a thing very remote. The hatred which the Pope had preserv'd for a long time against Cardinal Mazarin's person, gave a colour to Charrier's deceit; and the interest of Monsignor Chigi, secretary of state, who has since been Alexander the Seventh, concurred likewise very effectually to it. Chigi was sure of the hat at the first promotion, which

niani, who were constantly at the Vatican, gave occasion to Pasquin to say to Marforio, ' se tu vuoi fare il Ruffiano, troverai ' donne al Vaticano.'

made

made him haften it as much as he could. Monfignor
Azolini, who was fecretary of the briefs, and who
had been attached to Panzirolo, had inherited from
him a great contempt for Mazarin, and a great deal
of good will for me. All this ferved to deceive the
Bailli de Vallancey our ambaffador, who had not fo
much as the leaft notice of my promotion, till after it
was over. Pope Innocent hath fince told me, that he
knew for certain, that Vallancey had in his pocket
the King's letter for the revoking my nomination, with
an order however not to deliver it but in cafe of neceffity, and at the opening of the confiftory in which
the Cardinals were to be declared; and the Abbot
Charrier had fent me two expreffes with the fame advice. What is certain, and what I have fince learnt
from Champfleury, captain of the guards to Cardinal
Mazarin, is, that as foon as his eminence had the
news of my promotion, which he received at Saumur,
he ordered him to go to the Queen in all hafte, and
to intreat her in his name that fhe would diffemble
and appear joyful at it.

I cannot help difcovering in this place, for the fake
of truth, my own imprudence, which had like to have
made me lofe the hat. I fancied to myfelf, and that
very wrongfully, that it was againft the dignity of the
poft I was in to ftay fo long for it; and that this delay
of three or four months, which they were obliged to
make at Rome for the regulating a promotion of fix-
teen Cardinals, went againft the promifes which I had
received from thence, and the manner in which I had
been courted to ftand for a candidate. I grew angry,
and I wrote a letter to the Abbot Charrier, which I
ordered him to make public, and which was writ in a
tone neither prudent nor decent. It was the moft to-
lerable piece for ftile of any I ever wrote. I have
looked for it to infert it here, but could not find it.
The prudence of the Abbot, who fuppreffed it at
Rome, gained me by the event fome reputation with
thofe that had feen it in France, who thought that I
owed my promotion to it; any thing high and bold
being

being always magnified when it is crowned with fuccefs. This did not prevent my being heartily
afhamed of it, in which fentiment I ftill continue;
and I fancy that I am in fome manner making amends
for the fault by publifhing it. I return to my narration.

I had carried it, as I remember, to the 16th of
February, 1652. There was an affembly of the
Chambers on the 17th, in which you will fee at once,
as in a kind of an abridgment, which is more than
fufficient in my opinion, all that paffed in the affemblies from that day to the firft of April, though they
were held pretty frequently. The Duke opened the
fitting, by reprefenting to the Company that the
Lettre-de-cachet, that had been read there upon the
15th, whereby he was taxed with favouring the entrance of the enemies into the kingdom, could proceed from no other caufe than the calumny he was
afperfed with, and to which the Queen was willing
to lend an ear ; that the troops which Mr. de Nemours led were Germans, and confequently could not
be called enemies. This was, properly fpeaking, the
only fubject which employed thefe affemblies. The
Prefident le Bailleul, who was at the head of them,
began commonly to enlarge upon the neceffity of de-
liberating on his majefty's Lettre-de-cachet : the conclufions of the King's council were all along for commanding the commons to oppofe Mr. de Nemours's
march : and the Duke continued conftantly to maintain, that the troops which he commanded were not
Spanifh, and that after the declaration which he made,
that as foon as the Cardinal was expelled the kingdom, they would enter into the King's pay, it was
altogether fuperfluous to deliberate upon that fubject.
This conteft was renewed every day, and even more than
once in a fitting ; and it is certain, as I have faid before, that the Duke fhifted it off all along. But it is
not lefs certain, that he was amufed by this pretended
advantage, which he was fo well pleafed to have obtained, when we had been of a contrary opinion, that

he

he would not so much as confider whether what he
had obtained was fufficient; that is, that he would
not enough diftinguifh between the parliament's con-
niving at, or declaring for, a thing *. - - - - -
- Except the contefts which I have given you an account of, and in which there were all along fome of
the contradictions which I have fo often mentioned,
nothing paffed in thefe affemblies of the chambers
worthy, in my opinion, of your curiofity. In fome
of them there were read the anfwers which moft of
the parliaments of France made at that time to that
of Paris, which were all of them conformable to its
intentions, in acquainting it with the arrefts which
they had put out againft Mazarin. The other affemblies were employed in providing for the prefervation
of the funds appointed for the payment of the town-
houfe annuities, and of the officers falaries. It was
refolved, in the affembly of the 13th of March, to
meet upon that fubject in the chamber of St. Lewis,
with the other fovereign courts. I was prefent at no
affembly from the firft of March, both becaufe the
ceremonial of Rome does not fuffer Cardinals to be
prefent at any public affemblies, till they have received the cap; and becaufe that dignity giving no
rank in the parliament, except when Cardinals accompany the king thither, the place that I could have
in his abfence being only that of coadjutor, which is
below that of the Dukes and Peers, had not well
agreed with the pre-eminence of the purple.

I muft confefs that I was extremely glad to have a
pretence, and even a reafon to go no longer to thefe
affemblies, which in truth were become not only
tedious, but infupportable. You will fee that the
affemblies which followed thefe, were pretty much of
the like nature; but before I fpeak of them, I muft
touch as lightly as I can upon fome particulars that

---

* The French copy begins in this place a new period, but it
being interrupted by a chafm which makes the fenfe imperfect, I
have left it out,

relate

relate to Paris, and say likewise something in general
in relation to Guienne.

You may remember what I have said of Mr. de
Chavigny in the second volume of these Memoirs, and
that I have told you that he retired into Touraine a
little after the King was come of age. He found not
the secret there of making himself easy, but on the
contrary he grew weary to a point, that he came back
to Paris upon the first pretence that was offered him.
That pretence was grounded upon the advice sent him
by Mr. de Gaucourt, which made it necessary for
him, as he said, to prevent the cabals I was forming
near the Duke against the interest of the Prince. Mr.
de Gaucourt was a gentleman of a very noble family,
being descended from the ancient and powerful Counts
of Clermont in Beauvoisis, so famous in our history. He
had wit and industry, but he had too much assumed
the character of a negotiator, which is not the best
qualification required in negotiations. He was attached to the Prince, and was his chief correspondent
at Paris. His principal care, at least as it appeared
to me, was to ruin my credit with the Duke; but
finding it no easy matter, he had recourse to Mr. de
Chavigny, who came back to Paris with all haste,
either for that reason, or taking that for his pretence.
Mr. de Rohan, who arrived at that time, very well
pleased with the manner in which he had defended
Angers, though he had done it but very poorly,
joined himself against me with the two others. They
attacked me in form as a secret favourer of Mazarin,
and whilst their emissaries were working upon such
of the mob as might be won with money, they omitted nothing to move the Duke by their calumnies,
which were supported with all the cunning learnt at
Court, in which art Ravai, Beloi, and Goulas, belonging to the Duke, but partisans of the Prince,
were not ignorant. I experienced, in this occasion,
that the most refined courtiers may be easily deceived,
when they rely too much on their conjectures. Those
which these gentlemen made upon my promotion

were,

were, that I had obtained the hat by means only of the engagement which I was entered into with the Court. This was the ground on which they went; they reviled me with the Duke upon that account. His Royal Highnefs, who knew the whole truth, made a jeft of it. Inftead of ruining me, they eftablifhed me with him; becaufe in refpect to calumny, all that does not hurt the perfon calumniated, is advantageous to him; as in this cafe, where you fee that thefe gentlemen fell themfelves into the trap which they had prepared for me. I was one day faying to the Duke, that I could not conceive how he did not grow weary of all the impertinencies which were fo often repeated to him againft me; his anfwer was: ' Do you count ' for nothing the pleafure one has of difcovering every ' morning people's wickednefs hid under the name of ' zeal; and every evening their impertinence under ' the difguife of penetration?' I told the Duke, that I received with refpect that faying of his, which I looked upon to be a good leffon for all thofe who had the honour to approach great Princes.

What the Prince's partifans were working with the people againft me, had like to have coft me dearer. They had fome hired perfons, whofe bawling incommoded me more at that time than when I went abroad accompanied by a great number of gentlemen, and of fervants, before whom they durft not appear. For, as I had not yet the cap, which the French Cardinals receive only from the King, to whom the Pope difpatches an exprefs for that purpofe, I could now go abroad only incognito, according to the rules of the ceremonial; fo that when I went to his Royal Highnefs, it was always in a plain coach without any liveries; and I even went into the library by the little ftaircafe that is next the gallery, that I might avoid the great ftair-cafe, and the great apartment. One day that I was there with the Duke, Bruneau came in, all in a fright, to inform me that there were in the court two or three hundred of thefe bawlers, who faid that I betrayed his Royal Highnefs, and that they would kill me.

3

The

The Duke appeared ftruck down at this news. I
obferv'd it, and the example of the Marefchal de
Clermont, killed in the arms of the Dauphin, whofe
fright could at moft but equal that which I faw the
Duke in, coming to my remembrance, I took a refolution, which I thought to be the fafeft, though it
appeared the moft hazardous; becaufe I made no
doubt but that the leaft appearance of fright in his
Royal Highnefs would occafion my being murdered;
and becaufe I ftill made lefs doubt, that the apprehenfion of difpleafing thofe that were bawling againft
Mazarin, whofe murmurings he dreaded to a degree
that was ridiculous, not to mention his temper, that
made him ftart at the leaft thing, would create in him
a much greater fright than was needful for my undoing. I intreated him to let me do as I would, and
that he would immediately fee what contempt one
ought to have for thefe mercenary rafcals, that were
paid for doing what they did. He offered me his
guards, but after a manner that made me judge that
my refufing of them would be very acceptable.. I
went down, though, the Marefchal d'Etampes had
thrown himfelf down upon his knees to prevent my
going; I went down, I fay, with only Chateau-Renaut and d'Haguevjlle, and going directly to that
troop of feditious mob, I afked them who was their
chief? One of their crew, who had an old yellow
feather in his hat, anfwered me infolently, ' 'Tis I.',
I then turned to the gate that leads into the Rue de
Tournon, and calling to the guards, I bid them hang
that rafcal at the iron rails. At this the rogue making me a low bow, told me, that he had no thought
of doing any thing againft the refpect which he owed
me; that he came with his comrades, only to tell me
that there was a report of my carrying his Royal Highnefs
to court, and of reconciling him there with Mazarin;
but that they were far from believing it; that they
were my humble fervants, and ready to die for my fervice,
if I would promife them to be always a good Frondeur.
They offered to accompany me (but I did not want

their convoy) to the place where I was going, which was not far off. It was to Madam de la Vergne's, who had married for her second husband the Chevalier de Sevigné, and who lived at the same house where Madam de la Fayette her daughter lives now. This Madam de la Vergne was at the bottom an honest, woman, but covetous to the last degree, and more susceptible of vanity for her managing all manner of intrigues, without exception, than any woman I have ever known. That which I proposed at that time to her, and for which I wanted her service, was of a nature to startle a prude at first. I seasoned however my discourse with so many protestations of having nothing dishonest or uncivil in my thoughts, that what I proposed was not rejected; it is true, that she would not hearken to it but upon my promising her most solemnly, that 1 would never require any thing of her that should extend beyond what she could do in conscience towards procuring a good, chaste, innocent, and holy friendship. I promised whatever was required of me; my word was relied upon, and Madam de la Vergne was even well pleased with herself to have met with an occasion, very likely to break in time my commerce with Madam de Pomereux, which was not thought so innocent. That into which I was to enter was to be altogether spiritual and angelical; for it was to be with Mademoiselle de la Loupe *, whom you have known since under the name of Madam d'Olonne. She had pleased me very much at a little assembly, which had met some days before in the Dutchess of Orleans's closet. She was handsome, and had besides a reserved and modest air. She lodged just by Madam de la Vergne, and was such an intimate friend of her daughter's, that she had a door made in a wall to come to her the more easily. The attachment which the Chevalier de Sevigné had for

---

* Who married the Count d'Olonne, and became famous for her gallantries, of which the Count de Bussy Rabutin speaks so much in his Histoires Amoureuse de Gaules.

me,

me, my going frequently to his houfe, and what I knew of his wife, contributed much to my hopes. But thefe hopes proved vain by the event; for though I had not my eyes pulled out, though I was not ftifled for want of leave to vent my fighs, though I could perceive by certain airs that the lady was not difpleafed to fee a Prince of the Church fubmit to her charms; the lady preferved all along a feverity, or rather a modefty, which kept my tongue tied, though it ufed to give itfelf liberty enough; which will appear furprifing to thofe who have not known Mademoifelle de la Loupe, and have only heard talk of Madam d'Olonne. This ftory, as you fee, is not much to the advantage of my gallantry. I pafs for a moment to what was doing in Guienne.

As I pretend only to give you a precife account of what I have myfelf feen, I will touch but very lightly on the affairs of that province, and no further than it is neceffary for your underftanding better what happened there that had any relation to the affairs at Paris. I am even in doubt whether the little I intend to fay will be very juft, having it only from accounts, the exactnefs of which I dare not warrant. I have done all I could to get from the Prince of Condé the particulars of his actions that related to the war, the leaft of which have always been greater than the moft heroic ones of other men; and it would be a very great pleafure to me to have it in my power to adorn and honour thefe memoirs with them. He had promifed to give me an abftract of them, and I believe that he would have done it, if his averfion for relating his own wonders, and the trouble it would have put him to, were not as great as his inclination and ability for performing them.

I have told you that the Count d'Harcourt commanded the King's armies in Guienne, and that his troops were the beft difciplined of any in Europe. The Prince's forces were all new levies, except what Mr. de Marfin had brought from Catalonia, which did not make up a body confiderable enough to op-

pofe thofe of the King. The Prince, properly fpeaking, maintained his affairs merely by his own prefence. You have already feen how he had feized
upon Saintes. He left the Prince of Tarente to command there, and returning himfelf into Guienne,
he encamped his forces near Bourg. The Count
d'Harcourt followed him, and he detached the Chevalier
d'Aubeterre to reconnoitre his camp. That Chevalier
was repulfed by the regiment of Baltazar, which gave
the Prince time to poft himfelf upon a rifing ground,
where he made his body of troops appear fo great,
which was in effect but very little, that the Count
d'Harcourt durft not attack him. The Prince retired to Libourne after this action, which was that of
a very great general. He left fome foot there, and
he went to Bergerac, a place famous during the wars
about religion, and he caufed its fortifications to be
raifed up again. Mr. de St. Luc, Lord Lieutenant
of Guienne, thought that he might furprize the Prince
of Conti, who was lodged with fome new-raifed
troops at Caude-Cofte, near Agen, which made Mr.
de St. Luc advance that way, with 2000 foot and 700
horfe, of the beft that were in the King's army. He
was himfelf furprized by the Prince of Condé, who
was informed of his defign, and the Prince attacked
him in the midft of his quarters, before he had had
any news of the Prince's march. He ftood firm
however, and pofted himfelf on a rifing ground;
where he could not be come at but by a narrow pafs.
Almoft the whole day was fpent in fkirmifhing, whilft
the Prince was expecting three cannons, which he had
fent for to Agen. He had great need of them, for
he had in all with him, including the troops of the
Prince of Conti, but 500 foot and 2000 horfe, all
new-raifed forces. A weak condition does not commonly infpire boldnefs, but that of the Prince of
Condé went further on this occafion, for it infpired
him with a piece of vanity, which is, I believe, the
only time he ever gave way to that paffion. It came
into his thoughts, that if the enemy knew that he was
there

there in perfon, it might frighten them fo as to put them into diforder. He therefore fent fome prifoners back, who failed not to acquaint their own troops with it, and the Prince charging them at the fame time, they immediately gave ground; and it may be faid that they were defeated, rather by the terror of his name, than by the fhock of his arms.. Moft of their infantry threw themfelves into Miradoux, where they were immediately befieged. The regiments of Champaign and of Lorrain, whom the Prince would receive but at difcretion, defended that forry place with incredible valour, and gave the Count d'Harcourt time to come to their aid. The Prince fent back his artillery and baggage to Agen: he put garrifons into fome fmall places that might incommode the enemy; and in the evening he came himfelf to Agen, having with him Meffieurs de la Rochefoucaut, de Marcin, and de Montefpan, in order to obferve the defigns of the Count d'Harcourt, who on his fide left fome troops to befiege, if I am not miftaken, Staffort, and la Plame; and with the reft caufed fome fortifications that Meffieurs de Liflebonne, the Chevalier de Crequi, and Coudrai Montpenfier, had begun at one of the fuburbs of Agen, to be attack'd. The gentlemen, whom I have laft named, fignalized themfelves in this attack, which was made in the prefence of the Prince. The enemies were repulfed with an extraordinary vigour, and the Count d'Harcourt, to comfort himfelf for his lofs, went and took the two fmall places which I have mentioned.

The Prince of Condé, who had formed the defign of returning to Paris, for the reafons which you fhall prefently fee, refolved to leave the Prince of Conti, his brother, to command in Guienne, with Mr. de Marcin for lieutenant-general under him; but he thought it neceffary, before he left that province, to fecure entirely the town of Agen, which had indeed declared for him, but having no garrifon, might change its fide at every inftant. He prevailed with the jurates, who confented to fuffer the regiment of

Conti to be received into the town ; but the inhabitants not being of the same mind with their magiftrates, rofe up in arms and fet up barricadoes. The Prince has been heard to fay, that he ran a greater rifk on this occafion, than he would have done in a battle. I have forgot the particulars, and all that I remember is, that Meffieurs de la Rochefoucaut, de Marfillac, and de Montefpan, made fpeeches in the town-houfe, and appeas'd the fedition to the fatisfaction of the Prince, of whofe journey to Paris I am now to fpeak.

Meffieurs de Rohan, de Chavigny, and de Gaucourt, were every day preffing him by letters not to mind fo entirely the affairs of the provinces, as to neglect thofe of Paris, which, as it was the capital city, were in every refpect to be chiefly look'd after. Thefe were Mr. de Rohan's words, in a letter of his which I furprifed. Thefe gentlemen were perfuaded that I broke all their meafures with the Duke, who indeed, when there was any thing which he would not do for the fervice of the Prince, excufed himfelf upon the regard which my poft at Paris obliged him to have for me. His Royal Highnefs has fometimes confeffed to me, that he made ufe of that excufe on fome occafions; and, it is certain, that upon others, he even forced me, by his perfecuting me, to give fome appearances which might confirm what the Duke would perfuade to thefe gentlemen. I reprefented feveral times to him that he would carry matters to a point that would oblige the Prince to come to Paris, which was the thing in the world that he feared moft. But weak perfons being always moved by prefent objects, more beyond comparifon than by abfent ones, though never fo near, he chofe rather to believe that it would be long before the Prince could undertake that journey, than to deprive himfelf of the prefent eafe he found in charging me as the caufe of the murmurs and complaints which the Prince's minifters were making him at each inftant on a thoufand things. But thefe gentlemen
finding

finding themfelves more fatigued than fatisfied with
the Duke's fhifts, earneftly preffed the Prince to come
with all poffible hafte to their affiftance; and their inftances received a mighty fupport from the news which
the Prince had at that fame time from Mr. de Nemours, the particulars of which it is neceffary for me
to touch upon.

Mr. de Nemours entered into France at that time
without any refiftance, all the King's forces being
divided; and though Mr. d'Elbeuf and Meffieurs
d'Aumont, d'Igby, and de Vaubecourt, had forces
fpread up and down, he penetrated as far as Mantes,
and paffed the Seine upon the bridge there by the
leave of the Duke de Lude governor of that town,
who was difcontented with the Court, becaufe the feals
had been taken from his father-in-law. He encamped his forces at Houdan, and came himfelf to
Paris with Mr. de Tavannes, who commanded fuch
of the Prince's troops as he had been able to keep
together, and with Clinchant, who was a general
officer in Mr. de Nemours's army.

This was the firft falfe ftep that they took; for if
that army had marched without refting, and if Mr.
de Beaufort had joined it with the Duke's forces, as
he did fince, they might have paffed the Loire without
any difficulty, and had very much embarraffed the
King's march. Every thing contributed to this delay: the uncertainty of the Duke, who could not
determine himfelf upon doing even what had been
moft firmly refolved upon; Mr. de Beaufort's love
for Madam de Montbazon, which detained him at
Paris; the childifhnefs of Mr. de Nemours, who was
glad to fhew to Madam de Châtillon his general's
ftaff; and the falfe policy of Chavigny, who thought
that he would be much more mafter of the Duke by
dazzling his eyes with the fight of fo many regimental
fcarfs all different one from another. This was what
he told Croiffi, who was imprudent enough to impart
it to me, though he was much more in the Prince's
intereft than in mine. I did not keep the thing hid

E 4   from

from the Duke, who was very much piqued at it. I
took that time to entreat him to suffer that I should
convince these gentlemen in his presence, that it was
foolish in them to pretend to dazzle any one's eyes,
though weaker beyond comparison in every respect
than those of his Royal Highness. As he was about
to make me explain myself, he was informed that
Messieurs de Beaufort and de Nemours were waiting
for him in his chamber. I went thither along with
him, though against my rule, because I had not yet
the cap; and the conversation being become public
(for there was company even to a crowd) I put my
hat on as soon as he had his on his head.' His Royal
Highness observed it, by reason both of what I had
just then said to him, and because I had always refused to do it, though he never failed to command it
me. He was very glad of it, and he affected to keep
up the conversation for a full hour, after which he
took me in private, and brought me back into the
gallery. You may well think that he was angry, for
I believe there were in his chamber above fifty red
scarfs, besides the Isabella ones. His anger lasted all
that evening, for he told me the next day, that
Goulas, his secretary, and an intimate friend of Chavigny's, being come to tell him, with great eagerness,
that all the foreign officers grew mighty jealous of the
long conversations that I had with him, he had re-
buked him very sharply: saying to him, ' Go to the
' devil, you and your foreign officers ; if they were
' as good Frondeurs as the Cardinal de Retz, they
' would be at their posts, and would not spend their
' time in the taverns of Paris.' They at last rejoined
the army, more certainly by my instances, than by
those of Chavigny, who believed all along that I made
it my business to retard them. For the Duke soon
took care to repair what he had let slip unawares
whilst he was angry ; because it was convenient for
him (or at least he fancied so) to make use of me
sometimes as a pretence to what he did, and almost
always to what he did not. I shall tell you which

f   way

way the troops took their march, after I have given
you an account of what happened at Orleans at this
time.

It was natural that this important city should be
much in the dependance of the Duke, being his apen-
nage, and the Duke having made it his most ordinary
place of residence ; the Marquis de Sourdis besides
(who was governor of it) being in his interest. The
Duke had however taken care to send thither the
Count de Fiefque, to oppose the efforts of Mr. le
Gras, master of requests, who did his best to perfuade
the inhabitants to open the city gates to the King, to
whom that place had certainly been very useful.
Messieurs de Beaufort and de Nemours, who saw best
what confequence it was of, becaufe having taken
their march that way, they were nearer at hand to
make their obfervations, wrote word to the Duke that
there was in the town a powerful faction for the Court,
which made his prefence there extremely necessary.
But you may well judge that it was still much more
necessary at Paris. The Duke therefore chofe, without any hefitation, to stay there, which he was advised to do by every one without exception. * Mademoifelle offered to go herfelf to Orleans, which the
Duke confented to, but very unwillingly, both becaufe he thought it against decency, but much more
becaufe he relied but little upon her conduct. I remember, that the day that Princefs took leave of her
father, he said to me : ' This knight-errantry would
' be very ridiculous, if the good fenfe of Madam de
' Fiefque, and of Madam de Fratenac, were not a
' fupport to it.' Thefe two ladies went with the
Princefs, and with them Mr. de Rohan, and Messieurs
de Croiffi and de Bermont, counfellors of the parliament of Paris. Patru faid a little too freely, that as
the walls of Jericho fell at the found of trumpets, fo
would the gates of Orleans open themfelves at the
noife of fiddles. This was a rub upon Mr. de Rohan,

* The Duke of Orleans's daughter.

E 5   who

who was faid to be a little too fond of them. However all this ridicule fucceeded at laft by the courage
of Mademoifelle, which certainly was very great;
for though the King was very near with fome troops,
and that Mr. Molé, Lord-keeper and firft Prefident,
was at the gate, requiring entrance in the King's
name, that Princefs paffed the river in a fmall boat;
fhe obliged the watermen, who are always in great
number upon the key, to break open a poftern gate,
that had ftood walled up for a long time; and fhe
marched with the concourfe and the acclamations of
people directly to the town-houfe, where the magiftrates were affembled to deliberate whether they fhould
let the Lord-keeper in. You may imagine that the
Princefs had the cafting vote. Meffieurs de Beaufort
and de Nemours came immediately to her, and they
refolved jointly with her to feize either upon Loris or
Gien, which are but fmall towns, but which have
bridges over the river Loire. That of Gien was vigoroufly attacked by Mr. de Beaufort, but was ftill
more vigoroufly defended by Mr. de Turenne, who
had juft taken upon him the command of the King's
army, having however the Marefchal d'Hocquincourt
for partner. The Duke's army was obliged to quit
this enterprize, having loft in it Baron de Sirot, a
gentleman of reputation, and who ferved there as
lieutenant-general. That gentleman boafted, and I
believe it was true, that he had exchanged piftol-fhots
both with the great Guftavus King of Sweden, and
with the brave Chriftian King of Denmark *.

Mr. de Nemours, who had a natural averfion and
contempt for Mr. de Beaufort, though they were
brothers-in-law, complained of his conduct to Mademoifelle, as if he had been the caufe that the defign
upon Gien had not fucceeded. They had fome words

---

* See Mr. le Vaffor's Hiftory of Lewis XIII. who fays, that
both the Kings were fo taken with his bravery, that they defired
to be acquainted with a gentleman whofe courage and virtue they
fo much efteemed.

upon

upon that account in Mademoiſelle's anti-chamber. Mr. de Beaufort, who pretended, upon very ſlight grounds, at leaſt as it was ſaid at that time, that the other had given him the lie; returned Mr. de Ne-mours a box on the ear, as Mr. de Nemours pre-tended: for I have heard perſons that were preſent ſay, that he received it only in imagination. It was at leaſt as doubtful as thoſe which Mr. Paſcal ridicules in his letters againſt the Jeſuits. Mademoiſelle made up the matter, at leaſt outwardly; and after a great conteſt, which had been no ſmall occaſion of begin-ning the quarrel, it was reſolved that they ſhould go to Montargis, an important poſt in the preſent con-junéture, becauſe that by that means the army of the Princes, being betwixt Paris and the King, would be in a condition to countenance every thing. Mr. de Nemours, who paſſionately wiſhed to ſuccour Mouron, was of opinion, that it would be better to paſs the Loire at Blois, that they might be behind the King's army, to whom the fear of abandoning too much the provinces beyond the Loire to the diſcretion of the army of the Princes, would make it ſtill more difficult to reſolve upon advancing towards Paris, than it would be by the obſtacle that Montargis would be to it. The other opinion was carried in the council of war, both by number and by the authority of Made-moiſelle; and I have heard gentlemen that underſtood theſe matters ſay, that the reaſon of the thing ought likewiſe to have carried it, becauſe it would have been ridiculous to abandon all the places near Paris to the King's forces, whoſe only deſign, as it was clearly perceived, was to approach that capital, either to win it, or to frighten it. Chavigny ſpoke to the Duke very much in favour of the opinion that carried it, as the Dutcheſs, who was preſent, told me the next day; and I cannot comprehend what ground people could have to imagine that there was any conteſt about it at the Duke's palace. His Royal Highneſs, in that caſe, had not failed to extol to me his reſiſting the advice of thoſe that were attached to the Prince. But

E 6 every

every one was of the like opinion; and Goulas railed openly at the conduct of Mr. de Nemours, who will, said he, lose Paris for the saving of Mouron. I return to the Prince of Condé's journey to Paris.

I have already told you that those who managed his interests with the Duke, pressed his coming back to that place, and that their instances were strongly supported by the necessity he thought there was of helping, or rather repairing, by his presence, the harm which the incapacity and misunderstanding of Messieurs de Beaufort and de Nemours did, in lessening the weight which the valour and experience of the troops under their command ought to have given their party. The Prince having almost the whole kingdom to cross, found it necessary to keep his march extremely secret. He only took along with him Messieurs de la Rochefoucaut, de Marsillac, de Levi, Guitaut, Chavagnac, Gourville, and another whose name I don't remember. He passed with an extreme diligence through the provinces of Perigord, Limousin, Auvergne, and Bourbonnois. He narrowly escaped being taken near Châtillon sur Loire, by St. Maure, a pensionary of the Cardinal's, who followed him with 200 horse, upon advice given to the Court by somebody who knew Guitaut. The Prince met in the forest of Orleans with some officers of his troops who were in garrison at Loris, and he was received by the whole army with all the joy you may imagine. He dispatched Gourville to the Duke to give him an account of his journey, and to assure him that he would be with him in three days time. The instances of the whole army, which was fatigued to the last degree by the ignorance of the Generals, detained him longer. He was besides naturally inclined to stay at places where it was likely that some great action might offer; and I am going to speak of one of the bravest he ever performed.

It appeared by the first step that the Prince took, as soon as he had joined the army, that the opinion of Mr. de Nemours, of which I have spoken, was not

right;

right; for the Prince marched directly to Montargis, which he took without striking a blow. Maudreville, who had thrown himself into the castle, with eight or ten gentlemen and 200 foot, surrendered immediately. The Prince put a garrison into it, and without losing one moment of time, he marched directly to the enemies, who were quartered separately. The King was at Gien; Mr. de Turenne had his general quarters at Briare, and those of Mr. d'Hocquincourt were at Bleneau.

The Prince being informed that the forces of this last were dispersed in the neighbouring villages, he advanced towards Chateau-Renaut, and fell like lightning in the midst of these dispersed troops. He cut in pieces all the horse that were there, belonging to the regiments of Maine, of Roque-epine, of Beaujeu, of Bourlamont, and of Moret, who were endeavouring to get to the dragoons quarters, as they were ordered to do, but too late. The Prince broke even through the dragoons quarter, sword in hand, whilst Tavannes was doing the like through the Croats * quarter. He pursued those that fled as far as Bleneau, where he met with the Mareschal d'Hocquincourt, who had 700 horse in good order, with whom he vigorously charged the Prince's men, who, during the obscurity of the night, having engaged too far, were dispersed, and even against their General's command were busy in pillaging a village. The Prince rallied them, and drew them up in battalia in the enemy's sight, though they were much stronger than he, and though he was obliged, by the great resistance they made at his first charging of them, to look to himself, having had a horse killed under him. His second charge was so vigorous, that he put them entirely to rout, insomuch that it was not in Mr. d'Hocquincourt's power to rally them. Mr. de Nemours was very much wounded on this occasion, wherein Messieurs de Beaufort, de la Rochefoucaut,

* Or Croatians.

and

and de Tavannes, fignalized themfelves. Mr. de Turenne, who had fent notice in the morning to Mr.
d'Hocquincourt, that his troops were too much difperfed, and too much expofed, and that the Prince
was coming to him; Mr. de Turenne, I fay, came
out of Briare, and drew up his forces in battalia, near
a village, named, I think, Oucoi. He put 50 horfe
into a wood that ftood betwixt him and the enemy,
and through which they could not pafs without de-
filing. He made thefe horfe to retire immediately,
with a defign thereby to oblige the Prince to engage
himfelf in that defile, by making him believe that
the retreat was occafioned by their fright. This ftra-
tagem fucceeded, for the Prince threw three or four
hundred horfe into the wood, who at their coming
out of it were overthrown by Mr. de Turenne; and
they could hardly have efcaped, if the Prince had not
ordered fome foot to advance, which ftopped thofe
that were purfuing them. Mr. de Turenne pofted
himfelf on a rifing ground behind the wood; he placed
his artillery there, which killed many men in the
army of the Princes, and, among others, Maré, brother to the Marefchal de Grancey, who belonged to
the Duke, and who ferved as lieutenant-general in his
troops. The two armies remained the whole day in
fight of each other, and towards evening they both
retired to their camps. It is a difficult matter to judge
who got moft honour that day, whether the Prince or
Mr. de Turenne. It may be faid in general, that
they both did what the two beft Generals in the world
could have done. Mr. de Turenne faved the Court,
which had ordered, upon the news of Mr. d'Hocquincourt's defeat, the baggage to be packed up,
without knowing precifely where they could find a
retreat; and Mr. de Senneterre has fince told me
feveral times, that it was the only occafion on which
he had feen the Queen dejected and afflicted. It is
certain, that if Mr. de Turenne, by his great capacity, had not maintained matters, and that if his
army had had the fate of that of Mr. d'Hocquincourt,

I   there

there had not been a town but would have ſhut their
gates againſt the Court. It was what the Queen herſelf ſaid that day, with tears in her eyes, to Mr. de
Senneterre.

The advantage which the Prince got over the Mareſchal d'Hocquincourt was not near of ſo great uſe
to his party, becauſe it was not puſhed on afterwards,
ſo far as the Prince himſelf would have probably done
had he ſtaid with his army. You will ſee what paſſed
there in his abſence, after I have given you an account of the firſt effect which the Prince's coming to
Paris produced, and of ſome particulars relating to
me.

You have already ſeen that the Prince had ſent
Gourville to the Duke, as ſoon as he had joined his
army, to inform him that he would be at Paris in
three days time. This news was a thunderbolt to
him. He ſent immediately for me, and at my coming he cried out, ' You had foretold it ; what new
' trouble on our hands ! what a misfortune ! We are
' now worſe than ever.' I tried, but in vain, to put
him in heart again ; and all I could gain of him was,
that he would ſet a good face upon the matter, and
keep his ſentiments hid from every one, as he had
done from Gourville. He performed this very exactly,
for at his coming out of the Dutcheſs's cloſet, he appeared with a moſt gay countenance, and publiſhed
the news of the Prince's coming, with great demon-
ſtrations of joy, though a quarter of an hour after he
ordered me to omit nothing to ſpoil the ſport, that is,
to bring, if poſſible, matters to a point, that might
oblige the Prince to make but a ſhort ſtay at Paris.
I begged of his Royal Highneſs not to charge me with
this commiſſion, ' which (ſaid I to him) will not be
' for your ſervice, for theſe two reaſons : the firſt,
' becauſe I cannot execute it without giving the Car-
' dinal an advantage which will prove inconvenient
' to you ; and the ſecond, becauſe you will never be
' able to ſtand it out, conſidering the temper which
' it has pleaſed God to form you of.' This way of
                                                    ſpeaking

speaking to a son of France, will, without doubt, appear to you a want of respect; but I desire that you would observe, that St. Remi, lieutenant of his guards, had used the same expression to him two or three days before, upon a 'trifling subject; that the Duke had been pleased with it, and that he repeated it, speaking of himself on all occasions. The truth is, that it was not improper on this conjuncture, as you will presently see. Our contest upon this was pretty great, and I resisted for a long while; but I was obliged to submit and obey. I had more time to go about this piece of work than I expected; for the Prince, whom the Duke had been as far as Juvify to meet, upon the first of April, thinking he would come that day to Paris, arrived there but on the 11th. By that means I had leisure enough to prevail with Mr. le Fêvré, Prevost-des-Marchands, who was indebted to me for that post, and who was my particular friend. He spoke about it to the Marefchal de l'Hôpital, Governor of Paris, who being well affected to the Court, was easily persuaded. They called for an assembly at the town-house, in which it was resolved, that the Governor, with the Prevost-des-Marchands, should wait on his Royal Highness, to tell him, that it appeared to the assembly that it was against order to admit the Prince into the city, before he had purged himself in respect to the King's declaration against him, which had been verified in the parliament.

. The Duke, who was in a transport of joy at this speech, answered, That the Prince came only to confer with him about some private affairs, and would not stay above twenty-four hours at Paris. As soon as the deputies were gone, 'You are (said he to me) 'a gallant man: "havete fatto polito:" how will 'Chavigny be surprized at this!' To this I answered immediately, 'Sir, I never served you so ill in my 'life: remember what I tell you.' Mr. de Chavigny, who was told at the same time both of the deputies speech and the Duke's answer, reprimanded his Royal

Highness

Highnefs for it, ufing of bravadoes, which he carried
to infolence, and even to rage. He declared to the
Duke, that the Prince was in a condition to ftay at
Paris, as long as he pleafed, without being obliged to
afk any body's leave. By means of Pêche, one famous
for being a feditious man, he formed a troop
of 100 or 120 fcoundrels upon the Pont-neuf, who
had like to have pillaged the houfe of Mr. du Pleffis-
Guenegaut; and he frightened the Duke to a degree,
that he obliged him to make a public reprimand, both
to the Marefchal de l'Hôpital and to the Prevoft-des-
Marchands, for having regiftered at the town-houfe
the Duke's anfwer, which he affirmed to have been
given them only in private, and as a fecret. As I
was about infinuating to the Duke that I was in the
right in what I had faid to him, he interrupted me
haftily, and faid, ' 'Tis wrong to judge of things by
' the event. I was yefterday in the right; you are
' in the right to-day: what muft be done with thefe
' fort of men?' He ought to have added, ' and with
' me?' which I took the liberty to do myfelf. For
when I found, that notwithftanding all the expe-
riments he had made, the continued in the fame conduct, which, fpeaking to me, he had condemned a
thoufand times, fince the Prince had left Paris to go
into Guienne, I thought that I had reafon enough to
include him among the fort of men of whom he complained. I therefore refolved to meddle as little as
poffible with his affairs; which conduct, it is true,
would be wrong with fome fort of men, in times that
are very full of trouble, but which I thought neceffary
for me to follow, confidering the Duke's temper, which
I could not redrefs; and confidering likewife the ftate
I was in at that prefent conjuncture, which I muft beg
leave to explain to you a little more at large.

I am obliged to tell you for the fake of truth, that
as foon as I was made a Cardinal, I began to feel the
inconveniencies of that dignity, becaufe I remembered
what I had fo often reflected on, of my having been
too much tranfported at the fplendor of the poft of
Coadjutor.

Coadjutor. One of the caufes of the abufe whicĥ men commonly make of their dignities, is their being dazzled with them at their firft obtaining them, which occafions the firft errors into which they fall, and which are always the moft dángerous for a great many reafons. The ftatelinefs which I had affected as foon as I was made Coadjutor had a good fuccefs, becaufe my uncle's meannefs had made it neceffary. But I clearly perceived, that had it not been for that confideration, and for fome other feafonings which the difpofition of the times rather than my own addrefs, gave me room to accompany it with, that ftatelinefs would not have been an effect of good fenfe, or at leaft would not have been attributed to it. The time I had had to reflect on this, obliged me to give a particular attention to my prefent dignity, which is apt enough to turn the heads of moft of thofe that are honoured with it. The moft vifible, and in my opinion the moft palpable illufion it fubjects new-created Cardinals to, is the pretenfion of preceding the Princes of the Blood, who may at every inftant become our mafters, and who in the mean while remain almoft always fo, in refpect to our neareft relations, by the confideration they are in with them. I preferve a gratitude for the Cardinals of my family, who have from my childhood taught me this leffon by their example; and I met with a pretty favourable opportunity of practifing it on the very day that I received the news of my promotion. Chateau-Briant, whofe name you have already met with in thefe Memoirs, faid to me in the prefence of a great many gentlemen that were in my chamber: 'Now, Sir, we 'fhall ceafe to falute firft.' This he faid, becaufe that though I was upon very ill terms with the Prince of Condé, and that I commonly went well accompanied, I faluted him, as you may well judge, whereever I met him, with all the refpect due to him from fo many confiderations. I anfwered Chateau-Briant, 'Pardon me, Sir, we fhall always falute firft, and 'lower than ever. God forbid that the red hat fhould

'turn.

'·turn my head to that point, as to difpute the prece-
' dency with the Princes of the Blood. It is enough
'·for a gentleman to have the honour to ftand by their
'·fide.' Thefe words, which in my opinion preferved
afterwards in France the rank of Cardinals, by the
condefcenfion of the Prince of Condé, and the friendfhip he had afterwards for me; thefe words, I fay, produced a good effect, by leffening the envy which was
conceived againft me, which is the greateft of all
fecrets.

To attain that end, I made ftill ufe of another
means. Cardinal Richlieu and Cardinal Mazarin,
who had incorporated the dignity of Minifter into that
of Cardinal, had annexed to this laft a fort of ftatelinefs which can become neither of thefe dignities, but
when they are joined together. It would have been
difficult however, in the poft I had at Paris, befides
the Cardinalfhip, not to have allowed me the fame
ftatelinefs. But I parted with fome of it of my own
accord, and in a manner which made it impoffible to
attribute it to any thing but my own moderation,
having declared openly that I would receive in publick
no other honours than thofe which had been rendered
to Cardinals of my family. And as all depends upon
right management, I ordered my matters fo, that I
gave the upper-hand to nobody without exception. I
waited on the Marefchals of France, the Dukes and
Peers, the Chancellor, the foreign Princes, the ille-
gitimate Princes, who came to fee me, no further than
to the top of the ftairs, and every body was well
pleafed.

The third means which I thought upon, was to
omit nothing which decency could permit me, to recall
all thofe to my fervice, who had parted from me, by
reafon of the different parties. It was impoffible but
that there muft be a good number of them, becaufe my
fortune had been fo variable and in fuch agitation,
that part of thofe that were attached to me, were afraid
at certain times to find themfelves involved in it, and
that others had oppofed my interefts on fome occafions;

to·

to whom muſt be added thoſe that had conceived hopes
of making their court at my coſt. I ſhould tire you,
if I entered into particulars, and it is enough for me
to tell you, that Mr. de Berci came to my houſe at
midnight; that I ſaw Mr. de Novion at Father Dom.
Carouge's, a Carthuſian; that I ſaw the Preſident le
Coigneux, at the convent of the Celeſtins. Every one
was glad to reconcile himſelf to me, when to the dignity of Coadjutor they ſaw one, added of a much
ſuperior kind. As for me, I was glad to be reconciled
with every one, at a time when my advances could
only be attributed to my generoſity. I found a benefit
by it; and the gratitude of ſome to whom I had ſaved
the ſhame of the firſt advances, has recompenced me
more than enough, of the ingratitude of ſome others.
I maintain that policy requires as much as civility, of
thoſe that are in the higheſt poſts, to ſave that ſort of
ſhame to thoſe that are under them, and to offer them
their hand, when they dare not preſent theirs.

The conduct which I followed with application
upon theſe ſeveral heads, agreed in more than one
manner with the reſolution I had taken to enjoy as
much as poſſible the quiet which the great dignities
that fortune had aſſembled in my perſon might naturally
enough, in my opinion, have procured me.

I have already told you that the incorrigibility (if I
may uſe that word) of the Duke had diſcouraged me
to ſuch a degree, that I could no longer ſo much as
imagine that he could in the leaſt be relied upon.
The incident that follows will convince you that I muſt
have been very blind if I had been capable of reckon-
ing upon the Queen. You may remember what I have
ſaid towards the end of my ſecond volume, of an imprudence of Mademoiſelle de Chevreuſe, in reſpect to
a part which I acted with the Queen, in concert with
Madam de Chevreuſe. She imparted it to her daughter, againſt my advice, and the daughter underſtood
the jeſt at firſt extremely well; I even remember that
ſhe took pleaſure in making me repeat the comedy of
the Switzer, for ſo ſhe uſed to call the Queen. It
hap-

happened one evening, that the company being very
numerous at the Hôtel de Chevreuſe, moſt of them fell
a laughing, and to tell. you the truth, I can give you
no reaſon why I did not laugh with the reſt. Mademoiſelle de Chevreuſe, who was the moſt capricious
perſon in the world, took notice of it, and ſaid to
me, that ſhe did not wonder at it, after what ſhe had
obſerved ſome time ſince, which was, as ſhe fancied,
that I was grown much colder in reſpect to her, and
that I had even a correſpondence with the Court, which
I kept hid from her. I fancied at firſt that ſhe was in
jeſt, there being not the leaſt ſhadow of probability in
what ſhe ſaid; and I did not diſcover that ſhe was in
earneſt, till ſhe had told me that ſhe was in no manner
ignorant of the errand upon which a certain footman
of the Queen's came every day to me. It is true, that
there was ſuch a footman that had for ſome time been
pretty often at my houſe, but it is likewiſe true, that
he had no errand for me, and that he came only to ſee
one of my ſervants who was related to him. I cannot
tell by what chance ſhe became acquainted with it,
and much leſs what could oblige her to draw from it
the conſequences ſhe did. But ſhe did draw them,
and could not forbear her murmurings and threatnings.
She ſaid in the preſence of Seguien, who had been
valet-de-chambre to her mother, and who had ſome
employment either with the King or the Queen-
Mother, that I had confeſſed a thouſand times, that it
was impoſſible for me to conceive how any body could
be in love with that Switzer. In ſhort, ſhe managed
her matters ſo, that it came to the Queen's ear that I
had called her Majeſty Switzer, ſpeaking to Mademoiſelle de Chevreuſe. I was informed that ſhe was told
of it three or four days before the Prince's coming to
Paris, and it is what ſhe has never forgiven me, as will
appear by the ſequel. You will eaſily imagine that
this circumſtance, which ſhewed that there was no
great room for me to expect good uſage at Court, was
no hindrance to the reſolution I had taken to live for
the future more retired. My place of retreat had
nothing

nothing very dreadful; and I had besides the Arch-Epifcopal Mitre, and the Cardinal's Hat, to defend me againſt the bad weather. I was full of the advantages of this quiet life, which if I did not enjoy, I can aſſure you that it was by no fault of mine, but only becauſe fortune would not have it ſo. I return to my narration.

The Prince arrived at Paris on the 11th of April, and the Duke went to meet him a league out of town. Upon the 12th, they went together to the parliament. As ſoon as they were entered into the Grand Chamber, the Duke told the company, that he had brought the Prince his couſin to aſſure them, that he had not, nor ſhould ever have, any other intent than that of ſerving the King and the State; that he would always follow the company's advice; and that he offered to lay down his arms, as ſoon as the arreſts given out againſt Mazarin were executed. The Prince ſpoke himſelf afterwards to the ſame purpoſe, and he even required that the publick declaration which he made of it ſhould be inſerted in their regiſters.

The Preſident le Bailleul made anſwer; That the company took it always as an honour to ſee him there; but that they could not diſſemble the great ſorrow they had of ſeeing him with his hands ſtained with the blood of the King's men, who had been killed at Blexeau. A noiſe aroſe at that word from thoſe of the inqueſts, which was like, by its impetuoſity, to have blown down the poor Preſident de Bailleul; fifty or ſixty voices were heard at once diſowning of what he ſaid; and I believe that they had been followed by a great many more, if the Preſident de Neſmond had not ſtopped and appeaſed the noiſe, by the report he made of the remonſtrances which he, together with the other deputies of the company, had carried in writing to the King, who was at Sully. The remonſtrances were very ſtrong and vigorous againſt the perſon and the conduct of the Cardinal. The King cauſed the Lord-Keeper to anſwer the Deputies, that he would conſider of them after the company had ſent him their informations; his Majeſty being willing to give a

judg-

judgment upon them himself. The President de Nesmond having made his report, the King's council were called in, who presented to the company a declaration, and a Lettre-de-cachet, signifying that order to the parliament, and likewise that of regiftring without delay the declaration whereby that of the 6th of September, and the arrests given against the Cardinal were superseded. Upon this the King's council being called again, they concluded, after a sharp invective against the Cardinal, that new remonstrances should be made to represent to the King the impossibility there was for the company to register this declaration, which against all manner of rules and forms submitted to a new judiciary proceeding, susceptible of a thousand objections, the most authentick declaration in the world, and that bore the greatest marks of the royal authority, and which consequently could not be revoked but by another declaration as authentick, and bearing the same characters. ; They added, that the new Deputies ought to complain to his Majesty that the first Deputies were refused to have their remonstrances read in his presence; that they ought to insist upon this, as well as upon the reasons for not sending the informations which the Court required; and that all the transactions of that day in the parliament should be registred, a copy of which should be sent to the Lord-Keeper. These were Mr. Talon's conclusions, which he spoke with wonderful vigour and eloquence. After this the company began their deliberation, which for want of time was put off to the 13th. The arrest followed without any contest, conformably to the conclusions, with these additions however; that the declaration which the Duke of Orleans and the Prince of Condé had made, should be carried to the King by the Deputies; that a copy of the remonstrances, and of what had been registered, should be sent to all the Sovereign Courts in Paris, and to all the parliaments of the kingdom, to invite them to send likewise Deputies to the King from their several bodies; that a General Assembly should incessantly be held at the Town-house,
where

where the Duke and the Prince should be invited to come and to make there the same declaration that they had done in the parliament; and that in the mean while the King's declaration against Cardinal Mazarin, and all the arrests given against him, should be executed.

The Assemblies of the Chambers, of the 15th, 17th, and 18th, were almost wholly employed in discussing the difficulties which offered about the regulating that General Assembly at the Town-house: For example; Whether the Duke and the Prince should be present at the deliberation there, or whether they should withdraw after having made their declarations? Whether the parliament had the power to order that assembly, or whether they ought only to invite the Prevost-des-Marchands, with the other town-officers, and the chiefest citizens of every ward to assemble.

That assembly was held upon the 19th in the afternoon, at which sixteen deputies of the parliament were present. The Duke and the Prince made there their declarations in the like form as those they had made in the parliament; and after they were withdrawn, and that the King's attorney for the city had taken his conclusions, which were, that most humble remonstrances should be made to the King, both by word of mouth and in writing, against Cardinal Mazarin; Mr. Aubry, President in the Chamber of Accounts, and the eldest City Counsellor, rose up and said, That it was too late to begin the deliberation, and that it was necessary to put off the assembly to the next day. He was in the right all manner of ways, for the clock had struck seven, and he held intelligence with the Court.

The Duke and the Prince went to the parliament upon the 20th, and the Duke told the company that he was certainly informed that the Marechal de l'Hopital, Governor of Paris, and the Prevost-des-Marchands, had received a Lettre-de-cachet, forbidding them to continue the assembly; that that letter was
insigni-

infignificant, being the work of Mazarin ; and that
he defired the company to fend immediately for the
Prevoft-des-Marchands and the echevins, and to
injoin them to have no manner of regard to it.
There was no need of fending, for they came of themfelves to acquaint the company with this Lettre-de-
Cachet, and likewife that they had call'd an affembly of the city common-council, to advife about
what was beft to be done. They were defired to withdraw that the company might deliberate, and being
again called in, they were told that the company did
not difapprove of the affembly which they had called,
becaufe it was according to order and to cuftom ;
but that the company gave them notice, that a general affembly which was called upon fuch important
matters, ought not, nor could not be ftopped by a
fingle Lettre-de-Cachet. The company after this had
their letter to all the parliaments of the kingdom, read.
It was fhort, but decifive and preffing. That fame
day in the afternoon the general affembly was held at
the town-houfe, as the common-council had ordered
it in the morning. The prefident Aubry's advice
was conformable to the city attorney's conclufions.
An apothecary, named Defnots, who fpoke very well,
added, That they ought to write to all the towns in
France, that were either the feats of parliaments, or
of bifhops, or of prefidial courts ; inviting them to
hold affemblies like unto theirs, and to make the
like remonftrances againft the Cardinal. That opinion, which had a majority of above feven voices that
day, had the minority at the next affembly, which
was held upon the 22d. Some having faid in that
affembly, That that union of all the towns was a
kind of league againft the King : this brought the
majority to the advice of the prefident Aubry, which
was only for making remonftrances to the King about
the removal of Cardinal Mazarin, and his Majefty's
return to Paris. That fame day the Duke and the
Prince went to the chamber of accounts, where they
caufed the like declarations to thofe they had made

at the parliament and at the town-houfe to be regiftred. That chamber refolved likewife upon fending remon-ftrances againft the Cardinal.

Upon the 23d, the Duke told the parliament, That Mazarin's army having poffeffed themfelves, under pretence of the King's approach, of Melun and of Corbeil, againft the promife made by the Marefchal de l'Hopital, that the troops fhould keep at twelve leagues diflance from Paris, he was obliged to make his army advance likewife. After this he went with the Prince to the court of aids, where matters were carried on as in other places.

Though I can anfwer for the truth of the facts which I have mentioned, in refpect to the affemblies that were held at that time, that is, from the 1ft of March to the 23d of April, becaufe there is not one but what I have verified myfelf with the regifters of the parliament, or of the town-houfe, I have not thought that the truth of hiftory required that I fhould infift upon them with the fame attention or reflection, as I have done in relation to the affemblies of the chambers, where I had been prefent in perfon. The difference between a narration writ upon memoirs, though never fo good, and a narration of facts which one has one's felf feen, is as great as between a pic-ture drawn upon hear-fays, and one drawn from the life. All that I could meet with in thefe regifters can be at moft but the body of the thing, for as to the fpirit of the deliberations, it is impoffible to dif-cover it by the bare reading of them. It is often much better difcerned, by a look, a gefture, an air, fometimes even almoft imperceptible; than by the fubftance of things that appear the moft important, which, however, is the only matter of which the regifters ought to give us an account. I defire that you would take this obfervation, as a mark of the exactnefs I have, and always will have, to be want-ing in nothing that may ferve to the explanation of a fubject upon which you have commanded me to write. The account which I am going to give you,

of

of what I was obferving at that time of the fecret fprings which gave motion to thefe feveral machines, is a thing which I am better able to perform, and which I hope I fhall do pretty exactly.

It is impoffible that after having feen the unanimous confent of all thefe bodies, confpiring together the ruin of Cardinal Mazarin, you fhould not be perfuaded that he is upon the very brink of the precipice, and that nothing lefs than a miracle can fave him. The Duke was as much perfuaded of it as you can be, at his coming from the town-houfe, and he bantered me, in the prefence of the Marefchal d'Eftampes and of the Vifcount d'Autel, on the opinion I all along had, that the parliament and the city would fail them. I confefs now, as I confeffed to him at that time, that I miftook in that point, and that I was furprifed beyond what you can imagine, at the ftep that the parliament had taken. Not but that the Court contributed to it as much as lay in its power; and the imprudence of the Cardinal, which precipitated the company into it againft their will, was certainly more than fufficient to excufe, or at leaft diminifh the fhame which I might have, to have formed fuch a wrong judgment. It came into his head to command the parliament, in the King's name, to revoke and annull, properly fpeaking, all that that company had done againft him, juft at the inftant that the Prince arrived at Paris; and the man in the world that was the leaft afhamed of making ufe of illufions, and who loved them beft when they were unneceffary, affected to reject them on an occafion in which I believe that a man of the greateft probity might have ufed them without fcruple.

It is certain that nothing was in itfelf more odious than the Prince's coming to the parliament, four days after having cut in pieces a good part of the King's army; and I am convinced that if the Court had not been over-hafty, and had forbore doing any thing at that inftant, all the feveral bodies, who in truth began to be weary of the civil war, had foon given

figns

signs of their weariness at the sight of the Prince, who
came only to engage them the more openly into it.
That conduct in the Court had been wise, but they
took one quite opposite to it, which did not fail to
produce a quite contrary effect; for by exasperating
these bodies, they reconciled them in an instant to
the Prince. He ceased from that moment to be the
man that had routed the King's troops, and was now
only looked upon as one that came to Paris to oppose
Mazarin's return. These representations of things,
so different from one another, entered even into the
head of those who would have sworn that they could
not confound them. In a time of such a general pre-
vention, none but philosophers can distinguish these
sorts of ideas right. But such men are few in number, and are besides counted for nothing, because they
are never seen with a halbert in their hands. The
busy men that make a noise with the people, and
harangue in assemblies, are those that confound these
ideas. This is exactly what the imprudence of Mazarin brought about; and I remember that Bachaumont,
whom you know, was telling me, the very day that
the King's council brought to the parliament the last
Lettre-de-Cachet which I have spoken of, that the
Cardinal had found out the secret of making Boisleve
a Frondeur. In saying that he said all, for Boisleve
was the arrantest Mazarinian that ever was known.

You will without doubt believe that the Duke and
the Prince did not fail of making use of this imprudence of the Court. Not at all; on the contrary,
they let not one opportunity slip of neglecting and of
spoiling all; and it is particularly on this occasion
that it must be owned that there are faults that are
more than humane. You will not be surprised at
those into which the Duke fell, but I am still wondering at those of the Prince, who was, even at that
time, naturally the man in the world the most incapable of committing them. His age, his birth, his
courage, might have made him commit errors of
another nature, which nobody would have wondered

at.

at. Thofe which I am going to fpecify, could proceed from none of thefe caufes; much lefs could they
proceed from oppofite ones, to which it is impoffible
for any body to attribute them; from whence I conclude, that that fort of blindnefs fo often mentioned
in Scripture, is even fometimes eafily perceived in
men's actions. Was there any thing more natural to
the Prince and more agreeable to his inclination,
than to have pufhed on his victory and reaped from
it the advantages which in all likelihood he might
have done, if he had continued to command his own
army in perfon? But inftead of doing that, he aban-
dons it to the conduct of two novices; and Mr. de
Chavigny's unquietnefs, which recalls him to Paris
upon a pretence, or a reafon which had no reality at the
bottom, overweighs with him what his warlike inclination and his true intereft ought to have led him to,
which was to ftick to his troops. Was there any
thing more neceffary to the Duke and to the Prince,
than the fixing, if I may fay fo, the happy moment
in which the imprudence of the Cardinal had delivered
into their hands the firft parliament of the kingdom,
which hitherto had hefitated about declaring itfelf,
and had from time to time taken fteps, not only weak,
but dubious? Inftead of making ufe of that inftant,
by binding the parliament entirely to them, they occafioned a fort of fright in that company, which never
fails to difguft at firft, and afterwards to create averfion; and they fuffer them to take a fort of liberty,
which at firft accuftoms them to refiftance, and which
infallibly produces it at laft. I explain myfelf. As
foon as the news came of the approach of the Prince,
there were papers pofted up, and a great commotion
upon the Pont-neuf. The Prince had no hand, nor
could have any, in it, for he was not arrived at Paris
when it happened, which was upon the fecond of
March; it is true, that it was done by order of the
Duke, as I have mentioned before.

Upon the 25th of April, the office for the toll at the
gate of St. Anthony was broke open and pillaged by

the

the mob; and Mr. de Cumont, counfellor of the
parliament, who happened by chance to be there,
coming to the Duke in his library, where I was with
him, and acquainting him with it. received this anfwer : ' I am forry for it, but it is not amifs that
' the people fhould now and then awake. There is
' no body killed ; the reft is no great matter.'

. Upon the 30th, the Prevoft-des-Marchands, and
other town-officers, who were coming back from the
Duke's, were like to have been murdered at the end
of the ftreet de Tournon ; and they complained the
next day to the parliament that they had received no
affiftance, either from the Duke or the Prince, though
they had fent to require it.

Upon the 10th of May, the King's attorney for the
city, and two echevins, had been killed in the parliament-hall, had it not been for Mr. de Beaufort,
who had much ado to fave them.

Upon the 13th, Mr. Quelin, counfellor of the
parliament, and captain of his ward, having brought
his company to the parliament for its ufual guard,
was deferted by all the citizens that compofed it,
who cried aloud that they were not affembled to guard
Mazarinians ; and upon the 24th Mr. Molé de St.
Croix complained in full parliament, that upon the
20th he had like to have been cut in pieces by the
feditious.

- You muft obferve, that the mob, that alone committed all the diforder, had nothing in their mouth
but the name and the fervice of the Princes, who
never failed to difown their doings the next day in
the affembly of the chambers. That difowning,
which was commonly very fincere, occafioned the fharp
arrefts which the parliament put out on all occafions
againft the feditious ; but it did not prevent the company from believing, that thofe that difowned the
fedition, were themfelves the authors of it; and confequently it abated nothing of the hatred which many
counfellors conceived at it; and it accuftomed the
company to give out arrefts which were not, at leaft

as

as they thought, pleasing to the Princes. I am not ignorant, and I have said it elsewhere, that in weak and troublesome times that inconvenience is inseparable from popular power, and no body has more experienced it than I. But it must likewise be owned, that neither the Duke nor the Prince had all the necessary application for salving the appearances of things which they did not in effect command. The Duke, who was a weak man, was afraid of offending the people by repressing with too much violence the seditious; and the Prince, who was an intrepid man, did not reflect enough upon the ill and powerful effects that these commotions caused with those that feared him.

I must confess myself in this place, and own to you, that as my interest led me to weaken the credit of the Prince with the public, I made use for that effect of all the colours which the conduct of many persons of his party furnished me with in abundance. Never was any man less capable than the Prince himself of following that conduct; and nothing was ever easier than to charge him with the envy and the appearances of it. Pêche was every day in the Court of the Hôtel de Condé, and the commander de St. Simon was always waiting in the anti-chamber. You may judge that this last had played some very strange trick, since I made no scruple, notwithstanding his quality, to confound him with such a wretch as Pêche was. It is certain that I made a very advantageous use of these two names against the interest of the Prince, who was in truth no otherwise to blame in respect to them, than in not being attentive enough to their foolish doings. But without being wanting to the respect I owe his Highness, I dare say that he was less excusable in not opposing at first certain liberties, which some private members of all the courts of justice took, to resist him openly, and even to attack him personally. I know that the Duke of Orleans's natural softness, and the continual jealousy he entertained of the Prince, obliged this last to dissemble; but I

like-

likewife know that he was himfelf too foft on thefe
occafions, and that if he had fpoke and acted as he
might have done when the Court offered him fo fair
an opportunity, he had brought Paris, and the Duke
himfelf, to fubmit to his will without ufing any
violence. But my love for truth, which has obliged me
to obferve the fault, obliges me likewife to admire
the principle from which it was derived. It is fomething fo fine in the man in the world of the moft
heroic courage to have fallen into faults out of an
excefs of goodnefs, that what he has not fucceeded in,
in refpect to politicks, ought at leaft to be admired
and exalted by all honeft people in refpect to his
morals. It is neceffary to mention thefe particulars
in few words.

Mr. Fouquet, attorney-general, and known for a
Mazarinian, though he declaimed againft the Cardinal in his turn, came into the grand chamber on
the 17th of April, and in the prefence of the Duke
of Orleans, and of the Prince, required of this laft
in the King's name, to give him a communication of
the feveral affociations and treaties which he had
made both without and within the kingdom; adding,
that in cafe the Prince refufed to do it, he demanded
of the company an acknowledgment in writing of
what he had requefted, and of the oppofition he made
to the regiftring the declaration of the Prince, about
his laying down his arms as foon as Cardinal Mazarin
fhould be removed.

Mr. Menardeau declared publickly at the great
affembly held at the town-houfe on the 20th of April;
that his opinion was, that no remonftrance ought to
be made againft the Cardinal, till the Princes had
laid down their arms.

Upon the 22d of that fame month of April, none
of the prefidents of the chamber of accounts, except
the firft, met at their chamber, upon fome pretence
or other, which appeared at that time a very flight
one: I do not remember the particulars. Mr. Per-
roches, an inftant after, told the Princes to their
face, that an arreft ought to be iffued out to forbid
                                                    the

the levying any troops without the King's leave;
and on the same day Mr. Amelot, first president of
the court of aids, said openly to the Prince, that he
wondered to see at that place a Prince who after
having so often triumphed over the enemies of the
state, had lately united with them. I mention these
only as samples of what was then doing. There
were every day others of the like nature, and there
was none, however inconsiderable it might appear at
that instant, that did not leave in the minds of the
people some of these sorts of impressions that are not
felt for the present, but that are afterwards remembered. It is indeed prudent in the head of a party to
bear with things which it is best for him to dissemble; but too much easiness in such cases, accustoms
not only bodies, but private persons, to resistance.
The Duke, led by his humour, and by the jealousy
which the Prince gave him at every instant, was
unwilling to displease any body. The Prince, who
was in the faction only by force, did not study with
application, enough the principles of a science, which
the Admiral de Coligny used to say, that no body
could ever be master of. In this manner both the
Duke and the Prince left not only to every one the
liberty of delivering their opinion, but even suffered
them to carry it to licentiousness. They thought in
all the occasions which I have mentioned, that it was
enough for them to have carried it by a majority of
votes, as indeed it had, if the matters in question
had been such as are decided by the ordinary course
of the law. They did not distinguish timely enough
the difference there is between speaking freely, and
speaking licentiously; and they could not persuade
themselves that a speech pronounced with authority,
with judgment, and in a decisive manner; and made
besides at convenient times, and at such critical
moments as are now and then to be met with, might
have produced that distinction, without the least sha-
dow of violence. By that means they all along suffered a certain air of a party opposite to theirs, to

F 5 remain

remain at Paris, which never fails to grow to a body when it is supported by the royal authority. If it had pleased the Duke and the Prince to remove from Paris, any one of those that had been wanting to the respect due to them on the occasions I have spoken of, which they might have done in a civil manner, the companies of which they were members had not opposed it. The court of aids disowned publicly what Mr. Amelot, their first president, had said to the Prince; that company would have consented to his removal, if the Prince had required it; they had even thanked his Highness for it the first day, and the next day they had trembled. The secret in matters of this nature, is to keep people to their obedience, by apprehensions which they have themselves occasioned, and been instrumental to; these sorts of fears being commonly the most effectual, and always the least odious. You will see what the contrary conduct produced. But that which was of great help to induce them to a contrary conduct, was the itch of negotiating (so old St. Germain called it) which was, properly speaking, the epidemical disease of the Prince's party.

Mr. de Chavigny, who had been brought up to state affairs from his infancy, thought of nothing else but of getting into them again at what rate soever. Mr. de Rohan, whose only talent, properly speaking, was dancing, knew very well that the court was his only element. Goulas had no other will but that of Mr. de Chavigny. These gentlemen, you see, could not but be very susceptible of proposals and negotiations. The Prince was, by his inclination, his education, and his maxims, more averse to a civil war than any man I have ever known, without exception. And the Duke, whose predominant character was to be always full of fear and of distrust, was, of all men I have ever seen, the most capable of falling into false steps, by the dread he had of falling into them; being in that like unto hares. These dispositions made both the Duke and Prince no less susceptible of hearkening

kening to proposals and negotiations. The quality
in which Cardinal Mazarin excelled, was to go about
the bush; to give to understand; to feed with hopes;:
to cast a mist before one's eyes; to offer proposals,.
and afterwards to entangle them. This sort of genius
was altogether fit for making use of the illusions,.
which those that have in hand the royal authority
are never without, to engage people in negotiations.
It was indeed what he did with every one; and these
engagements were in part the cause of the conduct
which I have explained, because they amused people
with the false hopes of an accommodation: but the
worst effect they produced, and which made the conduct I have spoken of altogether pernicious, was that
they gave courage to those in the city and the parliament who were well inclined to the Court; and that
they took it away from those who were sincerely
attached to the opposite party. I will explain these
particulars, after I have given you an account of the
motion of the armies of both sides, and of that which
I was obliged to make in this conjuncture, against
both my inclination and resolution.

The King, whose design, as I believe I have already
told you, had all along been to approach Paris, left
Gien immediately after the fight at Bleneau, and took
his way by Auxerre, and by Melun, as far as to Corbeil; whilst Messieurs de Turenne and d'Hocquincourt,
who advanced with the army as far as Moret, were
covering his march; and whilst Messieurs de Beaufort and de Nemours, who had been obliged to quit
Montargis for want of forage, were gone to encamp
at Estampes. The Court coming afterwards as far as
St. Germains, Mr. de Turenne posted himself at Pa-
laiseau, which obliged the Princes to put garrisons
into St. Clou, Port de Neuilly, and Charenton. You
will easily judge that all these motions of troops were
not made without a great deal of disorder and pillaging,
which last being looked upon at the parliament as no
better than robbing on the highway, occasioned every
day some scene there, that had not been unworthy to

be

be inferted in the ingenious fatire written againſt thé
league.   The fcene in which I was aſting my part at
the Duke's palace, was of another nature.   I went
thither every day without fail; both·becaufe the Duke
would have it fo, to let the Prince fee that in cafe of
need he might always reckon upon me; and becaufe
it was likewife advantageous to me to let the publick
fee that what thofe of the Prince's party were every
day faying againſt me, about my holding intelligence
with the Cardinal, was neither believed nor approved
of by his Royal Highnefs.   I kept always in the
library, becaufe not having yet received my Cap from
the King's hands, I did not appear in publick.   At
the time of my being there, the Prince was very often
either in the gallery, or in the chamber.   The Duko
was continually going to him, and returning back to
me, both becaufe he could never ſtay long in a place,
and becaufe he fometimes affeſted it for different·ends.
The common fort of people, who love always to be
myſterious, pretended that this continual motion,
which was natural to him, was the effeſt of the different impreffions which he received from the Prince
and me.   The Prince thought me the author of all
that the Duke did not do for the good of the party:
The little attention I had had for the offers made to
Mr. de Briffac, by the means of the Count de Fiefque,
had newly exafperated him.   There happened even
occafions where the Duke thought it was convenient
for him·that the Prince's anger againſt me fhould not
diminifh.   The truce betwixt us in refpeſt to writing
was broke.   Pamphlets began afrefh from his fide,
which I thought fit to anfwer; and it was on this
occafion, or at leaſt on fome others that followed it,
that I publifhed fome of thofe pamphlets which I have
mentioned in the fecond volume of thefe Memoirs
(though out of their place)·that I might not be obliged
to touch twice upon a matter too flight in itfelf to be
fpoken of fo many times.   I fhall only tell you by the
by, that the pamphlet entitled, ' The Difappointments
' of Mr. de Chavigny, firſt Miniſter to the Prince,'
                                                    which

which I dictated to Caumartin for a pastime, touched that haughty and vain man to such a degree, that he could not forbear shedding tears at it in the presence of above a dozen persons of quality that were in his chamber. One of them acquainting me with it the next day, I said these words to him in the presence of Messieurs de Laincourt and de Fontenay : ' I entreat ' you to tell Mr. de Chavigny, that being conscious of ' the many good qualities that are in him, I would ' write his panegyrick still more willingly, than I have ' done the pamphlet which he is so much touched at.'

I have already acquainted you with my resolution of keeping quiet as much as possible, it being certain that I could gain nothing, and could lose very much by stirring. I accomplished it in part, having hardly had any hand in any thing that was transacted at that time, because I was fully convinced that there would seldom happen any occasion of acting handsomely, and that even the few that might perhaps offer of acting wisely, would be missed by reason of the different and complicated views which every body had in this circumstance of time. I therefore rested myself upon my two great dignities, as being the surest foundation of my fortune; and I remember that the President de Bellievre telling me one day that I should bestir myself more than I did, I immediately answered him : ' We are in the midst of ' a great tempest, wherein it seems to me that our ship ' is sailing against the wind. I am provided with two ' good oars, a Cardinal's mace, and an Archbishop's ' crosier. I am unwilling to break them, and my ' business now is only to keep above water.'

You have seen that being obliged to wait very often on the Duke, I was forced to appear outwardly more active than I intended. Necessity even obliged me not to remain altogether quiet, because of the noise those of the Prince's party made by their pamphlets against me, wherein I was treated as a favourer of Mazarin. I was obliged to reply by other pamphlets, and the noise this made, added to my frequent visits to the Duke, which though they were publickly known,
appeared

appeared the more myſterious, becauſe I was obliged
for the reaſon I have more than once mentioned, to go
there only incognito, produced three very ill effects
againſt me. The firſt was, that it occaſioned even indifferent perſons to believe that it was impoſſible for me
to keep at reſt : The ſecond, that it perſuaded the
Prince that I was irreconcileable to him : And the
third, that it ſerved to exaſperate the Court more and
more againſt me, becauſe I could not reply ,to the
Prince's pamphlets, without inſerting in mine things
that could not be agreeable to the Cardinal. Theſe
inconveniencies could not be avoided without falling
into greater. For the only means I had for avoiding
the firſt, was an entire retreat from the world, which
had been unbecoming at a time that it had been attributed to the pretended fear I had of the Prince,
and which had been againſt the reſpect and the ſervice
that I owed the Duke, at a time when my preſence,
at leaſt as he fancied, was neceſſary to him. I could
avoid the ſecond, only by reconciling myſelf with the
Prince, or by ſuffering him to take with the publick
all the advantages which he pleaſed againſt me : This
laſt had been fooliſh, and the firſt was impracticable,
both by reaſon of my engagements with the Queen
upon that account, and of the diſpoſition of the Duke,
who would always keep me as a reſerve to help him in
caſe of need. I could not avoid the third without
taking ſteps towards the Court, which the Cardinal
would not have failed to make uſe of to ruin me, as
the following example will ſhew.

As ſoon as I had received the news of my promotion,
I ſent Argentueil to the King and to the Queen to give
them an account of it ; and I charged him expreſsly
not to viſit the Cardinal, to whom I was, as you have
ſeen, very far from thinking myſelf indebted for it,
and whom I was beſides willing to mark by a circumſtance of this nature, with the parliament and with the
publick, for my enemy. The Duke was ſo kind or
ſo prudent to tell me himſelf, that he owned that it was
neceſſary for me to give Argentueil that order, but
that

that I ought however to do it with a proviſo, and that in the ſtate in which things were or would perhaps be at his arrival at Saumur, where the Court was at that time, he thought it beſt that Argentueil ſhould not be kept within too ſtrict bounds, and that I ſhould leave it to his diſcretion to ſee the Cardinal in ſecret if he required it, and if the Princeſs Palatine, to whom I recommended Argentueil for the introducing of him to the Queen, thought it uſeful. ‘ Who knows, ‘ added he, if by the event, this may not be good ‘ for ſomething, even for the main of our affairs ? ‘ Prudence requires that one ſhould not loſe any op- ‘ portunity that offers of amuſing, when one has to do ‘ with thoſe that make it their buſineſs to amuſe. ‘ Mazarin will without doubt render Argentueil’s con- ‘ ference with him publick ; but where’s the harm ? ‘ Mazarin is an errant lyar whom nobody believes, and ‘ true or falſe he will publiſh it.’ Theſe were the Duke’s words, which proved a kind of prophecy. The Cardinal would ſee Argentueil in the night-time at the Princeſs Palatine’s. He told him, (moved without doubt with an exceſſive kindneſs for me) that if I had been fooliſh enough to order that he ſhould have viſited him publicly, he would, with an intent of ſerving me, have mended that fault of mine, by a public refuſal. He ſhewed a mighty regard for every thing that concerned me, and he would have made Argentueil believe that he was reſolved to ſhare the miniſtry with me.

It is certain however that before Argentueil was returned to Paris, the Duke was informed by Goulas, not of what had really paſſed in reſpect to that viſit, but of all that would have paſſed if it had been of my own ſeeking, and made unknown to his Royal High- neſs, with a deſign of differving him. This I think is ſufficient to ſhew you what was working againſt me, and may ſerve to juſtify the conduct I followed at that time.

It is by your order that I am writing the hiſtory of my life, and the pleaſure I take in obeying you faithfully,

faithfully, is the cause that I have spared myself so little, for you may hitherto have observed that I have taken no pains about making my apology. But I now find myself obliged to do it, because it has been on this occasion that my enemies have found it the most easy to impose upon the credulity of the vulgar. I know that people were saying at that time : ' Is it ' possible that the Cardinal de Retz is not satisfied to ' be at his age a Cardinal and Archbishop of Paris ? ' How can it come into his head that he can obtain ', by force of arms the first place in the King's coun- ' cil ?' I know that the pitiful gazettes, of that time are still full of these ridiculous ideas,) I confess that these ideas had still been much more ridiculous than they are made appear in these papers, if I had really entertained any such views or such hopes. But it is certain that I was very far from doing it, not only by the unreasonableness of the thing, considering the circumstances ; but even by my own inclination, which carried me with such a rapidity, both towards pleasure, and towards reputation, that the post of minister, which is a great obstacle to pleasure, and always renders reputation odious, was still more against my taste, than above my capacity. I do not know whether I am making my apology in, speaking to you after this manner, but I am sure at least that I am not making my panegyrick. I consider that I am obliged above all things to say the truth, which indeed will not serve me much with posterity for excusing myself, but which will at least be of some service to shew that the greatest part of ordinary men that judge of the actions of persons in great posts, ought at least to be stiled presumptuous fools. I begin to perceive that I have made this digression too long, which you will perhaps attribute to vanity. I believe it does not proceed from that principle, and that the pleasure I take in justifying myself has no other cause but my desire of receiving your approbation.

It

It is impoffible that when you reflect on the fituation I was in at the time which I have defcribed, but
that you muft remember what I have told you more
than once, that there are conjunctures wherein it is
impoffible to act well. The Duke of Orleans was I
believe repeating thefe words a hundred times in a
day, fighing and lamenting more than you can imagine, for not hearkening to me when I was repre-,
fenting to him that he would himfelf fall into this
ftate, and caufe every body to fall into it with him.
But my fituation was ftill the worfe by reafon of
fome domeftic difappointments (for I believe I may
call them by that name) that happened to me at this
time.

You have already feen that Madam de Chevreufe,
Noirmoutier, and Laigues, had begun in fome fort to
keep divided from me; and that under pretence that
they could neither directly nor indirectly come into
the intereft of the Prince, they had, in effect, abandoned that of the Duke, though they continued to
obferve outwardly all the meafures of civility and
refpect they owed his Royal Highnefs. Their meafures with the Court became much clofer. The
Abbot Fouquet had fucceeded Bertet in this negotiation, as I learnt from the Duke himfelf, who obliged
me, or rather forced me, to dive into it more than I
had done if I had not had his exprefs order; for in
truth, fince what had paffed at the Hôtel de Chevreufe
when the Cardinal re-entered the kingdom, I had
ceafed to rely in any wife upon them, and I continued to go thither, only becaufe I faw Mademoifelle
de Chevreufe there, who had not failed me. I
thought myfelf obliged to the Duke for his giving no
manner of credit to what Chavigny and Goulas were
faying againft me from morning to night, about the
commerce there was between the perfons I have named
and the Court, which in effect opened a large field
to calumniate me, and I thought myfelf thereby the
more obliged to watch them myfelf. This confideration made me enter, againft my inclination, into
fome meafures with the Abbot Fouquet. I fay
againft

against my inclination, for the little I had seen of
that gentleman at Madam de Guimené's, where he
went pretty often to see Madamoiselle de Meneffin, a
relation of his, had given me no great opinion of
him. He was very young at the time of his going
thither, but he had even then a certain air of a rash,
paffionate man, which I did not like. I saw him
two or three times, in the evening, at a friend of his
named le Fevre de la Barre, who was son to the
Prevoft-des-Marchands, upon pretence of conferring
with him about breaking the cabals which the Prince
was making to render himself master of the people.
Our correspondence lafted not long; both becaufe
I drew immediately from him all that I wanted to
know; and becaufe he grew quickly weary of converfations that anfwered not his purpofe. He would
have had me at the firft inftant to become as great a
Mazarinian as he was himfelf, not conceiving it fit
to preferve any meafures. He may, for ought I
know, have become fince an able man, but I can
affure you that at that time he fpoke no better than
if he had been but juft come from college. I believe
that that might be of no differvice to him with
Mademoifelle de Chevreufe, with whom he fell in
love, and fhe with him. Little de Roye, who was
a pretty German woman belonging to her, informed
me of it. I comforted myfelf eafily enough with the
waiting-woman of the infidelity of the miftrefs, whofe
choice, to tell you the truth, did not humble me.
I took however the liberty to break fome jefts at the
Abbot, who thought, or who feemed to think, that
I had carried them too far, and that I had threatened
to have him cudgelled. I never thought of any fuch
thing, and yet he had preferved as great a refentment
for it, as if it had been true. He contributed much
to my imprifonment; and Mr. le Tellier has told me
at Fontainebleau, after my return from foreign parts
into France, that he had offered feveral times to the
Queen, to kill me. My anger againft him went not
near fo far, and was not greater than my jealoufy,
                                            which

which was but moderate. Mademoiselle de Chev-, reuse had only beauty, of which one grows weary when nothing is joined to it. She had wit only for the man she loved, but as she never loved long, her wit lasted but a little while. She grew angry at her lovers as she did at her cloaths. Other women grow weary of theirs, she burnt hers, and it was with the utmost difficulty that her women could save a petti- coat, a hood, a pair of gloves, or a point de Venise. I believe that if she could have burnt her lovers too when she grew weary of them, she had done it with all her heart. Her mother, who would have set her at variance with me, when she resolved to unite intirely with the Court, lost her labour, though she had ingaged Madam de Guimené to shew her a billet under my hand, writ to that lady, whereby I gave myself up to her, body and soul, as witches do to the Devil. In the quarrel that I had with Noir- moutier and Laigues, at the time that the Cardinal entered into France, she took my part in the most passionate manner; but in two months time she changed, without knowing any reason why. She grew of a sudden passionate for Charlotte, one of her women that was very pretty, and who would stick at nothing; but this lasted but six weeks, after which she became in love with the Abbot Fouquet, and to that degree that she would have married him, had he been willing. It was at that time that Madam de Chevreuse, finding herself idle at Paris, resolved to leave it and retire to Dampierre, being drawn thither by the hopes that Laigues (who had been at Court) had given her, that she would be very well received there. I had an eclaircisement with Made- moiselle de Chevreuse, to whom I opened my grie- vances, which, to say the truth, I did not much stomach, and which did not hinder me from sending all the gentlemen and all the horse I had by me, to convoy both the mother and the daughter as far as Dampierre. I cannot finish this slight sketch that represents the state in which I was at that time, without

out doing the Prince of Condé the juftice I owe him for his generofity. Angerville, who belonged to the Prince of Conti, came from Bourdeaux, with a de-fign of attempting againft my life, as the Prince at leaft believed or fufpected. I am afhamed that I can give you no exact account about the particulars, becaufe one can never enter too much into the detail of good actions, chiefly of thofe one ought to keep a grateful remembrance of. The Prince meeting Angerville in the Rue de Tournon, told him, that he would order him to be hanged, if he did not leave the town within two hours to rejoin his mafter.

Some days after the Prince being at Prudhomme's, who lodged in the ftreet called d'Orleans, and having by him in that ftreet his company of guards, and a great number of officers, Mr. de Rohan came to him all in a fweat, to tell him that he had juft left me in a fad plight ; that I was at the Hôtel de Chevreufe, having with me only the Chevalier d'Humieres, cor-net of my Gens d'Armes, and not above 30 horfe. The Prince anfwered him with a fmile, The Cardinal de Retz is either too ftrong or too weak. Much about that time Marigny told me, that being in the Prince's chamber, and having obferved that he was reading a book with great attention, he had taken the liberty to tell him that it muft be fome very fine piece, fince he took fo much pleafure in reading of it ; and that the Prince anfwered him, ' 'Tis very true that I ' read this with great pleafure, becaufe it tells me ' my faults, which is more than any body dare ven- ' ture to do.' You muft obferve, that what he was read-ing was a pamphlet of mine, intitled, ' What is true ' and what is falfe in the Prince of Condé, and in the ' Cardinal de Retz ;' which might eafily have piqued and angered the Prince, becaufe I fincerely own that I had been wanting in it to the refpect I owed him. What the Prince faid on this occafion is great, wife, and noble, and may be called an Apophthegm, of which Plutarch had not failed to take hold with plea-fure to honour ancient times with.

I return

I return to what was paffing at that time in the affembly of the chambers, of which you have already feen the beft part in the obfervations I have made, and on which I have even dwelt pretty long. I have mentioned to you the itch of negotiating as a difeafe that reigned in the party of the Princes. Mr. de Chavigny had actually, but fecretly, a negociation on foot with the Cardinal, by the means of Mr. de Fabert. It came to nothing, becaufe the Cardinal was at the bottom againft an accommodation, and wanted only the appearance of one to difcredit, with the parliament and with the people, the Duke of Orleans and the Prince of Condé. He made ufe to that effect of the King of England, who propofed to the King of France a conference at Corbeil. It was accepted at Court, as it was likewife at Paris, by the Duke and by the Prince, to whom the Queen-mother of England propofed it. The Duke acquainted the Parliament with it upon the 26th of April, and he fent the next day Meffieurs de Rohan, de Chavigny, and Goulas, to St. Germain's, where the King was gone from Corbeil. I took the liberty that evening to afk the Duke if he had fome certainty, or at leaft fome view, that that conference would be to any purpofe; and he anfwered me, whiftling betwixt whiles, ' I ' don't believe it; but who can help it? Every ' body is negotiating: I will not be left by my- ' felf.' You muft give me leave to mark that anfwer, becaufe it contains at once the whole conduct of the Duke in refpect to all the negotiations which are to follow. He never had any other view in any of them. He negotiated merely becaufe he faw others negotiate; he ufed no other art, no other cunning than that. He made no other anfwer, whenever I happened to reprefent to him the inconveniencies of that conduct, which however I never did, till after I had his repeated command for it, above five or fix times.

I believe that you will ceafe to wonder that I would not concern myfelf in all this. You will ftill be the lefs furprized at it, when I have told you that after

the

the negotiation, of which I have been speaking, which only served to discredit the party, as you will presently see, there were five or six others, or rather a chain of them, which Messieurs de Rohan, de Chavigny, Goulas, Gourville, and Madam de Châtillon, had in hand one after another. I gave however my helping hand to their work, which I embroidered with all the colours which might be of use to me with the public. As my business was to cast upon that party the hatred and envy of Mazarinianism, which those that composed it tried to charge me with on all occasions, I did my very best to discover and expose publicly the private advantages which these several negotiators were earnestly seeking for in their treaties. The proposals of the government of Guienne for the Prince of Condé, of that of Provence for the Prince his brother, of that of Auvergne for Mr. de Nemours, of 100,000 crowns, which were asked for Mr. de la Rochefoucaut, of the staff of Mareschal of France for Mr. du Doignon, of a patent of Duke for Mr. de Montespan, of the superintendancy of the Finances for Mr. du Doignon, of the impowering the Duke of Orleans to make a general peace, and the Prince of Condé to name the ministers, were painted out with all the liveliness and extent possible. I thought it no imposture in me to publish that all that I have mentioned had been proposed, because it is certain that I had such advices from Court, though I would not swear that some articles were not amplified. What I know to be altogether true is, that the Cardinal gave room to every one to expect, that whatever they demanded should be granted, without ever intending, for any single instant, to grant any thing at all. He gave himself the pleasure of exposing in public Messieurs de Rohan, de Chavigny, and Goulas, conferring with him, both in private and before the King, at the very instant that the Duke and the Prince were saying publicly in the assembly of the chambers, that a previous article to all treaties was the having no manner of commerce with Mazarin. The Cardinal acted a

comedy

comedy in the prefence of the gentlemen whom I
have named, in which, whilft he was kneeling to the
King, intreating him to give him leave to return into
Italy, he had contrived that his Majefty fhould publicly command him to ftay; which command the poor
Cardinal was forced to obey. He had the pleafure to
fhew Gourville to all the Court, though he caufed
him to come by a private ftair-cafe. He had the
pleafure likewife to amufe Gaucourt, who, by his profeffion of negotiator, gave the negotiation. ftill a
greater luftre. In fhort, things came to that point
that Madam de Châtillon went publicly to St. Germain's; upon which Nogent faid, that when fhe entered the caftle fhe wanted only to carry an olive-
branch in her hand. She was in effect received and
treated there as a Minerva. But the difference betwixt that goddefs and her was, that Minerva in all
likelihood would have forefeen the fiege of Eftampes,
which the Cardinal undertook at that fame inftant,
and in which he was prevented, but by a very little
matter, from ruining entirely the whole party of the
Prince. You will fee by and by the particulars of
that fiege, which I have touched upon here, only becaufe it ferved to put an end to the feveral negotiations of which I have fpoke, and which I have been
glad to mention together, that I might not be obliged
to interrupt fo frequently the thread of my narration.

But I doubt you are yourfelf interrupting of it at
this inftant, to tell me that Cardinal Mazarin. muft
be a man of great fkill, to deceive people, in a manner fo ufeful to him, by fo many appearances of advantageous accommodations. To this my anfwer is,
that thofe who have in their hands the royal authority,
find an incredible facility in amufing thofe who have
a great averfion to make war againft the King. I am
in doubt whether I am excufing or praifing the Prince.
I am fpeaking the truth, which I have taken the liberty to fpeak to himfelf. There had like to have
been fome ftirring in the parliament upon the day that
the Duke fpoke of the conferences which Meffieurs de

3   Rohan,

Rohan, de Chavigny, and Goulas, had had at St. Germain's with the Cardinal.

This happened at the parliament on the 30th of April. The murmur was such, that the Duke, who was frighted at it, said publicly, that they would never see him there again till the Cardinal was out of France. The company resolved that the attorney-general should be sent to Court to sollicit the necessary passes for the deputies that were to make the new remonstrances, and to complain of the disorders committed by the soldiers in the neighbourhood of Paris.

- Upon the 3d of May the attorney-general made his report of what he had done at St. Germain's, in pursuance of the orders of the company. He said that the King would hear the remonstrances on Monday the 6th of that month, and that his Majesty was very sorry that the conduct of the Duke of Orleans and of the Prince of Condé should oblige him to keep his army so near Paris. The town-house ordered that day the city-gates to be guarded, which they would not do however, before they had first a Lettre-de-Cachet to command them to do it. The Court sent that order, because they knew there that the Duke would at last oblige them to do it of his own authority. It was certainly a very necessary thing, tumults and disorders visibly encreasing at Paris every day.

Upon the 6th, the remonstrances of the parliament and of the chambers of accounts were made to the King with a great deal of vigour.

- Upon the 7th, those of the court of aids and of the town-house were likewise made. The King's answer to all these remonstrances was, that he would order his troops to retire, when those of the Princes were removed further. The Lord-keeper, who spoke in his Majesty's name, did not so much as pronounce the name of the Cardinal.

Upon the 10th, it was resolved in the parliament, that the King's Council should be sent again to St. Germain's, to demand an answer about the removal
of

of Cardinal Mazarin, and to infift further upon the army's retiring from the neighbourhood of Paris.

The Prince came to the parliament upon the 11th, to inform the company that the bridge of St. Cloud was attacked. He caufed as many citizens as he found willing to take up arms, and he carried them as far as the Bois de Boulogne, where he had notice that thofe who had reckoned upon taking the bridge of St. Cloud without any oppofition, meeting with refiftance there, were retired. He made ufe of the ardour of the citizens to feize upon St. Dennis, where 200 Switzers were in garrifon. He took them fword in hand, and without any form of a fiege, having himfelf got the firft over the ditch ; and he came back the next morning to Paris, having left at St. Dennis the regiment of Conti, if I am not miftaken, to guard that place. But what he had done proved fruitlefs ; for Remeville, or St. Megrin, I don't remember precifely which, retook it two days after with all manner of facility, the inhabitants having declared for the King. La Lande, who commanded there for the Prince, made a pretty great refiftance in the vaults of the church belonging to the abby, which he defended for two or three days.

There was a great commotion at the parliament upon the 14th. Many confufed voices were heard, demanding that the company fhould deliberate upon finding out means for preventing the infolences and the feditions that happened daily in the town, and even in the parliament-hall. The Duke, who was informed of it, and who was afraid that under that pretence the Mazarinians of the parliament would oblige the company to take fome fteps contrary to his intereft, came to the parliament pretty unexpectedly, and he propofed that the company fhould give him a full power. This propofal, which was infpired to the Duke by Mr. de Beaufort, in a heat, without any, view, and upon very flight grounds, produced three ill effects ; the firft of which was, that the whole company was perfuaded that it was done upon mature

deli-

deliberation: the fecond, that it leffened the Duke
very much, his birth and his poft, confidering the
conjunctures, having no need of a borrowed authority: and the third, that the prefidents took fo
much courage at it, that they durft tell the Duke to
his face, that none were ignorant of the refpect they
owed him, and that for that reafon they thought it
proper to forbear to infert his propofal in their regifters. Nothing is fo dangerous as propofals that appear myfterious, and are not fo; becaufe they raife all
the envy which myfterious things never fail to do,
and that they are even an obftacle to the advantages
which it is fuppofed they will bring.

The Duke, upon the 15th, had a fad experience of
that truth, for he had the vexation to fee a printer
fummoned to appear before the Chambers, for publifhing a pamphlet, wherein it was faid that the parliament had refigned all their authority, and that of
the whole city, into the hands of the Duke. He told
me that evening, fwearing, that he no longer wondered that Mr. de Mayenne, during the League, was
not able to bear the impertinencies of that company,
adding even to that expreffion another ftill more licen-
tious. I anfwered him fomething which I have forgot, but I remember that he fmiled at it, and fet it
down in his table-book, faying to me, I will para-
phrafe it to the Prince.

Upon the 16th, the Prefident de Nefmond made his
report about the remonftrances, which the King had
ordered, after fome difficulties, to be read in the prefence of the deputies, to whom he faid that he fhould
order an anfwer in writing to be made to them in two
or three days. After the Prefident de Nefmond had
fpoke, the Attorney-General gave an account of his
deputation, faying, that having demanded that the
troops fhould retire ten leagues off of Paris, and having
explained the declaration which the Princes had made
for caufing likewife thofe they had at the bridge of
St. Cloud, and at Neuilly, to retire, the King had
named on his fide the Marefchal Hopital, and had
                                                    fent

fent a pafs with a blank to infert the name of the
gentleman that fhould be fent by the Duke, to confer together with the Marefchal of the means of proceeding to that removal.   He added, that the Count
de Bethune, who had been chofen by the Duke to that
effeſt, had conferred with Meſſieurs de Bullion, de
Villeroi, and le Tellier, and that his Majefty, out of
regard for his good city of Paris, yielded to grant that
removal, provided that the Princes fhould execute on
their fide what they were engaged to on the fame account.   The attorney-general, who was affifted by
Mr. Bignon, advocate-general, prefented afterwards
to the company a writing, figned by the King, and
counter-figned by a fecretary of ſtate, importing that
his Majefty would, without delay, fend for two prefidents and two counfellors, out of each chamber, to
inform them of his will in refpeſt to the remonftrances.   Upon this the parliament ordered new ones
to be made, in which the Cardinal's name fhould be
mentioned with ſtill a greater aggravation.

. Nothing confiderable paſſed in the aſſemblies of the
chambers of the 24th and 28th of May.   .

Upon the 29th, the deputies of the inqueſts came
into the grand chamber, demanding an aſſembly of
the chambers to deliberate about the means of raiſing
the fum of one hundred and fifty thoufand livres, promifed to the man that fhould bring the Cardinal dead
or alive.   Juſt at that time, the vicar-general to the
Archbifhop coming into the bar of the King's council, to confer about the expoſing the fhrine of Sainte
Genevieve, le Clerk de Courcelles faid wittily enough
on that occaſion, ' We are this day ordering a double
' holy-day; a folemn proceſſion of our patronefs's
' fhrine, and the aſſaſſination of a Cardinal.'   It is
time to fpeak of the fiege of Eſtampes.

You have feen that it was agreed on both fides
that the troops fhould be removed ten leagues off of
Paris.   Mr. de Turenne, who fome time before had
ufed thofe of the Princes pretty roughly at the fuburbs
of Eſtampes, where the regiments of foot of Bur-

gundy, and of horfe of Wirtemberg and of Brow, had, fuffered very much, refolved upon crufhing of them altogether in the town itfelf ; and the weaknefs of the place, as well as that of the generals, made him believe that the thing was not impracticable. The Count de Tavannes, who commanded there for the Prince, (Meffieurs de Beaufort and de Nemours being at Paris) made one of the fineft and moft vigorous defences that has been feen in our days. There was much blood fhed on both fides. The Chevaliers de la Vieuville and de Parabere were wounded there. The attacks were frequent and vigorous, and the defence was anfwerable. The fmall number had at laft yielded to the ftronger, if the Duke of * Lorrain had not come very a-propos to oblige Mr. de Turenne to raife the fiege. This march of Mr. de Lorrain's deferves to be explained to you.

The Spaniards had been for a pretty long time preffing of him to enter into France for the affifting the Princes. The Duke and Dutchefs of Orleans had been earneftly folliciting of him to the like effect. His anfwer to the Spaniards was, demanding money of them ; and to the Duke and Dutchefs of Orleans was, his demanding the towns of Jametz, Clermont, and Stenay, which had formerly belonged to him, and which the King had fince given the Prince of Condé. The Duke forced me one day to dictate to Fromont an inftruction for Le Grand, whom he was fending to Bruffels, in order to perfuade the Duke of Lorrain ; and I may fincerely fay, that it is the only thing of that nature that I did during the whole courfe of that war. I was continually telling the Duke, that I would preferve the fatisfaction of being able to think inwardly, that I had nothing to do in an affair where every thing went ' † a la peggio ;' and I had almoft ufed him even to ceafe to afk my opinion upon what paffed, by anfwering him always with monofyllables. He

* Charles the fourth, Duke of Lorrain.
† At random.

was one day chiding me for it, when I added, ' 'Tis
' true, Sir, and that monofyllable is always the fame,
' always No.' I could not obferve the fame conduct
in refpect to the Duke of Lorrain's march; for the
Duke of Orleans defired abfolutely, and the Dutchefs
ftill more than he, that I fhould draw up the inftruction which I have juft now mentioned. I don't know
whether it found the Duke of Lorrain already inclined
that way, but he marched with his army, which was
compofed of 8000 men, all veterans and good foldiers.
He left them at Ligni, and came himfelf to Paris,
entering the city on horfeback, with an incredible
applaufe of the people. The duke of Orleans and
the Prince of Condé went to meet him on the laft of
May, as far as Bourget, and were accompanied by
Meffieurs de Beaufort, de Nemours, de Rohan, de
Sully, de la Rochefoucaut, de Gaucourt, de Chavigny,
and Don Gabriel de Toledo. It happened by chance
that thefe two laft marched a-breaft in the entry. The
Duke, who hated Chavigny, told it me in the evening, tranfported with joy at it; and my anfwer was,
that I wondered what could occafion his furprize;
that Mr. de Chavigny did no more than what the
Prefident Jeanning, who had been one of the ableft
minifters of Henry IV. had formerly done; that the
only difference was, that the Prefident Jeanning had
fquadroned with the Spaniards before he was a minifter,
and Mr. de Chavigny did it not till after he had been
one. The Duke was very well pleafed with the apology, which he got to be writ down, and had feveral
copies of it malicioufly difperfed up and down, in a
manner that I found one upon his ftair-cafe, and another at the Cours a quarter of an hour after. I kept
myfelf very referved in refpect to the Duke of Lorrain; and though he was brother to the Dutchefs of
Orleans, to whom I was very particularly attached,
all I did was to fend a gentleman to affure him of
my fervices. The Duke of Orleans defired that I
fhould fee him, in which there was fome difficulty,
the Dukes of Lorrain pretending to take the upper

hand

hand of Cardinals they go to visit. We met at the
Dutchefs of Orleans's, and afterwards in the Duke's
gallery, where there is no rank obferved, and where,
befides, fuppofing there had been any, no difficulty
had arofe, becaufe he did not difpute me the rank
in a third place. This conference was wholly fpent
in civilities and in railleries, in which he was inex-
hauftible. He took a fancy, two or three days after,
to fee me at the novices houfe at the Jefuits, where I
met him at the Dutchefs of Orleans's defire. I began
by telling him, that I was very forry that the Roman
ceremonial had not given me leave to pay him my
refpects at his houfe, as I fhould have wifhed ; and
he immediately repaid me in the fame coin, by faying, that he was forry at heart that the ceremonial
of the empire fhould have hindered his waiting on me
at my houfe, and his ufing me as he could have
wifhed. He afked me afterwards, without any pre-
amble, whether I thought his nofe fo proper to be
filipped ? and then going on, he railed at the Arch-
duke, and at the Duke and Dutchefs of Orleans, who
made him receive a dozen filips on the nofe every day,
by obliging him to come and fuccour the Prince of
Condé, who detained what belonged to him. From
this he entered into a detail of propofals and overtures,
of which I proteft I underftood not one word. I thought
that my beft way was to anfwer him by a difcourfe,
which, I can affure you, he could make but little of.
He has remembered this as long as he lived ; and
when he returned into Lorrain, the firft compliment
he fent me, by the Abbot de St. Michael, was, that
he did not doubt but that we fhould for the future
underftand one another better than we had done at the
Jefuits at Paris. To tell you the truth, I had been to
blame, if I had fpoke more clearly than he, being fo
well informed of what was paffing every where in
refpect to him. I had fure notice that the Court
offered him in a manner carte-blanche ; and I was
not ignorant, that though he might fill it almoft as

he

he pleafed, he gave ear however to much lefter propofals.

Madam de Chevreufe, who had not left Paris at
that time, told him, rather in jeft than ferioufly, that
he might perform the gallanteft action in the world, ·
by obliging Mr. de Turenne to raife the fiege of
Eftampes, which would fully fatisfy both the Duke
and the Spaniards; and by returning immediately·
after with his army into Flanders, which would to the
laft degree pleafe the Queen, whofe particular fervant
he had all along profeffed himfelf to be. This propofal, which might pleafe both fides, agreed very well
with his wavering way. He refolved upon it without
any more ado, and Madam de Chevreufe valued herfelf for it at Court, where they were not forry to
cover the neceffity they were in of raifing the fiege
of Eftampes, with fome· appearance of a negotiation, which they magnified among the public, with
a thoufand particulars, that are always honoured by
vulgar reafonings as fo many myfteries. Nothing in
the world however was lefs myfterious than what
paffed on thefe occafions; and though'I was at that
time not at all in the confidence either of Madam or·
Mademoifelle de Chevreufe, as you have already feen,
I was well enough informed of it, againft both their
wills, to affure you of the certain truth of what I
have faid. The conduct which the Duke of Lorrain
followed, the next day after the fiege was raifed, was
a fure mark that I was not deceived, or was at leaft
a proof that he remained not long fatisfied with himfelf in refpect to that action. For though he fpoke
to the Duke of the fervice he had done him in obliging the Court to raife the fiege of Eftampes, in the
higheft terms, it appeared to me foon after, that he
was afhamed of the treaty he had made, and that that
was the reafon that obliged him to grant the Princes
what they afked of him, which was to delay his
marching away, and to ftay at Villeneuve St. George,
till the troops that marched out of Eftampes were got
into fome fafe place.

Mr.

Mr. de Turenne finding that the Duke of Lorrain did not keep the word he had given him to return into the Low Countries, marched to Corbeil, with a defign to pafs the Seine there, and to fight him. There were goings backward and forward about explaining what had been either promifed or not promifed, during which the troops of Lorrain intrenched themfelves. Mr. de Turenne being advanced with the King's army, having paffed the river Yerre, and having drawn up his army in battalia, in the prefence of the Lorrainers, every body was expecting that both armies would have given the fignal for a battle, which certainly had been bloody, confidering the goodnefs of the troops on both fides, but which would probably have turned to the advantage of thofe of the King; becaufe the Lorrainers wanted ground. At that critical inftant, my Lord Jermin came to Mr. de Turenne, acquainting him that the Duke of Lorrain was ready to execute what had been agreed upon, on fuch and fuch terms. A negotiation was immediately entered into; and the King of England, who, upon the likelihood of a battle, had joined Mr. de Turenne, went himfelf backward and forward. It was agreed that Mr. de Lorrain fhould depart the kingdom in fifteen days, and remove from his poft the very next day; that he fhould put into Mr. de Turenne's poffeffion, the boats which had been fent him from Paris to make a bridge over the river; that Mr. de Turenne fhould make no ufe of thefe boats to pafs the Seine, and ftop the paffage of the troops that were marched out of Eftampes; that what troops belonging to the Princes were in the Prince of Condé's camp, might fafely come into Paris; and that provifions fhould be furnifhed by the King's order to the Duke of Lorrain's troops during their retreat. Thefe two laft articles received not much oppofition, Mr. de Turenne faying, that he was perfuaded that the Duke of Lorrain's army would fave the King the trouble and expence of furnifhing them with provifions, becaufe they would take care to provide for themfelves upon

the

the road; and as for the liberty that was asked for
the troops of the Princes to get safely into Paris, Mr.
de Turenne granted it with joy, because he was sure
that that would more alarm than encourage the city.
Mr. de Beaufort, who had brought to his camp five
or six hundred voluntiers from among the citizens,
told the Duke the next day in the evening, that they
had been so much frightened, that he was troubled for
fear they should alarm the whole city. The Prince,
who was sick at that time, was for that reason against
their going out of the city at that conjuncture. I return to the parliament.

I have had so little share in the last assemblies of the
chambers, and in the affairs I have last mentioned,
that I have been for some time in doubt with myself
whether I should insert them in a work that ought to
be, properly speaking, but merely the account which
you have commanded me to give you of my actions.
It is certain that my promotion happened just at a time
when the state of things, as I have been explaining to
you before, had prevented my acting almost in any
manner, though I had continued to assist at the deliberations of the parliament. I was now deprived by
my dignity to sit and speak there, and as you have
seen before, I spoke but little at the Duke's palace.
As for the movement I gave myself there, I can assure
you very sincerely, that it was more imaginary than
real, and such only as speculative men were pleased to
fancy. But as they were pleased to fancy all manner
of things upon my account, I was continually exposed
to the distrust of some, to the apprehension of others,
and to the reasonings of all. The part I acted, which
was to keep unactive, or at most merely on the defensive, is always a dangerous part to act, and is not easy
to be described, because one can hardly do it without
an appearance of vain-glory, and self-love. It looks
as if one incorporated one's self with every thing considerable that happens in a state, when, in a work
that ought to relate only to one's own person, a man
dwells upon matters in which he has had no share.

From

From that confideration I have looked out with care
how to diftinguifh things of that nature, from others
which really belong to thefe memoirs; but it has been
impoffible for me to do it, becaufe the figure I have
made (though but a middling one) in the times that
went before and that followed thefe, in which I remained unactive, gives them fuch a relation and con-
nection one with another, that it would be a hard tafk
to fet them before your eyes in a true light, if they
were entirely diftinguifhed. This obliges me to go
on with what was paffing at that time, in which I intend however to be as fhort as poffible, becaufe I never
write upon other people's memoirs but with an extreme repugnance. I will only mention matters of
fact, without any obfervations of my own, and only
relate what appears the moft weighty to me, paffing by
the moft flight matters; and in what relates to the
affemblies of the parliament, I fhall take notice of the
dates, in refpect only to the moft confiderable deliberations. I fhall forbear even mentioning the others,
being perfuaded that it is more than fufficient to tell
you, that they were wholly employed in declamations
againft the Cardinal, in complaints and in arrefts
againft the infolencies and the feditions of the people,
and in the Prince's difowning thefe feditions, which
for the moft part were indeed but too natural an effect
of the people's difpofitions.

Upon the firft of June the Duke fent to the parliament to know what feat they would give the Duke of
Lorrain in the affemblies of the chambers. The company anfwered unanimoufly, That the Duke of Lorrain being an enemy to the ftate, they could give him
no feat at all there. The Duke, who honoured me
with a vifit two or three days after, upon account of a
defluxion I had in my eyes, faid to me, ' Could you
' have believed that the parliament would have made
' me that anfwer?' To which I replied, ' I could
' have much lefs believed, Sir, that you would have
' run the hazard of afking them the queftion.' He replied in an angry tone, ' If I had not ventur'd it, the
                                                        ' Prince

' Prince had faid that I had been a Mazarinian.' This word difcovers the principle of all the Duke's actions at that time.

There was a great commotion at the parliament upon the 7th, on account of the approach of the troops of Lorrain, who were come on this fide of Lagny, and who committed great diforders in Brie. This was fpoken of in the parliament with the fame furprize and horror, as if there had been no manner of divifions in the kingdom.

Upon the 10th, the Préfident de Nefmond reported what had paffed in the deputation fent to the King, who from the beginning of the fiege of Eftampes had advanced as far as Melun. His Majefty's anfwer was, That the company might fend whom they pleafed to confer with thofe whom he fhould name, about re-eftablifhing the public quiet. The company delibe-rated upon this, and they refolved to fend the fame deputies back to Court to be better informed of the King's will, but to renew however the remonftrances againft Mazarin. Both the Duke and the Prince had been againft this refolution, maintaining that no pro-pofals about a conference ought to be hearkened to, except the firft article was actually and effectually for the removing the Cardinal.

The complaints were renewed upon the 14th, againft the approach of the troops of Lorrain, and were car-ried fo far as to occafion the fending for the King's council, whofe conclufions were, that the Duke of Orleans fhould be defired to oblige them to retire. A counfellor, whofe name I don't remember, having faid, that he could not imagine how the retreat of thofe troops could be of fervice to the company, confider-ing upon what terms they were with the Court; Me-nardeau anfwered, That that reafon obliging the com-pany ftill the more to take off all manner of pre-tences that might be made ufe of for calumniating them with the King, his opinion was, that they fhould put out an arreft injoining the commons to fall upon them. A further deliberation upon this was however put off

till

till the Duke fhould be prefent. It is likely that you imagine that the Duke of Lorrain's retreat, of which I have fpoken, and which was known at Paris upon the 16th, made no great impreffion upon people's minds, having been fo generally wifhed for. That impreffion was however incredible, and I obferved that many of thofe who had highly exclaimed againft his approach, were thofe that made the greateft noife againft his retreat. It is not extraordinary that men fhould not know themfelves: there are times where it may be faid, that they have loft all feeling.

Upon the 20th, the Prefident de Nefmond reported what had paffed in the deputation fent to the King at Melun, and got his Majefty's anfwer to be read to the company, the fubftance of which was; That though his Majefty could not be ignorant that the demand that was made about the removal of Cardinal Mazarin, was no more than a pretence, he might perhaps be induced to grant a thing, which the Cardinal himfelf was every day preffing him to, (after having repaired his honour by fuch declarations as his innocence required) if his Majefty was affured that he might have good and fubftantial fureties on the part of the Princes, for the execution of what they had offered in cafe of that removal: That his Majefty defired therefore to know:

1. Whether in that cafe they will renounce all manner of leagues and affociations made with foreign Princes?

2. Whether this will put an end to their pretenfions?

3. Whether they will attend on his Majefty?

4. Whether they will fend back the foreigners that are in the kingdom?

5. Whether they will difband their forces?

6. Whether Bourdeaux will fubmit to its duty, as well as the Prince of Conti, and Madam de Longueville?

7. Whether the places which the Prince has fortified will be put into their firft ftate?

Thefe

These are the chief of the twelve questions, on which the Duke of Orleans spoke with a great deal of emotion, saying, That it was a thing unheard of, that a son of France, and a Prince of the blood, should be brought in this manner upon the stool to be asked questions, as if the declaration they both of them had made of laying down their arms as soon as Cardinal Mazarin should be out of the kingdom, was not more than sufficient to content the Court, supposing that their intentions there were good. The company began to deliberate on this, but they could not make an end, and so the deliberation was put off till the next day.

The Duke not being able to come to the parliament upon the 21st, by reason of a great fit of the cholic, which he had had in the night, nothing was debated there in the presence of the Prince, but how to find out a fund for the subsistence of the poor, who suffered very much in the city, and about raising the sum of 150,000 livres, which was the price set upon the Cardinal's head. It was proposed about this last article, to make with speed an inventory of what household goods were remaining, belonging to the Cardinal. Mr. de Beaufort committed that day a blunder worthy of him. There having been in the morning a great commotion in the palace-yard, in which Messieurs de Vanau and Partial would have been killed, if it had not been for him, he thought that the best way for diverting the mob from coming to the parliament, was to assemble them at the Place-Royale, where he gave them a rendezvous for the afternoon. He gathered there four or five thousand beggars, to whom he made a kind of sermon, in which indeed he had no other end than to exhort them to the obedience which they owed to the parliament. I was informed of all the particulars by persons whom I had sent thither on purpose, and who might be credited. Fear, which had already possessed most of the Presidents and of the Counsellors, made them believe that that assembly was intended only for their undoing. This fear redoubled

redoubled at the speeches which they fancied that Mr.
de Beaufort was making, and it became so great, that
it was not in the power either of the Duke, or of the
Prince to remove it, and to oblige them to go to the
parliament. What happened that same day to the
President de Maisons, in the street called de Tournon,
did not serve to raise their courage. He was very near
being killed by a multitude of people as he was coming out of the Duke's palace, and it was with a great
deal of difficulty that the Prince and Mr. de Beaufort
could save him. What happened on this occasion
shewed that Mr. de Beaufort was not aware that the
assembling the mob together is always the putting them
in a commotion. It appeared by experience to be so,
for two or three days after his fine sermon, the sedi-
tion grew stronger than it had yet been; and the President de Novion was even pursued in the street, and
run the greatest risk possible.

On the 25th the Princes declared in the assembly of
the chambers, that as soon as the Cardinal was out of
the kingdom, they would faithfully execute all the
articles which were asked of them in the King's answer, and would afterwards send deputies to conclude
what should remain undone. Upon this the company
gave out an arrest, ordering that the deputies of the
parliament should incessantly return to Court to carry
the Princes declaration to the King.

Not any of the Presidents went to the parliament on
the 26th.

On the 27th the President de Novion went thither,
and gave out a cutting arrest against seditious persons.

The other sittings were spent in giving the necessary
orders for the safety of the city, which occasioned no
small trouble, those of the guards being themselves
often enough the authors of the seditions. It is time
to return to the war affairs.

The Prince, who had had some fits of a tertian
ague, went as far as Linard to meet his troops, which
were coming from Estampes; and as the Court had in

no manner of way obferved what had been promifed there, in refpect of their removing theirs from the neighbourhood of Paris, he thought not himfelf obliged to remove his, which made him poft his fmall army at St. Cloud, a confiderable poft, becaufe of the bridge, by means of which he might, in cafe of need, remove it wherever he pleafed.

Mr. de Turenne, who was with the King's army about St. Dennis, whither his Majefty was likewife come in perfon to be nearer Paris; Mr. de Turenne, I fay, built a bridge of boats at Epinal, with an intent to come and attack the enemy before they had time to retire. Mr. de Tavannes had notice given him of it, and fent the like to the Prince, who came to his camp with all diligence. He marched off in the evening, and came towards Paris, intending to arrive at Charenton by break of day, to pafs there the Marne, and take a poft from whence he might not be diflodged. But Mr. de Turenne gave him not time to do it, for he attacked his rear-guard in the fuburb of St. Dennis. The Prince loft there but a few men of the regiment of Conti, and he fent the Duke of Orleans word by the Count de Fiefque, that he might rely upon his reaching the fuburb of St. Anthony, in which he fhould, he faid, have more room to defend himfelf. It is on this occafion, more than on any other, that I am forry that the Prince has not given me, as he had promifed, an account of his actions. What he did that day was one of the fineft of his whole life. I have heard from Laigues, who underftood war affairs, and was with him all that day, though he was more difcontented at him than all the world befides, that he fhewed fomething in this occafion beyond human valour, and human capacity. I fhould be inexcufable if I undertook to give you the detail of the greateft and moft heroic action in the world, from the memoirs that were publifhed, which I have heard officers fpeak of with contempt. I fhall only tell you, that after the moft bloody and obftinate fight in the world, he faved his troops, which were but a handful of men, though attacked by

Mr.

Mr. de Turenne, reinforced by the army of the Marefchal de la Ferté. He loft there the Count de Boftu, a Fleming, la Roche Giffart, Flammarin, and de Hacqueft, of the houfe of Montmorency. Meffieurs de la Rochefoucaut, de Tavannes, de Cogny, the Vifcount de Melun, and the Chevalier de Fort were wounded there. On the King's fide, Efclainvillier was wounded, and Meffieurs de St. Megrin and Mancini were killed. I cannot exprefs to you the Duke's agitation all the time the fight lafted. All poffible events filled up his thoughts for a while, and were fucceeded, as is ufual in fuch cafes, by a view of all impoffible events. Jouy, whom he fent feven times to me in lefs than three hours, told me that there were moments in which he was afraid that the city would revolt againft him; and others, wherein he feared that it would declare too much for the Prince. He fent perfons unknown to fee what was doing at my houfe, and nothing encouraged him thoroughly, but the hearing that I had only my Switzer to guard my door. This I was told by Bruneau the next day, who concluded from it, that there was no great danger fince I was no better guarded againft it. Mademoifelle, who had done her utmoft with the Duke to oblige him to go into the ftreet called St. Anthony, to caufe the gate to be opened to the Prince, who began to be extremely preffed in the fuburb, took the refolution to go thither herfelf. She went into the Baftille, the entrance of which, Loüviere *, out of refpect, durft not refufe her. She caufed the cannon to be fired upon the troops of the Marefchal de la Ferté, which were advancing with a defign to take in flank thofe of the Prince. She afterwards harangued the guard that was at the gate of St. Anthony, which was opened to the Prince, who entered the city with his army, of which the foldiers, though much difabled, appeared covered with more glory ftill than wounds. This famous fight happened upon the 2d of July.

---

* Son to Brouffel, and Governor of the Baftille.

A general

A general aſſembly at the town-houſe, which had been ordered on the firſt of July by the parliament, to adviſe about what was to be done for the ſafety of the city, was held there upon the 4th in the afternoon. Both the Duke and the Prince aſſiſted there, upon pretence of thanking the city for giving entrance to their troops the day that the fight happened; but in reality, to engage the aſſembly to unite ſtill more ſtrictly with them. This was at leaſt what the Duke was made to believe; but there was another deſign, which I heard not of till four or five years after, when the Prince himſelf diſcovered it to me at Bruſſels. I do not preciſely remember whether he confirmed to me a report very current among the public, of an advice given him by Mr. de Bouillon, that the Court would never think of a real accommodation with him, till they were convinced there that he was in effect maſter of Paris. I know that I inquired of him about the truth of that report, but I cannot recall to my memory what his anſwer was. This is what he diſcovered to me about his deſign. He was perſuaded that I did him great diſſervices with the Duke, in which, as you have ſeen before, he was miſtaken. But he was likewiſe perſuaded that I did him a great deal of prejudice in the city, in which he was in the right. I have acquainted you with the reaſons I had for acting ſo, in reſpect to him. The Prince had obſerved that I ſtood in no manner upon my guard, and that I made uſe, even with affectation, of the pretence of marching incognito, to which the ceremonial obliged me, to ſhew the confidence and the truſt which I repoſed in the people's good-will, in the midſt of the greateſt commotions. He reſolved very prudently to make uſe of that confidence of mine, to execute one of the wiſeſt and fineſt actions that had perhaps been imagined during that whole age. His deſign was to ſtir the people upon the morning of the day that the aſſembly was to be held at the Town-houſe; to come directly to my houſe about ten in the morning, which was known to be juſt the hour that I had leaſt company with me, be-

caufe it was the time I commonly employed about my
ftudies; to carry me away civilly in my coach out of
the city; and to forbid me at the gate; in due form,
to come into it again.   I am confcious to myfelf that
the game was fure, and that in the condition things
were in, the fame perfons that had taken up arms for
my defence, if they had had time to confider on it,
had approved the thing after its execution; it being
certain that in revolutions that are great enough to
keep the multitude in fufpence, thofe that get the ftart
are always applauded, provided they fucceed at firft.
I ftood upon no manner of defence.   The Prince
might have made himfelf mafter of the cloyfter without ftriking a blow; and I might have been carried to
one of the city gates, before any alarm ftrong enough
had been given to oppofe it.   Nothing could have
been better imagined.   The Duke, who would have
been ftruck down with the thing, had applauded it.
The affembly at the Town-houfe, whom the Prince
would have informed of it upon the fpot, had trembled
at it.   The Prince's civil manner of doing it had been
both praifed and admired.   I had fuffered by it a great
lofs of reputation, for keeping in a condition fo de-
fencelefs, and I muft have confeffed myfelf to have
been guilty of a great deal of temerity and of imprudence, not to have forefeen a thing fo feafible.   Fortune turned that fine defign againft the Prince, and
rendered it, by the event, as fatal as the blackeft of
all enterprizes could have been.

The commotion being begun towards the Place-
Dauphine, by forcing thofe that went by to put ftraw
in their hats, Mr. de Cumont, a Counfellor of the
parliament, and a particular fervant of the Prince's,
who had been obliged to do as the reft, went in great
hafte to give notice of this to the Duke, and to intreat
him to prevent the Prince, who was in the gallery,
from going out whilft that commotion lafted, which
Cumont fuppofed, as he told the Duke, to have been
raifed either by the Mazarinians, or by the Cardinal
de Retz, for deftroying the Prince.   At this the Duke
ran

ran after his Highnefs, who was going down the privy-
ftairs, and who had his coach ready to come to my
houfe and execute his defign. The Duke made ufe of
his authority, and even of violence to keep him from
going. He made him dine with him, and carried him
afterwards to the Town-houfe, where the affembly
was to be held. They ftaid there only to return their
thanks to the company, and to reprefent the neceffity
there was of finding out means to defend themfelves
againft Mazarin, after which they came away. The
fight of a trumpeter, who arrived juft at that time
from the King, with an order for the affembly to be
put off for a week, provoked the people who were in
the Greve, crying inceffantly, that the city ought to
unite with the Princes. Some officers, whom the
Prince had interfperfed in the morning with the mob,
not having received the orders they expected, were
not able to ftop their fury. The firft object it difcharged itfelf upon, was the Town-houfe. They fhot
at the windows; they fet fire to the doors; they entered in, fword in hand. They maffacred Mr. le Gras,
a Mafter of Requefts, and Mr. Miron, a Mafter in
the Chamber of Accounts, and one of the moft honeft
men, and of the beft credit with the people, that was
in Paris. There were, befides, twenty-five or thirty
citizens that perifhed in this occafion, and the
Marefchal de l'Hopital efcaped the danger but by a
miracle, and by the help of the Prefident Barentin.
A young man of Paris, named Noblet, of whom I have
already fpoken, in relating the encounter I had with
Mr. de la Rochefoucaut at the parliament, had likewife the good luck to be ferviceable to the Marefchal
on this occafion. You may eafily imagine what effect
the Town-houfe fet on fire, and the blood fhed, produced in Paris. The confternation was at firft general there; all the fhops were fhut up in an inftant.
Things remained for a while in that ftate, and it was
about fix in the afternoon before the citizens awaked
and came to themfelves in fome places, where they
fet up barricadoes to ftop the feditious, who difperfed

almoft

almoſt of themſelves. Mademoiſelle contributed however to it. She went herſelf, accompanied by Mr. de Beaufort, to the Greve, where ſhe found ſome of them left, whom ſhe drove away. Theſe wretches ſhewed more reſpect to her than to the hoſt, which the curate of St. John's preſented to them, to oblige them to extinguiſh the fire which they had ſet to the Town-houſe doors.

The Biſhop of Châlons came to my houſe in the height of this commotion, the fear he had for my perſon being ſtronger than that he ſhewed for his own in a conjuncture where nobody without exception could reckon themſelves ſafe in walking the ſtreets. He found me ſo little precautioned againſt the danger, that he made me aſhamed of it, and I cannot conceive even at this time what could oblige me to be ſo careleſs on an occaſion in which I had, or at leaſt might have, ſo great a need to look to myſelf. This has perſuaded me, as much as any other thing in the world, that men are often valued for actions, which they ought the moſt to be blamed for. The public praiſed my firmneſs, when it ought to have blamed my imprudence. This laſt was real, the other was only imaginary. The truth is, that I had made no manner of reflection upon the danger which I began to be ſenſible of as ſoon as I was made to perceive it. Mr. de Caumartin ſent at that inſtant to his houſe for a thouſand piſtoles, with which I made ſome ſoldiers, for he found me without money. I joined them to ſome reformed officers which I had always preſerved out of my Lord Montroſs's remains. The Marquiſs de Sabliere, colonel of the regiment of Valois, furniſhed me with a hundred of his beſt ſoldiers, commanded by two captains of his regiment that were domeſticks of mine. Querieux brought me thirty Gens-d'armes out of the company which he commanded, and Buſſy Lamet forty choſen men out of the garriſon of Mezieres. I furniſhed all my houſe and all the towers of Nôtre-Dame with granadoes. I took ſome meaſures, in caſe of an attack, with thoſe of of the Ponts of Nôtre-Dame, and of St. Michael, who were mighty well affected to me. In fine, I put myfelf in a condition to difpute the ground, and to be no more expofed to any infults.

This conduct appeared wifer than the blind fecurity in which I had been for fome time. And yet it was not fo in effect, compared at leaft with that which I fhould have followed, had I been capable of minding only my own intereft, by taking hold of the opportunity which fortune prefented me with. There was nothing more natural, both in refpect to my profeffion, and to the condition I was in, than to leave Paris, after a commotion which threw the public hatred upon a party that appeared at that time the moft oppofite to me. I had not loft by it thofe that were my friends among the Frondeurs, becaufe they had looked upon my retreat as upon a refolution to which I was brought by neceffity. I fhould infenfibly have reconciled myfelf with thofe that were lovers of peace, who could hardly have refufed to take my part, becaufe they had looked on me as on one that was exiled for a caufe which they had themfelves efpoufed. The Duke could not have complained of me for abandoning a place in which it appeared he was no longer mafter. Cardinal Mazarin had himfelf been obliged in that cafe, both in refpect to decency and to intereft, to preferve meafures with me; and it was even naturally impoffible but that the Court's animofity againft me muft have diminifhed confiderably, by a conduct that would have much contributed to blacken that of its enemies. My retreat might have been attended with circumftances which would have eafily prevented my fharing the public hatred that was born againft Mazarin. In order to that, my bufinefs would have only been to retire into the country of Retz, without going to Court; and that had even cleared me from the fufpicion of Mazarinianifm for the time paft. In that manner I had got off from the daily trouble in which I was, and from that which I forefaw for the future, with-

without feeing in what other manner I could ever be
able to difentangle myfelf from it. In that manner
I had patiently expected what it had pleafed Providence to order in relation to the fate of the two
parties, without running any of the rifks which I was
at every inftant expofed to from both fides. In that
manner I had appropriated to myfelf the love of the
public, which the horror that is conceived againft any
violent action, never fails to beftow upon him that
fuffers. In that manner I had found myfelf, at the
end of the troubles, a Cardinal, and Archbifhop of
Paris, driven away from his fee by the party that had
publicly joined with the Spaniards, cleared of the
faction by my retreat from Paris, and cleared of
Mazarinianifm by my retreat from Court; and the
very worft that could have happened to me from this,
was to have been facrificed by the two parties, in cafe
of a reconcilement and an union againft me, and to
have been fent as ambaffador to Rome, which employment they would have been glad at heart to make me
accept of, even upon my own terms, and which to a
Cardinal, Archbifhop of Paris, can never be a burthen, becaufe there are a thoufand occafions in which
he may always find room to leave it. I had all thefe
views in my thoughts, greater ftill, and more exten-
five than I have fet them down here. I ftood in no
manner of doubt but that they were right and good.
And yet I refolved, without hefitating in the leaft,
not to follow them. The intereft of my friends, who
fancied that I might at laft find in the chapter of
accidents room to ferve and to prefer them, made me
immediately confider that they would complain of me
if I followed a way that got me out of trouble, and
left them in it. I have never repented my fhewing
a greater regard for their interefts than for my own.
This conduct was indeed fupported by my pride,
that could hardly have fuffered that the public fhould
have thought that I had yielded meanly to the Prince.
I reproach myfelf with thefe fentiments, which were
however of great weight with me at that time. They
were

were both imprudent and weak; for I affirm that there is as much weakneſs as imprudence in ſacrificing a great and ſolid intereſt, to punctilios of glory which is always a vain-glory, when it hinders us from doing things greater than thoſe it propoſes. We muſt own ingenuouſly that nothing but experience can teach men not to prefer what tickles them for the preſent, to what would afterwards afford them a much more real pleaſure: I have made that obſervation an infinite number of times. I return to the parliament.

I will acquaint you in few words with what paſſed there from the 4th to the 13th of July. It had indeed but a very melancholy aſpect, all the Preſidents à Mortier and a great many counſellors having abſented themſelves for fear of the ſeditions, which the fire and the maſſacre at the Town-houſe had not diminiſhed. This ſolitude obliged thoſe that aſſiſted there to put out an arreſt, forbidding that any one ſhould forſake his poſt, to which arreſt little obedience was paid. The aſſemblies at the Town-houſe were, for the ſame reaſon, likewiſe very thin. The Prevoſt-des-Marchands, who had ſaved his life merely by a miracle, the day of the maſſacre, had ceaſed to aſſiſt there. The Mareſchal de l'Hopital kept cloſe and private at home. The Duke of Orleans, in a very thin aſſembly, got choſen in their room, Mr. de Béaufort for governor of Paris, and Mr. Brouſſel for Prevoſt-des-Marchands. The parliament ordered their deputies, who were at St. Dennis, to preſs the Court for an anſwer; and in caſe they could obtain none, to come back to their ſeats in parliament in three days time.

Upon the 13th the deputies wrote a letter to the company, to whom they ſent the King's anſwer in writing. It contained in ſubſtance: That although his Majeſty had room enough to believe that the inſtances made for the removal of Cardinal Mazarin were nothing elſe but pretences, he was willing to give the Cardinal leave to retire from Court, after the neceſſary things for the eſtabliſhing the public quiet had

had been fettled, both with the deputies of the parliament, as likewife with thofe whom the Princes
would be pleafed to fend. The Duke, as well as the
Prince, who had found out that the Cardinal never
propofed any conferences, but with a defign to difcredit them with the public, exclaimed at this propofal; the Duke faying warmly, that it was only a
trap laid for them, becaufe neither he nor the Prince
had any need to fend deputies in their own names,
confiding altogether, as they did, in thofe which the
parliament had fent. The arreft that was given upon
this was conformable to the Duke's fpeech; and it
ordered their deputies to continue their inftances for
the removal of the Cardinal. The Princefs wrote
likewife to the Prefident de Nefmond to affure him
that they would continue firm to their refolutions of
laying down their arms as foon as the Cardinal fhould
be effectually removed.

Upon the 17th the deputies fent word to the parliament that the King had left St. Dennis to go to
Pontoife; that he had commanded them to follow
him, but that upon their making a difficulty of it, he
had ordered them to remain at St Dennis.

Upon the 18th they acquainted the company that
they had received a new order from his Majefty,
commanding them to go to Pontoife. The company
grew very warm at this, and gave out an arreft
whereby it was ordered that their deputies fhould
return inceffantly to Paris. The Duke of Orleans,
the Prince of Condé, and Mr. de Beaufort, went out
themfelves with twelve hundred horfe to fetch them
back, to fhew the people the great danger they
refcued them from.

The Court were not idle on their fide. The Privy-
council there was every day iffuing out arrefts that
annulled thofe of the parliament. They declared null
and void, all that had been done, that was doing,
and that fhould be afterwards done, in the affemblies
at the Town-houfe; and they even ordered that the
money appropriated for the payment of the Town-

houfe

houfe rents, fhould, for the future, be brought only to the places where his Majefty fhould refide.

The Prefident de Nefmond reported to the company upon the 19th what he and the other deputies had done at Court. This report, which was filled up with objections and anfwers, contained, in effect, no more than what you have feen before, except an article of a letter writ by Mr. Servien to the deputies, importing, that in cafe that the Duke and the Prince continued to make a difficulty of fending deputies in their own name, his Majefty confented that they fhould truft thofe of the parliament with their intentions. There were affurances in that fame letter, that the King fhould remove the Cardinal from his councils, as foon as the articles that might be difputed in the conference fhould be agreed upon, and that he would not even ftay to do it till they were executed. The company began a deliberation upon this, which was not ended till the 20th. It was then declared that the King being detained prifoner by Cardinal Mazarin, the Duke of Orleans fhould be defired to take upon him the quality of Lieutenant-general to his Majefty, and that the Prince of Condé fhould be invited to take in hand the command of the armies for fo long as the Cardinal fhould remain in France; that a copy of this arreft fhould be fent to all the parliaments in the kingdom, who fhould be defired to give one in conformity to it. The other parliaments had no regard to that prayer, for excepting that of Bourdeaux, there was not one that did fo much as put the matter into deliberation : contrary to it, that of Britanny had fufpended all the arrefts they had before put out, till the Spanifh troops that were entered into France had entirely evacuated the kingdom. The Duke was not better hearkened to in refpect to the letters he writ to all the governors of provinces about his new dignity ; and he plainly owned to me fome time after, that not one of them, excepting Mr. de Sourdis, had anfwered his letters. The Court had given them notice of their duty by a

public

public arreſt given by the upper council, annulling
that of the parliament which inveſted the Duke with
his new dignity. His authority in reſpeet to it was
not ſo much as eſtabliſhed in Paris, at leaſt in the
manner it ought to have been; for two wretches
having been condemned to be hanged on the 23d
for ſetting ſire to the Town-houſe, the companies of
trained-bands that were ordered to ſee the thing done,
refuſed to obey.

A general aſſembly was ordered to be held at the
Town-houſe upon the 24th, to adviſe about the
means of finding money for the ſubſiſtance of the
troops, and of ſelling the ſtatues that were at the
Cardinal's palace, for a fund to pay the price ſet
upon the Cardinal's head.

Upon the 26th the Duke ſaid in the aſſembly of
the chambers, that his new dignity of Lieutenant-
general requiring that he ſhould have a council to
adviſe with, he deſired that company to name two
of their own body to be of that board, and that they
would likewiſe tell him whether they did not approve
that he ſhould deſire the Chancellor to aſſiſt there.
The company agreed to it; and even Mr. Bignon,
Advocate-general, and the Cato of his agè, did not
oppoſe it; for he ſaid in his concluſions, which were
admired for their ſtrength and eloquence, that the
parliament had not given the Duke the quality of
Lieutenant-general; but that he might take it of
himſelf in the preſent conjunéture, as belonging to
him by right of his birth, which naturally eſtabliſhed
him the firſt magiſtrate of the kingdom. In proof of
this he mentioned Henry the Great, who being firſt
Prince of the blood, had taken that quality upon
him in a diſcourſe he made in the time of the
troubles.

The council for the Duke was ſettled on the 27th,
and was compoſed of the Duke himſelf, of the Prince
of Condé, of Meſſieurs de Beaufort, de Nemours, de
Sully, de Briſſac, de la Rochefoucaut, and de Rohan;
of the Preſidents de Neſmond and de Longueil; of

1   Aubri

Aubri and l'Archer, Prefidents in the chamber of accounts, and of Dorieux and le Noir, Prefidents in the court of aids.

It was refolved on the 29th at the Town-houfe affembly, to raife 800,000 livres for increafing the troops of his Royal Highnefs, and to write to all the great cities of the kingdom to exhort them to unite with the capital. The King failed not to annul, by arrefts of his privy-council, all thofe of the parliament, and all the deliberations at the Town-houfe affembly.

I think I have acquitted myfelf exactly of my promife of troubling you but little with my reflections upon all that paffed in the time I have fpoken of, and which I have rather touched upon than defcribed. It is not, as you will eafily judge, for want of matter, and it is hardly poffible to find any, that better deferves to be reflected upon, and that would furnifh more reflections. The events are in themfelves odd, and uncommon; but as I was not an actor in them, and that I was even but a remote fpectator, I fear that if I fhould enter too far into the detail, I might with my views mix likewife my conjectures; and I have fo many times experienced that thofe that appear the beft grounded, are often falfe, that I think them for that reafon unworthy of a hiftory, and chiefly of one which is writ for a perfon to whom I ought upon fo many accounts to fay nothing but what is entirely and inconteftably true. I will however venture two reflections, which I take to be altogether of that kind.

The one is, that though I cannot explain in particular to you the feveral fprings that gave motion to what you have feen lately acted, becaufe I had no hand in it; I can affure you that the only one that caufed the Duke to act fo pitifully, was his being perfuaded, that every thing running at random as it did, the only way was always to follow the ftream: and that the only reafon which obliged the Prince to act as he did, was his averfion to a civil war, which fomented and even renewed at every inftant,

in

in the moſt ſecret receſſes of his heart, the hopes he
had of putting quickly an end to it by way of negotiation. You muſt obſerve that theſe movements in
the Princes had never any intermiſſion ; and though I
have already mentioned them in particular as the
cauſes of ſeveral of their actions which I have explained, I think it is in ſome meaſure neceſſary to
mention them again in general, in the courſe of a
narration that preſents you at each inſtant with incidents of which you would without doubt be willing
to know the reaſons, which I am forced to omit
becauſe I know nothing of the particulars.

I have already told you that I had tired the Duke
out with my monoſyllables, which I made uſe of
deſignedly, and which I left off merely on account
of his new dignity of Lieutenant-general to the King.
I oppoſed it with all my power, becauſe he forced
me to give him my opinion about it. I treated it as
an odious, a pernicious, and an uſeleſs thing, and
I explained myſelf upon it in ſo clear and plain a
manner, as to tell him that I ſhould be extremely
ſorry that all the world ſhould not be apprized of my
ſentiments in that reſpect, and that any body ſhould
believe that thoſe of the parliament over whom I had
any power, ſhould be capable of giving their vote
for it. I was in that as good as my word, and even
Mr. de Caumartin ſignalized himſelf in oppoſing it.
I thought myſelf obliged to follow that conduct, in
reſpect to the King, to the kingdom, and even to the
Duke himſelf. I was convinced, as I am ſtill,
that the ſame reaſons which allow in ſome caſes a
diſpenſation from a rigid obedience, will ever diſ-
allow the uſurpation of a title, which in reſpect to
royal authority is a thing moſt eſſential. To tell
you the truth, I acted in this manner becauſe I found
myſelf in a condition to maintain, not only my words,
but likewiſe my ſteps. The poſture in which I had
kept myſelf ſince what had happened at the Town-
houſe, had ſeized upon the imagination of people, and had made them believe that I was much

3   ſtronger

ftronger than I was in reality. Such a belief is
enough to increafe one's ftrength. I had experienced
it, and had found the advantage of ufing it, as well
as of the other means which I met with in abundance
in the difpofition in which Paris was. That city
was every day growing more and more exafperated at
the party of the Princes, by reafon of the taxes with
which it was threatened, of the maffacre of the Town-
houfe which had filled all people's minds with horror,
and of the pillage made by the troops, which fince
the fight at the fuburbs of St. Anthony were incamped
in the fuburbs of St. Victor, where they committed
diforders hardly credible. I made ufe of all thofe
outrages, which I took care to reprefent in a manner
that rendered me very agreeable to all that blamed
them ; and in that manner I was bringing again
over to me all the lovers of peace that were not pro-
feffedly attached to the Cardinal. In following that
way my fuccefs was fuch, that I found myfelf in a
condition to difpute the ground with every body, and
that after having kept three weeks at my houfe on the
defenfive, in the cautious manner which I have mentioned, I came out of it with a mighty pomp, notwithftanding the Romifh ceremonial. I went every
day to the Duke's palace, and I paffed in the midft
of the troops which the Prince had in the fuburb,
not doubting but that I might confide enough in
the people to ufe that conduct fafely, in which the
event at leaft fhewed that I was not miftaken. I
return to the parliament.

Upon the 6th of Auguft, Buchifert, fubftitute to
the Attorney-general, brought to the affembly of the
chambers two letters of the King, one directed to
the company, and the other to the Prefident de Nefmond, with a declaration from his Majefty importing the tranflation of the parliament to Pontoife.
They had taken that refolution at Court after they
had found that their ftay at St. Dennis had not prevented the parliament nor the Town-houfe from taking the fteps which you have feen. This news put

the chambers into a mighty commotion. The company went on to deliberate, and it was refolved that the letters and the declaration fhould be kept at the Rolls, to be duly confidered after the Cardinal fhould be removed out of France. The Parliament of Pontoife, which confifted of fourteen perfons, at the head of which were, the Prefidents Molé, Novion, and le Coigneux, who fome time before were got out of Paris · in difguife, made remonftrances to the King, tending to the removal of Cardinal Mazarin. His Majefty granted their demands at the inftance even of that good and difinterefted minifter, who in effeft left the Court and retired to Bouillon. This farce, very unworthy of the Royal Majefty, was accompanied with every thing that might render it ftill more ridiculous. The two parliaments of Paris and of Pontoife put out arrefts in which they thundered at one another.

Upon the 13th of Auguft, that of Paris ordered that thofe that fhould affift at the affembly at Pontoife fhould be razed out of their lift and regifter.

Upon the 17th that of Pontoife verified the King's declaration, enjoining to the parliament, to the chamber of accounts, and to the court of aids, that confidering the removal of Cardinal Mazarin, they fhould declare their readinefs of laying down their arms, provided his Majefty was pleafed to grant an amnefty, to remove his troops from the neighbourhood of Paris, to caufe thofe which were in Guienne to retire, to let the Spanifh troops retire in fafety, and to give the Princes leave to fend to his Majefty about adjufting what matters remained yet unfettled. That parliament gave afterwards an arreft whereby they ordered to return thanks to his Majefty for removing the Cardinal, and to intreat him moft humbly to return to his good city of Paris.

Upon the 26th the King caufed the parliament at Pontoife to verify the amnefty which he gave to thofe that had taken up arms againft him, but with fuch
reftric-

reftri&ions that but few perfons could find their fafety, in it.

Upon the 29th and 31ft of Auguft, and upon the 2d of September, nothing hardly was fpoken of in the aſſembly of the chambers at Paris, but of the refuſal which the Court had made to the Princes of the paſſes which they had aſked for the Mareſchal d'Eftampes, the Count de Fiefque, and Goulas; and of the King's anſwer to a letter of the Duke of Orleans to his Majefty. The fubftance of that anſwer was: That his Majefty wondered that the Duke had not confidered that after the removal of Cardinal Mazarine, he had nothing elſe to do, according to his promife and to his declaration, than to lay down his arms, to renounce all manner of aſſociations and treaties, and to cauſe the foreign troops to retire: after which, thoſe that he ſhould ſend him ſhould be very welcome.

Upon the ſecond of September that anſwer of the King's was examined, but the company had not time to finiſh their deliberation. All that they reſolved upon, was, that both the civil and criminal judges of the city of Paris ſhould be forbidden to publiſh any declaration from the King, without the parliament's order. The company came to that reſolution upon notice given them that theſe two judges had received the King's command to publiſh and ſet up, in the city, the amnefty that had been verified at Pontoiſe.

Upon the third the company finiſhed their deliberation upon the King's anſwer to the Duke of Orleans's letter. It was agreed that the company ſhould ſend deputies to the King, to return him thanks for the removal of Cardinal Mazarin, and to intreat him to return to his good city of Paris: that the Duke of Orleans and the Prince ſhould be defired to write to the King, to aſſure his Majefty that they would lay down their arms as ſoon as it had pleaſed him to ſend the neceſſary paſſes for the retreat of the foreign troops, and an amnefty in due form verified by all

the

the parliaments of France: that his Majesty should be entreated to receive the deputies of the Princes; that the chamber of accounts and the court of aids of Paris, should be invited to send deputies: that a general assembly should be held at the Town-house; and that letters should be writ to the President de Mesmes, who was likewise retired to Pontoise, desiring him to follicit for the passes.

Give me leave, I befeech you, to make a paufe here, in order to confider with fome attention the fcandalous and continual illufion with which a minifter makes a real jeft of the facred name and word of a great King; and with which, on the other fide, the moft auguft parliament of the kingdom, the court of peers, are in a manner making fools of themfelves, by acting perpetually in a contradictory manner, more like the levity of a college, than the majesty of a fenate. I have fometimes told you that men have no feeling of themfelves in thefe fort of fevers that agitate a ftate and have fomething of a phrenfy in them. I knew at that time fome honeft perfons that were perfuaded of the juftice of the Princes caufe, enough to have died for it, if it had been neceffary. I knew others of a difinterefted and confummate virtue, that would have laid down their lives with joy to have defended the caufe of the Court. The ambition of great men makes ufe of thefe difpofitions as it fuits with their intereft. They are firft a help to blind the reft of mankind, after which they blind themfelves in a more dangerous manner than they have done others.

Old Mr. de Fontenay, who had been twice ambaffador at Rome, who was a man of good fenfe and of experience, and whofe intentions for the ftate were right and fincere, deplored every day with me the lethargy into which domeftic divifions caufe even the beft citizens to fall.

As to our foreign war, the Archduke retook that year Gravelines, and Dunkirk. Cromwell, without any declaration of war, and with an infolence injuri-

ous to our crown, took, under I do not know what
pretext of reprifal, a great part of the King's fhips.
We loft Barcelona, all Catalonia, and Cafal, the key
of Italy. We faw Briffac under a revolt, upon the
point of falling again into the hands of the Houfe of
Auftria. We faw Spanifh colours and ftandards dif-
played upon the Pont-neuf. The yellow fcarves of
Lorrain appeared in Paris with the fame freedom, as
the Ifabel and blue ones. People were ufing themfelves to thefe fpectacles, and to the mournful news
of fo many loffes. This habit which carried terrible
confequences along with it, frightened me, and certainly much more for the ftate than for my perfon.
Mr. de Fontenay, who was touched to the quick
with it, and who was even moved to fee me fo much
concerned, exhorted me to awake from my lethargy;
' in which, faid he, you are yourfelf after your own
' mode. For in fhort, continued he, if you have no
' regard but to your own felf, you have chofen the right
' way. But if you confider upon the condition of
' this capital city, to which you are attached upon
' fo many accounts, do not you think yourfelf
' obliged to beftir yourfelf more than you do? You
' are moved by no private intereft, your intentions
' are good: muft you, by remaining unactive, caufe
' the ftate as much harm, as others do by their moft
' irregular motions?' Mr. de Seve-chatignonville,
whom you have feen fince of the King's council, who
was my very particular friend, and a gentleman of
great probity, had been making me the like inftances
even with eagernefs, for five or fix weeks before.
Mr. de Lamoignon, who is now firft Prefident of the
parliament of Paris, and who from his youth has had
all the reputation which his great capacity, joined to
a virtue nothing inferior to it, has juftly deferved,
was every day fpeaking to me after the fame manner.
Mr. de Valencay, counfellor of ftate, who came not
near the others in capacity, but who was, like them,
colonel of his ward, came to me every Sunday morning, whifpering in my ear: ' Save the ftate, fave
' the city; I do but wait for your orders.' Mr. de

H 5   Roches,

Roches, chanter of Nôtre-Dame, who was colonel of the Cloyſter, a man of little ſenſe,. but whoſe intentions were good, came two or three times a week to ſhed tears with me on the ſame account. What touched me more ſenſibly than all the reſt, was a diſcourſe of Mr. de Lamoignon's, whoſe good ſenſe I valued as much as his probity. ' I ſee, Sir,' (ſaid he one day as he was walking with me in my chamber). ' that with the moſt upright intentions in the world ' you are falling from the love of the public into the ' public hatred. The minds of the people, which in ' the beginning were all for you, have for ſome time ' been divided. You have regained ground by your ' enemies faults : I ſee that you begin to loſe it again. ' The Frondeurs believe that you ſupport Mazarin, ' and the Mazarinians that you ſupport the Fron- ' deurs. I know that this is not true, and I even ' judge that it cannot be true ; but what makes me ' afraid for you, is, that it begins to be believed by ' a ſort of perſons, whoſe opinion always forms in ' time the public reputation. Theſe perſons are thoſe ' who are neither Frondeurs nor Mazarinians, and ' who have nothing but the good of the ſtate in view. ' This ſort of perſons can do nothing in the begin- ' ning of the troubles ; they can do all towards the ' end.' Nothing can be fuller of ſenſe, as you ſee, than this diſcourſe ; but as there was nothing in it altogether new to me, and that I had many times before made reflections that came at laſt very near it, it made not near ſo much impreſſion on me, as what he added at laſt. ' Theſe conjunctures, ſaid he, are ' very odd. A wiſe man ought to extricate himſelf ' out of them, with all manner of haſte, and even ' with loſs, becauſe let him govern himſelf never ſo ' wiſely, he muſt, ſo long as he remains in that ſtate, ' run the riſk of loſing all his honour. I doubt much ' whether the Conneſtable de St. Paul * was as guilty,

* Lewis de Luxemburgh, Count de St. Paul, &c. was made conneſtable of France in the year 1456, by King Lewis XI. and was, by that King's order, beheaded at Paris, on the 19th of December 1475.

' and

‘ and had as bad intentions, as we are told.’ Thefe
laft words, which fhewed a right and a profound
fenfe, went the deeper in me, becaufe Father Dom
Carouges, a Carthufian, whom I had been to fee the
day before in his cell, had faid to me, in relation to
the conduct which I followed, ‘ It is fo clear, it is fo
‘ great, that all thofe who would not be capable of it
‘ in the poft in which you are, fancy that there is a
‘ myftery in it: and in troublefome and unhappy
‘ times, all that paffes for myfterious is odious.’ I
will give you an account of the effect which all thefe
difcourfes had upon my mind, after I have mentioned,
as briefly as ever I can, fome matters that deferve to
be remembered.

. I have already told you that the King, after having
fettled his parliament at Pontoife, was gone to Compiegne. He could not take along with him Mr. de
Bouillon, who died about that time * of a continual
fever ; but he ordered the Lord Chancellor to come to
him, that gentleman being got away from Paris in
difguife, becaufe he chofe rather to be of the King's
council than of the Duke's, in which indeed he
might, if he pleafed, have found room enough not to
have accepted a place. Nothing but his weaknefs can
excufe a ftep of this nature, in a Chancellor of France ;
but I am no lefs perfuaded, that nothing but the
weaknefs of the government under Cardinal Mazarin,
could have reftored to the head of all the council-
boards, and of all the courts of juftice in the kingdom, a Chancellor that had been capable of taking
fuch a ftep. One of the greateft evils which the miniftry of Cardinal Mazarin has brought upon the
kingdom, is his little care of preferving the dignity
of that poft. The contempt he fhewed for it was attended with fuccefs, and that fuccefs is a greater evil
even than the firft, becaufe it ferves as a cover and a

---

* The Duke de Bouillon died at Pontoife on the 9th of Auguft
1652,

palli-

palliative to the inconveniencies which fooner or later will infallibly happen to the state, by reason of that contempt which is now turned into an habit.

It was with a pretty deal of difficulty that the Queen, who was naturally haughty, could resolve upon recalling the Chancellor. But she was forced to submit to the Cardinal, who was the master, and to that degree, that when he took a fancy for Mr. de Bullion, into whose hands he even intrusted the finances, he answered the Queen, who advised him not to confide in such a fort of a man : ' It is pretty indeed, ' Madam, to fee that you take upon you to advise ' me.' I was informed of this particular three days after by Varennes, who had it from Mr. de Bullion himfelf.

I ought not to omit here the death of Mr. de Nemours, who was killed in a duel by Mr. de Beaufort. You may remember what I have told you of their quarrel at Orleans, which was revived by their disputing who should have the precedency at the Duke's council. Mr. de Nemours forced in a manner Mr. de Beaufort to fight : he was killed upon the spot by a pistol-shot in the head. Mr. de Villars, whom you know, was his second, and he killed Hericourt, Mr. de Beaufort's second, and lieutenant of his guards. I return to the Duke of Orleans.

You easily judge that the diforders of Paris did not contribute to put his court in good order. The death of Mr. de Vallois †, which happened on St. Lawrence's day, filled that Court with grief, which is always attended with confternation, at a time full of trouble and uncertainties. His Royal Highnefs was befides touched to the quick, by an advice which he received juft at that time from Madam de Choify, of a negotiation of Mr. de Chavigny's with the Court, of which I will by and by give you the particulars. This, added to the news which he received from all parts,

† Son to the Duke of Orleans.

and

and which was bad enough in relation to the party, put him in a greater agitation still than he was naturally. Persan had been obliged to surrender Mouton to Palluau, who was made a Marefchal of France after that expedition. The Count d'Harcourt had had almost all along the advantage in Guienne, and Bourdeaux itfelf was divided into fo many foolifh parties, that one could hardly rely upon it. Marigny ufed to fay, pleafantly enough, that the Princefs of Condé and Madam de Longueville, the Prince of Conti and Marcin, the parliament, the jurats, and the army, Marigny and Sarrafin, had each of them their factions there. He had begun to write a fatire, after the manner of that which was written in the time of the League, upon all that he had feen tranfacting there, which gave a very ridiculous idea of it. I am not enough acquainted with the particulars of that piece to bring it here as an entertainment for you. All that I can fay about it is, that what the Duke had heard of it, did not help to quiet his mind in the agitation he was in, nor to perfuade him that the party in which he was engaged was a good one.

Providence, which by fecret fprings, unknown even to thofe that give them a motion, difpofes means to their end, made ufe of the exhortations of the gentlemen whom I have named, to induce me to change my conduct, juft at the time that it found the Duke difpofed to change his, and to be led by me in the manner I fhould direct him. The greateft difficulty was to perfuade me to alter my fteps. For though I had in reality no intentions but what were very right and fincere towards the ftate, and though I defired only to come off with fome fort of honour, I was willing however to preferve a certain decorum, which it was very hard to hit rightly on in the prefent conjuncture. I agreed with thefe gentlemen, that it was fhameful to remain idle, and to fuffer the capital city, and perhaps the whole kingdom, to perifh ; but they likewife agreed with me, that fo great a change as the contributing to the reftoration of a minifter, odious

to

to the whole kingdom, and in whofe removal I had
fo much diftinguifhed myfelf, would not be much to
my honour. There was no room for any of us to
doubt, but that every ftep we fhould take towards a
peace, would infallibly, though indirectly, produce
that effect; becaufe we could not be ignorant that
that reftoration was the only thing the Queen had in
view. Mr. de Fontenay convinced me at laft, in a
converfation we had together as we were walking one
afternoon at the Charter-houfe : ' You fee,' faid he
to me, ' that Mazarin is but a fort of a Jack in a box,
' who is one day hiding himfelf, and fhewing himfelf
' the next; but you fee likewife, that whether he
' keeps hid or fhews himfelf, the fpring that makes
' him appear or difappear, is that of the royal autho-
' rity, which is not like to be fo foon broken, confi-
' dering the manner which is taken to break it.
' Even many of thofe that have appeared the moft op-
' pofite to Mazarin, would be very forry to fee him
' deftroyed. Many others will be very eafily com-
' forted to fee him faved. There is not one that goes
' in earneft about ruining him thoroughly, and you
' yourfelf, Sir, do it but weakly, becaufe you meet
' with a great many occafions, in which the terms
' you are upon with the Prince, do not give you leave
' to act againft the Court fo freely and fo fully as you
' would do. From this I conclude, that it is impofiible
' that the Cardinal fhould not be reftored, either by
' a negotiation with the Prince, who will carry the
' Duke along with him whenever he pleafes to come
' to an accommodation with the Court; or by the
' wearinefs of the people, who perceive already but
' too clearly, that thofe of the party of the Princes
' underftand neither how to make war nor how to
' make peace. In both thefe cafes, which I look
' upon to be infallible, you muft be a great lofer.
' For if you don't get out of the briars before the war
' ends by an accommodation between the Prince and
' the Court, it will be hard for you to difintangle
' yourfelf from an intrigue in which both the Court
' and

' and the Prince will certainly think of ruining you
' If the peace proceeds from the wearinefs of the
' people, will you be any thing the better for it ?
' And may not that wearinefs, which always carries
' with it the hatred of the people againſt thofe who
' have been the moſt ſtirring during the faction, alter
' its courfe, and fall heavy upon you for your pru-
' dent way of keeping quiet, as you have done for
' fome time ? Thefe are, in my opinion, the incon-
' veniencies which you may forefee, but which you
' cannot avoid, except you do it before the civil war
' ceafes by one of the two means which I have fpoken
' of. I know that the engagements you are in with
' the Duke, and even with the public, in relation to
' Mazarin, do not permit you to do any thing towards
' his reftoration ; and you know that for that reafon
' I have declined propofing any thing to you fo long
' as he has kept at Court. He is now removed from
' it, and though that removal be only a jeſt and an
' illufion, it opens however a door to you to enter
' into meafures which will naturally prove ufeful to
' you. Paris, though in rebellion, paſſionately
' wifhes for the King's prefence ; and thofe that fhall
' take the firſt ſteps towards procuring it, will gain
' thereby the affections of the people. I own, that in
' this the people do not confider what they are wifh-
' ing for, the King's prefence being likely to bring
' hither Mazarin the fooner. But however, they wifh
' for that prefence ; and Mazarin being removed
' from Court, thofe that are the firſt to follicit for it,
' will not pafs for Mazarinians. This entirely does
' your bufinefs ; for being guided by no private in-
' tereſt, and wifhing at the bottom nothing but the
' good of the kingdom, and the prefervation of your
' credit with the people, you do the one without ob-
' ſtructing the other. I confefs, that if it was in
' your power to prevent Mazarin's being reſtored,
' the way I propofe would agree neither with politics
' nor morality, confidering that his being reſtored
' ought to be looked upon, for an infinite number
' of

' of reasons, as a public calamity. But taking it for
' granted, as you yourself do, that the ill conduct of
' his enemies has made his restoration infallible, I
' cannot conceive why the view of a thing which you
' cannot prevent, should prevent your getting out of
' the trouble you are in, by a door which opens to
' you a way to honour and liberty. Paris, of which
' you are Archbishop, groans under its load; the
' parliament is now but a mere phantom; the town-
' house is a desert; the Duke and the Prince are masters
' only during the pleasure of those of the mob that are
' the maddest; the Spaniards, the Germans, those of
' Lorrain, are in our suburbs, and pillage our very
' gardens. You that are the pastor of this city, and
' that have been its deliverer in two or three occasi-
' ons, have been obliged to guard yourself in your
' own house for three weeks together; and you know,
' that even at this day, your friends are concerned
' when you walk the streets without being armed.
' Do you reckon the putting an end to all this misery
' to be nothing? And will you miss the only moment
' which Providence offers you for putting an end glo-
' riously to it? The Cardinal, who loves to disap-
' point people, may come back to Court when he is
' least expected; and if that should happen, the way
' I propose would be more impracticable to you than
' to any man alive. Don't therefore lose moments
' that ought for a contrary reason to be more precious
' to you than to any other man. Take your clergy
' along with you; go to Compiegne; return your
' thanks to his Majesty for the removal of Mazarin;
' invite him to return to his capital city; act in con-
' cert with the gentlemen of the several chambers,
' that are wishing only for the good of the kingdom,
' who are most of them already your particular friends,
' and who look already upon you, by your dignity,
' as their most natural chief, on an occasion which is
' so becoming and so proper to your character. If
' the King comes back to town, the people of Paris
' will owe his return to you; if he refuses to come,

' they

' they will however think themfelves obliged to you
' for your good intentions. If you can but bring the
' Duke to approve of this, you fave the whole ftate,
' becaufe I am perfuaded that if he knew but how to
' act his part well on this occafion, he would bring the
' King back to Paris, and keep Mazarin from ever
' returning thither. But fuppofing that he fhould re-
' turn in fome time, you may prevent the rifk which
' I perceive you are in fear of, by reafon of the
' people's reproaching you about it, by the employ-
' ment at Rome, which I have heard you feveral
' times fay that you would fooner refolve to accept
' than the having any thing to do here with him.
' You are a Cardinal; you are Archbifhop of Paris;
' you have the love of the public; you are but thirty-
' feven years old; fave this city, fave the ftate.'
This is the fubftance of what Mr. de Fontenay faid
to me, with a rapidity quite oppofite to his natural
coldnefs; and it is certain that it moved me: for
though he faid nothing which I had not already
thought upon, as you have feen by the reflections I
made when the town-houfe was fet on fire, I felt
however a greater emotion at his reprefenting it to me,
than at what I had faid to myfelf about it, or what I
had heard from others on the fame fubject.

'This deputation of the clergy had been for fome
time before in agitation between Mr. de Caumartin
and me, and we had often been examining, both the
manner of performing it, and the confequences it
might have. I muft do Mr. Joly the juftice to fay,
that he was the firft that thought of it, immediately
after Cardinal Mazarin's leaving the Court. We all
of us together added to the fubftance of the thing the
circumftances which we thought the moft ufeful, and
the moft neceffary. The firft, and in every refpect
the moft important, was to bring the Duke to approve
at leaft this conduct; and the difpofition which I
have already told you he was in, gave us room to believe that we might fucceed in our attempt with him.
I made ufe for that effect of the reafons which I knew

he

he would like best, among those which Mr. de Fontenay had mentioned to me. I added to them the advantages which he would himself reap by procuring to the parliament and to the city, an amnesty, good, sincere, and not fallacious, which he would certainly obtain, if he shewed the Court a sincere desire of an accommodation. I represented to him, that his retreat to Blois, which he had for so long a time wished for, being preceded by his care of seeking in the peace the sureties necessary both to the public and to every one in particular, could not but be glorious to him, and would so much the more appear so, that it would be looked upon only as the effect of his firm resolution of having no manner of hand in restoring the minister : that my retreat to Rome, which I had resolved to make before the coming back of the Cardinal, might be attributed to necessity; because many persons would believe that I should be forced to it, by the fear of finding no safety for me after his being restored : that he was by his birth above such talk and such suspicions; and that if he did for the public before his retreat, what he might certainly do easily with the Court, he would remain at Blois, attended but with a very few guards, cherished, respected, and honoured, both by Frenchmen and foreigners, and would be even in a condition to take advantage for the good of the state whenever he pleased, of all the faults of the several parties.

I must desire you to observe, that at the time that I spoke to the Duke in this manner, I was informed by a good hand, that five or six days before my last conversation with him, he had been under an apprehension that I should reconcile myself to the Prince. He had said enough, though indirectly, in that conversation, to let me perceive the fear he was in. But Jouy, to whom he had made a full confidence of it, upon some advice or other which he had had that Mr. de Brissac was again busy about it, had told me that the Duke had cried out, ' If that be true, the ' civil war is to last for ever.' You may be sure that
this

this circumstance did not deter me from trying him, of which I had no reason to repent ; for as soon as I had opened the matter to him, he came of himself into every thing I said. He rallied me upon my ceasing to speak nothing but monosyllables, which was a certain sign with him that he approv'd of what I said. He afterwards added to my reasons others of his own, which was another convincing sign of his being pleased. Then in a seeming surprize, as if some sudden thought had but just entered his head, which was always his way, chiefly when he had the thing in his head before; he said to me, ' But what shall ' we do with the Prince ?' I answered him, ' Your ' Royal Highnels, Sir, ought to consider upon what ' terms you are with him, for honour is preferable to ' every thing. But as I have reason to think that the ' several negotiations that are on foot, are made in ' common between you two, I suppose that there may ' be the like understanding between you in this mat- ' ter, as there has been in all the rest.' ' I find you ' jest,' replied the Duke ; ' but I am not so much ' embarrassed upon this subject, as you believe. The ' Prince is more impatient, to be out of Paris than ' you can be ; and he would rather be in the forest ' of Ardenne, at the head of four squadrons, than ' to command millions of such people as we have ' here, without excepting the President Charton.' What the Duke said was true ; and Croissi, who was one of the men in the world the least capable of keep-ing a secret (a defect pretty rare among persons used to great affairs) was every day telling me, that the Prince was consuming with grief, and was so weary of the parliament, the court of aids, the assemblies of chambers, and the town-house, that he often said that his grandfather could never be more so with the ministers of Rochelle.

I found however by what the Duke said to me, that he was seeking for reasons that might satisfy him, in relation to the Prince. But for my own satisfac-tion I affected to furnish him with none, nor to help
· him

him to find out any. I kept myself tied up to my monofyllables upon that particular point, though the Duke did what he could to make me speak more at large, not only upon that subject, but likewise upon the several negotiations which, right or wrong, were always reported to be on foot. All that I did with the Duke was the receiving his orders about my going to wait on the King, which I was forced to digest myself, and to put into a form; this is the substance of what I wrote down. The Duke commanded me to make a general assembly of all ecclesiastical societies, and to cause deputies to be named out of each; to go myself at the head of that deputation to entreat his Majesty to give peace to his people, and to return to his good city of Paris; to try, by means of my friends, to oblige other bodies and corporations to send deputies to the same effect; to let the Court know by means of the Princess Palatine (but without sending any letter that might at least be shewn) that his Royal Highness had been the first promoter of this deputation; to enter however into no particulars relating to a negotiation, till I was myself at Compiegne, where I should tell the Queen, that it was visible that the Duke would not cause, or even suffer the steps that were now taken by the several bodies of the city, except his intentions were very right and very sincere; that he was for a peace, and was so from the bottom of his heart; that his public engagements against Cardinal Mazarin had not given him leave to conclude it, or even to begin it, so long as he staid at Court; but now that he was gone from it, he passionately wished to convince her Majesty that nothing but that obstacle had prevented his going heartily about that work: that he made use of me to declare to her Majesty that he renounced all personal interest, either in respect to himself or to any of his party; that all he asked was in respect only to the public safety, which might be done by explaining only some articles of the amnesty, and giving a form to the whole, which would prove by the event to be as much

for

for the fervice of the King, as for the fatisfaction of
particular perfons; that as foon as he had had the
pleafure to fee the King at the Louvre, he would retire to Blois with as much joy as readinefs, with an
intent to think upon nothing elfe than to live quiet,
and to mind the good of his foul; and that all that
fhould be done afterwards at Court fhould be no
longer upon his account, provided they would be
pleafed not to charge him with it, but would leave
him in his folitude, where he very fincerely promifed
to remain. This laft paragraph was, as you fee, a
fubftantial one. The Duke added to his inftruction
a precife and particular order to affure the Queen,
that if the Prince was not content with the liberty of
remaining quiet in his government, with the full en-
joyment of all his penfions and all his places, he
would forfake him. As I was reprefenting to him,
that to my thinking he might and ought even to
foften that expreffion; ' No falfe generofity,' replied
he, in an angry tone; ' I know what I fay, and fhall
' be able to maintain and juftify it.'

This is precifely what paffed between the Duke and
me; after which I left him. I executed his orders
literally; in doing which I met with no manner of
obftruction, except from thofe which I ought not to have
expected it from. What I am going to relate is incredible. After I had taken all the previous measures
neceffary to an affair of this nature, I fent either Argenteuil or Joly (I don't well remember which) to the
Princefs Palatine, to confer with her about it. She
approved of it entirely; but fhe wrote me word, that
if I really defired that it fhould fucceed, that is, that
it fhould procure the King's coming back to Paris, it
was neceffary that I fhould furprize the Court; becaufe that if I fhould give them time there to confult
the oracle, his anfwer would be only fuch as the priefts
of the idols fhould infpire and dictate to him: ' And
' thefe priefts,' added fhe by way of cypher (for we
had one which we never thought could have been de-
cyphered) ' had rather that the whole temple fhould
' perifh,

' perifh, than to fuffer you to lay a fingle ftone for
' the repairing of it.' She afked only for five days
time to write herfelf to the Cardinal about 'it, and fhe
managed him fo well, that he was in a manner forced
to give his confent to my propofals, and to write to
the Queen that fhe ought at leaft to receive my deputation favourably.

As foon as the Telliers, the Serviens, the Onde-
deis, and the Fouquets, had notice of it, they oppofed it with all their power, faying, that it could
only be a trap which I had prepared for the Court to
fall into; that if I had had right and fincere intentions, I had begun by a negotiation, and not by a
propofal, which would either oblige the King to
come back to Paris before he had taken fufficient
meafures for his fafety, or draw upon him the complaints of the whole city for his not coming. The Princefs Palatine, who thought herfelf fufficiently ftrong,
by having in hand the Cardinal's order, anfwered
them, that it would not be poffible for me to act
otherwife than I did, fuppofing that my intentions
were never fo fincere; becaufe it was much lefs fafe
for me to expofe myfelf to a negotiation, in which
I might meet with a thoufand fnares, than to a deputation, of which the worft that could happen could
only be my having fhewn a good intention, which
had proved unfuccefsful. Ondedei pretended that
the only end of my propofal was the liberty of coming fafely to receive the hat from the King's hands.
To that the Princefs anfwered, that that was but a
mere ceremony, which I looked upon, as it was true,
with the greateft indifference poffible. Then came on
the Abbot Fouquet, who alledged, that the correfpon-
dences he had in Paris were fufficient to bring the
King back there in a little time, without being obliged to
perfons who propofed to recall him with no other view
than to be in a better condition to oppofe him afterwards. Meffieurs le Tellier and Servien, who had at
firft fided with the others, came over at laft to the
Princefs, moved to it, as well by her folid way of
                                          reafoning,

reasoning, as by the Cardinal's order; and the Queen,
who had kept the Abbot Charrier, whom I had sent
to her for passes, three whole days at Compiegne,
even since she had promised them, granted them at
last, even with an addition of many civilities for me.
I began my journey as soon as I had the passes, having with me the deputies of all the ecclesiastical bodies of Paris, and near 200 gentlemen, of which
number fifty were of the Duke's guards. I was informed at Senlis, that they had resolved at Court not
to lodge my train there; and Bautru, who was himself of the number, having taken that opportunity to
get out of Paris, whose gates were kept shut, told me
that he would not advise me to appear at Court with
so great a retinue. I answered him, that I could
hardly believe that he would advise me to go thither
accompanied only by curates, canons, and monks,
when the country was filled with soldiers of all parties. He owned that I was in the right, and he went
himself before to inform the Queen of the reasons I
had to go accompanied by that retinue, which people
had taken care to increase in a very ridiculous manner. All that he could obtain was lodgings only for
80 horse, and you must observe that I had 112 belonging only to the coaches. I only laughed at these
silly manners; but what gave me some umbrage was,
that I did not meet in my way the detachment of life-
guards, which in those days used to meet Cardinals
the first time they made their appearance at Court.
My distrust would have turned into fear, if I had
known what I was told at my return to Paris; that
the cause why this honour was not paid me, was their
being yet unresolved what they should do with my
person; some maintaining that I ought to be arrested,
others, that it was necessary to have my life taken
away; and others saying, that the violating the public faith on this occasion would be attended with too
many inconveniencies. Prince Thomas of Savoy
caused Father Senault of the Oratory to tell my father,
the very day that I returned to Paris, that he had been

of

of this laſt opinion ; that he would- name no body ;
but that there were people in the world that were
great villains. The Princeſs Palatine did not inform
me that they had carried the matter ſo far ; but ſhe
told me, the very next day after my arrival there, that
ſhe had rather have me at Paris than at Compiegne.
The Queen however received me very well, and ſpoke
angrily in my preſence to the exempt of the guards
for miſſing me upon the road, by loſing his way, as
ſhe ſaid, in the foreſt. The King gave me the cap
the next morning, and audience in the afternoon. I
made him a ſpeech, which is printed.

· The King's anſwer was civil, but in general terms
only, and it was even with difficulty that I could get
a copy of it*. - - - - - - - - - - - -

᾿ This is what appeared publicly of my journey to
Compiegne ; I will now tell you what paſſed in
ſecret.

: I told the Queen, in the private audience which
ſhe gave me in her cloſet, that I was come to Compiegne, not only as a deputy of the church of Paris,
but that I had another deputation, which I valued
much more than the firſt, becauſe I thought it much
more advantageous to her ſervice : that this ſecond
was the being ſent as an envoy from the Duke, who
had commanded me to aſſure her Majeſty, that he had
taken the reſolution to ſerve her ſincerely, effectually,
readily, and ſpeedily. At this laſt word I ſhewed her
a billet, ſigned by the Duke, that contained the very
words I had ſpoken. The firſt movement of the Queen
expreſſed an extraordinary joy, and, in my opinion,
it was more to that joy than to any art ſhe uſed (not-
withſtanding what people have been pleaſed to ſay ſince)
that the following words which ſhe ſpoke to me were
owing: ' I knew, Sir, that the Cardinal de Retz
' would give me at laſt ſome marks of the affection he
' has for me.' As I was juſt entering into diſcourſe
with her, Ondedei ſcratched at the door ; and as I

* There are here ſome lines ſcratched out in the manuſcript.

was

was rifing from my feat to open it, the Queen took hold
of my arm, and faid, ' Stay here for me.' She went out
and ftaid with Ondedei almoft a quarter of an hour,
and at her coming back, fhe told me that he had
brought her a packet from Spain. She appeared to
me embarraffed and altered in her manner of fpeaking, beyond what I can exprefs. Bluet, whom I have
mentioned to you before, has fince told me, that Ondedei, who had been informed that I had afked a private audience of her Majefty, came to interrupt it,
by acquainting her that he had received an order from
the Cardinal to entreat her to forbear granting me any
fuch audience, which would only ferve to give a jealoufy to her faithful fervants. This Bluet has fwore
to me more than once, that he had feen the original
of that order in the hands of Ondedei, who received
it but juft at the time that I was locked up with the
Queen in the clofet. 'Tis certain, that when fhe
came back to me, I obferved that fhe carried me near a
window, whofe glafs came down to the floor, and
that fhe placed me in a manner that it was eafy for all
thofe that ftood in the Court to fee us both. What
I am relating to you is pretty odd, and I fhould
hardly have believed it, if all that I obferved afterwards had not convinced me that there was fuch a
general diftruft of one another amongft all at Compiegne, that one muft have feen it to imagine it.
Meffieurs Servien and le Tellier hated one another
exceedingly. Ondedei was fpy to both, and fo he
was to all the world. The Abbot Fouquet afpired to
the honour of being fpy in fecond. Bertet, Bracher,
Ciron, and the Marefchal du Pleffis, had each their
feveral fhares. The Princefs Palatine had given me
the particular map of Compiegne, but I own that I
could not have imagined that it was fo exactly drawn
as I found it. The Queen, however, notwithftanding Ondedei's order, could not help expreffing her
joy and her gratitude to me : ' But,' faid fhe, ' as
' private converfations would but occafion people to
' talk more than is convenient to the Duke and to

'‘ yourfelf by reafon of the meafures which ought to be
'‘ preferved with the public ; fee the Princefs Palatine,
‘ and agree with her at what time you may confer in
‘ fecret with Servien.’ Bluet told me afterwards that
·Servien was the man whom Ondedei had pointed out
to her for this conference, becaufe he had appeared
·the moft difaffected to me; but that Servien, who
was afraid of fome ill offices from the fubalterns, had
·refufed to enter into any private negotiation with me,
·except he had·for his colleague, or rather for a wit-
nefs to his behaviour, Mr. le Tellier : ‘ Who would
‘ not fail otherwife, faid he to the Queen, to infinu-
‘ ate to the Cardinal by fome way or other that I am
·‘ entering into meafures to his prejudice with the
‘ Cardinal de Retz ; and ’tis for that·reafon, Madam,
‘ that I moft humbly intreat your Majefty, that Mr.
‘ le Tellier may affift·at the conference.’ I know
·nothing of what·I am now writing about, but by the
means of Bluet, who indeed was a pretty good author
in refpect to thefe little particulars, being an intimate
of Ondedei’s. What makes me believe that he had
·not invented this, is that I really found at the Princefs Palatine’s, where I went between eleven and
twelve at night, Mr. le Tellier, with Mr. Servien, at
which I was pretty much furprized, becaufe I had
fome ground to believe that le Tellier was not over
well affected to me. The fequel will fhew you the
·reafons which·I had·to diftruft him.

It appeared to me that thefe gentlemen had already
been informed by the Queen of what I was to propofe to
them, of which this is the fubftance : That the Duke was
fincerely refolved to conclude a peace, and that to convince the Queen of the fincerity of his intentions, he
had been willing, againft all common rules ufed in
politicks, to begin rather with deeds than with
words : that perhaps the moft efficacious and fubftantial proof that he could have given of it was fuch a
folemn deputation as that from the whole church of
Paris ; which deputation was refolved upon and executed, in the fight of the Prince, and of the Spanifh
troops

troops lodged in the fuburbs; and that he offered, without hefitating, negotiating, or afking either directly or indirectly, for any private advantage, to declare himfelf againft all thofe who fhould oppofe the peace, or the King's returning to Paris; provided he fhould be impowered to promife the Prince that he fhould be left at peace in his governments, upon condition that the Prince, on his fide, fhould renounce all manner of affociations with foreigners; and provided that they would put out an amnefty, full, entire, and in no manner captious; which amnefty fhould be verified by the parliament of Paris.

· It was hard to imagine that a propofal of this nature fhould not have been, I don't fay accepted, but applauded; becaufe, fuppofing even that it had not been fincere, which they might fufpect, according at leaft to their corrupt maxims, yet they might have received advantages from it in more than one manner. What made me judge that their reafon for rejecting it, was not their diftrufting me, but their diftrufting one another, was their looking for a long while upon one another, expecting who fhould fpeak firft. The fequel of the conference, but chiefly a certain air which cannot be expreffed, fhewed me more than fufficiently that I was not miftaken in my conjectures. I could get from them words only, without any meaning; and the Princefs Palatine, who, though very well verfed in that Court, was furprized at it to the laft degree, owned to me the next morning that I was right in many of my conjectures. ' But, faid fhe to me, I am
' refolved at all events, if you agree to it, to fpeak to
' them as if I was perfuaded that the diftruft they have
' of you is the only caufe which hinders them from
' acting like men; for 'tis certain, continued fhe,
' that what I faw of them laft night, had nothing of
' man in it.' I confented to it, provided fhe fpoke only of herfelf; for after what had appeared to me of their way of acting, I thought not fit to go fo far as I had refolved, or as my inftructions impowered me. The Princefs made it up of her own felf. She told

the

the Queen not only what had paſſed at her houſe the
night before, but what might have paſſed if it had
pleaſed the two ſub-miniſters. In ſhort, ſhe aſſured the
Queen, that if what I propoſed was granted, the Duke
would forſake the Prince, and would retire to Blois,
and would afterwards meddle with nothing, whatever
happened. That was the eſſential point which ought
to have decided all. The Queen took it right, and
had a right ſenſe of it. But all the ſubalterns undertook to make it paſs only for a ſnare, by ſaying to her,
that the Duke made this ſhew only to draw the King
to Paris, and to keep him there, whilſt he was ingra-
tiating himſelf the more with the people, by the
honour he aſſumed of the King's return, which was
very agreeable to the public; and by the back-door
which it was viſible he reſerved to himſelf, by his not
explaining his mind in relation to Cardinal Mazarin.
I have already obſerved that I plainly ſaw that what
they alledged was not ſo much the effect of any diſtruſt
they had upon a point which the ſtate of things had
begun to clear ſufficiently, as of the fear they had each
of them in particular of making any advances which
the reſt might have interpreted to their prejudice with
the Cardinal. For it is eaſy to judge that if the conduct which they followed on this occaſion had proceeded from the diſtruſt, which they took care to in-
fuſe into the Queen, they would have looked out for
means that might have prevented their falling into the
ſnares they would have been afraid of, and which, on
the other hand, might have contributed to keep the
minds of people from growing more incenſed, and
affairs more imbroiled, at a time when it was ſo
neceſſary to appeaſe the one, and bring the other to
rights. The event, which proved favourable to the
Court, did indeed juſtify their conduct, and I know
that the miniſters have ſaid ſince, that they were ſo
well aſſured of the diſpoſition of Paris, that they had
no need of theſe precautions. You ſhall yourſelf
judge of it by what followed; but before I go upon it
you muſt give me leave to take notice of two or three

cir-

circumſtances, which, though of no great moment, will repreſent the ſtate which all theſe profeſſed ſpies whom I have mentioned, put the Court into.

The Queen was ſo ſubmiſſive to them, and was ſo much afraid of their reports, that ſhe intreated the Princeſs Palatine to tell Ondedeï, without any affectation, that ſpeaking to her, ſhe had made great railleries of me; and her Majeſty herſelf told Ondedeï, that I had aſſured her that the Cardinal was an honeſt man, and that I had no pretenſions to his place. I can aſſure you, in my turn, that I had not ſaid any ſuch fooliſh·words to the Queen. Neither did her Majeſty forget to make her court to the Abbot Fouquet, in joining with him to turn the great expence which this journey coſt me, into ridicule. I muſt own that for the little time it laſted that expence was immenſe. I kept ſeven tables ſerved at the ſame time, which coſt me 800 crowns a-day. But what is neceſſary is never ridiculous. The Queen told me, when I received her orders, that ſhe thanked the Duke, to whom ſhe thought herſelf much obliged; that ſhe hoped he would contribute all that was neceſſary for the King's return; that it was her requeſt to him; and that ſhe would not take one ſtep without concerting it with him. I anſwered her, that in my opinion it would be requiſite to begin immediately: but ſhe broke off the diſcourſe.

I had wherewithal to comfort myſelf of the Abbot Fouquet's railleries, by the manner in which I was received at Paris. I met there at my return with an incredible applauſe, and I went directly to the Duke's palace, where I gave his Royal Highneſs an account of my negotiation. I put him into a mighty ſurprize; he fell into a paſſion; he railed at the Court; he went twenty times into the Ducheſs's apartment, and came back to me twenty times. At laſt he ſaid to me haſtily: ‘ The Prince is reſolved to go; the Count de ‘ Fuenſaldagne writes him word that he is ordered to ‘ deliver up into his hands the whole Spaniſh forces, ‘ but we muſt not ſuffer him to go. Theſe people

I 3 ‘ will

' will come to Paris and cut our throats. The Court
' muſt hold intelligences here, which we are not
' aware of. Could they act in the manner they do, if
' they were not conſcious of their own ſtrength ?'
This was one of the ſhorteſt periods of a diſcourſe
which laſted above an hour. I let him go on without
interrupting him, and I even anſwered his queſtions
only with monoſyllables. At laſt he grew impatient,
and commanded me to give him my opinion, ſaying,
' I forgive you your monoſyllables, when I act to
' pleaſe the Prince, contrary to your advice. But
' when I follow your advice, as I have done on this
' occaſion, I will have you ſpeak out and explain
' yourſelf.' ' It is my duty, Sir, anſwered I, to
' ſpeak always in that manner to your Royal High-
' neſs, whatever advice you are pleaſed to follow. I
' do not diſown the advice I have given on this occa-
' ſion ; far from it, I don't repent of it, notwithſtand-
' ing the event. Fortune diſpoſes of that, but For-
' tune has nothing to do with good ſenſe. My ſenſe
' of things may be leſs right than that of others, be-
' cauſe I want their ability. But for this time I hold
' my advice to have been as good as if it had ſucceed-
' ed, and it will be no hard matter to me to convince
' your Royal Highneſs of it.' The Duke interrupted
me here, even haſtily ; and he ſaid to me, ' You have
' miſtaken my meaning; I know that we have acted
' reaſonably. But it is not enough, as the world
' goes, to have reaſon of one's ſide, chiefly when the
' thing is paſt. The queſtion is, what we muſt now
' do ? We are going to be trampled upon, and you
' ſee as well as I, that they are not ſo blind at Court
' as to act in the manner they do there, except they
' had either made their accommodation with the Prince,
' or were maſters of Paris without me.' The Dutcheſs,
who was impatient to know how this ſcene would end,
came at this word into the library where we were, and
to ſay the truth, I was very glad of it, becauſe that
when ſhe was not prepoſſeſſed ſhe judged always
right, though ſhe had but a mean underſtanding.
The

The Duke continuing to command me in her prefence
to fpeak my opinion, I begged leave of him to fet it
down in writing, which was always the beft way with
him, becaufe his vivacity made him at every inftant interrupt the thread of the difcourfe fpoken to him. I give
you here a copy of what I wrote down, tranfcribed
from the original, which I met with by great chance.

' I think that his Royal Highnefs ought to take it
' for granted that the haughtinefs of the Court pro-
' ceeds lefs from the knowledge they have there of
' their ftrength, than of the confufion which the
' abfence of the Cardinal, and the multitude of agents
' they have there, puts them into two or three times in
' a day. But as part of our prefent difcuffion ought to
' be grounded upon that principle, it is not juft that
' his Royal Highnefs fhould believe me upon my bare
' word. Which after all is itfelf grounded only upon
' what I think that I have difcovered at Compiegne,
' and in which I may confequently be miftaken. For
' that reafon I intreat his Royal Highnefs to begin by
' having that point cleared, and by being fatisfied
' whether what I think I have difcovered is well
' grounded. To explain myfelf better, I would have
' him be fatisfied whether the haughtinefs which I
' fancy I have obferved in the Court is really true,
' and whether it proceeds from the confufion which I
' have mentioned, or from the diffidence and the averfion
' they have there for my perfon. His Royal Highnefs
' may be fatisfied upon that point in two days time,
' by means of Mr. Damville, and by means of thofe
' gentlemen that belong to his Royal Highnefs, that
' are more agreeable to the Queen than I. If I have
' been miftaken, I fee nothing new that ought to
' hinder him from purfuing his point, and going on
' with the peace as he had refolved before by making
' ufe of perfons that are like to be heard at Court
' more favourably than I. If I am right in my con-
' jecture, the queftion is whether his Royal Highnefs
' ought to change his thoughts, to think no longer of
' an accommodation, and to make war effectually,

I 4   ' running

' running the rifk of all that may happen ; or whether
' he ought to facrifice himfelf to the public repofe
' and tranquillity. Thofe who receive his Royal High-
' nefs's command to fpeak their fentiments on this
' occafion, are much embarraffed, becaufe their fate
' muft be, to pafs either for men of a factious fpirit,
' who feek to render the civil war eternal ; or for
' traitors, that fell their party ; or for idiots, that
' treat of matters of ftate in the clofet of Princes, as
' they would do of cafes of confcience in the Sor-
' bonne. And the misfortune is that it will be
' neither their good or their ill conduct, nor their
' good or evil intentions, which will either give
' them thofe denominations, or preferve them from
' thofe titles. All will depend on fortune, or even
' on their enemies conduct. This obfervation
' fhall not prevent me from fpeaking to his Royal
' Highnefs on this occafion, with the fame liberty that
' I fhould ufe, fuppofing that I was nothing concerned
' in the matter, and that I did not find myfelf in a
' conjuncture where I am fure that nothing good can
' be faid, for the fame reafon that nothing good can
' be done. His Royal Highnefs has in my opinion,
' as I have already faid, but two ways to follow, fup-
' pofing that the Court is in the difpofition I believe
' them to be in. Thefe two ways are, either to yield
' to whatever they pleafe there, and to fuffer their
' coming back to Paris by their own means, without
' thinking themfelves obliged to his Royal Highnefs
' for it, and without giving the publick any manner
' of furety ; or to oppofe their return with courage
' and with vigour, and to oblige them, by a ftrong
' and bold refiftance, to enter into a treaty and to
' pacify the ftate by the fame means which have been
' always fought for at the end of civil wars. If the
' refpect I owe his Royal Highnefs gave me leave to
' count myfelf for any thing in fo great an affair as
' this, I fhould take the liberty to tell him, that the
' firft way would ferve my purpofe, becaufe it would
' lead me (perhaps amidft fome murmurs which would
                                                    ' at

' at firſt be raiſed againſt me) to the poſt which I am
' perſuaded would be no ill one for me. The Fron-
' deurs would at firſt ſay that my counſels would have
' been but weak. Pacifick men, whoſe number is
' always the greateſt at the end of civil wars, would
' ſay that they had been both wiſe and honeſt. I
' ſhould above all remain a Cardinal and Archbiſhop
' of Paris, though perhaps removed to Rome, but
' removed only for a time, and even during that time
' in the greateſt poſt there. The event would oblige
' politicians to look upon me with the ſame eye as
' pacifick men. The heat againſt Mazarin would
' either be extinguiſhed, or laid aſleep by his being
' reſtored. The murmurs raiſed at firſt againſt me
' would be forgotten, or would be only remembered
' to occaſion people's ſaying ſtill the more that I am
' an able and a gallant man for withdrawing myſelf
' ſo cleverly out of an ill ſtep. This is the manner in
' which the world treats private perſons, in reſpeſt to
' reputation. It is otherwiſe with Princes, becauſe
' their birth and elevation being always more than
' ſufficient to ſave from ſhipwreck their perſon and
' their fortune, their reputation is thereby the more
' expoſed. Suppoſing that his Royal Highneſs ſuffers
' the parliament to be removed, the aſſemblies of the
' town-houſe to be interdiſted, the canons of the ca-
' thedral to be forcibly taken away, half of the
' ſovereign courts to be exiled ; people will not ſay :
" What could he have done to have helped it ? The
" attempting any thing would perhaps have proved
" his ruin." They will ſay : " It was in his power
" to have helped it ; the thing was eaſy if he had had
" but the will." It may be objeſted for the ſame
' reaſon, that ſuppoſing that his Royal Highneſs makes
' a peace, that he retires to Blois, and that Cardinal
' Mazarin is reſtored ; people will ſay the like of him.
' But I maintain that in this laſt caſe, there will be a
' vaſt, nay an entire difference from the firſt ; becauſe
' as to the return of Mazarin, after a peace made by
' his Royal Highneſs, the people may eaſily think that

' his

‘ his Royal Highnefs had not forefeen it; but if his
‘ Royal Highnefs fuffers the Court to return without
‘ his leave, it cannot be faid that he has not forefeen
‘ all the evil that will enfue to Paris perhaps to-
‘ morrow, if he does not oppofe it.   I fear the return
‘ of Cardinal Mazarin for the body of the ftate.   I
‘ fhould not fear it,. at leaft for the prefent, in relation
‘ to Paris.   Neither his temper nor his intereft, would
‘ carry him to revenge himfelf upon this city, and
‘ there would, in my opinion, be lefs danger in
‘ refpect to that, by his prefence now at Court, than
‘ by his abfence from it.   What makes me tremble
‘ for Paris, is the animofity which is natural to the
‘ Queen, the violence of Servien, the hardnefs of le
‘ Tellier, the paffion of the Abbot Fouquet, the
‘ madnefs of Ondedeï.   All that this pack of men
‘ are. like to advife in the firft inftants of a reduction,.
‘ all that they will execute, will be charged to his
‘ Royal Highnefs’s account, whilft he himfelf is either
‘ ftill at Paris, or juft getting out of it.   But no fuch
‘ thing will happen if his Royal Highnefs comes to
‘ a reafonable treaty with the Court, wherein he takes
‘ care jointly with the parliament and other bodies,
‘ to take all poffible fureties, agreeable to an affair of
‘ this nature; for after fuch a treaty, and after his
‘ Royal Highnefs’s being retired to Blois, every thing,
‘ and even the return of the Cardinal, would be
‘ wholly charged to the account of the Court, and
‘ would turn to the clearing and even to the honour
‘ of his Royal Highnefs.   Thefe are my thoughts as
‘ to the firft way, and here follow my reflections upon
‘ the fecond, which. is. that of continuing, or rather
‘ renewing the war.

    ‘ It is, in my opinion, what his Royal Highnefs
‘ can no longer do, but by keeping the Prince near
‘ him.   The Court has gained a great deal of ground
‘ in the provinces, chiefly in thofe places where the
‘ heat of the parliaments is grown much cooler.   Paris
‘ itfelf is not now near fo zealous as it was; and
‘ though it is far from being fo much relaxed as fome
                                    ‘ would

‘ would perfuade the Court, it is certain, that it is
‘ neceffary to fupport peoples fpirits there, and that
‘ moments begin even to become precious. The
‘ perfon of the Prince is not beloved there; his
‘ birth, his troops, his valour, are ftill there of the
‘ fame weight. In fhort, if his Royal Highnefs
‘ follows the fecond way, the firft ftep he ought to
‘ take is to make himfelf fure of the Prince his
‘ coufin. The fecond ftep, in my opinion, is to
‘ fpeak his mind publickly and without delay, in the
‘ parliament, and at the town-houfe, and to declare
‘ his reafons for continuing the war ; to mention there
‘ the advances which he has made to the Court by
‘ my means, and the defign they have refolved upon
‘ there to return to Paris without giving any fureties,
‘ either to the Sovereign Courts, or to the city; to
‘ mention the refolution which his Royal Highnefs
‘ has taken to oppofe the Court with all his might,
‘ and to treat as enemies all thofe who fhall hold
‘ directly or indirectly any correfpondence there. The
‘ third ftep is, in my opinion, to execute thefe decla-
‘ rations with vigour, and to enter into war, as if his
‘ Royal Highnefs was never to think again of a peace.
‘ The power which his Royal Highnefs has with the
‘ people makes me believe without the leaft doubt,
‘ that all that I have here propofed is poffible ; but
‘ I muft add, that it will ceafe to be fo, the moment
‘ that his Royal Highnefs fhall ceafe to make ufe of
‘ all his authority, becaufe the contrary fteps which he
‘ has fuffered to be made towards the Court, have
‘ rendered thofe that are now neceffary, more difficult.
‘ It is his Royal Highnefs’s bufinefs to confider what
‘ he may expect or what he may fear from the Prince ;
‘ how far he is willing to engage with foreigners ;
‘ what meafures he will take with the parliament and
‘ with the town-houfe ; for except he comes to a fixed
‘ refolution upon all thefe points, with a firm defign
‘ of not departing from it ; except he refolves to reject
‘ for the future thofe mediums whereby he pretends to
‘ reconcile things contradictory and impoffible, his

I 6   ‘ Royal

' Royal Highnefs will again fall into all the inconve-
' niencies in which he has feen himfelf, and which he
' will find more dangerous beyond comparifon, than
' in time paft, becaufe the ftate in which things are,
' will render them decifive. It does not belong to me
' to decide upon a matter of this importance; I leave
' it to his Royal Highnefs to take his refolution.
' *Sola mihi obfequio gloria relicta eft.*'

This I writ haftily, and without ftopping, upon the
table of the library of the Duke's palace. His Royal
Highnefs, read it with great attention, and carried it
to the Dutchefs. The ground-work of it was examined all the evening long, but without coming to
any refolution by reafon of the Duke's continual
hefitating, without ever coming to a choice.

At my coming from this conference, I found
Mr. de Caumartin at the Prefident de Bellievre's, who
had caufed his people to remove him to a houfe in the
fuburb of St. Michael, by reafon of a defluxion he
had on one eye. I told Mr. de Caumartin the fubftance of what I had writ down at the Duke's. He
chid me for it, and faid: ' I cannot imagine what is
' your meaning; for you expofe yourfelf to the hatred
' of both parties, by fpeaking the truth too openly of
' them both.' ' I know (replied I to him) that I go
' againft politicks, but I act agreeably to morality,
' which I value more than the other.' ' Nay, faid the
' Prefident de Bellievre, even according to politicks,
' the Cardinal de Retz is in the right, confidering the
' ftate in which affairs are.' There is fo much uncer-
' tainty in them, chiefly in refpect to his Royal High-
' nefs, that a wife man ought not to take upon him to
' determine any thing.'

Two hours after this, the Duke fent for me to
Madam de Pomereux's, where I was, and I found a
page at the gate of his palace waiting to tell me, that
his Royal Highnefs defired that I would go to the
Dutchefs's apartment, and ftay for him there. He
was unwilling that I fhould go to the library, where he
was fhut up with Goulas, whom he was queftioning
upon

upon the fubject you fhall now fee. 'He came to me
fome time after, and faid : ' You were this day faying,
' that the firft ftep I ought to take in cafe I refolve
' upon continuing the war, is to make myfelf fure of
' the Prince : but how the devil can I do it ?' ' You
' know, Sir,' replied I, ' that in the terms I am in
' with his Highnefs, I cannot anfwer your queftion.
' Your Royal Highnefs ought to confider how far your·
' power extends in this cafe.' ' How would you have
' me know it ? (continued he) ; Chavigny has almoft
' finifhed a treaty with the Abbot Fouquet. Do you
' remember what Madam de Choify has lately told me
' upon that fubject in general terms ? I have been now
' informed of all the particulars. The Prince fwears
' that he knows nothing of the matter, and that Cha-
' vigny is a traitor ; but who can tell whether that be
' true ?' Thefe particulars were, That Chavigny was
treating with the Abbot Fouquet, and that he promifed
to ufe his utmoft efforts with the Prince to oblige him
to come to an accommodation with Mazarin upon
reafonable terms. A letter from the Abbot Fouquet
to Mr. le Tellier, which was intercepted by a party of
Germans, and carried to Mr. de Tavanne's, juftified
the Prince fully in refpect to Chavigny's negotiation ;
for it imported in exprefs words, That in cafe the
Prince would not fubmit to reafon, Chavigny engaged
his word to the Queen, that he would leave nothing
undone to fet him at variance with the Duke.

The Prince, who had the original of that letter in
his hands, carried his paffion againft Chavigny to a
great extremity, and called him traitor, fpeaking to
himfelf. Overcome by grief at this, Chavigny went
home to bed, and never rofe from it afterwards. Mr.
de Bagnols, who was his friend as well as mine, came
to defire me to go and fee him. I found him without
the ufe of his fenfes, and I paid to his family what I
would have paid to his perfon. I remember that Mademoifelle du Pleffis Guenegaut was in his chamber,
where he died two or three days after.

Much

Much about that time the Duke of Guife * came
from Spain, where he had been detained prifoner, and
did me the honour to come and vifit me the very next
day after his arrival. I intreated him that he would,
in regard to me, moderate the fharp complaints he
made againft Mr. de Fontenay, by whom he pretended
to have been ill ufed at the time of the revolution at
Naples, Mr. de Fontenay being then Ambaffador at
Rome. He yielded to my inftances with a civility
worthy of the great name he bore.

I had all along referved to treat in this place of the
affair of Briffac, which I have juft touched upon in
the fecond volume of thefe Memoirs, becaufe it was
likewife much about this time that the Prince d'Harcourt quitted the army and the fervice of the King, to
throw himfelf into that important place. But as it
has not been poffible for me to find a relation extremely
fine and fincere, which I had of it, and which was
writ by an officer of the garrifon, who was a man of
fenfe and honour, I rather chufe to pafs by the particulars, and I content myfelf to tell you in general
that the good genius of France defended and faved
the honour of that crown in that important and famous
poft, in fpight of all the imprudences of the Cardinal,
and of the infidelities of Madam de Guebriant, by
the good intentions of Charlevoix, and by the uncertainties of the Count d'Harcourt †. I return to my
narration.

The irrefolution of his Royal Highnefs was of a
fpecies altogether fingular. It often hindered him from
acting, at the time that acting was the moft neceffary,
and it put him fometimes upon acting, when it was moft

* Henry de Lorrain, fecond of the name, born in 1614. He
went in 1647 to the affiftance of thofe who had rebelled at Naples,
where, after he had behaved himfelf to admiration, he was taken
prifoner by the Spaniards, who kept him in their hands till about
this time. In 1654 he went, for the fecond time, on an expedition
to Naples, and he died in 1664. We have his Memoirs, which
are efteemed.

† The Count d'Harcourt was at that time Governor of Alfatia,
of which he formed the defign of making himfelf Sovereign.

neceffary to remain quiet. I attribute both thefe
effects to his irrefolution, becaufe they both proceeded;
as I have obferved, from the different and oppofite views he had, which made him believe that
he might make a ferviceable ufe to himfelf, though in
different manners, either of acting or not acting;
according as he was moved by thefe oppofite and
different views. But methinks I explain myfelf but
ill, and that you will underftand me better, by expofing to your view the faults which I pretend to have
been the effect of that irrefolution. I propofed to the
Duke upon the firft or the fecond of September, to go
fincerely about making a peace; and I reprefented to
him that nothing was of greater importance than the
keeping this defign entirely hid from the Court itfelf,
for the reafons you have feen before, to which the
Duke agreed. Upon the 5th, there was an affembly
held at the town-houfe, which the Prince himfelf procured, to make the people believe that he did not
oppofe the King's return, and it was the Prefident de
Nefmond, at leaft as I have been told fince, who perfuaded him that that demonftration was neceffary: I
have never remembered to fpeak to him about it. It
was refolved in that affembly, to fend a folemn deputation to the King to intreat him to return to his good
city of Paris. This was not at all agreeable to the
Duke's defign, who having refolved, as I have already
faid, to gain to himfelf the honour and the merit of the
deputation of the Clergy, at the head of which I was
to go, ought not to have fuffered that the city fhould
be before-hand with him; confidering befides that he
was not mafter of the fteps that might follow that
deputation. He engaged however, without any hefitation, not only to fuffer the affembly to meet at the
town-houfe, but to affift at it in perfon. I was informed of it but in the evening, and I mentioned it
freely to him as a falfe ftep he had made. 'Why
' (faid he) this meeting about a deputation will come
' to nothing. Who does not know the infignificancy
' of thefe affemblies? The Prince has defired this,
' be-

' believing it good for him to appeafe people's minds,
' whom the firing of the town-houfe has incenfed.
' But befides,' added he, (and thefe are the words,
which I would have you to obferve) ' who knows
' whether we fhall execute what we have refolved about
' the deputation of the Clergy ? We muft advance and
' draw back in thefe perverfe times as matters require,
', without minding regularity too much.' This anfwer
is, in my opinion, an explanation of the nonfenfe
you have feen before ; I will give you another example.
The King having refufed, as you fhall fee prefently,
this deputation of the town-houfe, old Brouffel, who
made a fcruple to fuffer that his name fhould be
alledged as an obftacle to the peace, went to the
town-houfe and declared there that he quitted his
magiftracy. Having had notice time enough of his
defign to have prevented it, I went to acquaint the
Duke with it, who after having mufed a little, faid to
me : ' If the Court had anfwered our good intentions,
' it had been well for us that Brouffel had quitted his
' poft ; but I own that for the prefent it is bad for us.
' But you muft own likewife, that if they come to them-
' felves at Court, as they muft do one time or other,
' it being impoffible that they fhould always remain
' blind ; we fhould not be forry that old Brouffel had
' loft his place.' You fee in this difcourfe the image
and the effects of uncertainty. I have mentioned thefe
two examples only as patterns out of a long feries of
actions of the like nature, which the Duke, who had
certainly a very clear underftanding, could not correct
himfelf of. It is true indeed that the Court afforded
him no room to reflect much upon his faults, for want
of taking advantage of them. The advantage they
received from them at Court was due to fortune alone,
and if the Duke and the Prince had made the ufe they
might have done, of their refufing there to receive the
deputation from the town-houfe, the Court would
have been in danger to have no deputation at all
for a long while. Their anfwer to Pietre, the King's
Attorney for the city of Paris, who went to demand
                                                    an

an audience for the Echevins, and the deputies of the
several wards, was that it could not be granted so
long as the city should acknowledge Mr. de Beaufort
for Governor, and Mr. de Brouffel for Provost-des-
Marchands. The President Viole said to me, as soon
as he had heard of this refusal: ' I did not approve of
' the deputation, fearing that it would prove more
' hurtful than beneficial to the Duke and to the Prince.
' But the imprudence of the Court has now turned it
' altogether to their advantage.' The voluntary ab-
dication of old Brouffel rendered that imprudence the
more solemn. It is certain that they might have used
mediums there, which even in preserving the dignity of
the crown, had not exafperated people's minds to the
degree this refusal did. If the Princes had made a
right ufe of it, the minifters would have repented for
a long time of their blundering manner of carrying
on this affair, as well as all others.

What is furprizing is, that the Court followed this
conduct, juft at the time that the party of the Princes
was receiving a very confiderable reinforcement. The
Duke of Lorrain, who thought that by removing out
of the kingdom, he had fulfilled his treaty made with
Mr. de Turenne at Villeneuve St. George, notified by
two cannon fhot that he was arrived at Vaneau-les-
Dames, which is in the Barrois. He came back
afterwards into Champaign with all his forces, which
were augmented with 3000 German horfe, commanded
by Prince Ulric of Wirtemberg. The Chevalier de
Guife commanded as Lieutenant-General under the
Duke of Lorrain, and the Count de Pas, whom I
have mentioned before in fome place or other, had, I
think, joined fome horfe to this army. The Duke of
Lorrain came flowly on towards Paris, enriching his
army by pillaging. He encamped near Villeneuve
St. George, where the Duke of Orleans's forces commanded by Mr. de Beaufort, thofe of the Prince (who
was fick at Paris) commanded by the Prince of Tarente and the Count de Tavannes, and thofe of Spain
commanded by Clinchant, in the room of Mr. de
Nemours,

Nemours, came to join him. They refolved all of them together to come nearer Mr. de Turenne, who having Corbeil, Melun, and all that is above the river, in his hands, wanted for nothing; when the confederates, who were obliged to feek for fubfiftance in the neighbourhood of Paris, pillaged the villages, and raifed confequently the price of provifions in the city. This confideration, added to their number, which was fuperior to that of Mr. de Turenne, obliged them to feek out for an opportunity to fight him. He avoided it with that capacity which is known and refpected all the world over, and the whole ended in rencounters and fkirmifhes, that left matters undecided. The imprudence, or rather the ignorance of the Cardinal, and of the fub-minifters, went near to ruin their party, by a fault which ought to have been beyond comparifon of more prejudice to them than even the defeat of Mr. de Turenne. Prevot, a canon of Nôtre-Dame, and a counfellor of the parliament, a man as mad as any one can be that is not fhut up, undertook to affemble together at the Palais-Royal all thofe that were true fervants to the King, (that was to be the diftinguifhing character). This affembly was made up of four or five hundred citizens, of which there were not fixty that were men of any fubftance. Prêvot acquainted them that he had received a Lettre-de-cachet from the King, by which he was ordered to put to the fword all thofe who fhould wear ftraw in their hats, inftead of paper, which was the diftinguifhing mark of thofe of the King's party. He read, in effect, that letter, and that was the beginning of the moft ridiculous enterprize thought of fince the proceffion of the league. The event was, that upon the 24th of September, as that affembly was coming out of the Palais-Royale, they were moft intolerably hiffed at; and that upon the 26th the Marefchal d'Eftampes, whom the Duke fent to the place where they affembled, difperfed them by fpeaking but a few words. The end of that expedition was, that they ceafed to affemble for fear of being hanged,

hanged, as they were threatened to be by an arreſt of parliament, forbidding upon pain of death to aſſemble and to wear any diſtinguiſhing marks. If the Duke and the Prince had made uſe of that opportunity in the manner they might have done, the King's party had that day been cruſhed in Paris for a long time. One le Maire, a perfumer, who was of that gang, came running into my houſe, trembling for fear, and as pale as death. I remember that it was not in my power to hearten him, and that he deſired that he might hide himſelf in my cellar. I had myſelf ground enough to be afraid; for being known not to be in the intereſt of the Prince, I might eaſily enough have been ſuſpeſted to have had a hand in that enterprize. The Duke, as you have ſeen, was not inclined to make uſe of ſuch conjunſtures; and the Prince was ſo weary of any thing that had to do with the people, that he did not think it worth his conſideration. Croiſſi has told me ſince that he endeavoured all he could to awaken the Prince on this occaſion, and to perſuade him that he ought not to loſe it. I never remembered to ſpeak of it to the Prince.

Here follows another fault, in my opinion not leſs than the firſt. The Duke of Lorrain, who was a great lover of negotiations, entered into one as ſoon as he was arrived. He told me in the preſence of the Dutcheſs of Orleans, that negotiations followed him every where; that when he left Flanders he was weary of negotiating with the Count de Fuenſaldagne, and that at Paris he muſt begin again to negotiate, whether he would or no: ' For (ſaid he) what elſe ' can one do here, when I ſee even the Baron du ' Jour thinks of making a ſeparate treaty for himſelf?' This Baron du Jour was a gentleman belonging to the Duke, and a very odd ſort of a man; ſo that the Duke of Lorrain could not better repreſent the multi-tude of negotiators, than by bringing this Baron into the number. But what made him further believe that that ſpirit of negotiating was come into the Duke's head, was his having obſerved that for ſome time

he

he had not preſſed him to cauſe his troops to advance,
as he had done before. His obſervation was true,
and it is certain that the Duke, who was ſincerely
for a peace, had good reaſons to be afraid that the
Prince ſeeing himſelf ſo conſiderably reinforced,
would put invincible obſtacles to it. The Duke was
extremely glad for that reaſon, to ſee the Duke of
Lorrain likewiſe inclined to negotiate, and to ſend
to Court Mr. de Jojeuſe St. Lambert, ‘ who will
‘ only have (ſaid the Duke to me) Mr. de Lorrain’s
‘ commiſſion, which will not hinder him from diſ-
‘ covering if there is nothing to be done for me.’
‘ He may, perhaps, Sir, (anſwered I) be more ſuc-
‘ ceſsful than I have been : I wiſh he may, though
‘ I do not believe it.’ I gueſſed right, for that gentleman ſtaid twelve days at Court without receiving
any anſwer. He reported one at his coming back, I
believe of his own making, in words ſo obſcure that
no body could underſtand the meaning of them,
except at Court, where it was diſowned. The Mareſchal. d’Eſtampes, whom the Duke had likewiſe ſent
thither upon the inſinuations given to the Dutcheſs of
Orleans by Mr. le Tellier’s means, that he would be
hearkened to there as a private man, upon all that he
might ſay in the Duke’s name, came back as much
diſſatisfied at leaſt as the other.

Upon the 30th of September Mr. Talon made an
end of letting the Duke and the Public into the true
intentions of the Queen, by ſending Mr. Doujat to
the parliament (he being himſelf indiſpoſed) with the
letters he had received from the Chancellor and the
firſt Preſident, in anſwer to thoſe he had writ to
them, conſequently to the deliberation of the 26th.
Theſe letters imported that the King having transferred
his parliament to Pontoiſe, and interdicted the counſellors at Paris from any manner of function there,
he could receive no deputation from them till they
had obeyed. I cannot expreſs to you the conſterna-
tion of the company. It went ſo far that the Duke
was afraid that they would have forſaken him, which
                                                    appre-

apprehenfion made him take a very falfe ftep, for it obliged him to draw a letter out of his pocket full of flattering expreffions from the Queen. The Marefchal d'Eftampes had brought him this letter, and though that gentleman was very well affected to, the Court, he could not imagine it to be fincere, no more than the Duke himfelf, who had fhewn it me' the day before, faying to me; ' The Queen muft take me ' for a great fool to write to me in this manner, at ' the time that fhe is acting as fhe does.' By this you may fee that he was not the dupe of this letter, or rather that he had not been fo to that moment. But he became in effect the dupe of it by his making a fhew of it to the parliament, becaufe it perfuaded the parliament that the Duke was treating of an accommodation for himfelf with the Court. By this means he threw a diftruft of his conduct among the members of that company, inftead of regaining a further credit with them. He could never diveft himfelf of that myfterious air on fuch occafions, and notwithftanding what 'the Dutchefs could fay to him, he thought it all along neceffary for his fafety, to prevent people, as he faid, from running into accommodations without him. That air of negotiating, added to the appearances of it which the party of the Prince was continually fhewing, was, in my opinion, what brought the peace about, much fooner than the moft real and effectual negotiations could have 'done. Great affairs depend ftill more upon imagination than fmall ones. The people's imagination alone is fometimes the caufe of a civil war. It produced the peace on this occafion ; for the peace ought not to be attributed to their wearinefs, which was far from being come to fuch a point as to oblige them to recall back or to receive Mazarin. It is certain that they fuffered his return only when they became perfuaded that they could no longer prevent it : but as foon as the body of the public perceived plainly that it was fo, then private perfons ran into it, and what perfuaded

both

both private perfons and the public that it was fo, was the conduct of the chiefs.

The Duke's myfterious manner of explaining him-felf in the late affemblies, in order to fhew the regard which they ftill preferved for him at Court, finifhed what was already very much advanced. Every body thought the peace certain, fo that every body was for making his feparate treaty. As foon as the gentle-man whom the Duke of Lorrain had fent to Court was come back, and that his negotiation was known, the parliament flackened, and gave publicly to under-ftand, that provided the King would grant a general and full amnefty, that fhould be verified in, the parliament at Paris, they would feek for no other fureties. They went not fo far as to declare this by a formal arreft, but what they did produced very near the fame effect, having intreated the Duke to feek himfelf for no other fureties, and to inform the King of it.

Upon the 10th of October Mr. Sevin having repre-fented that it would be neceffary to defire the Duke of Beaufort to refign the government of Paris, by reafon of the King's refufing to receive the deputies of the Town-houfe, fo long as he fhould affume that poft; Mr. Sevin, I fay, who at another time durft not have mentioned any thing like this, was now heard without being either repulfed or hiffed. It was even faid in that fame fitting, that the counfel-lors of the parliament who were officers of the trained-bands, might go, if they pleafed, to St. Germain's, where the Court was, with the deputation of the Town-houfe. Obferve however that among the inftances which this deputation was to make to the King for his returning to Paris, not a word was faid about the verification of the amnefty in the parliament at Paris. What nonfenfe was that!

Upon the 11th the Duke promifed the company to get Mr. de Beaufort to refign his employment; and Meffieurs Doujat and Sevin acquainted the company of the complaints they had made to the Duke of the diforders committed by the forces, contrary to the

pro-

promife which had been given that they fhould retire.
The Duke of Lorrain, whom I met that day in St.
Honoré's ftreet, and who had like to have been killed
by the citizens who guarded the gate of St. Martin,
becaufe he would have gone out of town, fet off
with all its colours the uniformity of this conduct.
He told me that he would write a book upon it, and
dedicate it to the Duke. ' My poor little fifter * will
' cry at it, faid he, but no matter: fhe will com-
' fort herfelf with Mademoifelle Claude †.'

'Upon the 12th the Duke made many excufes to
the parliament that the troops did not remove fo foon
as they would have done had it not been for the bad
weather. You are without doubt very much furprifed to hear the Duke fpeak in this manner of thofe
troops, which eight or ten days before appeared publicly in their red and yellow fcarfs, in a condition to
fight even with advantage thofe of the King. An
hiftorian who fhould write of times more remote would
feek for connections to incidents fo unlikely, and if I
may fay fo, fo contradictory as thefe were. There
was no greater interval of time than the few days I
have mentioned, between thefe doings, neither was
there any other myftery in it. All that vulgar politicians have been pleafed to imagine in order to reconcile thefe events, was nothing elfe than fiction and
chimeras. This brings me back to the maxim I
have laid down, which is, that by confequences
almoft inevitable, capital faults render thofe things
poffible which appear and are in effect the moft
unlikely.

Upon the 13th the colonels of the feveral wards of
the city had the King's order to come by deputies to
St. Germain's where Mr. de Seve, the eldeft of them,
fpoke for the reft. The King ordered a dinner to be

* The Dutchefs of Orleans.
† Claude de Lorraine, who married Cardinal Francis of Lorrain her coufin-german, and brother to that Duke of Lorrain, of
whom the Cardinal de Retz here fpeaks: from which marriage
the prefent Dukes of Lorrain are defcended.

pre-

prepared for them, and honoured them even with his presence whilst they dined. That same day the Prince left Paris with a joy beyond whatever you can imagine : he had formed that design long before. It has been the opinion of many, that his love for Madam de Châtillon had detained him there; but many others believed that he had, to the last, entertained hopes of coming to an accommodation with the Court. I cannot remember what he has told me upon that subject; for it is impossible that in the long conversations I have had since with him about matters past, I should not have mentioned this.

Upon the 14th Mr. de Beaufort made a short and bad compliment to the parliament, upon his having resigned the government of Paris.

Upon the 16th the Duke declared plainly to the parliament, that the King had disowned in every respect what the gentleman sent by Mr. de Lorrain pretended to have transacted at court; but he added, according to his usual stile, that he was every moment expecting some better news. The Duke seeing me wonder at his continuing this conduct, said to me : ‘ Would you be answerable from one quarter of an ‘ hour to another ? How do I know whether the peo- ‘ ple would not in an instant deliver me up to the ‘ King, if they thought that I kept no measures with ‘ the Court ? How do I know whether in another ‘ instant they would not deliver me up to the Prince, ‘ if it came into his head to return to Paris, and to ‘ cause there an insurrection ?’ When you see these principles of the Duke’s, I believe that you are less surprized at his conduct. It is said that one ought never to dispute against what is laid down for a principle. Those principles that are grounded upon fear ought less to be disputed and are less disputable than all others : they are unapproachable.

The Duke acquainted the parliament upon the 19th that he had received a letter from the King, informing him of his coming to Paris upon the 5th, which was the Monday ; and the Duke added, that
he

he was extremely furprized that their Majefties fhould not begin by fending an amnefty to be verified in the parliament of Paris. The company fell into the greateft confternation. They deliberated upon it, and it was agreed that they fhould intreat the King to do that act of grace both to the parliament and to his people.

His Royal Highnefs had received that letter upon the 18th in the evening, upon which he immediately fent for me. He told me that the conduct of the Court was incomprehenfible ; that they ventured there upon lofing all, and that he had almoft a mind to fhut the gates againft the King. I anfwered him, that the conduct of the Court was not at all incomprehenfible to me ; that they knew there that they ran no manner of hazard, knowing as they did his good and pacific intentions ; that in my opinion they acted (at leaft confidering the end they had) with much more prudence than they had done in the beginning ; that I could not fee what could hinder them from returning to Paris, after his having promifed ever fince the 14th to reftore the former Prevoft-des-Marchands and the Efchevins, as the Court had ordered it without ever concerting the thing with him. The Duke uttered five or fix oaths one after another ; and after having mufed a little, ' Go, faid he, I will ' be left for two hours to myfelf ; come again this ' evening about eight.' I found him at that time in the Dutchefs's clofet, and I found her catechifing or rather exhorting of him, for he was in the greateft tranfport poffible, and fpoke as if he had been on horfeback, armed cap-a-pe, and ready to cover the plains of St. Dennis and Grenelle with blood and flaughter. The Dutchefs was frightened, and I muft confefs that though I knew the Duke well enough to prevent my being over hafty in imagining him fo bloody minded, I fancied however that he was more moved than ordinary. The firft thing he faid to me was : ' Well, Sir, what fay you to this ? Do you ' think there is any fafety for me to treat with the

' Court?' ' None at all, Sir, anfwered I, except
' you look to yourfelf, and provide for your own
' fafety; her Royal Highnefs knows that I never
'. fpoke otherwife to you.' . ' 'Tis certainly fo,' faid
the Dutchefs. ' But had you not told me,' continued
the Duke, ' that the King would not return to Paris
' without concerting the matter with me?' ' I had
' told you, Sir, replied I, that the Queen had told
' me fo, but that her manner of faying it obliged
' me to give your Royal Highnefs notice, that you
' ought by no means to rely upon her word.' ' He
' has given you but too much notice,' faid the
Dutchefs, ' but. you would not believe him.' ' I
' own it, replied the Duke, and I complain only of
' the curfed Spanifh woman.' ' Complaints are out
' of feafon, faid the Dutchefs; it is high time to act
' fomething one way or another. You was for peace
'. when it was in your power to make war; you
' are now for war, when it is not in your power to
' make either war or peace.' ' I will make war to-
' 'morrow,' replied the Duke in a warrior's tone, ' and
' more eafily than ever. Afk the Cardinal de Retz.'
The Duke thought that I would have oppofed that
propofition; I perceived that it was the thing he
wifhed, to have it in his power afterwards to fay, that
he would have done wonders if he had not been kept
back. I gave him no room for it, for I anfwered
him gravely and without the leaft emotion: ' No
' doubt of it, Sir.' ' Am I not ftill', continued the
Duke, ' mafter of the people?' ' Yes, Sir,' faid I.
' At my calling the Prince back, will he not return?'
' I believe he will, Sir,' faid I. ' Will not the
' Spanifh army advance if I require it?' ' In all
' appearance it will,' replied I. You expect after
this that he would have entered into fome great refolution, or at leaft into fome great deliberation.
Nothing like it, and I cannot give you a better account
of the end of this conference, than by defiring you
to remember what you have fometimes feen at the
Italian comedy. The comparifon fhews indeed but
                                              little

little respect, and I should not take the liberty to
make it, if it was of my own inventing. But it
came into the Dutchess's head presently after the Duke's
going out of her closet, and she told it me half laughing and half crying. ' Methinks, said she, that I
' see Harlequin telling Scaramouche : What fine
' things I would have said, if thou hadst not had wit
' enough to contradict me !' The conversation ended
in that manner, the Duke concluding that though it
was very bad that the King should return to Paris,
without doing it in concert with him, and without
an amnesty verified in parliament, it would however
agree neither with his duty or reputation to oppose it,
because there was no body but knew that it was in
his power to do it if he pleased, so that all the world
would do him justice in acknowledging that his regard
for the quiet of the state was the only thing that
could oblige him to follow a conduct, which, as to
his particular, ought to be grievous to him. The
Dutchess, who was however of his opinion at the
bottom, at least in regard to the thing itself, for the
reasons you have seen before, could not allow him
that expression. She said to him with firmness, and
even with anger; ' This way of reasoning, Sir,
' might become the Cardinal de Retz, but not a son
' of France : but that question is now over, and all
' we have to do now is to submit with a good grace
' to the King.' He exclaimed at that word as if she
had proposed to him to throw himself headlong into
the river. ' Retire then, Sir, immediately,' added
she. ' And where the devil shall I retire ?' said he.
He left her at this word, and went to his own apartment, whither he commanded me to follow him. It
was to ask me if I had had no notice from the Princess
Palatine about the King's return : I told him that
I had not; which was true: but it was not long
before I heard from her, for an hour after I received
a billet of her's importing that the Queen had commanded her to acquaint me with it, and to tell me
that her Majesty made no doubt but that I would

finish

finiſh in this conjunĉure what I had ſo well and ſo
happily begun at Compicgne. That Princeſs made
me many excuſes in a billet apart writ in cypher, for
giving me this notice ſo late. ' You know the ſtate
' of things here, added ſhe; the Court is at St. Ger-
' main's the ſame it was at Compiegne.' This was
telling me enough. All that I have related arrived
upon the 20th of Oĉober.

The King, who lay that night at Ruel, came to
Paris upon the 21ſt. He ſent from Ruel, Nogent and
Mr. d'Amville to the Duke, to invite him to come
and meet him. His Royal Highneſs could never
reſolve upon doing it, though theſe two gentlemen
preſſed him extremely. They were in the right, and
I am ſtill perſuaded that the Duke was not in the
wrong. Not that there was any deſign againſt his
perſon, at leaſt as I have heard the Mareſchal de
Villeroy ſay : but I believe that if he had been to
meet the King, and that the King had had a deſign
to have ſecured him, he might have done it, conſidering the diſpoſition in which the people were. I
own that at the bottom the people were very well
inclined to the Duke, and better inclined to him
beyond compariſon than to the Court ; but the minds
of people were in an agitation, and in a flutter
that might in my opinion have been turned to any
thing ; and if the weight of the Royal Majeſty had
been made uſe of in that conjunĉure, I do not know
whether it would not have carried it. I ſpeak doubt-
fully upon the matter, becauſe it is certain that upon
the whole the Duke had ſtill for him all the meaner,
and even all the middling people. But, in ſhort,
there were, in my opinion, good reaſons to prevent
his running the riſk, chiefly out of the walls of Paris.
My wonder was much greater that the miniſters
ſhould expoſe the perſon of his Majeſty to the diſcon-
tent, the diſtruſt and the fright of the Duke; to the
fear of a parliament that had room to believe that the
Court came with a deſign to cruſh that company ;
and to the caprice of a people who continued their

    attack-

attachment to perfons of whom the Cardinal was far from being affured. The event has fo well juftified the conduct which the Court followed on this occafion, that it is almoft ridiculous to blame it. I think neverthelefs that it was imprudent, rafh, and inconfiderate, beyond what it is poffible to imagine. I will not fay upon this head what I have faid upon the other, that I am doubtful ; I will fay pofitively and to my certain knowledge, that if the Duke had pleafed, the Queen and the fub-minifters had that day been feparated from the King.

Courtiers will always fuffer themfelves to be amufed by the acclamations of the people, without confidering that they are only things of courfe on fuch occafions. I heard fome perfons at the Louvre that evening that were flattering the Queen upon thefe acclamations, whilft Mr. de Turenne, who was behind me, at the circle, was whifpering me in the ear; ‘ They did almoft the like lately for the Duke of ‘ Lorrain.’ I had furprized that gentleman very much if I had told him, that in the midft of thefe acclamations there had been many perfons who had propofed to the Duke to oblige the King to go to the Town-houfe and take up his lodging there. This was very true, and Mr. de Beaufort himfelf had preffed him about it with twelve or fifteen counfellors of the parliament. There are fome of them who are ftill living, whom people would very much wonder at if I fhould name them. The Duke would not hearken to it, and I oppofed it to my utmoft when the Duke told me of that propofal. It was, in my opinion, a thing poffible as to the prefent fuccefs, it being certain that any town-officer that would have made the leaft appearance againft the Duke’s orders, had been maffacred by his own foldiers ; but fetting afide refpect, confcience, and what elfe you can imagine, the propofal was foolifh, confidering the circumftances and the confequences, as you will perceive at once by what I have faid before. It was certainly by a principle of duty only that I oppofed it,

K 3   for

for I thought myself in much greater danger than I
have ever done in my life. I went to wait for the
King at the Louvre, where I staid two or three hours
before he came, with Madam de Lesdiguieres, and
Mr. de Turenne. This last asked me aloud, without
any ill meaning, but rather moved by his concern,
Whether I thought myself safe there? I squeezed his
hand, because I perceived that Frelay, who was a
great Mazarinian, had heard him, and I answered,
' Yes, Sir, and all manner of ways: Madam de Les-
" diguieres knows that I am in the right to think so.'
This however was only bragging, for I am persuaded,
that if I had been arrested that day, it had occasioned
no manner of stirring. What I have been telling you
of what was possible on either side, will without doubt
appear contradictory to you, and I confess that it can
be well conceived only by those who have seen not only
the outside, but the inside of what passed.

The Queen received me admirably well, and she
desired the King to embrace me as being the man
to whom he chiefly owed his return to Paris. These
words, which were heard by a great many, caused me
a real joy, because I thought that the Queen would
not have spoke them publicly, if she had had a design to
have had me arrested. I staid at the circle till the
Queen went to council. As I was coming away, I
met Jouy in the anti-chamber, who told me that the
Duke had sent him to know whether it was true that
they had admitted me at the council-board, and to
command me to come to him. I met, as I was
entering the Duke's palace, Mr. d'Aligre coming out,
who had been sent by the King to bid the Duke in
his name to leave Paris the next day, and to retire to
Limours. This blunder has likewise been consecrated
by the event, but in my opinion it is one of the
greatest and most signal faults that has ever been committed in politics. You may tell me that they knew
at Court what sort of man the Duke was; to which
I will answer, that they knew him so little on this
occasion, that he was just upon the point of resolving,

OR

or rather of executing what he had really refolved; which was to poſt himſelf in the market-place, to make barricadoes even to the gates of the Louvre, and to drive the King away from thence. I am perſuaded that he had ſucceeded even with eaſe, if he had gone about it, and that the people had not ſtood heſitating if they had ſeen his Royal Highneſs in perſon, and his Royal Highneſs taking up arms only to prevent his being exiled. I have been accuſed to have ſtirred up the Duke very much on this occaſion. Take what follows as a true account of what I did.

At my coming to the Duke he appeared to me very much caſt down, becauſe he had put it into his head that the order which he had juſt then received from the King by Mr. d'Aligre, was only to amuſe him, and make him believe that there was no thought of arreſting him. It is impoſſible to expreſs the agitation he was in. He fancied that every muſket-ſhot he heard (and upon ſuch occaſions there are always many muſket-ſhots) came from the regiment of guards that was ſent to inveſt his palace. All thoſe he ſent to enquire, brought him word that all was quiet, but he would believe nobody, and he was at every inſtant looking out at window, that he might the better hear whether there were any drums beating. At laſt he recovered a little courage, enough at leaſt to aſk me whether he might depend upon me? To which I anſwered only by this piece of a verſe out of the Cid of Corneille: 'Any one beſides my father *.——This word ſet him a laughing, which was very extraordinary; when he was poſſeſſed with fear. 'Give me a proof 'of it, continued he, and come to a reconciliation 'with Mr. de Beaufort.' 'With all my heart, Sir,' replied I. He embraced me, and went himſelf to open the door of the gallery that joined to the door of

---

* The verſe alluded to in this place is in a ſcene of Corneille's play, called Le Cid, where a father having lately received an affront, aſks his ſon if he has courage, the ſon anſwers, *Tout autre que mon pere, l'eprouveroit ſur l'heure.* Any one but my father ſhould have immediate proof of it.

his

his bed-chamber, where he then was. I saw Mr. de Beaufort coming out of it, who took me round the neck, saying: ' Afk his Royal Highnefs what I was juft now ' faying to him upon your account. I can diftinguifh ' honeft men. Come, Sir, let us drive away the ' Mazarinians for good and all, and let us fend them ' to the devil.' The converfation opened in this manner, and the Duke went on with it by an ambiguous fpeech, which in the mouth of Gafton † of Foix had been the fore-runner of fome great action, but in the mouth of Gafton of France, was to me only the prefage of nothing at all. Mr. de Beaufort maintained, to the utmoft of his power, the neceffity and the poffibility of the propofal he made, which was that the Duke fhould march at break of day directly to the market-place, and that he fhould fet up barricadoes there, to be carried on where it fhould be thought beft. At this the Duke turned to me, faying as they do at the parliament, Your advice, Sir, as being eldeft counfellor. I will fet down here the very words I fpoke, and the whole converfation, which I have tranfcribed from the original, as I dictated it to Montrefor at my coming home from the Duke's, and which I have ftill by me written with his own hand.

' I think, indeed, Sir, that I ought to fpeak in this
' conjuncture after the manner of the eldeft counfellor
' of the parliament, that is, after the manner he did
' when he moved for publick prayers for forty hours
' together. I know but of few conjunctures where
' there has been fo much need of them. They would
' ftill be, Sir, much more neceffary to me than to
' any other, becaufe I can give no advice but what
' muft be attended with very difmal appearances, and
' even with terrible inconveniencies. If I advife you
' to bear with the injurious treatment which you have
' met with, will not the publick, which is always
' inclined to think evil, have a reafon or a pretence

† Gafton of Foix, Duke de Nemours, was one of the braveft men of his time. He was killed at the battle of Ravenna in the year 1512, upon Eafter-day, aged about 23.

' to

‘ to fay that I betray your intereft, and that in giving
‘ you this advice I do but go on with the obftacles I
‘ have put to the defigns of the Prince ? If I advife
‘ your Royal Highnefs to difobey, and to follow
‘ Mr. de Beaufort's views, will it be in my power to
‘ prevent people from thinking me to be a man who
‘ blows hot and cold ; who is for peace when he is in
‘ hopes of gaining fome advantages in treating of it ;
‘ who is for war when he has been refufed to treat of
‘ peace ; who advifes to deftroy the city with fire and
‘ fword, and to fet that fire to the gates of the Louvre,
‘ by enterprizing againft the King's perfon ? This is,
‘ Sir, what will be faid of me, and what you may
‘ yourfelf believe at certain inftants. I might have
‘ room, after having foretold your Royal Highnefs
‘ perhaps above a thoufand times, that your uncer-
‘ tainties would bring you to the condition you are
‘ now in ; I might have room, I fay, to intreat you
‘ with all the refpeft I owe to your Royal Highnefs,
‘ to excufe me from fpeaking upon a matter, which I
‘ have already faid more upon than any body living.
‘ I will however make ufe but of half the right which
‘ I think I have, that is, that though I do not defign
‘ to determine the way which your Royal Highnefs
‘ ought to follow, I will expofe to your view the in-
‘ conveniencies of both ways, with the fame freedom
‘ as if I had any thought of chufing one of the two
‘ for myfelf. If your Royal Highnefs obeys, you are
‘ anfwerable to the whole kingdom for all that it will
‘ afterwards fuffer. I will not pretend to judge of
‘ what that fuffering may come to, for who can fore-
‘ judge of an evil that depends on the punctilio's of a
‘ Mazarin, on the impetuofity of an Ondedei, on the
‘ impertinence of an Abbot Fouquet, and on the vio-
‘ lence of a Servien ? But, in fhort, you will be an-
‘ fwerable for all that they fhall do againft the publick,
‘ becaufe the publick will be perfuaded that it has
‘ been in your power to prevent it. If you do not
‘ obey, you run the rifk of overturning the ftate.’—
The Duke interrupted me at that word, faying with

great eagernefs: ' You do not come to the point,
' which is to know whether I am in a condition to
' difobey ?' ' I believe fo, Sir, anfwered I, for I do
' not fee which way the Court can go about to make
' you obey. The King muft come in perfon to attack
' you here, which will be no eafy matter.' Mr. de
Beaufort enlarged upon the impoffibility of the attempt, and faid fo much that I perceived that the
Duke began likewife to think fo, in which cafe he was
altogether like to refolve upon fitting idle, his inclination leading him always that way. I therefore
thought myfelf obliged by all manner of reafons to
clear that point to him, which I did by telling him,
that there was a diftinction to be made ; that I owned
that the people were not likely to fuffer for the prefent
that the Duke fhould be taken forcibly away from his
own palace, but that the King might in time bring matters to a pafs that fhould enable him to do it; that by
accuftoming the people to acknowledge his authority,
I made no doubt of his fucceeding in it, and even
quickly, becaufe I made no doubt but that by ufing
prudent meafures, he would quickly accuftom his
people to obey his power ; that that power would
encreafe at every inftant; that it was already greater at
ten at night, which was the hour that his watch had
juft then ftruck, than it was at five in the afternoon,
and that the proof of this was evident by the King's
rendering himfelf mafter of the gate of the conference,
which he caufed to be peaceably guarded, without any
body's murmuring at it, by the fingle regiment of
guards, who certainly durft not have come near it, if
the Duke had pleafed to have caufed it to be fhut for
a quarter of an hour only, between three and four in
the afternoon; that if his Royal Highnefs fuffered all
other pofts of Paris to be taken poffeffion of in like
manner; if he fuffered the parliament to be abufed,
as it would be perhaps the next morning, I believed that
perhaps the next afternoon there would be no great
fafety for him. This brought the Duke again into
his firft fright, and made him cry out : ' You mean
                                                    ' that

" that I cannot keep myself on the defensive?' ' No,
' Sir, answered I; you can do what you please, from
' this time till to-morrow morning; but I would not
' answer for what you can do to-morrow night.' Mr.
de Beaufort, who thought that what I said was with a
design to propose and to countenance the offensive
part, was offering to second me, but I stopped him
short by saying: ' I perceive, Sir, that you do not
' take me right. I speak to his Royal Highness in
' the manner I do, only because I have observed that
' he thinks he may securely stay in his palace against
' the King's will. I have no advice to give, in the
' state in which matters are. It has always belonged
' to the Duke to determine. It even belongs to him
' to propose, and our business is only to execute. It
' shall never be said that I have advised him, either to
' suffer the treatment he meets with, or to set up bar-
' ricadoes to-morrow morning. I have already ac-
' quainted him with the reasons I have to follow this
' conduct. He has commanded me to expose to his
' view the inconveniencies which I perceive on both
' sides, and I have done it.' The Duke gave me
leave to speak as much as I would, and after having
taken two or three turns about the chamber, he
came back to me and said: ' If I resolve to dispute
' the ground, will you declare for me?' ' Yes, Sir,
' answered I, and without any hesitation. I ought to
' do it; I am attached to your service; do but com-
' mand, and you shall certainly see me obey. But I
' shall be grieved at heart at it, because in the con-
' dition things are in, it is impossible for an honest
' man not to be grieved, whatever you resolve upon.'
The Duke, who was no otherwise good, than because
he was an easy man, and who was not naturally tender,
was moved however at what I told him. Tears came
to his eyes; he embraced me, and of a sudden he
asked me whether I thought that he might render himself master of the King's person. I told him that
nothing in the world was more impossible, the gate of
the conference being guarded as it was. Mr. de Beau-

fort

fort propofed fome means which were impracticable in every refpect. He offered to go and poft himfelf at the entrance of the Cours with the Duke's houfhold. In fhort, he faid many foolifh things in my opinion. I perfifted to fpeak and act in the manner I had done, and I perceived before I left the Duke (and to fay the truth, I perceived it with pleafure) that he would chufe to obey, for I obferved in him all the appearance poffible of joy for my forbearing to countenance the offenfive part, notwithftanding which he fpoke of nothing elfe the reft of the time we ftaid with him, and he even commanded us to get our friends in a readinefs, and to come to his palace all of us at break of day. Mr. de Beaufort perceived as well as I, that the Duke was againft doing any thing, and as we were coming down ftairs, he faid to me : ‘ This gentleman ‘ is not capable of a vigorous action.’ ‘ And much ‘ lefs capable, faid I, to go on with it, which makes ‘ me think you mad to propofe it to him in the ftate ‘ in which things are.’ ‘ I find you hardly know him ‘ yet, replied he ; if I had not propofed it to him, ‘ he would have reproached me with it for ten years ‘ together.’

I found at my coming home Montrefor, who was ftaying for me, and who made a mighty jeft of my fcruples, for fo he called all the regard I had fhewn in the converfation I had with the Duke, which he writ down as I was dictating it to him. That gentleman affured me very pofitively that the Duke had a greater defire to be at Limours than the Queen had to fend him thither, but upon the whole, he owned that the Court had committed a terrible fault in pufhing him to it, becaufe the fear of not thinking himfelf fafe there, might eafily put him upon undertaking what he would never have thought on, if the leaft regard had been fhewn to him. The event has likewife juftified that imprudence, which was fo much the greater, becaufe at Court, where they had ground to look upon me as upon a man exafperated and full of diftruft, they were, in my opinion, far from doing me the

juftice

juftice to believe that my fentiments for the ftate were
fo right as in truth they were. I am indeed convinced,
that confidering the Duke's humour, which it was
impoffible to change; confidering befides the divifion
of the party, to which no remedy could be found by
reafon of an infinity of circumftances, and of the
confufion, paft, prefent, and to come, occafioned by
that divifion; I am convinced, I fay, that it had been
impoffible to fupport any thing that had been undertaken, which reafon alone, fetting afide all others,
was fufficient to deter any body from advifing the
Duke to undertake any thing. But I am no lefs convinced that the Duke would for the prefent have fucceeded in his enterprize, and that he had driven the
King away from Paris. Many perfons will take what
I fay for a paradox, but all great things that remain
unexecuted appear always impracticable to thofe who
are incapable of any thing great, and I am fure there
were fome who were not furprized at the barricadoes
which the Duke de Guife fet up, who had looked
upon the thing as ridiculous if they had heard it mentioned a quarter of an hour before they were raifed.
I do not know whether I have not already faid in fome
place or other of thefe Memoirs, that what has made
fome men the moft remarkable by fome great actions,
is their having obferved before others the critical
minute which made the undertaking of them poffible.

I return to the Duke. He fat out for Limours a
little before break of day, and he even affected to be
gone an hour fooner than he had appointed Mr. de
Beaufort and me to come to him. We found Jouy,
expecting us by his order at the gate of his palace,
who told us from him, that he had had his reafons for
doing as he did, which we fhould know fome time or
other, and that we had beft come to an accommodation
with the Court if it was poffible. As for my part, I
was not furprized at his conduct: Mr. de-Beaufort
exclaimed much againft it.

Upon the 22d the King held his bed of juftice at
the Louvre. He caufed there four declarations to be
read.

read. The first was that of the amnesty; the second was for the recalling the parliament to Paris; the third was an order for Mr. de Beaufort, as well as for Messieurs de Rohan, Viole, de Thou, Broussel, Portail, Bitaud, Croisi, Machaut, Fleury, Martineau, and Perraut, to leave Paris; and in that same declaration the parliament was forbidden to meddle for the future with any matters of state; the fourth established a chamber of vacations. The parliament had agreed in the morning before they went to the King, that the company should make some instances to his Majesty about having those of their body who were exiled, restored to their functions. They all of them obeyed their orders that same day. I went to the Queen's in the afternoon, where, after her Majesty had staid some time at the circle, she commanded me to go with her into her little closet. She used me extremely well; she told me that she knew that I had softened both people's minds and affairs, as much as I had it in my power; that she believed that I had done it still more readily and more publickly, if I had not been obliged to observe many regards with my friends, who were not all of them in the same sentiments; that she pitied me, and would help me out of the trouble I was in. You find in all this a great deal of civility, and even of appearing kindness. But see what it tended to at the bottom. She was more incensed at me than ever, because Beloy, who belonged to the Duke, but who always was secretly attached to some other, and who had renewed his former measures with the Court since the affairs of the Prince had been declining, had sent her notice in the morning as soon as she was awake, that I had offered to the Duke to do whatever he would command me. Not that he knew any thing of the particulars of what passed the evening before between the Duke, Mr. de Beaufort, and me: But entring with Josi into the Duke's chamber as soon as we had left him, the Duke, whom they found both moved and troubled, said to them: 'I might, if I pleased, 'prepare a fine dance for the Spanish woman.' Beloy,
either

either malicioufly, or moved only by curiofity, anfwered
the Duke: ' But, Sir, can your Royal Highnefs depend
' intirely upon the Cardinal de Retz ?' ' The Cardi-
' nal de Retz, replied the Duke, is an honeft man,
' and will not fail me.' Jouï, who had heard this,
informed me of it in the morning, and I made no
doubt but that Beloy had likewife fent an account of
it to the Queen: But the Queen could not be informed
that at the fame time that I had offered to the Duke
what my honour obliged me to, I had omitted nothing
of what my honour likewife gave me leave to do, to
prevent the overturning of the ftate. At the very
moment that Jouï acquainted me with this, I made a
ferious reflection upon the fcruples which Montrefor
had made a jeft of and blamed me for, the night
before. It is true, that fuch fcruples meet with no
fuccefs in Courts, at leaft commonly; but there are
perfons who prefer to fuccefs, the inward fatisfaction
they find in themfelves.

You would have been furprized at the manner in
which I anfwered the Queen, if I had not given you
beforehand this little account, which contains the
reafons I had to fpeak to her as I did. I don't mean
as to matter of fincerity, for you have feen that even
before, I feldom failed of ufing the like in fpeaking to
her. I told her that I had a fenfible joy to have at
laft met with the moment, which I had for fo long a
time fo paffionately wifhed for, which was to ferve
her without any reftriction : that fo long as his Royal
Highnefs had been engaged in affairs, I could not follow
my own inclination by reafon of my engagements
with him, in which fhe knew that I had never deceived her : that if I had had the honour to fpeak in
private to her Majefty the day before, I would have
difcovered to her freely, as my cuftom was, the manner in which I was obliged in honour to behave myfelf with the Duke : that his Royal Highnefs having
left Paris, fully refolved to meddle no more with any
public affairs, had by that freed me from my engagements, and reftored me to the liberty of following

now my own inclination, which was fuch a pleafure to me that I could not well enough exprefs it to her Majefty. She anfwered me in the moft civil manner, but I perceived that fhe would fain have put me upon difcovering the difpofitions in which the Duke was. I eafily fatisfied her, and fhe was pleafed with what I faid; for I affured her, and it was certainly true, that the Duke was refolved to keep quiet in his folitude. ' We muft not fuffer him to ftay there,' replied fhe; ' he may be ufeful to the King and to the ' ftate: it is neceffary that you fhould go and fetch ' him back.' I was extremely furprized at this, becaufe I muft confefs that I expected nothing like it, and that at firft I could not well comprehend what her meaning was. But I quickly found it out, not that fhe explained it to me clearly, but by her giving me to underftand, that the Duke having fatisfied to what he owed to the King's dignity, by the obedience he had fhewn, it was in his power to re-eftablifh himfelf better than ever in the King's favour, by crowning the good conduct he had followed with juft and reafonable condefcenfions, in which he might even find his own account. You fee that there was nothing very obfcure in thefe expreffions. When the Queen perceived that I anfwered only in general terms, fhe clofed herfelf up, and appeared quite changed, not only in refpect to the matter we were upon, but to the manner in which fhe had at firft treated me. I faw her blufh, and fhe began to fpeak more coldly, which was always with her a fign of being angry. She came to herfelf however in a little time, and fhe afked me whether I continued to confide in Madam de Chevreufe? To which I anfwered, that I continued to be her very humble fervant. She took me up at that word very haftily, and, as I thought, fhe did it with fome pleafure. ' I underftand you,' faid fhe; ' you confide more in the Princefs Palatine, and you ' are in the right.' ' I put a great truft,' replied I, ' in the Princefs Palatine; but I befeech your Majefty to give me leave to rely on no body but your-
' felf.'

' felf.' ' With all my heart,' faid fhe, pretty kindly in appearance : ' adieu ; the whole nobility of ' France are within ftaying for me.'

I muft defire you to give me leave to inform you in this place of fome particulars that are neceffary to convince you, that perfons who are at the head of great affairs meet with no lefs trouble from thofe of their own party than from enemies. The enemies I had, though extremely powerful in the ftate, the one by his birth, his merit, and his faction, and the other by his favour, had not been able, with all their efforts, to oblige me to quit my poft ; and I may fay, without vanity, that I had kept it, and even with dig-nity, by failing only a little with the wind, if the different interefts, or rather the different chimæras of my friends, had not put me, againft my will, upon following a conduct which occafioned my ruin, becaufe it perfuaded the Court that I was refolved to hold it out againft wind and tide. To let you into thefe par-ticulars, which are pretty curious, it is neceffary, in my opinion, that I fhould let you likewife into fome particulars that relate to a certain number of perfons who were called my friends. I make ufe of that ex-preffion, becaufe many that went by that name were not really fuch.

I had not broke, for example, with Madam de Chevreufe nor with Laigues. Noirmoutier had left nothing undone to reconcile himfelf to me, and at the inftance of all my friends I had been obliged to receive him and to live civilly with him. Montrefor, who at all adventures had declared to me an hundred times in his life that he was in my intereft in depend-ance only of the houfe of Guife, pretended a right however to enter into my affairs, becaufe he had been let into the fecret of fome of them. That right, which confifts properly in having a hand in negoti-ations, he had in common with the perfons I have juft now named. He made not the like ufe of it in this laft conjuncture as the others did, though he fpoke as much and more about it. He was fatisfied

to appear difcontented, and to complain when he
came to me in the evening, but he took no ill fteps
towards the Court, as Mr. de Noirmoutier did, who
to gain fome credit with Cardinal Mazarin, whom he
went to fee upon the frontiers, fhewed him one of my
letters, the date of which he had falfified, and wherein
I had formerly charged him with a commiffion, which,
as he pretended, had relation to the prefent time.
The Cardinal fufpected the cheat, by reafon of fome
circumftances which I have forgot, and he never forgave it that gentleman. Madam de Chevreufe did not
ufe me in that manner, but having found at Court
neither the regard nor the truft which fhe expected,
fhe was feeking after fome intrigue, and fhe would
have been glad, at the King's coming back to Paris,
to have meddied with my concerns which appeared to
be of confequence, becaufe they were looked upon as
a thing previous and neceffary to the return of the
Cardinal. Laigues, who had treated me pretty freely
before my going to Compiegne, began to fee me
again regularly, and almoft upon the ancient foot;
and Mademoifelle de Chevreufe herfelf made fome
advances to be reconciled to me, by her mother's
order, if I am not very much miftaken. She had the
fineft eyes in the world, and a certain art of turning
them, that was admirable and altogether peculiar to
her. I juft took notice of them, and no more, the
evening fhe arrived at Paris, and I lived civilly both
with her and with her mother, as well as with Laigues,
and that was all. One might think that the conduct
I followed on this occafion would have been enough
to have ferved my turn; but it proved not fo, and
there was a reafon for it, which is, that the advances
that thofe who acknowledge their ill conduct make
to the great man they have offended, will infallibly
always turn to his difadvantage, if he rejects thofe
advances, or receives them but flightly, it being
hardly poffible that thofe who think themfelves flighted
fhould not preferve a refentment for it, and have a
fling at him, at leaft in their heat. I know that
Laigues

Laigues ufed me in that manner, and even grofsly, before feveral perfons and on feveral occafions. I have heard nothing like it of Madam de Chevreufe, which is not to be wondered at, becaufe fhe has a natural goodnefs in her, or rather a natural eafinefs. As for Mademoifelle de Chevreufe, fhe could not pardon me the refiftance I had offered to her eyes; and the Abbot Fouquet, who ferved at that time his quarter with her, faid, after that lady's death, to a perfon of quality from whom I had it, that fhe hated me as much as fhe had loved me. I can take my oath with all manner of affurance, that I had never given her the leaft occafion for it. The poor lady died of a malignant fever, that carried her off in four and twenty hours, before her phyficians fo much as dreamed that fhe was in the leaft danger. I faw her for a moment, with the Dutchefs her mother, who was by her bedfide, and who little thought that fhe was to lofe her daughter the next morning by break of day.

I had a fecond fort of friends, that is, perfons who kept themfelves wrapt up in the party of the Fronde, and who at the time that that party was fubdivided, had ftuck particularly clofe to me. This fecond fort was compofed of perfons of feveral degrees, who all agreed however in a point, which was, that they all expected that my accommodation with the Court would turn very much to their particular advantage; whereby they were already difpofed to believe, that if I did not do for them what they expected, it would be, not for want of power, but for want of will. Thefe fort of perfons are extremely troublefome, becaufe in a great party there is always a great number to whom it is impoffible to difcover all that the heads of the party are able or not able to do, and to whom it is confequently impoffible to juftify what is done. That evil is without any remedy, and is of the nature of thofe in which one ought to feek a fatisfaction in one's own confcience only. Mine has been all my life long more tender upon that article than it is convenient to a man who has meddled with fo great affairs.

affairs as I have done. There are but few matters
wherein fcruples are of lefs fervice. It is true, that
by the event I fuffered no inconveniencies in the prefent conjuncture; but I had already fuffered enough in
my imagination.

· The third fort of friends whom I had at that time,
was a chofen number of perfons of quality, who
were united to me both by intereft and by friendfhip,
who were in my confidence, and with whom I faithfully concerted what I was to do. Thefe were Meffieurs de Briffac, de Bellievre, and de Caumartin,
with whom Mr. de Montrefor, as I have already faid,
joined himfelf, by reafon of many paft affairs in which
he had had a fhare. There was not one in this little
number that had not a right to my friendfhip. The
quality of Mr. de Briffac, and his attachment to me
in my moft troublefome affairs, obliged me to have a
greater regard for his intereft than for my own, and
fo much the more that he had not had the advantage
ftipulated for him in relation to the government of
Anjou, at the time that the Princes were arrefted. I
can't fay however that it was either the fault of the
Court or mine, the treaty which he was entered into
failing only for want of the money which he could not
pay. But, in fhort, he had had nothing, and it was
juft, at leaft in refpect to me, that he fhould be provided for. The Prefident de Bellievre had had for
fome time the place of firft prefident in view, but
being a man of good fenfe, he thought no more of it
as foon as he faw the Court get the uppermoft; and
the very day that the Duke and the Prince fent Meffieurs de Rohan, de Chavigny, and Goulas, to St.
Germains, he faid thefe words to me, ' I muft do
' like the fnail, retire within my fhell; there is no-
' thing more to expect, and I defift from all preten-
' fions.' He was as good as his word; and a great
and dangerous defluction that fell at that time on one
of his eyes, ferved as a pretence to it, and made his
retirement not feem ftrange.

                                                    Mr.

Mr. de Caumartin went into Poitou to be married, a month or five weeks before the King resolved upon returning, and he continued there when the Court arrived at Paris. He had certainly had a greater share than any one in my most secret affairs, he had acted with a greater faithfulness and capacity, and even without any private interest, except that which his honour put him upon, on an occasion in which he knew better than any man living that there was nothing real in the case. The injustice done him upon that subject, obliges me to explain the particulars of it to you.

You have seen, in the second volume of these memoirs, that the Duke was drawn on by the Prince to ask the Queen for the removal of the sub-ministers, and that I had prevented his Royal Highness from taking that step, if he would have believed me, because it was in effect good for nothing at all, and worse for him than for any body else. Laigues, who looked upon the sub-ministers as on men undone, and who was the man in the world upon whose fancy these novelties worked the most, put it into his head to procure the place of secretary at war, which Mr. le Tellier had, to de Nouveau. Madam de Chevreuse mentioned that chimæra in the presence of the little Abbot de Bernay, who reported it to Mr. de Caumartin. This last was in the right to dislike the thing. He came to my house, and asked me if I knew any thing of that design. I smiled, and told him that he must take me for a madman by the question he asked me. That he was not ignorant that no body knew better than I that we were not in a condition to create secretaries of state * ; and besides, that if we were in a condition to do it, our choice would not fall upon Mr. de Nouveau. Caumartin exclaimed much against Ma-

---

* There are four secretaries of state in France, as has been explained before, of whom one hath the management of the war affairs, and is for that reason most commonly called secretary at war.

dam

dam de Chevreufe and Laigues, which he had a right to do : ‘ For though I am fully perfuaded, (faid he) ‘ that what they propofe is impertinent, it fhews how- ‘ ever that I am not to depend upon their friendfhip.’ ‘ You are much in the right, (anfwered I) and I will ‘ to-morrow tell them freely my opinion about it. ‘ At the time (added I) that I am doing my utmoft ‘ with the Duke to prevent his pufhing Mr. le Tel- ‘ lier too far, they will be the caufe by their ill-con- ‘ duct, that le Tellier will think that it is I that am ‘ working his ruin.’

I upbraided them both with it the next day, but they denied the fact ; this made a noife, and that noife came to the ears of Mr. le Tellier, who thought by it that we were already in difpute about his place. He never forgave it, as it has appeared to me fince, either to Mr. de Caumartin, or to me. Moft enmi- ties that are feen at Courts, have no better ground than this ; and I have obferved, that thofe that are the worft grounded are the moft obftinate. The rea- fon of it is plain ; for offences which occafion enmi- ties of this nature, confifting chiefly in the imagina- tion, never fail to grow bigger and bigger, in a foil which always abounds but too much in evil humours, the proper food of all enmities. Forgive me this fmall digreffion, which even is not unneceffary to the fub- ject I am treating of, fince it fhews you that I was ftill the more obliged not to forget Mr. de Caumartin’s intereft in my accommodation. It was not that gentle- man however that obftructed it. He very well knew that there was not ftuff enough left to be prodigal of. He had told me feveral times before he went into Poitou, that it was hard, but that it was neceffary that we fhould fuffer, even from the ill conduct of our enemies : that as for his part, he ceafed to look for any private advantage, and that the only thing to be minded now was to fave the fhip, in which he might again fet fail, as opportunities fhould prefent : that that fhip, which was myfelf, could not be faved in the ftate into which things were fallen by the irre-

folution

folution of the Duke, but by ftanding a-loof, and
failing eaftward, that is, towards Rome. I remember that the day he took his leave of me, before he
went into Poitou, he fpoke to me in this manner;
‘ You ftand now but upon the point of a needle, and
‘ if they knew at Court their power in refpect to you,
‘ they would ufe you as they will do others. Your
‘ courage makes you hold a countenance that deceives
‘ and difquiets them. Make ufe of this inftant to
‘ get what will be of fervice to you for your poft at
‘ Rome; they will do upon that article all that you
‘ defire.’

Of thefe few friends, Mr. de Montrefor was then,
the only one left; and he was continually faying,
That as for him, he had no kind of pretenfions. He
had even turned into ridicule a letter he had received
out of the country from Chandenier, who writ him
word that he made no doubt but that I fhould reftore
him to his poft *, and make him a Duke and Peer in
this conjuncture. It was, however, this Mr. de Montrefor who caufed all the trouble, and who did it
without being moved by any private intereft, but only
by a mere whim. One evening that we were all fitting round my fire, Joly, who was prefent, faid, upon
occafion of fomething that was fpoken in the converfation, that he had received a letter from Mr. de Caumartin. He read it, and that letter was full of the
fentiments which I have mentioned, and which were
even expreffed with a great deal of force. I obferved
that Montrefor, who did not naturally love him, appeared with an air full of myftery, mixed with four-
nefs, at the hearing it, and being extremely well acquainted with his manners and his humour, I let
fome words fall on purpofe to oblige him to explain
himfelf. It was no difficult matter, for he cried out
of a fudden, and even fwearing, ‘ We are not men
‘ to be led by the nofe; he is a villain that fays that

* Of captain of the Guards du Corps, or life-guards, of which
he had been deprived for fome time.

‘ his

' his Eminence ought or can come to an honourable
' accommodation except he procures something ad-
' vantageous for his friends. He that fays fo, has a
' mind to engrofs all for himfelf.' Thefe words, added
to the peevifh humour I had obferved in him for fome
days againft the Princefs Palatine, convinced me that
he thought that Caumartin, who was a particular
friend of that Princefs's, had taken fome private meafures with her, tending to his own profit, exclufively
of the reft. I did my beft to undeceive him, but
without fuccefs. He fucceeded better in deceiving the
others, for he brought the like fufpicion into the head
of Mr. de Briffac, who was indeed a man of wax, and
the moft fufceptible of any impreffions of any one I
ever knew. Mr. de Briffac infpired the like thought
to Madam de Lefdiguieres, who loved him entirely at
that time. Perfons who are in thefe bad difpofitions,
never fail to fupport them with all manner of ideas
that will ferve to perfuade them that a conduct, oppofite to that they ftand in fear of, is not only a thing
poffible, but even eafy. A like fancy gets into the
heads of others, and is communicated to the fubalterns of the party. The fecret is whifpered about
from ear to ear, and caufes at firft but a little murmuring ; that murmuring changes into a noife which
caufes three or four pernicious effects, both in refpect
to one's own patry, and in refpect to the party one
oppofes. This is exactly what happened to me, and
I was furprized to fee all my friends divided upon
what I fhould or what I fhould not do, as well as
upon what I could or what I could not do, which
brought the Court to look upon me as upon a man
who either pretended to fhare the miniftry, or to fell
my pretenfions very dear. I perceived and felt the
danger of the fituation I was in, and yet I refolved
to run all the rifk, to which I was moved by that fame
principle which has caufed me all my life long to
take too much upon me. There is nothing fo pernicious, according to the rules of politics. We feldom
have any thanks given us for it ; and it is certain
                                                    that

that of all things, good intentions ought the leaft
to be overftretched. I have met with great inconveniencies from not obferving that rule, both in matters
of ftate, and in domeftic affairs. But every body will
allow, that it is a very hard matter to forfake what
flatters at once our inclination and our morals. That
is the reafon why I could hardly ever repent the following that conduct, though it has coft me my imprifonment, and all the confequences of it, which
have not been little. If I had followed a contrary
one, by accepting the offers of Mr. Servien, I fhould
have got out of trouble, and have avoided all the
misfortunes which have fince almoft crufhed me. I
could not indeed have avoided at firft an inconvenience which always attends thofe, who being at the
head of great affairs, get themfelves out of them,
without procuring fome advantages to thofe who are
engaged with them. Time would have put an end
to their complaints, which fortune might even have
turned to my advantage by fome good events. I can
perceive all this, but without regretting it, having
been led with pleafure to an oppofite conduct, by the
motive which I have mentioned. And confidering
that, except religion and good manners, all the reft
ought, in my opinion, to be looked upon as indifferent, I think I may reafonably be well fatisfied with
what I have done. I refufed, as I have told you, Mr.
Servien's propofals, which were, that the King would
grant me the fuperintendancy of his affairs in Italy,
with a penfion of 50,000 crowns a year; that I
fhould receive 100,000 crowns towards paying my
debts, and 50,000 for the furniture of a palace at
Rome, where I was to ftay for three years, after
which I was left at liberty to return to my poft at
Paris. I did not, however, refufe Mr. Servien point
blank. I continued to live civilly with him; he
came to my houfe, and I went to his. We entered
into a negotiation, but he foon judged that it would
come to nothing, becaufe his power did not extend to
any thing that related to the intereft of my friends,

though I had felt his pulse upon that subject, to which he was opposite at the bottom. The Princess Palatine, in whom I confided most, was not fully persuaded at first, that nothing was to be done for my friends; but she perceived at last, that there was even something worse than that upon the anvil, and that the ill offices of Servien, and of the Abbot Fouquet, extended further than to the breaking my negotiation. She informed me of it, and she declared to me that she would no longer meet me at Joly's, where she was used to come to me in a hackney-chair, by a back-door, between ten and eleven at night. She convinced me that there was some danger for me in these secret conferences, and she frankly told me, that I ought to treat with the Cardinal himself, because all the subalterns were against me, one for one reason, another for another. Madam de Lesdiguieres sent me word, that all I had to do was to set a good face upon the matter, and to stay at my own house: that the Cardinal, who was amusing himself on the frontiers upon trifling matters in Mr. de Turenne's army, where you may be sure he had but little to do, and who was impatient to be at Paris, but who durst not come thither so long as I remained there, would build a golden bridge for my going out of it, and would grant me whatever I should ask him. The first President had spoke to Madam de Lesdiguieres in that strain, and had told her, that to his knowledge they wished for nothing more at Court than to come to an accommodation with me, which occasioned Joly, as I remember, to say to me, 'A new blow.' It was a blow indeed; for though all these reports did not persuade me, they were an obstacle to my concluding any thing with Servien, and they at last obliged me to follow the Princess Palatine's advice, which was to treat with the Cardinal himself. I wrote to the Bishop of Châlons, to desire him to go to his Eminence, and to declare plainly my demands to him, which were the government of Anjou for Mr. de Briflac, and some posts likewise for Messieurs de Montmorenci,

d'Argend'Argenteuil, de Chateau Brian, &c. There was no manner of difficulty as to thefe laft, and I am per-fuaded there had been but little in relation to Mr. de Briffac. I.anglade, who paffed juft at that time through Châlons, retarded undefignedly the Bifhop's journey, by telling him that the Cardinal was to be at fuch a place upon fuch a day. That delay was the caufe of my imprifonment, becaufe Servien and the Abbot Fouquet haftened it, by telling the Queen that there was too much danger in leaving things in the ftate in which they were. They never ceafed to buz in her ears that I continued my correfpondence with the annuitants, that I did my beft to inflame them, and that I was likewife forming cabals with the trained-band officers. An accident happened, on the 13th of November, which contributed very much to incenfe the Court. The King held his bed of juftice at the parliament, in order to have his declaration, whereby he declared the Prince of Condé guilty of high treafon, regiftred there; and he had fent to me, the day before, Saintot, lieutenant of the ceremonies, to command me in his name to be prefent there. My anfwer to Saintot was, that I moft humbly begged leave of his Majefty to reprefent to him, that confi-dering upon what terms I was with the Prince, I thought that it would be neither juft nor becoming, that I fhould give my vote in a deliberation upon which his condemnation depended. Saintot replied to this, that fomebody having told the Queen that I would ufe that argument to excufe myfelf, her Majefty had an-fwered that it was good for nothing; and that Mr. de Guife, who owed his liberty † to the inftances which

---

† The Duke de Guife had been taken prifoner at Naples by the Spaniards, and removed to Spain, where he was kept in pri-fon for feveral years, and in all likelihood had remained there longer, if the Prince of Condé, who had now joined the Spa-niards, had not interpofed his good offices with them in the Duke's behalf; notwithftanding which, the Duke, after he had recovered his liberty, refufed to join with the Prince, or to enter into his party.

the

the Prince had made in his behalf, would be present notwithstanding. I told Saintot upon this, that if I was of the same profession as Mr. de Guise, I should glory in imitating the great actions he had lately done at Naples. You can't imagine how much the Queen was exasperated at my excuse. It was explained to her as a convincing proof of the regard I had for the Prince, and what I did purely and sincerely out of a principle of civility, to which I am still persuaded that I was obliged, passed with her for a certain proof of the measures which I had already taken, or was upon the point of taking with him. Nothing was falser, and yet nothing was more believed; and the Queen was so strongly persuaded of it, that she resolved to play quit or double to get rid of me.

Touteville, a captain in the guards, and one of the Abbot Fouquet's Satellites, hired a house pretty near Madam de Pomereux's, in which he designed to put a set of men to attack me. Le Fay, an officer in the artillery, and one of those who had assisted at the ridiculous assembly at the Palais-Royal, insinuated himself with Pau, who was at that time clerk of my kitchen, and whom you have seen since my steward, in order to be informed of him at what hours I went out at night. Pradelle had an order, signed by the King's own hand, to attack me in the streets, and to take me dead or alive. That which was given to the Marechal de Vitri, when he killed the Marechal d'Ancre, was not more strict. I have heard of this order given to Pradelle only since my return into France, by means of the Archbishop of Rheims, who said two or three years ago to the Bishop of Châlons and to Mr. de Caumartin, that he had seen the original of it. I had some notice given me time enough of Touteville's design, but I looked upon it to be but the view of a hair-brained man, who complained of me for having favoured, to his prejudice, a friend of mine, who courted one Mrs. Darmet. I ought at least to have taken a greater notice about Le Fay's offers to the clerk of my kitchen, but I looked upon

it

it as an effect only of the unquietness of the subalterns, who would set a watch upon my actions. Mr. de Briffac told me one day, that I ought to look to myself with a greater precaution; that he received informations from all hands relating to me, and that he had that moment received a billet from an unknown hand, entreating him to prevent my going that day to Rambouillet, where we had taken a fancy to go and walk, though we were very far gone in November. I made no doubt but that this billet was writ by some body belonging to the court, with a defign to found both my courage and my strength. I went thither, accompanied by two hundred gentlemen, and I found there a great many officers of the guards, and among others Rubantel, a trusty confident of the Abbot Fouquet's. I don't know whether their defign was to attack me, but they found me in a condition not to be attacked. They saluted me with a great deal of respect; I entered into conversation with some of them whom I knew, and I came back to my house as well pleased with myself as if I had committed no fault. But what I did was certainly wrong, and was only likely to incense the Court the more against me. It is natural upon such motives to grow angry and to fall into passions, in which it is very hard to preserve a right conduct. What I am going to tell you will shew you further in what my conduct was defective.

I defigned to preach during the Advent, at least upon Sundays and holy-days; in the most considerable churches in Paris; and I began upon All-Saints day at St. Germain's, which is the King's parish. Their Majefties did me the honour to affift at my sermon, and I went the next day to return them thanks. But the informations I received about the danger I ran increasing daily, I ceased to go to the Louvre, in which I committed a fault, in my opinion; for I believe that that circumstance contributed more than any other to determine the Queen to cause me to be arrested. I only say that I believe it, it being impossible to know

it.

it for certain, except one knew firſt whether Cardinal
Mazarin had deſigned before-hand that I ſhould be
arreſted, or whether he only approved of the thing
after it was done.   It is what I could never preciſely
know, thoſe that belonged to the Court having ſince
ſpoken to me very differently about it.   Lionne has
all along told me, that the Cardinal had formed no
deſign againſt my perſon ; and ſome body, whom I
have forgot, has aſſured me, that he had heard Mr.
le Tellier ſay the contrary.   What is moſt certain is,
that had it not been for a circumſtance, which I ſhall
mention immediately, I had not gone to the Louvre,
but had kept upon my guard, ſo that notwithſtand-
ing the order given to Pradelle, I had in all likelihood puzzled the matter long enough at leaſt, to
expeＣt Cardinal Mazarin's anſwer.   I was adviſed
from all hands to keep at home, and I remember that
Mr. d'Hacqueville told me one evening, with ſome
anger, ' You have been able to keep within doors
' during three weeks upon account of the Prince : is
' it poſſible that you can't ſtay at home during three
' days upon account of the King ?'

, I will tell you what prevented me from doing it.
Madam de Leſdiguieres, whom I had reaſon to think
very well informed, and who was in effeＣt commonly
ſo, preſſed me extremely to go to the Louvre, ſaying,
that I could not but own, that ſuppoſing there was
no danger for me in going, it would be beſt for me
to go for many reaſons.   I agreed to what ſhe ſaid,
if indeed I might go there with ſafety, which was a
ſuppoſition I could not allow.   ' Are you,' ſaid ſhe,
' hindered from going by that conſideration only ?'
' By no other,' anſwered I.   ' Then you may go to-
' morrow,' replied ſhe, ' for I am very well informed
' of all the game that is playing there.'   That game
was, that they had held there a ſecret council, in
which, after great conteſts, it had been reſolved that
they ſhould come to an accommodation with me, and
ſhould even give me ſatisfaＣtion in relation to my
friends.   I am fully convinced that Madam de Leſdiguieres

diguieres did not deceive me, neither am I lefs perfuaded that the Marefchal de Villeroi did not deceive
Madam de Lefdiguieres. But the Marefchal was himfelf deceived, which has been the reafon that I have
never fpoke to him of it. I was drawn in this manner to go to the Louvre upon the 19th of December,
and I was arrefted in the Queen's anti-chamber by
Mr. de Villequier, who ferved his quarter as captain
of the guards. Mr. d'Hacqueville was very near to
have prevented it. He was walking in the court as I
came into the Louvre, and joining me as I came out
of my coach, we went together to Madam de Villeroi, where I defigned to ftay till the King could be
waited upon. That gentleman left me there, and
went up ftairs, where he met with Montmege, who
told him, that it was in every body's mouth that I
was going to be arrefted. Mr. d'Hacqueville hearing this, came down ftairs as faft as he could to inform me of it, and to carry me away by the kitchen-
court, which was next to Madam de Villeroi's apartment. I was gone up, but he miffed me but a moment, which moment had infallibly procured my
liberty. I am as much obliged to Mr. d'Hacqueville
as if he had got me fafe away; but I know that
gentleman too well not to be convinced that it was
otherwife with him. Mr. de Villequier carried me to
an apartment where the officers of the King's kitchen
brought me fome dinner. They took it mighty ill at
Court that I had dined very heartily, fo great is the
corruption and bafenefs of courtiers. I had more
reafon to take it ill to have my pockets turned infide
out, as they do to pick-pockets. Mr. de Villequier
had orders to do it, though it was an uncommon
thing. They found there nothing but a letter of the
King of England's *, who charged me to make fome
attempt at Rome towards raifing him a fum of money

---

* The whole account, in relation to this letter, is inferted in
the fourth volume, taken from the Earl of Clarendon's Hiftory
of the Rebellion.

there-

there. The noise of this letter was immediately
spread up and down the Court; and a man of quality, whose name I shall forbear to mention in regard
to one of his brothers who is my friend, thought to
make his court by saying, that it must needs be a
letter from the Protector and not the King of England. How base that was! About three in the afternoon I was carried all along the great gallery of the
Louvre, and I was brought down the stairs of the pa-
vilion of the Dutchess of Orleans. We met with one
of the King's coaches, into which I was put, having
with me Mr. de Villequier, and five or six officers of
the life-guards. The coach was driven at first towards
the city, but it turned of a sudden towards the gate
of the conference. It was guarded by the Marechal
d'Albret, at the head of the Gens d'Armes; by Mr.
de la Vauguyon, at the head of the light-horse; and
by Mr. de Vennes, lieutenant-colonel of the regiment of guards, who had with him eight companies
of that regiment. As they designed to carry me out
by the gate of St. Anthony, and as they must go near
two other gates before they got thither, they had
posted at each gate a battalion of Switzers, who presented their pikes to the town as we went by. You
see by this that there was a great deal of precaution
used, and that without any manner of need. Not
one soul stirred in the city. There appeared there
sorrow and consternation, but it was not carried to
any commotion, either because the consternation was
in effect too great, or because those that were well
affected to me were discouraged to find no body appear
that would head them. I have heard since people
speak differently about it. Le Houx, a butcher, but
a man of credit with the people, has told me that all
the butchers of the place Aux-Veaux were upon the
point of taking up arms; and that if the Duke de
Brissac had not assured them that that was a sure way
to have me murdered, he had set up barricadoes at
that quarter with the greatest ease possible. L'Espi-
nal has told me the like of the whole street of Mont-
martre.

martre. But as I think, the Marquis de Château-Renaut, who was that whole day very bufy in attempting to ftir up the people, has told me that he found no room to do it; and I know for certain, that Malclerc, who ran up and down, to the fame purpofe, over the bridges of Nôtre-Dame and of St. Michael, which were at my difpofal, found all the women there crying, and all the men in a fright, and incapable of doing any thing. However no body can be anfwerable for what might have happened, had there been but a fword drawn. When there is none drawn on thefe occafions, every body judges that nothing could have been done ; and if there had been no barricadoes at the taking of Mr. de Brouffel, thofe that had fpoke the leaft word, even of the poffibility of the thing, had been laughed at. I arrived at Vincennes betwixt eight and nine at night, and the Marefchal d'Albret having afked me as I came out of the coach, if I had no meffage to fend to the King ; I anfwered him, that I fhould think it a want of refpect in me if I took that liberty.

I was carried into a great room where there was neither hangings nor bed. The bed that was fet up about eleven at night was of Indian filk, which was not very proper for the winter feafon. I flept very well, which ought not to be attributed to any firmnefs, becaufe misfortunes naturally produce that effect on me *. I have experienced in more than one occafion, that it keeps me awake in the day-time, and inclines me to fleep at night. This is not, as I have faid, the effect of any firmnefs of mind, having obferved after a thorough examination, that it proceeds from the heavinefs into which I fall, when the reflections I make upon any thing that troubles me, are not diverted by my ftruggling againft them.

* Mr. de St. Evremont, fpeaking of Mademoifelle de Beverweert, fifter to the late Countefs of Arlington, &c. fays, that fhe never flept fo well as when fhe was under fome great affliction. See the Works of St. Evremond, publifhed in Holland by Mr. des Maizeaux, volume the fourth, p. 55.

I take :

I take a mighty pleafure in unfolding myfelf to you,
if I may ufe that expreffion, and in giving you an
account of the moft fecret motions of my heart.

: I was obliged to rife the next morning without any
fire, there being no wood to make any ; but the three
exempts of the guards that were with me when I
came firft to the caftle, were fo kind as to affure me
that I fhould have fome the next day. He that was
left to ftay in the room with me, kept the next day
the wood for himfelf, and fo he did for a whole
fortnight together, that I was left without any fire at
Chriftmas in a room as big as a church. That
exempt's name was Croifat, he was a Gafcon, and
had been, at leaft as the report went, valet-de-chambre to Servien. I do not believe that it had been
poffible to have found his like in the whole world.
He took away from me my linen, my cloaths, my
fhoes, and I was fometimes obliged to ftay in bed for
eight or ten days together, for want of any thing to
put on. I do not believe that I could have been
treated in that manner, without an exprefs order for
it, and without a formed defign to kill me with
grief. I armed myfelf againft that defign, and I
refolved not to die at leaft that fort of death. I
diverted myfelf at firft in compofing the life of my
exempt, who was as great a rogue, without any
exaggeration, as Lazarilles of Tormes *, or Bufcon.
I brought him at laft to ceafe to torment me, by taking no manner of notice of whatever he could fay or
do. I never appeared angry at him, I never complained of any thing, and never gave him the leaft
room to think that I was offended at any thing he
faid, though he faid not one word but with an intent
to vex me. He caufed a little garden of two or three
fathom to be made in the yard belonging to the
tower, and as I was afking him what he intended to
do with it, he told me that he defigned to have afpa-

* Two Spanifh rogues, whofe lives and actions have been
written in Spanifh, and have been tranflated in moft other
languages.

ragus

ragus in it, which you muſt obſerve are three years
a growing. This was one of his ſofteſt ſayings, and
I was regaled every day with twenty ſuch, which I
took care to ſwallow with as much eaſe as poſſible,
but that did but increaſe his brutiſhneſs, becauſe he
ſaid that I laughed at him. -

The inſtances of the chapter of the cathedral, and
of all the Curates of Páris, who acted for me to the
utmoſt of their power, though my uncle, who was
the weakeſt man in the world, and jealous of me even
to the making himſelf ridiculous, ſupported them but
very faintly ; their inſtances, I ſay, obliged the Court
to explain themſelves about the cauſes of my impri-
ſonment, which was done by the mouth of the Chancellor. That magiſtrate declared to theſe ſeveral
bodies, in the preſence of the King and of the Queen-
mother, that his Majeſty had cauſed me to be arreſted
for my own good only, and to hinder me from executing what there was room to believe I had in view.
The Chancellor has told me ſince my return into
France, that it was he that perſuaded the Queen to
approve that he ſhould give that turn to this affair,
under pretence of eluding more plauſibly the demand
which the church of Paris made in a body, either
to bring me to a trial, or to ſet me at liberty ; and
he added, that his true deſign had been to ſerve me,
in obliging the Court to acknowledge my innocence,
at leaſt as to matters paſt.

It is certain that my friends made a mighty uſe of
that anſwer of the Chancellor's; which was ſet off as
it ought, in two or three very ingenious pamphlets.
Mr. de Caumartin did, in this conjuncture and in
thoſe that followed; all that the moſt ſincere friend-
ſhip and the moſt refined honour could inſpire him
with. Mr. d'Hacqueville redoubled his care and his
zeal for me. The chapter of Nôtre-Dame cauſed an
anthem to be ſung every day publicly, and expreſly
for my liberty. Not one of the curates, except that
of St. Bartholomew, forſook me. The Sorbonne ſignalized itſelf, and even many of the regulars declared

L 6   openly

openly and vigorously for me. The Bishop of Châlons warmed the hearts and the minds of others, by his reputation and his example. This kind of general stirring obliged the Court to use me a little better than they had done at first. I was allowed a certain number of books, but without any ink or paper, and I had likewise a valet de chambre and a physician granted me; upon which occasion I must not omit a circumstance somewhat remarkable. This physician, who was a man of merit and of reputation in his profession, and whose name was Vacherot, told me the same day that he arrived at Vincennes, that Mr. de Caumartin had charged him to inform me, that Goisel, an advocate who had foretold the liberty of Mr. de Beaufort, had assured him that I should have mine in the month of March, but in an imperfect manner, and that I should not have it fully and intirely till the month of August. You will find by the sequel that the prediction was true.

I applied myself very much to study during the whole time of my imprisonment at Vincennes, which lasted fifteen months, and I employed in it not only the days, but even the nights. I made a particular study of the Latin tongue, to which I found that it is impossible to apply one's self too much, because that study comprehends all others. I made some observations upon the Greek tongue, and upon the ninth decade of Livy, which I had very much liked formerly, and in which I met again with a new relish. In imitation of Boëtius, I composed the Consolation of Theology, wherein I shewed that every prisoner ought to endeavour to make himself the Vinctus in Christo, which St. Paul speaks of. I gathered in a kind of Silva a great many things upon different subjects, and among others an application for the use of the church of Paris, of what was contained in the book of the acts of the Church of Milan, and I intitled that work Partus Vincennarum. My exempt omitted nothing to interrupt the quiet of my studies, and to give me as much vexation as he thought he could. He told me

one

one day, that the King had ordered him to carry me upon the plat-form to take the air. When he thought that I took some pleasure there, he then told me with a joy that he could not have diffembled if he would, that he had received a counter-order. My anfwer was, that it came very pat, becaufe the air which was too fharp upon the platform, had brought a pain into my head. Four days after he propofed to me to go down and fee my guards play at tennis. I defired to be excufed, becaufe the air would be too piercing, but he forced me to go, faying that the King, who took a greater care of my health than I imagined, had commanded him to make me ufe fome exercife. Ceafing afterwards to carry me thither, he told me for his excufe, that he had fome reafons for it which he could not difcover to me. I had indeed put myfelf above thefe little chicanes, which I defpifed at the bottom, and was not moved with. But I confefs that I had not the fame ftrength of mind, in refpect to the fubftance of the thing, which was my imprifonment; and when I came, every morning when I was awake, to confider that I was in the power of my enemies, I found nothing in me that relifhed of the Stoick. I kept this trouble hid from every foul, and that was the reafon that it became extreme. The hiding of it was an effect of that pride which is natural to man, and I remember that I was twenty times a day thinking to myfelf that an imprifonment for ftate matters was the very worft fort of imprifonment.

You have already feen that I made ufe of ftudy to divert my trouble. I fometimes made ufe likewife of other means. I had fome rabbits upon the platform; I kept turtles in one of the turrets, and pigeons in the other. The continual inftances of the church of Paris procured me from time to time thefe innocent diverfions, which, though mixed with a thoufand chicanes, amufed me however, and the more agreeably, becaufe I had often thought upon them, when it came into my mind to confider what I fhould pafs my time in, if ever I came to be arrefted. Thefe diverfions

fions however did not amufe me fo much as to hinder
me from thinking earneftly upon the means of efcaping out of prifon, and the correfpondence which I had
all along with my friends gave me room to think of
it, and to hope for fome fuccefs.

The ninth day of my imprifonment, one of my
two guards named Carpentier, approached near me
whilft his comrade was afleep (for I was watched both
night and day at leaft by one of the two) and he flipt
a note into my hand, which at firft fight I knew to
come from Madam de Pomereu. The note contained
only thefe words : ' Truft the bearer, and write a
' line by him.' He then gave me a pencil, and a
bit of paper, on which I only writ that I had received
the note. Madame de Pomereu had found means to
become acquainted with the wife of this Carpentier,
and had given her 500 crowns for this firft fervice.
The hufband was ufed to that fort of trade, and had
not been unferviceable to Mr. de Beaufort in procuring his liberty. He is dead himfelf, and fo are likewife his wife and family, which gives me room to be
the more free. But confidering that fome unforefeen
accident may bring to light whatever is fet down in
writing, you muft give me leave to enter into no
particulars that relate to the other manner of corref-
ponding with my friends, which I had befides this,
and in which fome of the perfons concerned are ftill
living. It is enough that I tell you, that notwithftanding the changing of three exempts, and of 24
life-guardmen, who fucceeded one another during
the 15 months I ftaid at Vincennes, my correfpondence was never interrupted.

I received twice a week regularly letters from Madam
de Pomereu, and from Meffieurs de Caumartin and
d'Hacqueville, which tended all towards feeking out
means to fet me at liberty. The fhorteft way was to
efcape out of my prifon. I made two attempts towards
it, one of which was fuggefted to me by my phyfician, who underftood mathematicks. He took it
into his head to file off the bar of the grate of a little
window

window that was in the chapel where I heard
mafs, and to tie to the window a fort of machine;
with which I might, 'tis true, have got down
eafily enough from the third ftory wherein I was
lodged, into the ditch. But confidering that I muft
from thence climb up the wall, from whence there
was no way afterwards of getting down, he quitted
that thought, which indeed was impracticable, and
we ftuck to another which in all likelihood would
have done, if it had not pleafed Providence to prevent
the execution of it. I had obferved at the time that
I was carried upon the platform, that there was at the
very top of it a cavity, the ufe of which I could never
guefs. It was about half filled up, but there was
room enough left to get down into it, and to hide
one's felf in it. This brought a thought into my
head, that upon the day that Carpentier was to guard
me, and whilft all the reft of the guards, except his
comrade, were at dinner, it would be an eafy matter
to make that comrade drunk. The man, whofe
name was Tourville, was old, and a few glaffes of
wine were enough to make him dead drunk, as Carpentier had experienced it more than once. I propofed to make ufe of that moment to go upon the
platform, and to hide myfelf in the cavity which I
have mentioned, with a provifion of fome loaves,
and of fome bottles both of wine and water. Carpentier owned that this firft ftep was not only poffible,
but even eafy, and what made it the more fo, was
that the two guards who were to relieve his comrade
and him, had always had the civility not to come
into my chamber, but ftay at the door till they thought
I was awake; for I had ufed myfelf to fleep in the
afternoon, or at leaft to make my guards think fo.
Carpentier was to have tied two cords to the window
of the gallery, through which Mr. de Beaufort had
efcaped, and to have thrown into the ditch a woven
engine, which Mr. Vacherot had been working upon
all night long in his chamber, by means of which it
might have been thought that I had got up the wall,
which

which had been made fince Mr. de Beaufort's efcape.
This trufty guard was at the fame time to have given
an alarm, as if he had feen me pafs into the gallery,
and to have fhewn his fword ftained with blood, as
if he had wounded me in purfuing me. This alarm
would have gathered together the whole guard, who
had found the cords tied to the window. They
would have perceived in the ditch the engine I mentioned, ftained likewife with blood. Eight or ten
men on horfeback were to have appeared in the wood
that furrounds Vincennes, with piftols in their hands,
ready to receive me. A man with a red calot on his
head was to have been feen as running out of Vincennes, and after having joined thofe that were waiting for him, he was to have marched with part of
them towards Mezieres, whilft the others would have
marched another way. The guns were to have been
fired at Mezieres three or four days after, as if I was
actually arrived there. Who would ever have thought
that I had been in the hole I have mentioned? They
would in all likelihood have removed the guards from
the caftle of Vincennes, and would have left there
only the foldiers that were ufually in it, who had
given leave to the inhabitants of Paris to come in for
two-pence a-piece to fee the window and the cord I
efcaped by, as they did thofe of Mr. de Beaufort.
My friends had come thither out of curiofity as well
as the reft, they had difguifed me in a woman's or a
monk's habit, or what elfe you pleafe, and I had got
away without the leaft fufpicion. I do not think that
any thing could have rendered the Court more ridiculous than my efcaping in this manner. It was fo
extraordinary, that it may appear impoffible, notwithftanding which it was certainly eafy, and I am
fully perfuaded that the fuccefs would have been
infallible, if one of the guards, whofe name was
l'Efcarmouche, had not fpoiled it by mere accident.
He was fent to Vincennes in the room of another who
fell fick, and being an old hard-hearted and obferving man, he told the exempt, that he did not conceive

why

why he did not caufe a door to be made at the foot
of the little ftair-cafe that went up to the platform :
the door was fet up there the next morning, and fo
my projeƈt came to nothing. That fame l'Efcarmouche told me in a very friendly manner that fame
evening, that if his Majefty was pleafed to order it,
he would ftrangle me.

I did not apply myfelf fo entirely to the finding out
the means of efcaping from Vincennes, as to negleƈt
thofe which might oblige my enemies to fet me at
liberty. The Abbot Charrier, who went for Rome
the very next day after my being arrefted, found Pope
Innocent incenfed at it even to a rage, and ready to
thunder out excommunications upon the authors of a
deed, for which he had the examples of what his pre-
deceffors had done in fome like cafes. He explained
himfelf upon it with an extreme refentment to the
ambaffador of France. He fent Mr. Marini, Archbifhop of Avignon, as nuncio in extraordinary, to
demand my liberty. The King, on his fide, refolved
upon maintaining his royal authority. He fent to
forbid Monfignor Marini to come further than Lyons.
The Pope grew afraid of expofing both his own power
and that of the church, to the rage of a madman,
meaning Mazarin, for he ufed that expreffion, fpeaking to the Abbot Charrier ; to whom he faid further :
' Furnifh me with an army, and I will fend a legate
' at the head of it.' It would have been no eafy
matter to have furnifhed him with an army, but the
thing would not have been impoffible, if thofe that
were obliged to ftand my friends on this occafion had
not failed me.

You have feen in the fecond volume of thefe memoirs
that I might have reckoned upon the town of Mezieres *, becaufe Buffi-lamet, who was governor of it,

* The towns of Mezieres and of Charleville are both in
Champaign, and fituated on the river Maeze, and at a very fmall
diftance one from the other. The place called Mont-Olimpe
lies over againft Charleville, on the other fide of the river.

was my particular friend; and that I had likewife a
right to reckon upon Charleville and the Mont-
Olimpe, becaufe Mr. de Noirmoutier had been made
governor of thefe two places, by my means only.
You have likewife feen that this laft had failed me at
the time that Cardinal Mazarin came back into
France. He thought it fufficient for his juftification
to tell every body that he would ferve me to all intents
and purpofes in what concerned my perfon; and there
being hardly any thing that touches the perfon of a
man nearer than imprifonment, Noirmoutier joined
himfelf publicly to Buffi-lamet, as foon as I was
arrefted, and they wrote a letter jointly to the Cardinal, whereby they declared that they fhould be
forced to carry matters to all manner of extremities,
if I was detained longer in prifon. The places of
which thefe two gentlemen were governors, are not
to be attacked when they are of the fame party, and
are confequently of an extreme importance; but what
made them be at this time ftill of a greater, was that
the Prince, who at the firft news he had of my deten-
tion, declared that he would do without exception
all that my friends fhould defire of him towards procuring my liberty, had offered the two governors to
fend the whole forces of Spain to their affiftance.
Belle-Ifle befides, of which Mr. de Retz was mafter,
was no contemptible place, becaufe of its nearnefs to
England, on which France could not depend at that
time; and Bourdeaux, as well as Brouage, were ftill
at that time holding out for the Prince. This and
many other circumftances of that nature, as for
example the difpofition of the Count d'Autel, who
was in Bethune, and who would have certainly ftirred
in my favour, if he had feen any enterprize well
formed; this, I fay, made many people believe that
there was wherewithal to have formed fuch an enterprize, that is, that there was a fufficient quantity of
ftuff, but by ill luck there was nobody capable of
making a right ufe of it. The intentions of the
Duke de Retz, my brother, were good, but he was

unfit

unfit for any great defign, and he was befides kept, back by his wife, and by his father-in-law. The; Duke de Briffac, who had been ordered to retire,· was not a man at all fit to head an affair. The Duke de Noirmoutier was the moft venturefome, but he was brought over at firft to the Court party by Madam de Chevreufe, and by Laigues, to whom the Cardinal faid in exprefs terms, that they fhould be anfwerable to him for the actions of their friends, and that if they caufed a fingle gun to be fired, they fhould fee how it fhould fare with them both. Mr. de Noirmoutier, whofe friendfhip for me, as you have already feen, was not over violent, yielded to the inftances of his friends, and of his lady, who is not one of the beft of her fex, and he promifed the Court * that, he would give me only appearances, but would in, reality do nothing for me.

That gentleman was as good as his word; he did not any ways traverfe the fiege of Stenay,· which the King made at that time. He eluded all the propofals of the Prince, and he contented himfelf with, continuing to fpeak and write in my behalf, and having many guns fired when my health was drank. He could hardly however have acted that part long, if Buffi-lamet, who was a man of fenfe and refolution,, had lived, This laft fpoke to Malclerc, whom my friends had fent to him, in this very manner: ' Noir-, ' moutier defigns to amufe me, but I fhall bring him ' to declare himfelf, or I fhall get mafter of his ' place.' The poor gentleman died of an apoplexy that very night. The Chevalier de Lamet; who was a major in the place, being become the mafter of it by the other's death, the Vifcount his eldeft-brother threw himfelf into it, and remained very faithfully attached to my intereft. The Abbot de Lamet, their

---

* The Marefchal de Villeroy gave notice of that engagement with the Court to Madam de Lefdiguieres upon the 14th day of my imprifonment. N. B. This note, which I have fet down as it is in the French copy, feems to have been written by the Cardinal de Retz himfelf,

coufin

cousin and mine, and who was master of my chamber [*], staid all the while at Mezieres, and served me there with all the zeal imaginable; but one place being able to do no good without the help of the other, nothing was done, and Mezieres, Charieville, and the Mont-Olimpe, were for me without being useful to me. It cost me however a large sum of money, which Mr. de Retz, my brother, lent for subsisting the garrison, and which I have repaid since with interest.

You may judge that all these particulars, which I was punctually informed of, did not give me a little trouble, but the greatest was my hiding the knowledge I had of them; and I remember that Mr. de Pradelle, who commanded the French and Switz guards that were in the castle, and who had the liberty to see me, as well as Mr. de Maupeou de Noisi, who was a captain in the guards; I remember, I say, that Mr. de Pradelle told me one day that he was grieved at heart at a piece of news which he thought himself obliged to mention to me, and that was the death of Mr. de Bussi-lamet. I appeared surprized at it, though I knew it as well as he. This Mr. de Pradelle was so kind as to comfort me in this same conversation, against the fear I might have that they would undertake something at Mezieres against his Majesty's service, and he assured me that that place was in the hands of the officer whom the King had sent to command there. Observe, I beseech you, that I had received the day before a billet from the Viscount Lamet, who assured me that he was master of it, and that I might rely upon him. I received however for truth whatever Pradelle was pleased to tell me upon that account, as well as most of his other discourses, which were such as are commonly used towards prisoners of state. I say, that I received most of his other discourses for truth, because there were some.

[*] An officer who introduces persons into a Cardinal's presence, and who has the direction of his chamber.

which.

which I could not appear to take in that manner.
That gentleman, whose talk was commonly about the
weather, or about matters past before my imprisonment, took it once into his head to acquaint me with
the happy return of Cardinal Mazarin to Paris. He
embellished his relation with all the ornaments which
he thought might displease me, and he magnified
extremely the fine reception that was made him at the
town-house. I had already been informed of it, and
that Mr. Vedeau had harangued him with all the
meanness possible. I answered Pradelle, that I was
not surprized at it : ' Nor will you be sorry, Sir, re-
' plied he, when you know how much regard the
' Cardinal has for you : he has commanded me to
' wait on you, and to assure you of his most humble
' services ; and he begs that you would believe that he
' will leave nothing undone to serve you.' I seemed
as if my head had been full of other things which
prevented my taking notice of this compliment, and
I asked him I do not know what question, upon a
subject that was altogether foreign to the Cardinal.
He began to mention the thing afresh, and as he was
pressing me to give him an answer, I told him that I
would not have failed to have shewn my gratitude
when he spoke first, if I had not been persuaded that
the respect which a prisoner owes the King takes away
from him the leave of explaining himself in any
manner upon any thing that relates to his liberty, till
it has pleased the King to restore it him. He understood what I meant ; he tried to persuade me to send
the Cardinal a more obliging answer ; but he lost his
labour.

The advices which Cardinal Mazarin received from
Rome, and the heat people appeared in, and which
even increased in Poitou and at Paris, in respect to my
imprisonment, obliged him to give at least some outward
demonstrations of his intending me my liberty, and
he made use to that purpose of the credulity of Monsignor Bagni, the Pope's Nuncio in France, a man of
probity, and of a distinguished birth ; but an easy
man,

man, and altogether fit to be deceived. The Cardinal sent him to me, accompanied by Messieurs de Brienne and le Tellier, with proposals for granting me my liberty and great advantages, in case I would resign the Coadjutorship of Paris. My friends having sent me notice that this step would be taken, I heard the proposal, and answered it in a set speech, very much becoming an ecclesiastick, and which even shamed Monsignor Bagni, and brought upon him afterwards a very sharp reprimand from Rome. This speech, which had been sent me by Mr. de Caumartin, and which was very fine and very much to the purpose, was printed at Paris the next day. The Court was extremely vexed at it. I had another exempt and other guards, but this change brought no interruption to my commerce with my friends.

The instances which the chapter of Nôtre-Dame made, obliged the Court to give leave to a canon of that body to be with me, and the chapter chose one who was of the family of Mr. de Braguelone, who had been bred up with me at the college, and to whom I had even given my prebend. The prison became too tiresome for him, though he had shut himself up in it with joy, for my sake. He fell into a deep melancholy, of which I took notice, and did what lay in my power to persuade him to leave me, but he would never hearken to it. He was seized with a fever, in the fourth fit of which he cut his own throat with a razor. They had the civility in the castle, during the whole time I staid there, to hide from me the manner in which he died ; but the tragical end of that poor gentleman was enlarged upon by my friends, which did not diminish the compassion which the people had for me, nor did that compassion diminish the fears of the Cardinal. These fears brought into his head the thought of transferring me either to Amiens, or to Brest, or to Havre-de-Grace. I was informed of it, and I counterfeited an illness. Vesou was sent to see whether I was really sick. I was differently informed about the report he made. What prevented

3   my

my being removed was the death of the Archbishop of Paris my uncle, which stirred up the minds of the people to such a degree, that the Court thought it fitter to appease them than to increase their discontent. The manner in which I was served in this affair, has something in it very wonderful.

My uncle died at four in the morning, and at five the possession of the Archbishoprick was seized in my name, by virtue of a letter of attorney from me, which appeared to be in very good form * ; and Mr. le Tellier, who arrived at Nôtre-Dame at five and a quarter, to oppose it in the King's name, had the satisfaction to hear my bulls fulminated † in the lobby. Whatever is surprizing stirs up the people. This scene was surprizing to the last degree, nothing being more extraordinary than the conjunction of the necessary formalities to an action of that nature, at a time when nobody thought it possible to have observed any one of them. The curates grew still warmer than usual ; my friends blowed the fire ; the people wanted their Archbishop ; the Nuntio, who thought he had been doubly abused by the Court, spoke very high, and threatened them there with ecclesiastical censures. A pamphlet was published, which proved, that all the churches must be shut up. The Cardinal was seized with fear, and his fears inclining him always to negotiate, a negotiation was begun. He was not ignorant of the advantage those have who negotiate with others that are not well informed how matters go. He thought half the time that I was of that number, and he believed it in this conjuncture. He got a hundred proposals to be made to me of permutations, of rich abbeys, of governments, of being restored to the King's favour, and of a solid union with the minister. Pradelle and my exempt spoke of nothing else from morning till night. I had a greater liberty allowed me than ordinary,

* All this was done by the contrivance of Mr. de Caumartin. See Joli's Memoirs, Vol. II. p. 61.

† This verb, which is often taken in another sense, is likewise used for the executing any deed coming from the court of Rome.

They

They would no longer fuffer me to ftay in my chamber, if the weather could in the leaft permit that I
might walk upon the platform. I feigned as if I reflected not in the leaft upon all this change, being
informed by my friends of what was acting underhand.
They fent me word to keep myfelf clofe, and not to
open myfelf in any manner to any body, becaufe they
knew for certain, by the informations they had, that
there was nothing folid at the bottom of the negociation, and that the Court intended only to make me
explain myfelf in a manner which they might take
hold of there; as if the refigning my Archbifhoprick
was not a thing impoffible, that the zeal of the clergy,
and of the people for me, might thereby grow cooler. I
followed exactly my friends inftructions*, infomuch that
Mr. de Noailles, captain of the guards in waiting,
coming to me by the King's order, and making me a
fpeech far different from his manners and from his inclination, which had nothing in it but fweet and civil
(for Mazarin obliged him to fpeak to me much more
like an Aga of the Janizaries, than like an officer
of a Chriftian King) I defired his leave to give him
my anfwer down in writing. I cannot remember the
words, but I know that it expreffed a fovereign contempt for the Cardinal's threats, as well as for his
promifes, and an unalterable refolution not to refign
the Archbifhoprick of Paris.

I received a letter from my friends the very next
day, which informed me that they had got my anfwer
to Mr. de Noailles immediately printed, and what admirable effect it had produced.   They likewife fent me
word, that the Prefident de Bellievre was ordered to
come and make a fecond attempt upon me the next
day.   He came, and offered me in the King's name,
the abbeys of St. Lucien de Beauvais, of St. Meddard
de Soiffons, of St. Germain d'Auxerre, of Barbeau,

---

* Joli, in the account he gives of this whole tranfaction, differs
very much from the Cardinal de Retz, whom, according to his
ufual cuftom, he reprefents as a weak man, which is not at all the
character given him by other writers.

of

of St. Martin de Pontoife, of St. Aubin d'Angers,
and of Orcan : ' provided (added he) ' that you re-
' nounce the Archbifhoprick of Paris, and provided.
' that'——he ftopped at that word, and looking upon
me, he faid : ' I have hitherto fpoke in a manner
' anfwerable to my commiffion, but it is time for me
' to begin to laugh at the Sicilian, who is weak
' enough to employ me in a work of this nature :
' And provided (continued he) that you give twelve
' of your friends for fureties that you will ratify your
' renunciation the moment that you are fet at liberty.
' ——This is not all (added he) I am to be one of
' the twelve, as are likewife Meffieurs de Retz, de
' Briffac, de Montrefor, de Caumartin, d'Hacque-
' ville, &c. Hear me fpeak (faid he) and do not
' anfwer me, I beg of you, till I have faid all I have
' to fay. Moft of your friends are perfuaded, that
' your only bufinefs is to hold out, and that the Court
' will grant you your liberty, and be fatisfied with
' getting rid of you, and fending you to Rome. That
' is a miftake. The Court is for having your renun-
' ciation any way. When I fay the Court, I mean
' Mazarin, for the Queen is grieved at heart to hear
' your liberty fo much as mentioned. Le Tellier fays,
' that the Cardinal muft be out of his wits. The
' Abbot Fouquet is enraged ; and Servien confents to
' it, only becaufe the others are againft it. We muft
' therefore lay down as inconteftably true, that Maza-
' rin is the only man that is for your liberty, and that
' he is for it, only becaufe he thinks himfelf fufficiently
' revenged of you, by making you lofe the Arch-
' bifhoprick of Paris. This is, at leaft, the pretence
' he makes ufe of, for at the bottom it is not what de-
' termines him. It is only the fear he is poffeffed
' with at this inftant, in refpect to the Nuntio, to the
' chapter, to the curates, to the people : I fay, at this
' inftant of the death of the Archbifhop, of which
' the confequence can at moft be an infurrection,
' which not being fupported, muft fall to nothing.
' But I fay more, for I maintain that it will produce

VOL. III. M ' no

' no such consequence. The Nuntio will threaten, and
' do nothing more; the chapter will make remon-
' strances that will be of no use; the curates will be-
' wail you in their pulpits, and that will be all; the
' people will make a noise, but will not take up arms.
' I am near at hand to see all these things, the event of
' which will be your being transferred either to Havre-
' de Grace, or to Brest, there to remain in the hands,
' and at the disposal of your enemies, who will after-
' wards do what they please with you. I know that
' Mazarin is not a man that loves blood, and yet I
' tremble when I consider what Mr. de Noailles has
' said to you, That they were resolved to dispatch
' matters, and to follow the steps which have so often
' been taken in other countries. Their resolving at
' Court to speak in this manner, is what makes me
' tremble. Great souls do it sometimes to serve their
' ends, but without any intent to execute what they
' say. Mean souls had rather do the thing than speak
' the words. From what I have said you will conclude,
' that I am for your resigning your post. Far from
' it. I am come hither to tell you that you will bring
' a disgrace upon yourself if you do it, and that you
' are obliged in this conjuncture, to answer at the
' expence of your life, and of your liberty, which I
' know to be dearer to you than life, the great expec-
' tation people are in upon your account. The time
' is come, when you ought more than ever to practise
' the maxims which we have so often bantered you
' upon : *I stand in fear neither of sword nor poison :*
' *Nothing but what is within me can move me : Death*
' *is to be met with every where.* These have been
' your frequent sayings, and they are now to be used
' in the answer you are to give those who shall speak to
' you about your renunciation. You have hitherto
' discharged your duty in a worthy manner, and no-
' body can reasonably find fault with your behaviour.
' I should therefore be to blame if I should undertake
' to persuade you to change your measures. It is not
' what I require of you. The thing I would ask of

' you

' you is, that you would tell me plainly whether you
' would accept of your liberty if it was offered you
' for a trifle ?' Seeing me fmile at that word : ' Stay,
' (faid he) and I will convince you that the thing is not
' impoffible. Do you reckon a refignation of the
' Archbifhoprick of Paris, dated in the caftle of Vin-
' cennes, where you are detained prifoner, as a valid
' act ?' ' No, (anfwered I) and therefore my enemies
' are not fatisfied with that, but will have fureties for
' the having it ratified afterwards.' ' But if I can
' find any room,' (replied the Prefident de Bellievre)
' to make the Court defift from their requiring fureties,
' what will you then think ?' ' I will refign the Arch-
' bifhoprick to-morrow,' (anfwered I.) He then explained to me all that he had done ; he told me, that he
would never undertake to come to me with any propofals, till he had clearly perceived that the real intent
of the Cardinal was to fet me at liberty, and till he
had found him likewife difpofed to defift from requiring
any fureties. He added, that befides this propofal of
having fuch fureties as were now demanded, there
were no manner of ways that he had not thought upon
to make my act of refignment a valid act. That his
firft thought had been to get a writing figned by the
chapter, the curates, and the Sorbonne, whereby they
fhould engage to difown me for their Archbifhop, in
cafe I fhould refufe to ratify my deed of refignment,
after my being fet at liberty. That the fecond had
been, to have me brought to the Louvre, to affemble
there all the ecclefiaftical bodies of the city, and to
make me engage my word to the King in all their
prefence, that I would ftand to my deed. ' In fhort,
' (faid the Prefident) there are no ways whatfoever
' but what have come into his head to fatisfy his
' diftruft. You may perceive it by what I have faid,
' though I have not faid half of what I have feen.
' Knowing him as I do, I have not thought fit to con-
' tradict him in any thing. But he has of himfelf
' rejected thefe ridiculous fancies, except that of the
' twelve fureties, which is indeed more practicable

' than

‘ than the others.   It will, however, get out of his
‘ head likewife, provided you remain firm in rejecting
‘ it.   I fhall be forced to infift upon it with obftinacy,
‘ and you muft refufe it with courage, as thinking it
‘ fhameful for you.   By this means we fhall bring the
‘ Sicilian to accept of an expedient which he will be well
‘ pleafed with, becaufe he will think it very proper to
‘ deceive you.   This expedient will be to truft you in
‘ the hands either of Mr. d’Hocquincourt or of Mr.
‘ de la Meilleraie, till the Pope hath accepted of your
‘ refignation.   The Cardinal will think that refig-
‘ nation good, if it is once accepted of by the Pope,
‘ and he is fo ignorant in our laws, that he was faying
‘ fo to me no longer ago than yefterday.’

I interrupted the firft Prefident, to tell him that
this expedient was good for nothing, becaufe the
Pope would refufe to accept it.   ‘ No matter, (re-
‘ plied he) that is the worft that can happen, and
‘ there is even a remedy to that.   When that expe-
‘ dient is propofed, in accepting of it you muft
‘ ftipulate, that happen what will, you fhall not be
‘ put again into the King’s power, but upon my
‘ direction; and I fhall take care to get a writing in
‘ good form, from the gentleman in whofe hands you
‘ are intrufted, not to deliver you up but upon my
‘ order.   You ought to truft me: Follow my direc-
‘ tions, and my heart gives me that God will perfect
‘ the work.’

We difcuffed the matter to the very bottom; we
examined thoroughly which of the two we fhould
chufe, Mr. d’Hocquincourt, or Mr. de la Meilleraie.
We agreed upon every thing, and the firft Prefident
left the caftle, telling Mr. de Pradelle with tears in
his eyes: ‘ I find in him an invincible obftinacy: I
‘ am forry at heart.   Not that he cares now for the
‘ Archbifhoprick; that would not be an obftacle.
‘ But he thinks his honour wounded by the propofals
‘ that are made to him of fureties and guarantees.
‘ He will never yield, and I will meddle no longer in
‘ it: There’s nothing to be done.’

3   Pradelle,

Pradelle, who was much more devoted to the Abbot Fouquet than to the Cardinal, and who knew that the Abbot was in no manner for my being set at liberty, acquainted him immediately with this piece of news, upon which he was ordered by the Abbot to mention to me indirectly and without affectation, in the conversation we should have together, the Archbishoprick of Rheims, and other immense recompences, with an intent that when proposals of a lesser sort should be offered me, I should appear more stiff, in hopes that my stiffness would offend Mazarin the more. I perceived easily enough what they drove at, by comparing together what I knew to be true, because I had it from Mr. de Bellievre and my other friends, and what I heard from Pradelle, and from d'Avanton, who was my exempt. This last spoke to me ingenuously, being altogether a dependant on Mr. de Noailles his captain, who went himself roundly to work, and had nothing in view but the service of the King. But Pradelle's design being to hinder me from accepting the offers that were to be made me, by putting me in hopes of obtaining something better, continued to dazzle my eyes with bright prospects; but I resolved to oppose artifice to artifice. I told d'Avanton, That I could in no manner conceive what the meaning of the Court was: That though I was a prisoner, I did not find my prison so very burdensome, as to wish to get free from it at any rate whatsoever: That it was best to go roundly to work with every body, and with prisoners as well as with others: That I had proposals made to me at the same time, opposite to one another: That the first President offered me seven abbies, whilst Mr. de Pradelle was mentioning to me Archbishopricks. D'Avanton, who desired nothing more than to see this negotiation come to a good end, failed not to give his captain an account of my complaints. Cardinal Mazarin, who was kept in a mortal fright by the curates and the confessors of Paris, and who for that reason was impatient to the last degree to finish the thing, was extremely angry at Pradelle's conduct, and he he ufed him very rudely upon it, fufpecting, as it was true, that what he did was by the Abbot Fouquet's orders. The vexation this gave him to find his own dependants oppofing his will, contributed much, as Mr. de Bellievre told me the next day, to make him confent to make an end of the matter by accepting my act of refignation, dated in the caftle of Vincennes, for which I was to have the feven abbeys which I have mentioned. He likewife confented that I fhould be put into the hands of Mr. de la Meilleraie, to be kept in the caftle of Nants, of which he was governor, and to be fet at liberty as foon as his Holinefs had accepted of my refignation: But that, whether the Pope accepted of it or no, I fhould not be put again into the King's hands, till the Prefident de Bellievre fhould fend a writing under his hand for his confenting to it; and that for greater furety of this laft claufe, the King fhould impower the Marefchal de la Meilleraie to give a promife under his hand to Mr. de Bellievre, not to deliver me up till he had the Prefident's order. All this was performed, and the Monday following they came both of them to Vincennes, and accompanied me in one of the King's coaches as far as the Port-à-l'Anglois.

The Marefchal being very lame of the gout, could not come up to my chamber, which gave an opportunity to Mr. de Bellievre to warn me, as we were coming down ftairs, againft entering into an engagement which would be required of me, and which was, that I fhould not try to efcape from the confinement which I was to be kept under at Nants. The Marefchal propofed it to me, and my anfwer was, That prifoners of war might give fuch promifes, but that I never heard that they were required from prifoners of ftate. The Marefchal grew angry at it, and he told me plainly, that he would take me under his care only upon that condition. Mr. de Bellievre, who had found only the opportunity of whifpering me a word about this, becaufe of the prefence of my exempt, of Pradelle, and of my guards, began now to fpeak.

' You

' You do not underſtand one another (ſaid he) the
' Cardinal does not refuſe to give his word of honour,
' if you will confide in it entirely, and give him no
' guards. But if you keep him under guard, Sir,
' what will ſuch a promiſe ſignify? Does not the
' keeping him under reſtraint free him from it?' The
Preſident played a ſure game, being well aſſured that
the Queen had made the Mareſchal promiſe that I
ſhould always have ſome guards to watch me. The
Mareſchal looked upon Mr. de Bellievre, and ſaid:
' You know that I cannot act in the manner you pro-
' poſe; come, Sir, ſaid he, turning to me, there is no
' avoiding the giving you guards, but I ſhall guard
' you in a manner that ſhall give you no manner of
' room to complain.' We left Vincennes, and we
marched away, accompanied by the Gens d'Armes,
the light-horſe, and the mouſquetaires of the King's
houſehold. Cardinal Mazarin's guards, who in my
opinion ought not to have appeared there, were
likewiſe of the company, and made even a mighty
figure.

We parted with the firſt Preſident at the Port-à-l'Anglois, and we continued our march as far as Baugency,
where we embarked, after my guards had been relieved
by new ones. The horſe returned to Paris; and Pradelle,
who had Morel for his enſign, that belongs now, I
think, to the Dutcheſs of Orleans, came in the ſame
boat with me; and in another boat that followed ours,
there was a company of the regiment of guards. The
next day after my arrival at Nants, all my guards left
me, and I was left entirely to the keeping of the Mareſchal de la Meilleraie, who was as good as his word,
for nothing could exceed his civil uſage. Every body
had the liberty of ſeeing me, all means poſſible were
ſought to divert me, and I had a play acted before me
almoſt every evening. All the ladies of the town were
preſent at it, and often ſupped in the caſtle. Madam-
de la Vergne, who was married a ſecond time to the
Chevalier de Sevigné, and lived in Anjou with him,
came to ſee me, and brought her daughter with her,

who is now Madam de la Fayette. She was very
agreeable and very lovely, and she had befides much
of the air of Madam de Lefdiguieres. I had a great
liking to her, but the truth is she had but little to me,
either becaufe her inclination did not lead her that
way, or becaufe of the diftruft that both her mother
and father-in-law had filled her with betimes, and
carefully, in refpect to me and to the inconftancy of
my amours. Her cruelty caufed me no great trouble,
it being natural for me in fuch cafes to be pretty eafily
comforted, and the freedom which Mr. de la Meilleraie
fuffered me to live in, with the ladies of the town,
was befides a great help to comfort me. It is true,
that the exactnefs with which he guarded me, was
equal to the civility he ufed towards me. I was never
left without fome body that watched me narrowly,
except when I was retired into my chamber, and then
there were always fix men that guarded the door.
There was in the chamber only a very high window,
that looked down into a yard, in which there was
always a numerous guard; and one of the fix men that
guarded the door, and who always accompanied me
when I went to walk in a little garden, which is upon
a kind of baftion or ravelin, built juft by the river-fide,
pofted himfelf upon the terras of a tower, from whence
he watched all my fteps. The Duke de Briffac, whom
I met at the Marefchal de la Meilleraie's when I arrived
there, and Meffieurs de Caumartin, d'Hacqueville,
the Abbot de Pont Carré, and Amelot, who came
thither foon after, were more furprized at the ftrictnefs
of my guard, than pleafed at the civilities fhewn me,
though never fo great. I own that I was myfelf very
much troubled at it, chiefly when I heard by an exprefs
fent me by the Abbot Charrier, that the Pope would
not give his approbation to what I had done, which
approbation had not made my act of refignation one
jot more valid, and yet would have procured me my
liberty. I difpatched immediately to Rome, Malclerc,
who has the honour to be known to you, with a letter
for the Pope, wherein I gave his Holinefs an account

of

of what my true intereſt required. I gave to Malclerc beſides a large inſtruction of all the expedients whereby the dignity of the Holy See might be reconciled with the accepting of my reſignation. But nothing could perſuade his Holineſs, and he remained inflexible. He thought that his reputation would lie too much at ſtake, if he ſhould conſent for a ſingle inſtant to a violence ſo injurious to the whole church ; and the Pope ſpoke in this manner to the Abbot Charrier and to Malclerc, who were preſſing him with tears in their eyes : ‘ I know that my approbation would not vali-‘ date a reſignation which has been extorted by vio-‘ lence ; but I likewiſe know that it would diſhonour ‘ me, when people ſhould ſay that I have given my ‘ conſent to a reſignation dated in a priſon.’

You will eaſily believe that this diſpoſition of the Pope's brought many ſerious reflections into my head, which worked afterwards the more upon me by the diſpoſition of the Mareſchal de la Meilleraie, who was of all men the moſt cringing to the Court. His being brought up at the Court of Cardinal Richlieu had made ſo ſtrong impreſſions upon his mind, that though he had a great deal of averſion for Cardinal Mazarin, he trembled at the hearing of his name mentioned. His fear redoubled at the firſt news that came from Rome. He appeared to be moved at it even beyond what decency allowed him. After the Cardinal had ſent him word that he knew for certain that the difficulty which the Pope made came from me, he could not contain himſelf any longer, but he reproached me with it, and inſtead of giving an ear to my reaſons, which were grounded merely upon truth, he affected to believe that I diſguiſed my true intention from him. I made then no doubt but that he would ſeek out for pretences to ſurrender me to the Court, when it ſhould be convenient for him to do it. This conduct is common to all thoſe who act with more cunning than prudence, but it does not ſucceed with thoſe whoſe impetuoſity is greater than their pro-bity. I made the Mareſchal diſcover his intentions by putting him infenfibly into a heat, and he betrayed himfelf very imprudently in the prefence of all thofe that were with us in the court belonging to the caftle. He read me a letter, which informed him that they had received advice at Court of my promifing the Duke of Orleans, who was at Blois, to bring the Marefchal de la Meilleraie over to his intereft, and that I did not even defpair that he would give him a retreat in Fort Louis. I told the Marefchal that he muft expect to be often troubled in this manner, and that the Court, which had no other view by removing me than to appeafe the people at Paris, thought now upon nothing elfe than to get me out of his hands by their artifices there. At this he turned towards me like a man poffeffed, and he faid to me in a loud voice and all in a heat, ' In fhort, Sir, I would have ' you to know that I fhall never make war againft the ' King upon your account, I will be true to my pro- ' mife, but the firft Prefident muft likewife do what ' he has promifed the King.'

This put me ferioufly upon finding out the means to make my efcape. I was preffed about it by the firft Prefident, upon whom the Court had already made a kind of trial, and Montrefor got a lady of Nantes to put a little note into my hands, in which I found thefe words written : ' You are to be removed to Breft at ' the end of this month, if you don't prevent it by ' making your efcape.' The thing was very difficult, and the firft ftep towards it was to amufe the Marefchal. Joly fhewed him the decyphering of letters, which appeared very genuine ; and I obferved on this occafion, that perfons the moft diftruftful are often the moft eafily deceived. I difcovered my defign to Mr. de Briffac, who came to Nantes from time to time, and who promifed to ferve me. He went always with a very great equipage, and had many mules to carry his trunks. This brought a thought into my head, that it would not be impoffible for me to be conveyed away in one of thefe trunks. There was one made for that purpofe, a little bigger than ordinary,

ordinary, and with a hole to let in some air. I tried
it, and I found that way of escaping natural and
practicable. Mr. de Briffac went for two or three
days to Machecoul, from whence he returned altogether altered. He discovered the thing to the
Dutchess of Retz, my sister-in-law, and to her father,
who dissuaded him from it; the first because she hated
me, and the second because of his ill-nature. Mr.
de Briffac said for his excuse, that he was sure that I
should be stifled in the trunk; but the truth is, that
he was touched with a scruple, which they had put
into his head, that by doing a thing of this nature he
would violate in too open a manner the laws of hof-
pitality. I represented to him as much as I could,
that in suffering me to be transferred to Breft, he
would violate in no less a manner the laws of friendship. He owned it, and he promised to help me to
escape any other way than this. I entered into measures with him upon a project, which I had thought
of, as soon as the first had failed.

I have already told you, that I went and walked
sometimes upon a kind of ravelin by the river-side,
and I had observed that (being in the month of Auguft) the river did not come up to the wall, but left
a little space of dry ground between it and the baftion. I had likewise observed, that between the
garden which was upon the baftion and the terrafs on
which my guards ftaid whilft I was walking, there
was a door, which Chaluçet had caufed to be fet up
to prevent the foldiers coming into the garden.
Upon thefe obfervations I formed my defign, which
was to draw unaffectedly that door upon me as I came
into the garden, which being made with crofs-bars,
was no obftacle to the guards from looking on me, but
would ferve however to prevent their coming to me.
I defigned afterwards to get down the wall by means
of a cord, which my phyfician and the Abbot Rouf-
feau, brother to the fteward of my family, were to
hold faft at the top; to have horfes ready by the river-
fide, both for myfelf and for four gentlemen whom I
defigned

M 6

defigned to take along with me. This project was
extremely difficult to execute. It was of an extraordinary kind, and all that are fuch are never thought
poffible by thofe that are capable of forming only
ordinary ones, but when they fee them executed. I
have made that obfervation above a hundred times ;
and if I am not miftaken, Longinus, that famous
Chancellor to Queen Zenobia, has obferved it · before
me, in his treatife on the Sublime. In fhort, there
had been nothing more remarkable in our age than
the fuccefs of an efcape like mine, if, in breaking my
fetters, it had ended in rendering myfelf mafter of
the capital city of the kingdom. Mr. de Caumartin * brought that thought into my head, and I embraced it very eagerly. The firft prefident de Bellievre approved of it ; and as foon as the Chancellor
and Servien, who were at Paris, heard that I was
marching that way, they had no other thought than
of quitting me the place, and of running out of it.
It was the firft word that Servien, who was not a
timorous man, faid, when he received an account of
it from the Marefchal de la Meilleraie. Add to that
the Te Deum that was fung for my liberty in the
church of Nôtre-Dame, and the bonfires that were
made in many places of the city, though they did not
fee me there, and judge of the effect which I had room
to hope that my prefence would have produced there.
I take this to be a fufficient anfwer to thofe who have
blamed my enterprize. I defire that thefe gentlemen
would examine ferioufly, and confider within themfelves, whether they would have thought that the declaration which I made in full parliament againft
Cardinal Mazarin, the next day after the battle of
Rhetel, would have fucceeded as it did, if it had
been propofed to them a quarter of an hour before
they faw the fuccefs of it. I am perfuaded that almoft all the great things that have been undertaken

* Joly fays, that it was he that firft propofed it to the Cardinal
de Retz.

are

are of this nature. I am perfuaded befides, that it is often neceffary to venture upon fuch undertakings; and I continue to be ftill perfuaded, that it was prudent in the occafion I am fpeaking of, becaufe the worft that could have happened was my embarking in an action of great moment, which I had pufhed on if I had found room, and to which I had given an air of moderation and of difcretion, if I had found matters not fo well prepared as I imagined. For my project was to enter into Paris with the appearance only of peaceable intentions; to declare both at the parliament and at the town-houfe, that I came with the defign only of taking poffeffion of my archbifhopric; to take in effect that poffeffion in my cathedral; to examine what effect fuch a fpectacle would have produced upon the minds of a people already inflamed by the ftate in which things were, Arras being befieged at that time by the Prince of Condé. My prefence at Paris would probably have prevented the King from attacking the lines as he did. The partifans of the Prince, who were numerous in the city, would certainly have joined with my friends. The flight of the Chancellor and of Servien had difcouraged the Mazarinians; the collufion of the firft Prefident de Bellievre had been a fignal advantage to me. Mr. Nicolaï, firft prefident of the chamber of accounts, has declared fince, that the Court having obferved againft me not any one of the forms of law required, that chamber had not hefitated one fingle moment to do in favour of my poffeffion whatever lay in their power. I fhould have known by thefe firft fteps how far I ought or might have carried the fecond. If I had met, as I have obferved, with more obftacles in my way than I had fancied, it would have been eafy for me to have taken a ftep backwards, to have acted only the ecclefiaftical part, and after having taken poffeffion of the archbifhopric, to have retired into Mezieres, where two hundred horfe would eafily have convoyed me, all the King's troops being far off. The Vifcount de Lamet was in that place, and Noirmoutier himfelf,

himfelf, though reconciled fecretly to the Court, as
you have feen, had been obliged to preferve a greater
regard for me, to prevent his lofing entirely his reputation with the public; and even in refpect to his private intereft, Charleville and the Mont-Olimpe being
infignificant without Mezieres. That gentleman was
befides reconciled to me in fome meafure, fince I was
come away from Vincennes; for thinking that I
fhould be quickly fet at liberty, he had taken hold of
thefe inftants to make his peace with me, having fent
to that effect Blanchecour, a captain of foot of the
garrifon of Mezieres. Blanchecour brought me a
letter, figned by Noirmoutier and by the Vifcount de
Lamet jointly, who both expreffed that they had been
all along in my intereft, and would continue in the
fame mind as long as they lived. The Vifcount wrote
me word by a feparate letter, that the Duke de Noirmoutier affected a greater zeal for me than ever, in
order to gild over his paft actions with the fhew he
made now, which, as matters ftood, could no longer,
at leaft as he thought, be of any prejudice to him at
Court. My retiring into Mezieres would, it is
true, have produced no great matters, becaufe of my
miftrufting Noirmoutier, and becaufe, as I have faid,
that place is infignificant without Charleville and the
Mont-Olimpe. It would however have ferved as a
place for me to retire into, which at that juncture of
time was what I needed moft.

The whole project was overthrown in an inftant,
though none of the foundations failed on which it was
built. I made my efcape upon Saturday the 8th of
Auguft, at five in the afternoon. The door of the
garden, which I have mentioned, feemed as if it had
fhut naturally of itfelf. I got down the baftion,
which was forty feet high, by means of the cord. A
valet-de-chambre, who belongs ftill to me, amufed
my guards with fome bottles of wine. They were
befides amufing themfelves in looking at a Domini-
can fryar, who was got into the river to bathe, and
who was very near drowning. The centinel, who

was

was not above twenty fteps from me, durft not fire, becaufe, when I faw him preparing to do it, I cried to
him that I would have him hanged if he budged;
and he faid, when he was put to the rack, that hearing me threaten him in that manner, he thought that
the Marefchal favoured my efcape. Two little pages,
who were bathing, feeing me coming down the baf-
tion-wall, would have difcovered my efcape, if they
had been hearkened to; but every body that heard
their cry, fancied that they were calling for help to the
monk that wanted it. I met, at my coming down,
my four gentlemen, who waited there as if they had
been watering their horfes. I got on horfe-back before there was the leaft alarm given, and having forty
frefh horfes waiting for me upon the road between
Nantes and Paris, I fhould infallibly have reached
this laft place on the Tuefday morning betimes, had
it not been for an accident, which has proved fatal to
the remaining part of my life. I will give you an
account of it, after I have taken notice to you of a
remarkable circumftance.

I had a cypher with the Princefs Palatine, which we
ufed to call the undecypherable, becaufe we had always found it impenetrable, except to thofe who knew
the word agreed on. It was with that cypher that I
wrote to the firft prefident that I was to make my
efcape upon the 8th of Auguft, and he made ufe of
the fame to bid me do it whatever rifk I fhould run.
I gave, with the fame cypher, the neceffary orders
about my relais. By the fame means I agreed with
Annery and Laillevaux on the place where the gentlemen out of the Vexin fhould meet to come into Paris
with me. The Prince of Condé, who had with him
one of the beft decypherers in the world, whofe name
I think was Martin, kept that cypher fix weeks at
Bruffels; and when he gave it me back, he told me
that that man owned, that it was impoffible to decypher it. Thefe are great proofs of the goodnefs of
the cypher; and yet Joly, who made it not his bufinefs to decypher letters, found out the key, after having

ing thought a while upon it. I beg that you would forgive me this digreſſion, which you will find not to be unneceſſary. I return to my narration.

As * ſoon as I was got on horſe-back, I took my way towards Mauve, which, if I miſtake not, is five leagues diſtant from Nantes, by the river ſide, and where we had agreed that Mr. de Briſſac and the Chevalier de Sevigné ſhould ſtay for me, with a boat to croſs the river. La Ralde, gentleman of the horſe to the Duke de Briſſac, who rode before me, told me that we ought to gallop at firſt, for fear the Mareſchal's guards ſhould have time to ſhut up the gate of a little ſtreet of the ſuburb where they were quartered, and through which we muſt neceſſarily paſs. I was mounted upon one of the beſt horſes in the world, and which had coſt Mr. de Briſſac a thouſand crowns. I did not however give him the bridle, becauſe the pavement was extremely bad and very ſlippery; but one of my gentlemen, whoſe name was Bois-guerin, perceiving two of the Mareſchal's guards, who had not however any deſign upon us, and bidding us cock our piſtols, I did ſo, and I preſented mine to the guard who was neareſt to me, to prevent his ſeizing my horſe's bridle. The ſun, that was yet pretty high, ſhining upon the plate, the reverberation frighted my horſe, that was ſtrong and lively. He ſtarted at it, and of a ſudden fell upon his four feet. I eſcaped with the breaking of my left ſhoulder by the fall, and the putting of it beſides out of joint, againſt a great ſtone that lay before a door. Another of my gentlemen, named Beau-Cheſne, took me up and got me upon my horſe, and though I ſuffered an intolerable pain, and that I was now and then obliged to pull my hair to prevent my fainting away, I rode out the five leagues, before the Mareſchal de la Meil-

---

* In Joli's whole account of this matter, he repreſents the Cardinal de Retz in the worſt light imaginable, and as a man ſo much poſſeſſed with fear, that he knew neither what he ſaid or did.

leraie,

leraie, who (if Marigni's ballad is to be believed) was following me with full speed, with all the runners of Nantes, could reach me. I found, at the place of rendezvous, Mr. de Briſſac and the Chevalier de Sevigné, with a boat ready. I fainted away at the getting into it, but I came to myſelf by their throwing water on my face. I tried to get upon my horſe after we had paſſed the river, but I was too weak to fit on horſe-back, and Mr. de Briſſac was forced to have me put into a hay-mow, where he left me with one of my gentlemen, who held me in his arms. The Duke de Briſſac took Joly with him, and they went directly to Beau-Preau, with a deſign of gathering together the gentlemen of the country, and of coming afterwards to fetch me away.

I think myſelf obliged to relate two or three actions of ſome perſons that belonged to me, which deſerve not to be forgotten. Paris, a doctor in the univerſity of the college of Navarre, who had given the ſignal with his hat to the four gentlemen that aſſiſted me in this conjuncture, was found by the water-ſide by Coulon, gentleman of the horſe to the Mareſchal, who took hold of him and gave him ſome blows. The Doctor preſerving his wits, ſaid to Coulon, with a ſimple air, and like a Norman, ' I will tell the Mareſchal that ' you ſpend your time in the abuſing a poor prieſt, ' becauſe you dare not attack the Cardinal, who is ' armed with good piſtols.' Coulon took this for genuine, and aſked him where I was. ' Don't you ' ſee him,' anſwered the Doctor, ' entering into that ' village?' You muſt obſerve that he had ſeen me croſs the river, and this preſence of mind, which you will own to have been pretty extraordinary, got him away out of Coulon's hands. I will mention now an act of courage no leſs extraordinary. The gentleman whom the Doctor was ſhewing Coulon, as if it had been myſelf, was that Beau-Cheſne whom I have mentioned. His horſe was quite ſpent, which prevented his joining me. Coulon, who took him for me, ran to him, and perceiving many perſons ready

to

to join him, he came up towards Beau-Chefne with
a piftol in his hand. Beau-Chefne, who was expecting him in the like pofture, looking about him, perceived a boat that was not above ten or twelve fteps,
diftance from him. He flung himfelf into it, and
whilft he was ftopping Coulon by prefenting him
one of his piftols, he was holding the other at the
waterman, and obliged him to pafs the river. The
ftoutnefs he fhewed on this occafion did not only preferve him, but favoured my efcape ; becaufe the Marefchal; having miffed that boat, was forced to ride a
long way before he could crofs the water.

An action of another nature, but which contributed
ftill more to my liberty, was this : I have already
told you, that as foon as the Abbot Charrier had fent
me word that the Pope refufed to receive my refignation, I difpatched Malclerc to follicit his Holinefs
about it. The Court fent Gaumont at the fame time;
who was carrying the original act of my refignation to
the Cardinal d'Eft, with an order for him to follicit
that affair, becaufe there was at that time no ambaffador from France at Rome. Gaumont, at his arrival
at Lions with Malclerc, finding himfelf tired, refolved to go to Marfeilles and embark there for Italy.
That being the longeft way, and Malclerc, who went
through the mountains, being like to be the fooneft at
Rome, Gaumont thought fit to intruft him with the
pacquet he had for the Cardinal d'Eft. His fimpli-
city was great, as you may obferve, and it is like
that he had never ftudied a maxim which I have always practifed, and always preached to all thofe who
belonged to me; which is, never to mind, in affairs
of importance, either fatigue, danger, or expence.
Gaumont was punifhed for not following that maxim
on this occafion. The original act of my refignation
was not to be found in the pacquet, though none of
the feals feemed to have been broken. When Gaumont complained of it, Malclerc, who was a braver
man than he, complained on his fide, that what was
alledged was a contrivance. This difappointment
gave

gave room to the Pope to leave the Cardinal d'Eft in doubt, whether their doing nothing at Rome about that affair proceeded from want of good-will in his Holinefs, or from want of the original act of my refignation. Malclerc was ordered to entreat the Pope, in my name, that in cafe he would not admit of that refignation, he would fpin out the matter till I had found means to efcape; and what Malclerc had done, in relation to Gaumont, afforded, as you fee, a pretence plaufible enough. The Cardinal d'Eft being himfelf amufed, amufed likewife Mazarin; whofe inftances to the Marefchal de la Meilleraie, about his delivering me back into the King's hands, grew thereby lefs frequent and lefs preffing; and I had the fatisfaction to owe to the zeal and to the prudence of two perfons who belonged to me (for the Abbot Charrier had his fhare in this intrigue) the full time I wanted to provide for my efcape.

I return to the place where I was hid. I remained for above feven hours in fuch an anguifh that I am not able to exprefs it. I had my left fhoulder both broken and put out of joint, and extremely bruifed befides. I was feized with a fever about nine in the evening, and the thirft it occafioned was ftill cruelly increafed by the heat of the new hay. Though I was by the river-fide, I durft not drink; becaufe if Montet (that's the perfon's name that was with me) and I had come out of the hay-mow, we had no body to put it again in order at our coming back into it, which might confequently have afforded room to thofe that ran after me to have fearched it. We were continually hearing people on horfeback, that were riding on the right and on the left, among whom we knew by his voice Coulon to be one. The uneafinefs occafioned by thirft is incredible, and inconceivable to thofe who have never experienced it. Mr. de la Poife St. Offanges, a man of quality of thofe parts, whom Mr. de Briffac had acquainted with my misfortune, came about two in the morning to fetch me away, after having obferved that the coaft was perfectly clear.

He

He caufed me to be put upon a hand-barrow, which they ufed to remove dung with, and two country-men carried me into the barn of a houfe belonging to him, that ftood a league off. I was likewife covered up with hay there, but not wanting drink, that made me eafier.

The Duke de Briffac came with his Dutchefs feven or eight hours after, having with them about twenty horfes, and they carried me to Beau-Preau, where I found the Abbot de Belebat, who was come to vifit them. I ftaid there but one night, till all the gentlemen of the country were affembled. Mr. de Briffac was very much beloved there, and in a little time he got together above two hundred gentlemen. Mr. de Retz, who was ftill more beloved in his parts, joined him four leagues from thence with three hundred more. We paffed almoft within fight of Nantes, from whence fome of the Marefchal de la Meilleraie's guards came out to fkirmifh. They were vigoroufly repulfed to the field-gate of the town, and we arrived fafely at Machecoul, which is in the country of Retz. But this piece of good luck happened not without being allayed with domeftic troubles. Madam de Briffac, who had all this while acted the part of an heroine, prefenting me at parting with a bottle of imperial water, faid to me, ' Nothing but your mif-
' fortune hath hindered me from mixing poifon with.
' it.' She made me anfwerable for the piece of treachery done me by Mr. de Noirmoutier upon her account, which I have fpoken of before *. It is impoffible for you to conceive how much I was touched at hearing thefe words ; and I felt beyond what I am able to exprefs, that an honeft heart carries its fenfibility to the greateft excefs of weaknefs, at the complaints of a perfon to whom he thinks himfelf obliged. I was not near fo fenfible at the hardnefs of the

* In the fecond volume; but in a manner fo imperfect, that the paragraph relating to it was not tranflated, as it is there taken notice of.

Dutchefs

Dutchefs of Retz, my fifter-in-law, and that of her father. They could not hide from me their want of good-will, as foon as I came. The Dutchefs complained that I had not intrufted her with my efcape, though fhe had left Nantes but the day before I made it. The father exclaimed pretty openly at my obftinacy, for refufing to fubmit to the King's pleafure, and he did whatever he could with Mr. de Briffac, to oblige him to perfuade me to fend to the Court the ratification of my refignation. The truth is, that both the father and the daughter were extremely afraid of the Marefchal de la Meilleraie, who being enraged at my efcape, but more ftill at his being abandoned by all the gentlemen of the province, was threatening to deftroy all the country of Retz with fire and fword. Their fright was fuch, that they fancied to themfelves, or were at leaft willing that other people fhould fancy, that my complaints about my fhoulder were an effect only of my tendernefs; that there was nothing broke or out of joint; and that the whole amounted only to a contufion. The old Duke's furgeon, who fided with them, faid the like to every body; adding, that it was very hard that for the fake of my tendernefs I fhould expofe the whole family, which was upon the point of being invefted at Machecoul. I was in my bed all this while, where I felt incredible pains, and where I was not able fo much as to turn. But hearing thefe people fpeak in this manner, I grew fo impatient, that I refolved to leave them, and to throw myfelf into Belle-Ifle, from whence I might at leaft get away by fea. The paffage to it was very hazardous, becaufe the Marefchal de la Meilleraie had caufed all the coaft to be guarded with men in arms. I ventured upon it however. I embarked at the port de la Roche, which lies about half a league from Machecoul, in a floop, of which la Gifclaie, a captain of a man of war, and a good feaman, would be the pilot. The weather obliged us to caft anchor at Croify, where we were in danger of being difcovered by a floop, which came to us in the night. La Gifclaie,

claie, who fpoke the country language, and knew all
thefe parts, came off very well. We failed away the
next morning at break of day, and we difcovered fome
time after a long bark of Bifcay, which gave us the
chafe. We run from it out of regard to Mr. de Briffac, who would not have liked to have been carried into
Spain, becaufe he was not, like me, efcaping out of
prifon, and that fuch a voyage might have been
looked upon as criminal in him. The long bark
coming full fail upon us, and being even near getting the wind of us, we thought that it would be beft
for us to land in the ifland of Retz. The bark
feemed as if it would have followed us thither, and
we faw it coaft along for a pretty while, till at laft
we faw it bear off. We got again on board of our
floop at night, and we arrived at Belle-Ifle at break
of day.

I fuffered, during this paffage, all the pain that a
man is able to bear, and I had need of all the ftrength
of my conftitution to preferve the contufion I had on
my fhoulder, being fo great as it was, from the gan-
grene, having applied to it all this while no other
remedy than falt and vinegar. I met not at Belle-
Ifle with the fame difguft as at Machecoul, but at the
bottom I met not there with a much greater firmnefs.
They fancied, in the country of Retz, that the commander de Neuf Chaife, who was at Rochel, would
receive inceffantly an order for invefting me in Belle-
Ifle, and they likewife heard there, that the Marefchal de la Meilleraie was preparing at Nantes two
long barks for that purpofe. Thefe advices were in
the main right and true, but the execution of them
was not by much fo near at hand as they thought,
and it required a longer time than had been needed
for the curing of my fhoulder. But the fright they
were in at Machecoul had an influence upon thofe
of Belle-Ifle, and I perceived it by their being inclined
to think there, that my fhoulder was not really out
of joint, and that the pain which the contufion caufed
me made me fancy that my ail was greater than it
really

really was. It is impoffible to imagine the trouble
which thefe forts of murmurings caufe when they
are unjuft. The Chevalier de Sevigné, a man of
courage, but felf-interefted, was afraid of having his
houfe pulled down ; and Mr. de Briffac, who thought
that he had made fufficient amends for the lazinefs,
rather than weaknefs, which he had fhewn during my
imprifonment, was glad to put an end to the thing,
and not expofe his quiet about it for ever. I was
not lefs impatient than they were, to fee them
difintangled out of a trouble in which they had engaged only for my fake. The difference was, that I
thought not the danger fo great, either for them or
for me, as to be deprived of the neceffary time which
I fancied might have been allowed me for curing my
fhoulder, and about providing myfelf with a fhip
which I might be fafe upon. They would have perfuaded me to have put myfelf on board of an Ham-
burgh fhip, which lay in the road, ready to fail
for Holland, which I thought not fit to do, the
mafter, who was a ftranger, knowing who I was, and
having it in his power to carry me to Nantes, as well
as Holland. I propofed to them to fend for the long
bark of Bifcay, which I have mentioned, and which
had caft anchor in fight of Belle-Ifle ; but they were
afraid that to have fuch an intelligence with the Spaniards would be imputed to them as a crime. I embarked at laft in a fifher-man's bark, in which there
were only five mariners of Belle-Ifle, and I had with
me only Joly, two of my gentlemen, and a valet-
de-chambre, whom my brother had lent me. The
bark was loaded with pilcherds, which was a good
for us, becaufe we were very bare of money. My
brother had fent me fome, but the man that carried it
had been arretted by thofe that guarded the coaft. His
wife's father had not been fo civil as to offer me any.
Mr. de Briffac lent me eighty piftoles, and the officer
who commanded in Belle-Ifle forty. We left our
cloaths, and took fome tattered ones, which the foldiers of the garrifon furnifhed us with, and we put to

fea

sea in the beginning of the night, with a design to
sail to St. Sebaſtian, which is in the Guipuſcoa.
The diſtance to that place was great enough for ſuch
a bark as ours was, it being eighty long-leagues ; but
it was the neareſt of all thoſe where I could land with
ſafety. The weather was very ſtormy all night long,
but it grew calm at break of day, which was no great
matter of comfort to us, becauſe we loſt the only mari-
ner's compaſs we had. It fell into the ſea by I don't
know what accident. Our mariners found themſelves
at a great loſs, and being very ignorant men, they knew
not whereabouts they were. They followed no other
courſe than that which a ſhip that gave them chace
forced them to take. They diſcovered, by its garb,
that it was a Sallee rover. Perceiving, in the evening,
that they were ſtriking ſail, we judged by it that they
were afraid of the land, and conſequently that we
could not be far from it. Little birds that came to
perch upon our maſt made it beſides plain enough.
The queſtion was what land it might be, for we were
as much afraid of that of France as of that of the
Turks. This made us keep off from ſhore all that
night and all the next day, and a ſhip which we
ſpied, and would have come near to inform ourſelves,
fired thrice at us, which was the only anſwer we received. We had but little water on board, and we
were afraid of being ſurprized by foul weather, there
being already ſome appearance of it. The night
however was calm enough, and at break of day we
perceived a ſloop at ſea. We came near it with
much ado, thoſe upon the ſloop fearing that we might
be rovers. We ſpoke Spaniſh and French to three
men whom we ſaw on board, but they underſtood
neither of theſe languages. One of them cried aloud
San Sebaſtian, to let us know that they belonged to
that place. We ſhewed him money, and anſwered
San Sebaſtian, to give them to underſtand that we
would land there. He came on board of us and
conducted us thither, which was eaſy for him to do,
becauſe we were near it.

We

We were no fooner landed than thofe of San Sebaftian afked us for our charter party, which is a
thing fo neceffary at fea, that it is a hanging matter
for any mafter of a fhip to be found without one.
The mafter of our bark had not confidered of this,
thinking that I fhould have no need of it. The want
of fuch a paper, and our ragged cloaths, obliged the
guards of the port to tell us that we were like to be
hanged the next morning. Our anfwer was, that we
were known to the Baron de Vatteville, who commanded for the King of Spain in the Guipufcoa.
This anfwer made them bring us to an inn, and Joly
went with one of their men to the Baron de Vatteville, who was at Port-Paffage, and who judged at
firft by his cloaths that he was an impoftor. He kept
however that thought to himfelf, and the next day he
came to vifit me at my inn. He made me a very long
compliment, but dark and entangled, and fuitable to
a man who was ufed, in the poft he was in, to meet
often with impoftors. The arrival of Beau-Chefne
began to give him a better opinion of me. I had fent
Beau-Chefne from Beau-preau to Paris, and my friends
had difpatched him immediately back to me to St. Sebaftian, as foon as they heard that I was to fteer my
courfe to that place. The Baron found him fo
well informed of the news, that he had room to believe that he was no falfe exprefs. His news indeed
was not very pleafing to the Baron, for he learnt from
him that the French had beat the Spaniards out of
their lines at Arras, and the advice which Mr. de
Vatteville fent immediately of it to Madrid, was the
firft they had there of that defeat. Beau-Chefne came
to St. Sebaftian with an incredible diligence upon a
fhip of Bifcay, which he found in the road of Belle-
Ifle, the mafter of the fhip being extremely glad to
find an opportunity of bringing that gentleman to me.
My friends fent him to perfuade me to take my way
towards Rome, rather than towards Mezieres, into
which place they were afraid I fhould throw myfelf.
Their advice was certainly the wifeft, though it did

not prove the moft fuccefsful. I followed it without any hefitation, but not without pain. I knew enough of the court of Rome to be perfuaded that the poft of a refugee and a fuppliant is not pleafing there ; and being as much incenfed as I was againft Mazarin, I felt motions within me which inclined me to go rather to fome place where I might have a larger field to exprefs my refentment. Not that I was ignorant that I ought not to have expected from the Duke de Noirmoutier every thing which might perhaps have been convenient for me for the time to come, but I was not ignorant neither, that being mafter in Mezieres, as I would have been if I had gone thither, it is probable that I might have engaged Mr. de Noirmoutier further than he himfelf intended ; that gentleman, after all, fhewing, outwardly at leaft, a regard for me, and having, as foon as he heard of my efcape, even difpatched me a gentleman, who came with Lamet's exprefs, to offer me a retreat in both their places. My friends did not doubt of my finding a fure retreat at Mezieres, but they were in fear as to Charleville ; and the fituation of thefe two places being fuch, that one of them is not very confiderable without the other, they thought, that confidering the difpofition of Mr. de Noirmoutier, I fhould do better not to chufe thefe places for my retreat. I repeat once more here what I have already faid of the probability of fucceeding better there than my friends believed, not that I ground this probability upon the good intentions of Noirmoutier, but upon the effect which my prefence might have produced upon him. The advice of my friends prevailed over my own views. They reprefented to me, that the natural fanctuary for a Cardinal and for a Bifhop, that was perfecuted, was the Vatican. But there are conjunctures, in which it is not difficult to forefee, that fuch a fanctuary may prove an exile. I forefaw it, and I chofe it; that choice being grounded on the deference I had for the advice of thofe I had obligations to, and I have never repented of it, though the fuccefs anfwered not their

expectation.

expectation. I fhould value myfelf more upon it if it had proceeded from my own moderation, and from my defire of applying myfelf to my re-eftablifhment by ecclefiaftical means.

It was not the Spaniards fault that I followed not other meafures. As foon as Mr. de Vatteville was convinced that I was the Cardinal de Retz, which the circumftances I have mentioned were a help to, and in which he was confirmed by a gentleman of Bourdeaux, who was his fecretary, and who had feen me at Paris feveral times; he took me to his houfe, where he kept me hid in a manner, that though the Marefchal de Grammont, who was not above three leagues diftance from San Sebaftian, had fent notice to the Court by an exprefs of my arrival at that place, he thought the next day that he was under fuch a miftake, as to oblige him to difpatch another exprefs to unfay what he had written. I kept my bed for three weeks without being able to ftir, and Mr. de Vatteville's furgeon, who was a very able man, would not undertake my cure, becaufe it was too late. I had my fhoulder abfolutely out of joint, and he condemned me to remain lame fo long as I lived. I fent Bois-Guerin to the King of Spain with a letter, wherein I intreated him to give me leave to pafs through his dominions to go to Rome. That gentleman was received both by his Catholic Majefty, and by Don Lewis de Haro, with a civility beyond what I am able to exprefs. He was fent back the very next day, with a prefent of a chain of gold worth 800 crowns. I had one of the King's litters fent me, and Don Chriftoval de Chaffembac, a German, but devoted to Spain, a fecretary for foreign affairs, and a great confident of Don Lewis, was difpatched to me. He ufed all manner of ways to oblige me to go to Madrid. I excufed myfelf from it, becaufe fuch a journey would be of no fervice to his Catholic Majefty, and might give a great advantage over me to my enemies. Thefe reafons, though very good, as I believe you will own, were not reckoned

                                        fuch,

such, which as I was wondering at, Vatteville, who in the presence of the secretary had been of the same mind openly with him, and even vehemently, said to me: ' This journey would cost the King 50,000 crowns, ' and would perhaps cost you the Archbishoprick ' of Paris, and yet it would be of no use at all. I ' must however speak as the other does, or they ' would resent it at Court. We act upon the foot ' of Philip the second, whose maxim was always to ' engage strangers by public demonstrations. You ' see in what manner we apply it, and you may ' judge of the rest by this.' These words are significant, and I have myself found them since more than once to be true, when I have examined the conduct of the council of Spain. It has appeared to me on several occasions, that they fall there into as great errors by keeping too obstinately attached to their general maxims, as they do in France by the contempt they shew there for any manner of maxims or rules.

When Don Christoval saw that he could not persuade me to go to Madrid, he tried by all manner of ways to oblige me to embark upon a frigate of Dunkirk, which was at St. Sebastian, and he made me immense offers, in case I would go into Flanders to treat with the Prince of Condé, and declare myself together with Mezieres, Charleville and the Mont-Olimpe, for the Spaniards. He was in the right to propose to me these measures, which would certainly have proved serviceable to the King his master. You have seen what reasons I had to refuse the proposal. What was very gallant and very civil in him, is, that notwithstanding my not accepting any of his offers, he caused however a little trunk covered with velvet to be brought, in which there were 40,000 crowns in double doubloons. I thought not fit to accept of them, considering that I did nothing for the service of his Catholic Majesty, and I excused myself upon that account with all the respect which I was obliged to. But having no linen nor cloaths, either

.I   for

for myfelf or for thofe that were with me, and the
400 crowns * which I received out of the fale of the
pilchards, having been almoft fpent in what I gave to
Mr. de Vatteville's fervants ; I borrowed 400 piftoles
of that gentleman, which I gave my note for, and
which I have repaid him fince.

After my health was fomewhat reftored I left St.
Sebaftian, and took my way towards Valencia, with
an intent to imbark at Vivaros, where Don Chriftoval affured me that Don Juan of Auftria, who was at
Barcelona, would fend me both a frigate and a galley. I paffed through all Navarre in one of the
King's litters, under the name of Marquis de St.
Florent, having for my conductor Mr. de Vatteville's
fteward, who faid that I was a gentleman of Burgundy
that was going to ferve the King in the Milaneze.
At my arrival at Tudello, a pretty confiderable town,
which is beyond Pampeluna, I found the people there
in a pretty great commotion. They lighted fires there
in the night, and kept corps-de-guards. The country farmers of the neighbourhood had made an infurrection, becaufe they had been forbidden to hunt.
They had entered the town, and had ufed great violences there, having even pillaged fome houfes. A
corps-de-guards, which was placed at ten at night
before the inn where I lay, began to put me in fear
that the inhabitants had fome fufpicion of me. But
the King's litter, and the muleteers who wore the
King's livery, removed that fear. At midnight I
faw one Don Martin come into my chamber with a
very long fword and a large buckler. He told me
that he was the inn-keeper's fon, and that he came
to give me notice that the people were in a great
commotion ; that they believed that I was a Frenchman,
who was come to foment the revolt of the farmers ;
that the Alcade himfelf knew not what to think of it ;
and that it was to be feared that the worft fort of

* Joli fays 6co crowns, and that he received a like fum for
the fale of another par el of pilchards brought upon the fhip in
which Beau-Chefne came to St. Sebaftian.

mob might take hold of that pretence to rob and to murder me ; and that even the corps-de-guard, which had been set up before the inn, began themselves to murmur and to grow inflamed. I desired Don Martin to shew them without affectation the King's litter, and to bring them to speak with the muleteers, and with Don Pedro, Mr. de Vatteville's steward. This last came into my chamber at that same instant to tell me that they were Endemoniados *, who understood neither rhime nor reason, and that they had threatened to murder him himself. We passed the whole night in this manner, having for serenadoes a multitude of confused voices that sung, or rather howled songs against the French. I thought fit the next morning to shew these men by our assured countenance, that they were mistaken in taking us for Frenchmen. But as I was offering to go out to mass, I met a centinel at the door, who made me get into my chamber again hastily enough, by putting the but end of his musket to my head, and by telling me that he was ordered by the Alcade to command me in the King's name to keep where I was. I sent Don Martin to the Alcade to tell him who I was, and Don Pedro went along with him. The Alcade came immediately to me. He left his wand at the door, and kneeling to me, he kissed the skirt of my coat ; but he declared that he could not let me go till he had an order for it from the Count de San Estevan, viceroy of Navarre, who was at Pampeluna. Don Pedro went to him with an officer of the town, and they came back with many excuses from the viceroy. They gave me a convoy of 50 soldiers mounted upon asses, who accompanied me as far as Cortés.

I continued my journey through Sarragossa, the capital city of Arragon, a large and fine town. I was surprized to the last degree to hear in the streets every body talking French. There is indeed a vast number of French in that place, most of them are

---

* Persons possessed.

artizans,

artizans, who are more attached to Spain than even
the Spaniards themfelves. The Duke de Monteleon,
a Neapolitan of the houfe of Pignatelly, viceroy of
Arragon, fent a gentleman to meet me upon the road
at three or four leagues diftance from the town, and
to tell me that he would have come himfelf with all
the gentry, if the King his mafter had not fent him
word to obey my orders, which he knew would be
againft his coming. This compliment, which, as
you fee, was very civil, was accompanied with all
poffible marks of kindnefs, and with all manner of
refrefhments which I met with at Sarragoffa. Before
one enters the town on the fide on which I went, one
fees the Alcaçar * of the ancient Kings of the Moors,
which belongs at prefent to the inquifition. There
is near it a walk of trees, in which I faw a prieft
walking. The gentleman belonging to the viceroy
told me, that that prieft was the curate of Occa, a
very antient town in Arragon, and that the curate
was there performing quarantain, after having buried,
three weeks fince, his laft parifhioner, who was in
reality the laft man of twelve thoufand who had died
of the plague in his parifh. The fame gentleman
of the viceroy's fhewed me all that was remarkable at
Sarragoffa. I went all this while under the name
of Marquis de St. Florent, but the gentleman did not
reflect that Nueftra Senora del Pilar, which is the
moft famous fanctuary of all Spain, could not be feen
under that title. They never difcover to the fight of
any body, that miraculous image, except to fovereign Princes, and to Cardinals. The Marquis de
St. Florent appeared to be neither, fo that when I
was feen within the banifters, with a black velvet
coat, and a cravat on, the multitude of people
that had been brought thither by the found of a bell
that never rings but upon account of that ceremony,
thought me to be the King of England. I believe
that there were above two hundred coaches full of

* Palace.

ladies, who all expreſſed the greateſt civilities to me, to which I could make a return but in very indifferent Spaniſh. That church is fine in it's ſelf, but its ornaments and riches are immenſe, and its treaſury magnificent. I was ſhewed there a man who was employed to light the lamps, the number of which is prodigious, and I was told, that he had been ſeen at the door of that church for ſeven years together but with one leg, whereas now he had two. The dean and all the prebends aſſured me, that the whole town had ſeen it as well as they; and that if I would ſtay but two days longer, I might ſpeak to above 20,000 perſons from the neighbourhood, who had ſeen him, as well as thoſe of the town. He had recovered his laſt leg (as he ſaid) by anointing himſelf with ſome oil out of the lamps. They keep there a yearly holy-day, in memory of that pretended miracle, with an incredible concourſe of people; and the truth is, that at the diſtance of a day's journey from Sarragoſſa, I ſtill met the roads full of perſons of all qualities running to it.

From the kingdom of Arragon I came into that of Valencia, which may not only be called the whole-ſomeſt, but likewiſe the fineſt country in the world. Pomegranate-trees, orange-trees, and lemon-trees, ſerve there for palliſadoes to all the great roads. The fineſt and cleareſt waters run along them like canals. The whole country round, which is ena-melled with millions of different ſorts of flowers, exhale millions of different ſorts of odours of a charm-ing ſmell. I arrived through that country, at Viva-ros, where Don Ferdinando Carillo Zuatra, general of the galleys of Naples, joined me the next day with the admiral galley of his ſquadron, an excellent and fine ſhip, and reinforced with the beſt part of the galley-ſlaves, and of the ſoldiers, belonging to the vice-admiral's galley, that had been in a manner diſarmed for that purpoſe. Don Ferdinando brought me a letter from Don Juan of Auſtria, as finely writ, and as well turned, as any one I have ever ſeen.

He-

He left it to my choice either to make ufe of that galley, or of a frigate of Dunkirk of 36 guns, that was in that port. This laft was the fafeft to pafs the gulf of Lions, in fo far advanced a feafon, for we were in the month of October. I chofe the galley, which (as you will fee) was not wifely done of me. Don Chriftoval de Cardonna, a knight of St. James's, arrived at Vivaros a quarter of an hour after Don Ferdinando Carillo, and he told me that the Duke de Montalte, viceroy of Valencia, had fent him to offer me all that he had in his power; that he knew that I had refufed his Catholick Majefty's prefent at St. Sebaftian; that he durft not for that reafon prefs me to accept what the Pagueloi of the galleys was ordered to bring me; but that knowing that the precipitancy with which I had left France, had not given me time to take much money with me; knowing befides, that being very liberal, I fhould not be forry to give fome regale to the people on board the galley; he hoped that I would not refufe fome little refrefhments to that purpofe. Thefe refrefhments confifted of fix great chefts full of all forts of fweet-meats made at Valencia; of twelve dozen pair of Spanifh gloves, of an exquifite fmell; and of a perfumed purfe, in which there were two thoufand pieces of gold coined in the Indies, which were worth two thoufand five or fix hundred piftoles. I accepted the prefent without any manner of difficulty, and my anfwer was, That as I did not find myfelf in a condition to do his Catholic Majefty any fervice, I thought that I fhould have been wanting to my duty all manner of ways, if I had accepted the confiderable fums which were brought to me from him at St. Sebaftian, and which were offered me at Vivaros by his order; but that I fhould think likewife I was wanting to the refpect I owed to fo great a Monarch, if I fhould refufe to accept this laft prefent, which he was pleafed to honour me with. This was the reafon of my accepting of it; but before I embarked I prefented the captain of the galley with the fweet-meats, I gave

the

the gloves to Don Ferdinando, and I sent the gold
by Don Pedro to the Baron de Vatteville, with a
letter importing that having heard him say several times how imbarrassed he was by reason of the
great expence which he was put to for finishing the
building the admiral's ship for the West-Indies,
which was upon the stocks at St. Sebastian, I sent
him a small grain, as a remedy against his head-ach,
for so he called the pain which the building of that
ship cost him. My manner of acting on this occasion was a little over-strained. I was in the right to
give the refreshments to the captain, and as for the
gloves it was a thing indifferent to keep them for myself, or to give them to Don Ferdinando; but it had
been prudent in me to have kept the gold. The
Spaniards have never forgiven it me, and have attributed to my aversion, a refusal which was in effect
but the natural consequence of the resolution which I
had taken of never accepting money from any body.

I imbarked at the second watch of the night, the
wind being high, but going before it, it did not
incommode us much. Our ship ran fifteen miles an
hour, and we arrived the next day at Majorca. The
plague being in Arragon, all the ships that came from
the coast of Spain were obliged to call at that island.
It was with a pretty deal of difficulty that we could
obtain leave to have any communication with the
town, the magistrates opposing it with vigour. The
viceroy, who is not near so absolute in that island as
other viceroys are in Spain, and who had received an
order from the King his master to do me all the
civilities possible, obtained at last by his instances,
leave for me, and for those that belonged to me, to
come into the town, upon condition that I should not
lie in it. We thought this, you may be sure, pretty
odd, because the contagious air may be carried to a
place, though you do not lie in it. I was saying it
in the afternoon to a gentleman of Majorca, who
made me the following answer, which I took notice
of, because it may be applied to a thousand occasions

ffons one may meet with. ‘ We are not afraid of your
‘ bringing here the contagious air, becaufe we know
‘ that you have not paffed at Occa ; but having been
‘ pretty near it, we are glad to make you an example,
‘ which will not incommode you, and of which the
‘ confequences will be of fervice to us.’ This has
fomething ftronger, and even more gallant, in the
Spanifh tongue than in ours.

· The viceroy, who was a Count of the kingdom of
Arragon, came to fetch me with 100 or 120 coaches,
full of perfons of diftinction, having the beft air of
any in Spain. He carried me to mafs at the Leo,
which is a name they give to all cathedrals. I faw
there between thirty and forty women of quality all
handfomer one than another, and what is wonderful,
is, that there is no ugly woman in all the ifland, or
at leaft they are very few in number. Their beauty
for the moft part is of the moft delicate kind, and
their complexion all lillies and rofes ; even the ordinary women that walk the ftreets are all fuch. They
have a particular fort of drefs, which is very becoming. The viceroy gave me a magnificent dinner in a
rich tent of gold brocade, which was fet up by the
fea-fide. He carried me afterwards to a concert of
mufic in a convent of nuns, nothing inferior in beauty
to the ladies of the town. They fang at their grate,
in honour of their faint, airs, and words more gallant and more paffionate than thofe of Lambert *.
Towards evening we walked round the town, and
faw the fineft country imaginable, and fuch as we had
feen in the kingdom of Valencia. After walking we
came to the vice-queen, who was as ugly as the Devil,
and who, being feated under a large canopy, and all
covered over with precious ftones, gave a marvellous
luftre to threefcore ladies that fat round her, who were
the choiceft beauties of the town. I was brought back
to the galley with fifty white wax flambeaux, whilft all

* A famous mufician of Paris, whofe daughter Signior Bap-
tifto Lully married.

3   the

the guns of the ramparts were difcharged, and whilft a vaft number of hautboys and trumpets were playing. I fpent in thefe diverfions the three days which the bad weather forced me to ftay at Majorca. I left that ifland upon the fourth with a frefh gale of wind behind us, which carried us fifty leagues in twelve hours, fo that I arrived fafely before night at Port-Mahon, which is the fineft port in the Mediterranean. The entrance into it is very ftrait, and I do not believe that two gallies could pafs in it at once. It widens on a fudden, and forms an oblong wet dock of a good half league broad, and a good league long. A great hill that furrounds it on all fides forms a theatre, which by the number and height of the trees that cover it, and by the waters that fall from it in great abundance, opens thoufands and thoufands of fcenes, more furprizing, without exaggeration, than thofe of our Operas. That fame hill, the trees, the rocks, guard the port againft all winds, fo that in the moft tempeftuous weather the water is always calm and fmooth. It is equally deep every where, and the Spanifh galleons can ride in it at four fteps diftance from the ground. This port is in the ifland of Minorca, which furnifhes more flefh, and more of all forts of provifions neceffary for fhips, than that of Majorca furnifhes pomegranates, oranges and lemons.

The weather grew extremely ftormy after our arrival in this port, which obliged us to ftay there for four days. We tried four times to put to fea, but the wind would not give us leave. Don Ferdinando Carillo, who was a young gentleman of quality, of twenty-four years of age, mighty civil and mighty kind, fought to procure me all the diverfion that that fine place would afford. We found there hunting of all kinds, and fifhing in abundance. A way of fifhing particular to that port was this: Don Ferdinando chofe a hundred Turks out of his fhip's crew, who were fet in rank, and were made to hold a very large cable. Four of the Turks dived to the bottom and tied the cable to a large ftone, which their companions drew

drew by that means upon the shore, after having used incredible efforts about it. The breaking of that stone with hammers, proved not much less difficult. They found in it seven or eight shell-fish, less than oysters in bigness, but of a higher relish beyond comparison.

The weather growing calmer we put to sea with a design to pass the gulf of Lyons, which begins there, and is one hundred leagues long and forty broad. It is extremely dangerous, as well because of the sands, which they say it abounds with, as because it has no port any where. The coast of Barbary which bounds it on one side, is often not approachable : That of Languedoc which joins it on the other side, is very bad. In short, that passage is not at all to be liked for gallies when the season is advancing towards winter, and it was pretty far advanced for us, the month of November being near approaching, when blustering winds are always blowing. Don Ferdinando, who was one of the most venturesome gentlemen in Spain, confessed to me that a small frigate had been better on this occasion than the strongest galley. We passed the gulph in thirty-six hours time with the finest weather in the world, and with a wind which at the same time that it served us, did not oblige us to set up any light upon our stern. We entered in this manner into the channel which is between Corsica and Sardinia. Don Ferdinand Carillo perceiving some clouds which made him fear a change of weather, proposed to me to go and cast anchor at Porto Condé, which is an uninhabited place in Sardinia, which I agreed to ; but his fear vanishing away with the clouds, he altered his mind, that he might not lose the fair weather, which was a great piece of good luck for me ; for Mr. de Guise, who was going to Naples with a French fleet, had cast anchor at that place with six galleys. Don Ferdinand Carillo, who was informed of it two days after, told me that he would have made but little account of these six galleys, having on board his own 450. men, which was enough to have resisted them.

But

But it had been however an encounter, which a man who was efcaping from prifon, would fooner ftill have avoided than any other. The fort of St. Boniface, which is in Corfica, and belongs to the Genoefe, fired forty gunfhots when they perceived us, and being at too great a diftance from the fort to take this for a falute, we judged that it was a fignal which they gave us, as it was true, for it was to give us notice of the enemies being at Porto Condé. We did not underftand it this way, and we thought that it was to let us know that a fmall frigate which we faw before us at the coming out of the channel, was a Turkifh pirate, as it appeared to be by the garb. Don Ferdinand took it into his head to attack it, and he told me that if I would permit him he would give me the pleafure of feeing a fight that would not laft above a quarter of an hour. He ordered his pilot to give chace to the frigate, which indeed feemed to make the beft of its way in order to avoid us. The pilot, who was intent upon nothing but the obeying that order, did not mind a fhelf which though it did not appear above water, is fo well known that it is even marked out in maps. Our galley ftruck againft it, and nothing being more dangerous at fea, every body began to lament. All the flaves rofe up, trying to undo their fetters and to efcape by fwimming. Don Ferdinand Carillo, who was playing at piquet with Joly in the ftern-room, threw to me the firft fword that he could find, crying to me to draw it out. He drew out his and flafhed all the flaves he met, as did likewife his officers and foldiers, being afraid that the whole crew of flaves, among whom there were many Turks, would make themfelves mafters of the galley, as it has fometimes happened on fuch occafions. After they had all taken again their ufual places, he faid to me with the greateft calm and affurance poffible: ‘ My order, Sir, is, firft ‘ of all to take care of you; I muft therefore provide ‘ for your fafety, and will afterwards fee whether the ‘ galley be damaged.’ He ordered, at this, four flaves to take me up, and to put me into the Felucca.

Thirty

Thirty Spanish soldiers came into it likewise by his order, whom he commanded to carry me upon a little rock which appeared near us, and on which not above four or five persons could find room. The soldiers were in the water to the middle, which I took compassion at, and finding that our galley was not damaged, I was for sending them back to it; but they told me that if those of Corsica, who stood upon the shore, perceived me to be without a good guard, they would infallibly come to pillage and murder me; these barbarians fancying that all that is cast away belongs to them.

The galley was not damaged, which was a kind of miracle. They were however above two hours in setting it to rights. The Felucca came to take me up, and I was glad when I found myself again upon the galley. As we were coming out of the channel, we still perceived the frigate, which was pursuing its way after having found that we had ceased to give her chace. But we began again to do it, and she to run away from us. We joined her in less than two hours time, and we found that it was in effect a Turkish ship, but that it belonged to the Genoese, who had taken it from the Turks and had set it out. To tell you the truth, I was very glad to see this adventure end in this manner, this sort of war being not to my liking. The weather growing somewhat foul, Don Ferdinand thought fit to go to Porto Vecchio, which is another uninhabited port of Corsica. A trumpeter came thither from the governor of a fort belonging to the Genoese, which is just by it, to give us notice, that Mr. de Guise was at Porto Condé with six French galleys; that it was likely that he had seen us pass by, and perhaps that he intended to come and surprize us there in the night-time. Upon this we resolved to put out to sea again, though the weather began to be very tempestuous, and that it was even somewhat dangerous to come out of Porto Vecchio during the night, because that at the mouth of it there is a rock from whence there descends a pretty troublesome current,

rent. The foul weather encreafed with the night, and we were perhaps attacked with the greateſt ſtorm that was ever feen at fea. The pilot in chief of the galleys of Naples, who was on board of us, and who had uſed the fea for fifty years, faid that he had never feen the like. Every body were at their prayers, or were confeffing themfelves; and none but Don Ferdinand Carillo, who received the communion every day when he was on ſhore, and who was a gentleman of an exemplary piety, forbore ſhewing any forwardneſs to proftrate himfelf at the feet of the prieſts. He left others at liberty to do what they pleafed, but he kept quiet himfelf; and he whifpered thefe words into my ear: 'I am much afraid that all thefe confeffions, 'extorted only by fear, are nought.' He remained all along upon the deck, giving his orders with a furprizing coolnefs, and heartening, but mildly and civilly, an old foldier who appeared a little frightened. I ſhall always remember that he called him Sennora-Soldado de Carlos Quinto. The private captain of the galley caufed, in the greateſt height of the danger, his embroidered coat and his red fcarf to be brought to him, faying that a true Spaniard ought to die bearing his King's marks of diſtinction. He fat himfelf down in a great elbow-chair, and with his foot ſtruck a poor Neapolitan in the chops, who not being able to ſtand upon the courfey of the galley, was crawling along, crying out aloud, *Sennor Don Fernando por l'amor de Dios confeffion.* The captain, when he ſtruck him, faid to him; *Inimigo de Dios piedes confeffion?* And as I was reprefenting to him that his inference was not right, he faid that that old man gave offence to the whole galley. You cannot imagine the horror of a great ſtorm; you can as little imagine the ridicule mixed with it. A Sicilian Obfervantine Monk was preaching at the foot of the great maſt, that St. Francis had appeared to him, and had affured him that we ſhould not perifh. I ſhould never have done, ſhould I undertake to defcribe the ridiculous frights that are feen on thefe occafions.

The

The great danger lasted but seven hours, after which we sought for a little shelter under the Piarouse. Finding the wind to abate, we got to Porto-longone. We spent there the feast of All-Saints and that of All-Souls, the wind being contrary for us to come out of the port. The governor, a Spaniard, shewed me all the civility imaginable; and finding that the wind continued to be contrary, he advised me to go and see Porto-ferraro. There is but five miles distance from one port to the other, and I went thither on horseback.

I have already told you that nothing so agreeable can be seen in the rural scenes of an opera, as the scene at Port-Mahon; and I may be allowed to tell you now with as much truth, that there is nothing so magnificent in the most stately scenes you ever saw there, as is to be seen at Porto-ferraro. None but a man versed in fortifications can well describe it, and I will only tell you that the strength of it surpasses its magnificence. It is the only place in the world that is impregnable, as the Marefchal de la Meilleraie confessed. He went to visit it, after having taken Porto-longone during the regency, and being an impetuous man, he told the commander Grifoni, who commanded in it for the Great Duke of Tuscany, that the fortification of it was good, but that if the King his Master commanded him to attack it, he would give him a good account of it in six weeks time. The commander Grifoni replied, that he took too long a term, and that the Great Duke was so much the King's humble servant, that a moment would suffice. The Marefchal was ashamed of having spoken so rashly, or rather so brutishly; and to make the commander some amends, he said to him: ' You ' are a gallant man, and I am a fool. I confess that ' your place is impregnable.' The Marefchal related this story to me at Nantes, and Grifoni, who still commanded in that place when I passed there, confirmed it to me.

The wind suffering us to come out of Porto-longone, we landed at Piombino, which is upon the coast of Tuscany. I left the galley at that place, after I had given

to the officers, to the foldiers, and to the crew of
flaves, all the money I had left, and even the chain
which his Catholick Majefty had given to Bois-guerin.
I bought it of him, and I fold it to the factor of
Prince Ludovifio, who is Prince of Piombino. I kept
but nine piftoles, which I thought would be fufficient
to carry me to Florence.

I am obliged to fay, for the fake of truth, that
never men deferved better to be gratified than thofe
who were upon that galley. Their difcretion in refpect to me is perhaps without example. They were
above 600 men, of whom there was not one but
knew me; and of all that number there was not one
that gave the leaft demonftration of it, either to myfelf or to any other. Their gratitude was equal to
their difcretion. They were touched to that degree
with the gratification that I gave them, that they all
wept when I left them to go to Piombino. This was,
properly fpeaking, the place where I recovered my
liberty, which till that time had run fome rifk, as the
adventures which I have related will fhew.

END OF THE THIRD VOLUME.

www.ingramcontent.com/pod-product-compliance
Lightning Source LLC
Chambersburg PA
CBHW030622030726
47497CB00006B/1601